THUNDER

To Harry

Ro Dalsh

 www.trafford.com

North America & international
toll-free: 1 888 232 4444 (USA & Canada)
phone: 250 383 6864 ♦ fax: 250 383 6804 ♦ email: info@trafford.com

The United Kingdom & Europe
phone: +44 (0)1865 722 113 ♦ local rate: 0845 230 9601
facsimile: +44 (0)1865 722 868 ♦ email: info.uk@trafford.com

10 9 8 7 6 5 4 3 2

Acknowledgement

For the person who was always there for me

CHAPTER ONE

It was a cold February morning. The black Jag drove through the London traffic with ease. The chauffeur looked briefly in the mirror at his boss reading the Times newspaper. The car drove along Birdcage Walk and stopped opposite the Home Office. The chauffeur opened the door, Carl Lightman got out. Without a glance at his chauffeur he pulled his coat around him, doing up the buttons. He took the bag the chauffeur handed him and walked off into St James' Park. The chauffeur leaned against the wing of the car and watched his boss disappear.

Carl Lightman was slightly built with sandy coloured hair that was thinning on top and going grey at the sides. His face was lined and he looked older than the three score years he was. His eyes had a haunted look. He looked straight ahead as he walked slowly and with purpose. Beneath the heavy overcoat was the expensive suit, the handmade shirt, the silk tie, the simple silver tie pin. He had an air of money and power. The bread bag swung as he walked; to and fro, to and fro. By the water's edge he stopped. On the water were ducks, geese and swans. Pigeons sat on the bank fluffed up against the cold. They all ignored him until he opened the bag and started throwing bits of bread. Soon he was surrounded by birds.

Bob Lowman walked across the park from the Mall. He was in his forties and very much the junior man in this uneasy alliance, although his heavily featured face showed years of hard graft, hard living and over indulgence. His frame was generously proportioned with broad shoulders and hips, topped by slicked back black hair and dark eyes. He also wore a black overcoat; his covered an expensive double breasted suit, an expensive diamond tie pin adorning a black tie over a crisp white shirt. He wore several pieces of heavy gold jewellery; an identity bracelet, a thick rope chain round his thick neck and several rings on his fingers.

He was very much the 'heavy' and the message plainly said 'don't mess with me or else'; here was a man who was not afraid of violence, a man who had in the past not been above doling it out himself, a man who would do so again if and when the need arose. Whereas Lightman would employ someone to do his dirty work, Lowman was not afraid to get his hands dirty. Although both powerful men in their own context, there was a vast difference between the two men.

Lowman stared ahead as he walked and looked to the world as if he saw and heard nothing, but he noticed the few people walking through the park and had heard the birds from yards off. He walked down the path to where Lightman was busy feeding the birds. For a couple of minutes Lowman stood and watched.

"Good morning, Lightman," Lowman said quietly, his gravel voice was pleasantly pitched, not the expected deep or menacing voice. It lulled you into a false sense of security - before his massive hands closed around your throat.

Carl Lightman looked over his shoulder. Lowman stood looking into the distance then pulled the collar of his coat up around his ears. Lightman straightened up. The birds flapped and fought over the remaining bread. The plastic bag hung limply in one hand. He emptied it onto the grass then stuffed it into one pocket and brushed the crumbs from his hands.

He walked over to Lowman and they shook hands. Lightman sunk his hands deep into his pockets. The weather had turned cold and he was always susceptible to the cold. Lowman wasn't wearing gloves and didn't seem to notice the cold at all, though the upturned collar might have suggested otherwise.

"Well Lowman? Was Thunder contacted as I requested?" Lightman's American accent hadn't blurred much over the years. There were rumours that he'd been forced to flee America, but no one knew for sure and it wasn't the sort of thing you asked him. He looked over Lowman's massive shoulders. There was few people about, all were huddled in coats, scarves and hats, hands in pockets or gloves as they hurried about their business. None gave the two men a glance.

"He's in Cairo on another job," Lowman replied, his London

accent sounded like gravel on glass. Lightman dragged his attention back to him. He frowned. "He'll be back soon," Lowman reassured him, his voice softened at the edges.

"I want the best!" Lightman snarled.

"Thunder is the best," Lowman replied softly; it belied the violence that Lightman knew him to be capable of, indeed was famous for.

"So I've heard. Palmerston-Smith is getting more powerful. He needs cutting down to size," Lightman said. He looked small beside the big man but his power was no less tangible. He looked at Lowman; colleagues, not friends; their tastes ran in opposite directions - Lightman to golf, Lowman to boxing. A mutual acquaintance had brought these two powerful businessmen together and it soon became beneficial for both; now another businessman was threatening their power. He had to be cut down to size, made more manageable, more on their wavelength, if necessary a puppet.

"Thunder will do whatever you ask," Lowman said. His quiet voice was reassuring. "For the right price,"

"He'd better. I want no hitches," Lightman replied bluntly.

"He will make contact when he is back in England," Lowman continued.

If Lightman believed he could sort out someone like Thunder he was either naive or an idiot. Lowman's enquiries had all said the same thing: no one crossed Thunder and lived to tell the tale; and if you were stupid enough to try it you'd best write your will, dig a hole and make the funeral arrangements. Even a reformed thug like Lowman knew better than to take on someone like Thunder.

"He comes from England then?" Lightman asked.

"Who knows. He seems to have been around for years. No one knows him and no one knows where he's from," Lowman replied.

"Except the Chinaman," Lightman stated.

"He is the contact. Kill him and no one will be able to find Thunder," Lowman's voice struggled to stay level and he pointed at Lightman to emphasise the point. Lightman ignored the warning voice and pointing finger. Lowman frowned. He looked straight at Lightman, noticed the flecks in his eyes, the hardness around the mouth and knew he was wasting his time; the man was both naive and an idiot. "BUT, he will find you," he said, his voice suddenly low and menacing.

Lightman looked at him and then looked away as he thought for a couple of minutes. Behind him the ducks and geese flapped and squawked. "Just get him for the job," he said lamely.

Lowman looked at Lightman for a few seconds thoughtfully, his face was impassive but his mind whirled. He nodded and turned on his heel. He walked back the way he came. In the Mall he hailed a taxi.

Lightman watched the birds for a minute then slowly walked back to his car. As he came into view the chauffeur stood up, uncrossed his arms and moved to the door. By the time Lightman reached the pavement, the door was open. Lightman hesitated for a second, looked back over his shoulder at the park, saw there was only a few people about and climbed in, the door being closed firmly behind him. He settled back and picked up the paper, resuming his reading while the chauffeur pulled off smoothly into the London traffic.

In a hot and dusty Cairo the object of their interest sat in a car, his fingers lightly encircled the steering wheel, his thumbs played out a drum beat as he quietly watched people going about their busy worlds. He stretched his arms above his head. Then shifted around, wiggling to get comfortable again, his long legs felt cramped from sitting in one position for hours. He ran his fingers through his hair and then wiped them on his jeans and hooded top with distaste; his hair, like the rest of him, needed washing. He looked in the mirror, cold dark eyes stared back. He saw the greasy slicked back hair, the unshaven face and momentarily frowned. He ruefully fingered his chin, it had three days or more growth. He tried to remember when he'd last had a decent meal, a bath and a shave but the days were hazy. He knew that it was two days since he'd grabbed the girl. Two days of driving aimlessly around. Two days of being watched and followed by a variety of people. Two days of pretending to look for the right place. Though in reality he had already picked the place. Now the time had come and all pretence vanished, he knew exactly what he was doing and where.

Thunder was about six foot with broad shoulders that topped a hard, toned rather than muscular body. His hair was dark from sweat, dirt and grease, slicked back from pushing his fingers through it too many times. His face was attractive in a rugged, lived in way; the face of a survivor. His expression was hard, distant, uncaring; he had lived life the hard way and had experienced both pleasure and pain. His eyebrows arched over quite beautiful but at the moment cold dark eyes. His emotions was kept strictly in check; yet he was capable of humour and compassion, even tenderness, as well as a dark ruthless side.

He had a quirky playful sense of humour, his mouth could twitch into a rueful smile and when he laughed, though rarely, it lit up his whole face, changing his whole personality. Thunder was not a man to be trifled with, he knew how to handle himself and was at home in riches or squalor; he had tasted both; if anything he was apt to be rather blasé about it all. A job was just a job, someone had to do it, he just happened to do it well.

Behind him on the back seat, tied up and gagged, was his 'victim' - a young Arab girl with big tearful eyes and dirty face, dressed in jeans and frilly top, her dark hair untidy, the band that had once held it in place now discarded on the floor along with her shoes. Thunder drove off, up one street, down another, all the time glancing in the mirror. The blue car behind him followed for several streets to be replaced by the black one, but he continued driving until he was satisfied that he had lead whoever a merry dance. He drove into a street and pulled up outside a large building. He went inside, looking neither left nor right, taking a kit bag with him. Ten minutes later he came out and carried the girl in over his shoulder. She was silent and submissive. He is glad. The last girl had managed to kick him where it really hurt! He'd limped for days. This time he made sure her feet were shoeless and tied together.

His latest tail - a beige car - pulled into the street and stopped further down. Their attention was taken by a man carrying boxes into a building half way between them and Thunder. He also had dark hair, wore jeans and a sweatshirt. Thunder stood in the doorway watching. It was obvious to him that the boxes held anything other than explosives, but he had lead them to this street again and again. They hadn't got close enough to have a good look at him so one dark haired man in jeans was as likely to be him as another.

"Far too obvious boys. You'll have to do better than that!" he muttered and thoughtfully returned inside. His voice betrayed no accent. He could have been any nationality. Came from anywhere. Or nowhere.

The girl sat on the floor against a wall, her legs under her. She looked wildly at him, breathing hard and struggling not to cry. Her wrists were red from struggling against the rope even though she knew it to be futile; she was tied up too securely for escape.

Thunder checked the ropes all the same, then stood up and looked down at her. He suddenly smiled, she looked up at him fearfully and was not reassured. He shrugged and crossed to the back of the building. He opened the door and peered out. A red car was parked outside. He looked up at the buildings and, when satisfied that no one was about, went out to the car and opened the boot. It was large and roomy. He nodded. Out of habit he again scanned the buildings but saw nothing.

He returned to the building and picked up the girl, laying her over his shoulder. She closed her eyes and tears slide down her face unchecked, marking the back of Thunder's top. The moment had come, the moment she had been dreading for the last two days, ever since he had snatched her while out shopping. In all those long hours Thunder had not said one word to her. That was the worst thing - the silence. But at least he hadn't touched her except to tie her up and carry her about.

He walked over to the door, looked out, then carried her to the car and laid her in the open boot. He pulled a blanket over her and gently tucked it in around her making sure that she wouldn't suffocate. She looked up, saw his grim face and heard muttered words just as he slammed the boot shut. He returned inside and finished setting the explosives around the base of the large wooden pillar in the centre which held up the floor and the building.

He looked out the front again. The men in the car were still watching the man with the boxes who had nearly finished; only two left. Thunder watched with a thoughtful look, then ducked back in, picked what he wanted out of the bag and shoved it inside his top. He stopped at the door for a second then pulled the hood over his head and strolled down the street, bouncing a bunch of keys in one hand, the other hand in his pocket. He whistled as he crossed the road near the car. Both men watched the street, ignoring the approaching scruffy individual. He walked right next to the car and still they didn't see him.

Near the end of the car he dropped the keys, stopped, bent down to retrieve them and put the bundle from inside his top beneath the car jammed up against the back wheel. The man on that side glanced briefly in the mirror but his attention was taken with the man who had just taken the last box in. Thunder continued down the street, crossed near the end and at the corner looked back. The man and the boxes had gone inside. He could see the two men in the car arguing, fingers pointing, shouting at each other.

Thunder quickly ran up the alleyway to the back of the building. He entered the back door, set the time, collected his stuff, shut the door and nonchalantly looked around once more. It was still deserted. He whistled again, this time a Beatles song, then got into the red car. A quick look at his watch and he drove off, tyres screeching, the girl safely in the boot.

Five minutes later the bomb in the building exploded. The ground floor blew out in a shower of dust. The top two floors collapsed in on itself like a pack of cards. Timbers burning threatened the buildings either side. The two men in the car looked on in disbelief as people ran into the street.

"What the hell?" the driver said. He looked at his partner.

"We've been watching the wrong building!" he retorted.

"So what now?" the driver retorted back.

His partner thought quickly. "Nothing. The job is done," his voice reverted to its normal pitch. "Let's go," He gestured to his friend.

Just as he reached for the key, the bomb under their car went off, sending the car, back end first, up into the air in a fireball. The car somersaulted, flipped onto its roof and crashed to the street in a ball of fire. People jumped back. From a distance a siren's wailing could be heard.

More sirens wailed as emergency services descended on the scene. People stood and watched in disbelief. It was reported back to the hirers. They smiled and shook hands. The job had been done: their rival effectively silenced; the tailers have unfortunately gone; the hired man too - he wasn't that good after all. Anyone who knew about the job was dead so the job couldn't be traced back to them. They paid off the families of the two dead men. All that was left was to arrange for the money advanced to be transferred back.

Miles away their rival, a wealthy Arab businessman, was welcoming his daughter back into the family. Thunder wore flowing Arab robes over his filthy clothes and head, so that only his eyes could be seen. Two holdalls of money were put in the boot of the red car. Thunder watched impassively, his eyes cold and distant. A final handshake, grateful thanks for the sixth time and Thunder quickly left, driving away at speed.

Once out on the road he pulled off the head dress. He smiled a thin smile as he imagined the faces of his hirers when they discovered that the money they had paid in advance had vanished and that not only had he kidnapped the girl as ordered but that he had delivered her back to her family and got paid handsomely for it. The extra bonus, as he saw it, was that the father was even now plotting his revenge. It would be an uneasy time for all concerned, but not for him.

As dusk fell he found a small hotel where he got a room and some food; the first decent meal in days. He lay back in the bath and scratched the hair on his chest as he thought. It had been a long day in a series of long days. He rubbed his throat and then his chin. He needed a shave. Three days growth had been good for hiding his face but now he didn't need to hide. He got out of the bath and wrapped a towel around himself.

He quickly shaved off the beard. He looked in the mirror

where two black eyes looked back. He carefully removed the lenses from his eyes and dropped them down the toilet. Then he washed his face vigorously, removing the last of the shaving foam and rubbed his itchy eyes with his knuckles. He looked up into the mirror. His eyes looked back at him. Grey/green. Like his mother. Out of habit he checked that the door and windows were all locked. He laid down on the bed, one arm behind his head and stared at the ceiling. Soon he was asleep.

The next morning he continued to Alexandria and the railway station. In a left luggage locker he pulled out his leather suit bag and went to the nearest toilet where he changed. Ten minutes later he emerged dressed in light coloured tailored jacket, crisp white shirt and black trousers. He returned to the car and then drove to a bank.

"I wish to make a large deposit," he told the cashier.

"How large?" he asked.

"Two bags," Thunder replied holding up the holdalls. The cashier looked surprised and motioned to a small office to the side of them. Thunder dumped the two bags on the table and sat on a chair with his back to the wall. The cashier opened one bag. His jaw dropped. He called the manager.

"Count it," the manager told the cashier when he saw what was in the bags. The cashier started to count, muttering the whole time. Thunder inspected his nails and generally ignored the entire proceedings.

"Pay it into this account and transfer it into English sterling," Thunder said when the counting had finished, handing over a piece of paper with bank details.

"Yes sir," the manager said. "Get a receipt for the gentleman,"

"Don't bother. I know how much is there," Thunder replied in an off-hand tone. The manager and cashier exchanged looks. "And I know roughly how much there should be in sterling," he added darkly.

The manager personally escorted him to the door. Thunder didn't look back as he strode off. The manager stared after him in wonder. He hadn't even said what his name was. He shook his head as he went back inside; these foreigners were very strange.

Thunder drove to the airport and parked the car. He took only
his suit bag with him, everything else he left locked in the boot.
Early the following morning he caught a plane to London. Once at
Heathrow he phoned Kit Chan. Shortly after Thunder had saved
Kit and his family and brought them to England Kit had started to
work for Thunder. Kit was small, very atypical Chinese and the
closest thing Thunder had to family. People who wanted to hire
Thunder contacted Kit who would find Thunder. Without Kit, no
one would be able to find Thunder, but you could be assured that
Thunder would find you if anything happened to Kit.

"How is the lotus blossom this week?" Thunder asked when
Kit answered.

"Fine. How was the weather?" Kit replied.

"Fine, how was it for you?" Thunder replied.

"Wet and stormy, it follows the monsoon," Kit said carefully.

Thunder frowned. Who would want to follow Kit? Unless
they were after him. Once before Kit had been followed and
unknowingly led them to Thunder. It was only quick thinking on
Thunder's part that had saved both men from certain death. There
was always going to be people who wanted to kill Thunder, it was
the nature of the beast.

"Where are the flowers falling?" Thunder said.

"In Shanghai," Kit replied.

The phone went dead. Kit now knew he had to get rid of his
tail before he met Thunder. He went out onto Gerrard Street and
walked around the shops buying, talking, passing the time of day.
Across the street a young Chinese man stood watching. A few
minutes later he disappeared into a restaurant. Kit walked across
casually and disappeared inside too. Kit followed the man
through the restaurant and into the kitchen. The cooks called out
greetings as he passed through and out the back door. Carefully
he looked round. The door closed behind him.

He walked out and down an alleyway to Shaftesbury Avenue
and away to Piccadilly Circus. A little way up Piccadilly he turned
into the church courtyard where a small market was set out. Kit
wandered about, looking at this and that, buying a few trinkets.

"You have another job for me," Thunder said behind him. Kit

handed some money to the stallholder who went to another stall to get change.

"Yes," Kit didn't turn round. Thunder stood next to him and picked up an object. He turned it over in his hands. "They want a girl kidnapped, possibly killed, they haven't decided," Kit added.

Thunder sighed. "Sounds exciting," he said dryly.

"Here are the details," Kit put a small note book down. Thunder picked it up and tucked it in his pocket.

"I'll be in touch," Thunder said.

Kit did not look at him. "We'll have dim sum together," he said quietly.

"Bank on it," Thunder replied and moved off. He wandered round for a few minutes and then went out onto Piccadilly. A bus came along, he jumped on, went upstairs and sat in the corner. He bought a ticket and looked blindly out the window.

As the bus lurched along he thought. Life was tedious. Rivals bringing down rivals, Arabs killing Arabs in petty battles, nothing to test his skill - and he did consider himself skilful. It was time to stop and live life properly, perhaps settle down. He pulled the notebook from his pocket and flicked through. There were details of the job and a phone number.

The hirers were a consortium of businessmen; the mark, Ray Palmerston-Smith, a wealthy businessman. He was their main opposition in an important deal which the consortium desperately needed to stay in the power league. The hirers wanted the mark out of the deal, cut down 'to a manageable size'. Thunder smiled wryly. He knew what that meant.

The consortium wanted Thunder to kidnap Palmerston-Smith's only daughter, Sarah and hold her hostage for three weeks forcing Palmerston-Smith to pull out of the deal, otherwise his daughter would die. However there was no mention of returning the girl and Thunder's terms were specific, these sort of details you specified; he didn't want an outraged father on his trail.

Thunder had killed many people in his career without much thought; if they deserved it, he did it without a qualm. Several years ago a kidnap job had gone badly wrong and he had unwittingly wiped out the entire family. His hirers had been very pleased, it had exceeded their expectations and had achieved what they wanted. Thunder had been so disgusted that he gave away the money and disappeared for a while until he felt clean enough to return to civilisation.

Ever since he hated kidnap jobs and had made his terms very clear; very specific; the return of the live kidnap victim was one detail on which he insisted on specification because the kidnap victim was nearly always some innocent tool. Occasionally he would have to kidnap someone who was corrupt in which case he had no compunction about killing them, but he preferred to return the innocent unharmed which was why the girl in Cairo had been returned to her family safe and the watching men had died. Thunder liked to balance these things out; it appealed to his sense of honour and appeased his troubled conscience - slightly.

He looked out the window, recognised where he was, stuffed the book back into his pocket, got off the bus and walked into the Red Lion pub. The landlord greeted him like an old friend. They chatted. Others came in and he spent an enjoyable, noisy evening there and thought no more of the job.

The next day in his flat in Wandsworth he looked again through the book as he drank coffee. Another thing bothered him - there was no photo, just a vague description. How would he know her? He phoned the contact.

"Hello, this is Thunder. I believe you have a job for me,"

"Ah yes, Sport," an exaggerated Australian accent boomed.

"How will I know her?" Thunder asked bluntly.

"You phone me on a certain day and I'll tell you what she is wearing and where she is going," Bruce said.

"You're close to her then?" Thunder frowned.

"You could say that," his contact drawled.

"What day? What time?" Thunder asked. The voice was beginning to grate.

"Ring me in a week. It will take time to set things up. Put a few suggestions into heads etc. You understand," Bruce said.

"A week then," Thunder replaced the phone.

Bruce opened his mouth to say more, then dangled the phone

from his fingertips. He smiled slowly. It would be easy to get rid of Palmerston-Smith. He rang Lowman and told him Thunder had been in touch.

"Good. I'll pass on the news. Just set it up from your end. I don't want any hitches," Lowman said. He disliked the Australian intensely. He was too smooth and his lack of loyalty bothered Lowman. If necessary he would have to be got rid of.

"I'll see to it. It will be a piece of piss," Bruce said smoothly.

"Good. Ring me when it is done," Lowman said and rang off. Bruce smiled slowly and made a list of things to do. In his mind he was already buying the ticket home.

Thunder spent the week sorting out paperwork, mostly bills and then he started to sort out his flat and threw out a lot of junk. Again he thought about a place in the countryside, somewhere to retreat to. He stayed away from Chinatown and Kit. It was safer for both of them. One night Kit turned up on his doorstep.

Thunder opened the door and looked at Kit with a questioning look. "What brings you out here?" he asked. Kit always considered south of the Thames to be a different world.

"A passing visit on an old friend," Kit replied as Thunder let him in.

"Are you still being watched?" Thunder asked.

Kit shrugged. "Who knows. They want you, not me," he sat in a big leather chair.

"They might kill you to bring me out into the open," Thunder said quietly.

"Oh that would bring you out into the open all right," Kit said with a smile. "But they wouldn't live very long to enjoy it,"

Thunder poured Kit his usual whisky and one for himself. He handed Kit the glass. Kit took a sip and looked at Thunder over the rim. Thunder flopped down into a chair opposite.

"Are you taking this job?" Kit asked suddenly.

"Yes. This is the last time. After this I quit," Thunder said. He felt tired. He ran his fingers through his hair. It felt clean. He looked up at his hand, a few hairs were trapped in his fingers, then he lowered his hand to his lap and looked at Kit.

Kit watched him with a fascination. Thunder always reminded

him of a snake, coiled and seemingly harmless until it struck its fatal blow. He laughed. "I've heard that before. You'll be back, flying to God knows where, blowing up something or someone," Kit was sceptical.

"No," Thunder's voice was cold, adamant. "This is the last time. This is a young man's game and I've been doing this too long. I feel old. Some bright young kid will catch me out and I'll be dead. I want to live longer than that,"

Kit shook his head in disbelief. Thunder had talked like this before. "Perhaps," was all he said. Thunder said nothing in reply.

For several hours they talked of general things. At eleven Kit went home. They had drunk most of the whisky between them. Thunder took the remainder to bed, but didn't get in. He lay with one hand behind his head, balanced the glass on his chest and thought about retirement.

He didn't fear death, he had lived with it for so long now, it held no fear for him, but he wanted to live longer, he was in his thirties now, it was time to quit while he was ahead. The days of intricate explosions, spectacular escapes and well planned battles were gone. Now it was petty quarrels and kidnaps. The only assassinations were of political people with minders, guards and strict security, and that set up had never been his idea of earning a living. He had made a good living at this job but now he was bored. It was time for a change.

He drained the glass, put it on the side table and turned out the light. He pulled the cover round him but couldn't sleep. Something nagged at him. He tossed and turned all night. He could feel a flaw in this. Eventually he slept.

A week later he rang the Aussie. "Which day? What time? Where?"

"Hello to you too. Ring me on Easter Saturday, in the morning. I'll find out what she's wearing and where she's definitely going," Bruce replied.

"Right," Thunder hung up.

Bruce thought for a few minutes. Easter Saturday was two weeks away. Plenty of time to arrange things. He phoned another number.

Lowman answered. "It's set for Easter Saturday. Thunder will call in the morning. I should know what she is wearing then," Bruce said.

"Good. Is everything else set up?" Lowman said.

"Of course," Bruce sounded supremely confident.

"Good. Let me know the details about the girl," Lowman said. "And Bruce, make doubly sure this isn't likely to go wrong. I wouldn't like to be in your Aussie boots if it does,"

"All right, all right," Bruce was irritated. If they could do better he thought, they were welcome to try.

"It had better be," Lowman continued. He had wanted to organise it, but Lightman had been adamant: Bruce would organise it and be the contact. Lowman was just the middle man.

"It will be. Thunder can charm the birds off the trees," Bruce said.

"It'd better. If anything goes wrong you will answer to me," Lowman said, his voice low and menacing.

Bruce swallowed. "Okay. I heard. Christ!"

"We don't want a repeat of the last time you worked for me," Lowman said.

"That wasn't my fault. Thunder is a true professional. You have the report on him," Bruce protested.

"Not a lot there. Is that all?" Lowman had been unimpressed. He'd been told Thunder was something special; the report wasn't convincing, yet all his contacts highly recommended him.

"No one knows Thunder, except the Chinaman and he's as close as a clam," Bruce said.

"I know that. Just don't fuck up Bruce," Lowman slammed down the phone. It made Bruce's ear hurt.

He was still muttering a hour later. He hoped this Thunder was the best. Certainly his contacts had said so but no one knew what he looked like, where he lived or where he came from; elusive was an understatement. He wondered if the tail on the Chinaman had produced anything of interest. He phoned there next but the tail on Kit had got bored very early on. As far as he was concerned one Chinaman looked like another and in Gerrard Street there were a lot of them. He had nothing to report.

In the two weeks up to Easter Thunder busied himself. He found somewhere to store his most precious possessions and spent the time packing them. The men turned up on the Thursday before Easter. For some reason Thunder kept adding things. He felt it was the end of an era. When it had all gone his flat looked quite bare, just a few essentials left. Thunder wandered around, a feeling of detachment. This was going to be the last job. He had decided, definitely.

On the Monday afternoon he had gone to the Palmerston-Smith address. It hadn't been too difficult to find, Palmerston-Smith turned out to be quite well known. He waited outside, leaning against a tree, studying the exterior. It was a large detached house on three floors. Few people came or went.

After a hour a tanned man strode out and down the road. He had a dark beard and dark hair with blonde dyed ends. He spoke brightly in an exaggerated Australian accent to a lady walking her dog. Thunder slowly followed him from across the road as he went to the shops and then the betting shop where he put down several large bets. Then he strolled back to the house and disappeared inside. After another hour Thunder gave up and went home. He had got one piece of information but still had no idea about the girl. There was something about this job that lay uneasy on his mind.

On the Tuesday he visited his accountants and left letters regarding his affairs should he die, which he had no intention of doing but it was something that he did occasionally. He spent Good Friday alone, resting. He packed a bag, got cash and went through the book again before destroying it. He felt very calm, he knew exactly what to do, now all he had to do was wait.

CHAPTER TWO

On Easter Saturday after a leisurely breakfast Thunder rang the Aussie. "Well?" he asked.

"Hello mate, how's things?" Bruce sounded irritatingly happy. When Thunder didn't answer he sighed and gave him the information he needed. "Okay Sport, she's wearing jeans, white sweatshirt, black leather jacket and boots. Carrying a black handbag and brown leather holdall. Dark shoulder length hair and glasses. She's catching the half two train to Brighton from Victoria Station today,"

"Fine," Thunder said.

"Right," Bruce tried to take control. "There's to be no violence or rough stuff. No hanky panky either. Softly, softly," If he could have seen Thunder's cold expression he wouldn't have bothered.

"Fine," Thunder repeated.

"If you hurt that girl, you'll answer for it," Bruce tried to sound menacing.

"You'll have to find me first," Thunder purred.

Bruce was about to say something else but the line was already dead. He called Lowman full of confidence. "He's got the message,"

"Good. No cowboys. Just the professional," Lowman said.

"Thunder is a professional," Bruce said.

"You'd better hope so Bruce! Or else!" the line went dead.

Bruce was now extremely irritated. He made another call and gave the same information he'd given Thunder.

Upstairs Sarah was happily finishing her packing. She was thinking what a good friend Bruce was. He'd arranged for her father to be away so she could be on her own for a whole week. She went out the side door quietly. It was a cold and windy day. She leaned on the door just long enough to look up at the grey sky, then zipped up her jacket to her throat. She put her black bag on one shoulder and picked up the brown holdall, then started off down the path. As she turned out of the gate she paused and hoisted the holdall to her shoulder, then walked off towards the nearest tube station. A week of freedom away from home beckoned.

As she walked down the road she saw no one she knew and as far as she knew, no one saw her. Anyone driving by would see a beautiful girl, her bobbed dark hair swinging with her stride. Sarah was carefully made up, she knew she was beautiful and the way she walked let everyone else know she knew. She could be, and was often called, vain - sometimes in the extreme. She had taken trouble to set this up, thanks to Bruce.

At Victoria Station Sarah climbed the steps that emerged just outside the station. She turned left, found somewhere out of the way of passers by and got out her mobile phone. A male voice answered.

"Hi, it's me," she said.

"Where are you?" the voice asked.

"Victoria. Everything set?" she said.

"Yes. I'll see you later. I'll pick you up," the voice said.

"Bye," Sarah shut the phone and started across Victoria Station.

Sammy Jones was short, had a weedy body, lank greasy hair and resembled a weasel. His face was pock-marked and spotty. He wore three earrings in one lobe, all different shapes and each bigger than the first. He wore cheap rings on fingers that were as nicotine stained as his teeth. Close to he reeked of cigarettes, bad breath and rancid sweat. His clothes were dirty and tatty, his fingers nails black with engine oil from tinkering with cars. He took off the bottle-bottomed glasses and wiped them on his t-shirt, only managing to smear them worse than before. He replaced them and peered at the girls walking by. He would be the first to admit that he wouldn't know a beautiful girl if she walked up to him; he was more interested in car engines, heavy metal music and boys. His mate, Joe was the ladies man. Women scared Sammy shitless.

Most days he looked like a tramp. Today, his hair was slicked back into a pony tail, he wore dirty oil-stained jeans, a denim jacket with patches and a faded black t-shirt, on his back was a small rucksack. He stood near the column outside Smiths opposite one of the underground entrances. For the third time in half a hour he pulled out his cigarettes. He looked at the no smoking signs and put them back with a sigh. Every so often he looked over his shoulder at Smiths with longing. He wished he was in there, looking at the magazines. Now and then he pulled a crumpled piece of paper from his pocket and read the list written there in his childish scrawl, then he scrutinised the girls walking by. He saw plenty of girls in jeans, but none matched his list, so he did nothing except occasionally hop from one foot to the other.

Shortly after Sarah entered the station Kate Bromham climbed the same steps and walked into the station heading towards Smiths and Sammy. He saw her and looked again. Could that be her? He checked the list again: jeans, white sweatshirt, black leather jacket, boots, black handbag, brown holdall, dark hair, glasses. Yes. That had to be her. He'd have to ask Joe if she was stunningly beautiful; this one looked nice but quite ordinary - well as far as he could tell, that is. He dismissed the thought that her hair actually went past her shoulders and was pinned back at the front but as everything else checked out according to his list, he was confident, it had to be her.

He shoved the paper in his pocket and followed her to the ticket office. He already had his ticket so he waited while she bought hers. He followed as she went off to look at the departures board. Kate dropped her holdall at her feet and looked up at the board, flexing her fingers as she did so.

On the other side of the station Sarah went into Smiths, picked up several magazines and then moved to a corner near the books. She replaced the glasses with shades and pulled a black hat from the holdall. She took a hair band from her pocket and tied her hair up, then jammed the hat down on her head. Sarah did not want anyone to recognise her. It would be just her luck to bump into someone in the middle of Victoria Station.

Having made her transformation she bought the magazines

and walked across Victoria Station. Sarah walked behind Kate still looking up at the board. She walked in front of Sammy who took absolutely no notice of her. His attention was wholly on Kate. Kate found the train to Brighton, saw it was on platform 16 and, picking up her bag, started off in that direction, with Sarah slightly in front of her. Kate took no notice of people around her including Sarah.

Suddenly Sarah turned right, going out the side entrance and leaving Victoria Station altogether. Once out on the street she turned left towards Victoria coach station. Kate carried on walking, Sammy following some distance behind.

At the ticket office Thunder had bought two first class tickets. He picked up his bag and walked towards platform 16. He saw Kate walking in the same direction of the platform but did not see Sammy, and certainly not Sarah who has just disappeared around the corner. He too mentally went through the check list. As Kate approached the side entrance someone stepped out in front of her. She stopped abruptly, stepped round the person, who has also stopped, and with a quick look over her shoulder to make sure the person was not moving in the same direction, walked off towards the platforms. That sideways glance was all Thunder needed to see that Kate was wearing glasses. He too believed she was probably Sarah Palmerston-Smith, even though he registered the difference in the hair. A thought fleetingly crossed his mind that this girl was supposed to be stunningly beautiful. However unlike Sammy, Thunder knew whether a girl was beautiful or not, but just as quickly as Sammy, he dismissed it. Keeping his eyes on Kate he walked casually towards the ticket barrier, slowing down to allow people in front go through.

Kate went through the barrier and strolled off down the platform. As Sammy approached the barrier he looked sideways to Joe standing by the shops. Sammy stroked the side of his nose with one finger. Joe nodded, folded up his paper and put it in his raincoat pocket. He picked up a small suitcase and moved towards the barrier. He did not notice Thunder, and Thunder, having given people there only a cursory glance, largely ignored him and Sammy, and like them kept his eyes on Kate.

Sammy went through the barrier first and hurried after Kate, followed by Joe at a leisurely pace. Thunder let several people through and then followed, also taking his time. Ahead, Kate walked down the platform looking for a quiet seat on the train. Probably because of the cold weather or the time of day the train was surprisingly empty. She got near the middle of the train and then walked back passing people hurrying towards the front or the middle of the train. Kate walked right back to the start of the train and got into the carriage divided into first and second class. She sat in a corner facing first class with her back to where she was going. She pulled a CD player from her bag, set it up and turned it on. She pulled out a book and started to read. Now she was set for the journey, totally unaware that she has been followed.

Sammy watched Kate walk down the platform and then back. He hung around near the end of the train ostensibly fiddling with his rucksack. He saw which carriage she got in and walked down the platform past her, heading for the next carriage. He looked at the no smoking signs and silently swore. He stood by the door at the end of the carriage. People walked up the platform, a couple gave him a filthy look but most just walked past him.

Joe Farrell, Sammy's mate got in the same carriage as Kate but at the other end. He stood in the doorway watching people walk by. He was stocky built, ginger haired, red faced, arrogant and firmly believed he was God's gift to women. He was quite unintelligent, although certainly smarter than Sammy, but mostly he belonged to the dirty mac brigand and always wore his now very dirty beige raincoat. It covered pale blue nylon slacks that have been snagged several times by his rough hands and a blue checked shirt. His speech, like his behaviour, was coarse and vulgar. He loved fighting and was as handy with his fists as a knife or a gun. However, he had a way with a certain sort of women that ensured he was never without one at any given time, and he tolerated Sammy's fondness for young men even though homosexuals disgusted him in the extreme and he had been known to beat them up without provocation. He saw Thunder approach, admired the clothes and wished he could afford to dress like that and when he saw him get in first class, wished he could afford to travel like that.

Thunder slowly walked towards the train. He had seen where Kate had got in. He stepped into first class and sat down facing the carriage. Sammy was now walking up and down the platform. He also saw Thunder, noted the expensive jacket and well cut trousers and that the leather holdall he carried had a designer label and was therefore expensive. He did not notice the face and later would only be able to describe the clothes. He also wished he could dress like that but only so he could attract a man dressed like that. He looked at Joe who gestured at him to get on the train. He hurried into the next carriage.

Joe watched the last couple of people hurry down the platform. A pretty blond girl in a red mini skirt and black fishnet tights encasing endless long legs caught his eye. Now that was more like it! he thought. He saw her get in the same part as Kate and smiled. Once the girl was safely secured perhaps he would have time for her. He grunted in anticipation.

Thunder put his bag on the seat next to him. He had a clear view of Kate. He looked down the carriage and saw Joe at the door. He saw him gesture at Sammy outside and Sammy get on the train. Thunder looked thoughtful, a newspaper on his lap. He looked out the window and saw the last few people walk past. He too noticed the blond and recognised her. Mini Skirt Sue. He had come across her a couple of times in the past. She was quite good, used her beauty to get near someone and then did her work. She never got caught and always had a cast iron alibi. He held up the paper, not that she actually knew him, they had never met, but he knew her well enough. Looking round the paper he saw her get into the same carriage as Kate. That was too much of a coincidence. He shrugged, when the time came, he would deal with it.

Kate took little notice of the girl in the mini skirt as she sat down across the train, expect perhaps to wish that her legs looked like that. Her concentration went back to the music in her ears and the book in her hand. She was so engrossed she missed the smile of satisfaction when the girl saw that there was just the two of them in that part of the carriage and hardly anybody else in the rest. Sue did not notice Joe still at the door nor did she see him sit down at the far end. The only thing Kate noticed was the sound of the doors shutting and the jolt as the train pulled out. She looked up briefly, saw the station slide by and returned to her book.

Soon Kate's eyes began to close and by the time the train left East Croydon she was asleep. Sammy came into the carriage and sat near Joe. A few minutes later they got up and walked up the carriage. Sue looked up from her magazine in surprise when a gun was waved in her face. She knew these two by sight, they obviously didn't know her. Joe sat down opposite her and kept the gun aimed at her. Sammy moved towards Kate.

Kate never knew whether it was instinct or some noise that abruptly woke her to find a man standing over her. Instinctively she screamed, then kicked him in the groin. Sammy yelled and rolled up in pain on the seat opposite clutching his groin. Joe looked over at Sammy. Sue went for him. He swotted her aside like a fly. She slumped back in her seat, unconscious.

Joe moved across the carriage towards Kate who tried to flatten herself against the wall. All she saw was the gun. Suddenly he toppled forward into oblivion as Thunder hit him across the back of the head. Her eyes followed him down to the floor. Thunder then hit Sammy once.

"I suggest you move into another compartment while I sort things out here," he said in a velvety voice. Kate looked up suddenly.

"Th... th... thank... thank you. I will," she said gathering up her belongings. Thunder stood to one side as she stepped over Joe and went through the door.

He laid Joe on the seat that Kate had been sat on, took a bottle of cheap whisky from his pocket and poured it down the two men's fronts, putting the bottle in Joe's hand. He put Joe's gun in Sue's bag and her head against the wall as though she was asleep. He pulled down Kate's holdall and returned to first class. Kate was sat next to the window, opposite his seat, the tears running silently down her face, her back to what was going on behind her. He put down her bag.

"Here, drink this," he offered her a hip flask. She shook her head and leaned her forehead against the cold window.

Thunder sat opposite her and waited. He felt a little annoyed that someone else had put a contract out on Sarah, or maybe it was the Aussie being over careful. Either way he didn't like his professionalism being questioned, he would have to speak severely to the boy when this was over. Mini Skirt Sue, he knew; she was quite good, but he didn't know the other two and their boorish behaviour marked them down as amateurs or worse; hired thugs. As far as he was concerned they were scrum.

Kate's fear died down leaving a rage at the two men and a question: why pick on her? She hardly looked rich enough to rob and the other girl was a far likelier target for rape. For the first time Kate turned to look at her rescuer. His eyes returned her stare steadily. She smiled uncertainly at him; there was something about him; in spite of herself she shivered.

"Thank you for helping me. Although I have no idea why they picked on me," Kate said quietly.

"Don't you?" he asked softly. Again that velvety voice. It was menacing; yet somehow reassured her. The shiver returned.

"No," Kate said. "Why should I?"

"Perhaps. It doesn't matter, you are safe enough for now," he said. Kate felt vaguely reassured. She put her CD player in her bag and picked up her book.

Is she really that innocent? he asked himself. Or just a very good actress? She certainly didn't look like the daughter of a rich man who was supposed to be akin to gangsters; and her voice was hardly that of a rich girl. Perhaps this was her way of throwing his wealth back at him. He could understand that. Still that little niggle at the back of his mind troubled him.

They settled down, Kate to her book until she fell asleep again, him to gaze thoughtfully out the window. Once Kate was asleep he produced a pad of cotton wool and a bottle from his bag. He kept a watchful eye on the girl but she slept on, unknowingly. He looked at his watch. It was nearly time. He tipped an amount on the pad and replaced the bottle in his bag. He carefully pressed the pad over her nose. She put up no fight and soon was unconscious slumped against him. He just had time to put the pad in his bag when he saw a guard coming through the carriage. He went to the door and showed two first class tickets.

"They were being very rowdy earlier, but they seem harmless enough now," he told the guard pointing at the two men and the woman. The guard frowned. He walked back through the carriage without bothering them. Thunder went back to the first class. He put their bags by the door.

They pulled into Haywards Heath soon after. He opened the door and threw the bags out. He looked at a guard and called him over. He put Kate over his shoulder and got off the train. The guard picked up the bags and followed him.

A police van appeared with four policemen who took the two men and Sue off the train, bundling them into the van. He imagined they would be taken to the nearest police station. No one gave him a look. He carried Kate to the car park and up to a black car. He laid her on the back seat while the guard put their bags in the boot.

"Will she be all right?" the guard asked eyeing Kate.

"Yeah, fine," Thunder replied. "She often has these fainting fits. A good sleep and she'll be fine,"

"Well if you're sure?" the guard was doubtful.

"Positive. Thank you for your help," Thunder said firmly. He gave the guard a tenner.

"Thank you sir," he pocketed the tenner and walked away.

Thunder got in the car and drove away. He turned out the town and into the countryside. He looked over his shoulder at Kate but she was still unconscious. He sped down country lanes until he came to a small airfield. He drove slowly up the lane to it. A helicopter was waiting, the pilot stood near by. When he saw the black car he started it up. Thunder parked near the building, carried Kate to the helicopter, returning for the bags. The pilot looked over his shoulder at Kate and then back to his controls. He was being well paid to see nothing.

They took off, flying south towards the Isle of Wight. Thunder kept a careful eye on Kate but she stayed unconscious throughout. He was becoming vaguely uneasy but couldn't put a finger on why. Again he had the same thought as Sammy. Sarah Palmerston-Smith was supposed to be stunningly beautiful and this girl was pretty enough. He shrugged, what was stunningly beautiful to one man wasn't to another, and he had never liked supposedly stunningly beautiful women, although he'd had more than his share of beautiful women in the past.

Once they had flown off a man came out of the building. He stood watching them disappear then got into the car and took his mobile phone out of his pocket. He rang Bob Lowman.

"They have taken off," he said when Lowman answered.

"Good," Lowman said. "Any problems?"

"None that I could see," the man said. "He had the girl drugged. She seemed okay,"

"What's he like?" Lowman asked out of curiosity.

"Well dressed, dark hair, tall, pretty ordinary really," the man said. It was the same description Joe was giving a policeman in Haywards Heath.

Lowman grunted. "I'll be in touch," he said and hung up. The man drove back to London.

The helicopter landed in open space near a farmhouse that was otherwise surrounded by woodland. Thunder carried Kate in, the pilot followed with the luggage. Thunder laid Kate on a bed and left her bag with her. He looked round the farmhouse, opening cupboards and windows. Besides the sitting room, there was a kitchen, scullery, hallway, bathroom and three bedrooms. In the master bedroom there was a double bed, the other bedrooms had two singles in each. It was usually let to at least six or eight people, the sofa converting to another double bed. There was a track leading to the house through the wood from a small lane so passing traffic were unlikely to be a problem. It was remote enough for his needs, there was plenty of food, heat and water, and a group of tourists weren't likely to appear on the doorstep.

While he looked round the pilot sat in the sitting room. Once Thunder was satisfied he sent the pilot back to the mainland and settled down to wait for a phone call and Kate to wake up. At eleven o'clock the phone rang.

"Have you the girl?" a voice asked. Thunder realised it was

not the Aussie. Perhaps his boss?

"Yes," Thunder's voice was quiet.

"Was she harmed?" the voice sounded anxious.

"No," Thunder replied quietly.

"Any problems?" the voice relaxed.

"There were two men and a girl also trying to grab her but I dealt with them," Thunder said.

"What?" the voice suddenly became anxious again.

"Don't worry I got rid of them," Thunder's voice dropped to a purr. "I expect the police will have a few questions for them," he sounded amused.

"I'll pass that on and get back to you tomorrow. Keep an eye on her, she's got quite a temper by all accounts," there was a noise in the background. Someone had come in. The phone went dead. Now it was a waiting game.

Thunder leaned back in the chair, cradling the handset and looked up at the ceiling. God, he hated this game. This was definitely the very last time.

"Should I know why first those two men and now you needed to kidnap me?" Kate demanded angrily. She was standing in the doorway leaning against the frame with folded arms and a frown.

He looked round as he calmly put down the handset. She could move very quietly, he hadn't heard her, which surprised him; and she looked pretty annoyed right now. Justifiably.

"Ah, you've woken up," was all he said.

"Obviously," she said sarcastically. He indicated the chair opposite him. She crossed the room and sat down reluctantly.

"Surely, you've guessed by now," he said gently.

"No," Kate was definite.

"Oh come on Sarah, you can't keep this pretence up for ever," Thunder decided to humour her.

"Sarah? My name is Kate," she said firmly. "Kate Bromham,"

"What?" he paused, momentarily thrown off balance. Then he gave a hollow laugh. "Oh very good Sarah. Nice trick, but it won't work," the last few words came out low and slow and utterly cold. Kate shivered involuntarily.

"Trick? I can assure you it's no trick. I am not called Sarah,"

Kate curled up in the chair, drawing her feet under her and refolded her arms.

Thunder watched her. He felt that he was seeing her for the first time. He went over the description again. Sarah Palmerston-Smith was supposed to be tall, slim and stunningly beautiful with dark shoulder length hair and glasses. He guessed from carrying her that this girl was more medium build and height and, although attractive, was not stunningly beautiful by anyone's standards. Her long dark hair hung past her shoulders with the front pinned back. She wore large glasses that didn't really suit her face, faded jeans and a baggy white sweatshirt with no make up and the only jewellery was a pair of gold studs and a black inexpensive watch. From what he had read about Sarah Palmerston-Smith, she wouldn't be seen dead without being immaculately turned out and right now be probably be throwing quite an impressive fit.

Sarah was the vain, spoilt daughter of a rich man and Kate most certainly didn't fit this description. In fact when Thunder looked at Kate properly there was not a shred of vanity to be seen and she did not fit the description at all. It was the similar clothes and the bags that had done it. The niggle that had been bothering him suddenly became very clear: dark hair, glasses, jeans, boots, white sweatshirt, black handbag, brown holdall. That description could have fitted half of London!

He thought for a few minutes as the knowledge sunk in, his eyes staring at Kate without seeing. The clock on the mantelpiece ticked away, ominously loud. Kate stared back at him steadily. She waited for him to speak. She could see him weighing things up and waited for her fate to be decided. Whatever it was she didn't much care.

Thunder looked at this girl and remembered that he hadn't heard her come down the stairs. She sat very still with her arms folded and hardly blinked. Here was someone who obviously kept her emotions and temper under a tight rein. Well he understood that, at least.

"I hope for your sake you are Sarah Palmerston-Smith," he stated.

"Why? I'm not," Kate replied coldly.

"Because if you're not, then I and the other three have picked the wrong girl and Sarah Palmerston-Smith is still free," he felt angry that he could have been so wrong, but then so had the others - and they certainly wouldn't be quite so calm right now if the position was reversed. He turned cold.

"Oh," Kate couldn't think of anything else to say as she digested this piece of information. "Three? What three?" she suddenly asked.

"The two men and the girl in the mini skirt," he told her.

"Girl? Oh her. I thought she was…," Kate trailed off, her voice dying.

"A stranger on the train?" Thunder said savagely. Kate nodded. "We all were," he said grimly.

"Oh," again.

"Well, we'd better get some sleep and work it out tomorrow," he said.

Kate looked at him sharply. "I think I've slept long enough,"

"Probably, but I haven't," he said coldly.

"Tough," Kate said savagely.

Thunder looked at her. He admired her cool, she was taking this fairly well, considering. "I could always put you out again," he said quietly.

"You could, but I can't think if I'm drugged," she retorted.

"Think? About what?" he asked her.

Kate swallowed and looked at him with more confidence than she actually felt. "How to extract myself with the least amount of trouble," she said. "I'm sure you can look after yourself," the last was said with sarcasm dripping. He resisted the temptation to smile. Kate looked at the phone. "Why don't you phone someone and find out what's going on?" she asked.

"They contact me," he said.

"Oh," Kate pondered the situation. Then she sighed. "Oh well, here is as good a place as any," she got up and started across the room. At the door she stopped and turned. "What do I call you, by the way?"

"Thunder,"

"Thunder?" she gave him a quizzical look.

"Thunder," he repeated just as coldly as the first time.

"Why? Do you 'thunder' around the place?" she asked with a smile.

"No. I cause thunder," he said. Kate frowned. "I've been known to blow things up," he explained.

"Oh. I see," Kate didn't sound too sure. "People too?" He nodded. "Nice," she was being sarcastic again. "I'll go to bed now,"

He followed her up and checked the windows. Kate stood at the door and watched, arms folded. "I doubt I'll be running anywhere," she told him.

"Just checking," Kate's humph told him she wasn't convinced. "Anyway," he said as he crossed the room. "It's a long walk in any direction," he stood very close to her. "And I doubt you know where you are," he added quietly.

She looked up at him. This close his eyes looked cold and lifeless, like glass. She felt like someone had just walked over her grave. "I couldn't care less where I am," she said.

"Good," he walked past her.

"Anywhere is better than home," she added quietly and shut the door.

He looked back over his shoulder but all he saw was the door closing. He shrugged and went to bed. He would have to wait for another phone call before he could decide what to do. One thing was certain, he wasn't about to kill a perfectly innocent girl because of his stupidity. Something did bother him though. Where was Sarah Palmerston-Smith? This obviously wasn't her, he was convinced of that.

CHAPTER THREE

The next morning Thunder woke about nine. From somewhere beneath him he could smell fresh coffee and bacon cooking. He rolled off the bed and looked out the window. The sky was grey and overcast and it was drizzling. He went downstairs. He could hear voices in the kitchen. He crept towards the door, gun in his hand.

Thunder silently pushed open the door. Kate was cooking breakfast, the radio blaring. He stood in the doorway and watched her deftly flip over some bacon, her back to him. He stepped into the room and let the door slam. She jumped and turned, the slice in her hand, threatening him. He looked at her amused.

"Oh very funny," she said. Then the colour drained from her face as she saw the gun in his hand. Her hand went to her throat as any retort that she might have said, died. "Oh my God," she whispered. He put the safety catch back on and laid it down on the worktop near the door.

"Not quite," he said quietly.

"I suppose you think it's funny frightening me half to death," she said angrily.

"Would you rather I frightened you totally to death?" he asked softly. "Something smells good,"

Kate looked at him for a minute or two and then turned her back on him, returning her attention to breakfast. He helped himself to a glass of orange juice and made a cup of black coffee. Kate put a large plate on the table with bacon, sausages, tomatoes and scrambled egg followed by a plate of toast. Kate poured herself a cup of tea. They sat opposite each other and ate in silence. Kate was too hungry to ask questions and Thunder didn't volunteer any information.

"Was there anything on the news?" Thunder asked after he

had eaten. The large plate was now empty. Kate was finishing off the toast.

She looked up from spreading marmalade, the knife in mid stroke. "No," she replied and went back to spreading the marmalade.

"Won't someone be missing you?" Thunder asked.

Kate licked the marmalade off her fingers. "I doubt it. I never planned to go away. I just got on a train and went. No one is expecting me to turn up. I'm not expected at home and I wouldn't be missed anyway. So no, no one will miss me," she said.

"I see," he said and made another coffee. "We'll have to stay here until I get told otherwise,"

"When will they tell you?" Kate asked finishing her toast.

Thunder shrugged. He expected a call at midday, it was now half ten. Kate stacked the breakfast things and started to wash up, ignoring him. He slowly got up and left, picking up the coffee and his gun. If Kate noticed he'd gone, she gave no hint.

He went into the sitting room and lit the fire. Outside it was still drizzling. He sat in the chair and watched the fire slowly burn, the coffee in one hand, the gun across his lap. Kate joined him a few minutes later.

She looked through the bookcase, found a book, flopped down on the sofa and started to read. However the words danced in front of her eyes and she soon closed it with a sigh and laid it down. She put her head back against the sofa.

"Care to talk?" Thunder asked. He hadn't looked at her once since she had entered the room and sat down. He kept his gaze on the flames.

"I was wondering what to have for dinner," Kate started. "I presume we'll still be here then,"

"No, not about dinner. Why were you on a train going nowhere in particular?" he looked at her. "No family or friends to spend Easter with?" He shifted slightly to get a clear vision of her. Kate moved her head and looked at him.

"No," she said sharply. "I wanted to be on my own,"

"Any particular reason?"

"No," she said again sharply. She twisted her hands, dropping her gaze to them in her lap. He watched her.

"You're hard work, you know that?" he said and could have been talking about himself.

"Sorry?" Kate looked up. Thunder looked at her with a questioning look. She smiled involuntarily. His expression told her she could trust him. His past behaviour didn't. She shivered.

"Are you cold? Come over to the fire," he indicated the chair opposite him. Kate did as she was told. They sat in silence and watched the fire burn.

"What about you?" Kate asked.

"I'm always alone," he said. "Actually I don't usually talk to my victims,"

"Should I feel honoured?" Kate asked coldly.

He smiled at her. "No. I am what I am. A hired person. I do what has to be done for people I never see who pay me well so they don't get their hands dirty. This job is a mistake I should have seen coming," he said. He put his head back and looked up at the ceiling. "I'm getting too old for this crap," he groaned. He looked sideways at her. "Perhaps it's time I did something else,"

"Like gardening?" she asked and then laughed. "I can't see you gardening,"

"Hardly," he agreed.

"So you're a paid assassin?" she asked.

"Sometimes. Or I blow things up," he was being very off hand, very blasé about it.

"Things? Or people?" Kate asked.

"Sometimes both. It's unfortunate for those caught up. I ask no questions and give no moral judgements," he said slowly. "Well not often," he added quietly.

Kate looked at him. Despite her initial horror, she felt a fascination. Lulled by his calm quiet voice, she was attracted in a morbid way, but entirely horrified by his cold description of his job. He could have been describing a boring job in the city.

"No regrets? No remorse? Nothing?" Kate asked.

"Nothing," he said tonelessly. He watched Kate, he could almost see her thoughts, her fingers played with the hem of her jumper.

"What happens now?" she asked.

"I get a phone call," he said.

"Then you act," she finished for him. He nodded. He looked at his watch. It was now ten to twelve.

"Not long now," he said.

They sat quietly, waiting, listening to the fire crackle and the rain outside against the windows. Suddenly the phone began to ring, a wail that went round and round. Kate jumped nervously. Thunder calmly picked it up.

"Hello," he listened, strangely detached.

"I have relayed the message," the voice said. "Stay there until I ring again,"

"There is a slightly complication," Thunder said.

"What?" the voice sounded irritated.

"The girl I have here is not the one you want," Thunder said calmly. He looked at Kate. She tried not to listen.

"What?" the voice suddenly became nearly hysterical and went up several notes in pitch. Thunder winced, pulling the phone from his ear.

"The right girl gave us all the slip," Thunder said calmly. "She wasn't on the train. The girl I have was,"

"What?" the voice was a little quieter but still near hysteria.

"You heard," Thunder said in that velvety voice that made Kate shiver.

There was silence at the other end of the phone. Kate found herself holding her breath. Thunder sat calmly and waited for the caller to speak. He could almost hear the person's brain whirling, the silence was so complete.

"Right, kill that girl," the voice said. "And get after the right one!" the voice yelled. Thunder winced again and looked at Kate. He hoped she couldn't hear this. "I can't send the 'copter so you'll have to make your own way back to the mainland," the voice was back under control. "Wait," he spoke to someone in the background. Thunder could hear a muffled voice but not what they were saying.

"Right," he was back. "Kill that girl, do whatever, then get out of there fast. There are others on your trail and they believe you have the right girl. Only they will kill both of you,"

"I see," Thunder's voice was cold. "And how do they know where to find me?" there was no answer. Thunder's eyes got hard. Whoever had hired him was going to regret not trusting him to do the job. "How do I contact you?" he asked.

"You don't. I'll make contact through the Chinaman. Don't get it wrong!" the phone line went dead. Thunder replaced the received, his face was hard, he looked annoyed. Kate waited for a few seconds more.

"We're leaving," Thunder said quietly.

"Not killing me then?" Kate asked.

"You have good hearing,"

"He had a loud voice,"

"Why should I?" he asked softly.

"I'm in your way," Kate stated.

"You are an innocent victim of my gross stupidity," he stated. "It serves nothing,"

"I will hold you up," Kate said. "You're in danger,"

"So are you," he said.

"Not dead, I'm not," Kate stated.

"Stop being a martyr and go pack. We're leaving in a hour," he said.

Kate looked like she was about to argue then got up and went upstairs. He replaced the book, straightened the covers on the chairs, put out the fire and laid a new one. He went upstairs. As he put his bag on the landing Kate appeared. She had on her boots and jacket, her handbag over her shoulder, carrying her holdall.

"I've tidied my room," she said.

"Good," he looked round the rooms and they went downstairs. In the sitting room Kate sat on the arm of the chair. Thunder pulled out a map and looked at it. He went into the kitchen. The back door was locked and there was no key. He went into the scullery and pulled the window off the hinges. He peered out. It led out into a covered alleyway which opened onto the back garden. In one wall was a door to the cellar. He turned round. Kate was standing at the door.

"We'll have to go out through here," he said.

"What's wrong with the front door?" Kate asked.

"We have to go through the woods at the back. I don't want to leave tracks round the house," he replied.

"Fine," she replied. "In that case we'll take this with us," she held out her hand. On the palm sat the front door key. "I've locked it,"

"Good idea," he said. He fetched their bags and threw them through the window. He helped Kate through the window and followed her. She stood at the end of the alleyway looking up at the sky.

Behind the cottage the garden was overgrown. The back lawn went into the wood. There was a line strung from the cottage to a tree. There was no path. He figured whoever was coming would do so by road up to the front. He picked up his bag and walked across the lawn trying not to leave tracks.

Kate put her handbag across her body, put her arms through the handles of her holdall and followed him closely. In the wood they were fairly sheltered from the rain. Thunder looked at her and did the same with his bag. They were much easier to carry that way. He kept the map in his jacket pocket and consulted it every so often. He started off. Kate followed.

The weather turned worse. The rain got heavier and soon, even with the shelter of the trees, they were soaked. The ground was becoming like sludge but at least their footprints were disappearing soon after they made them. Thunder looked at Kate. She trudged along behind him, head down, following his boots, putting her feet where his went, thoroughly wet and looking thoroughly miserable.

After a couple of hours they came to a village with one hotel. Thunder motioned to Kate to stay put. He walked off to the hotel. Minutes later he came out and waved at Kate. She trudged over. The landlady showed them into a twin bedded room with adjoining bathroom. She eyed their wet and filthy state sympathetically.

"I do hope your car gets fixed soon," she said. "You must be tired after walking so far," Kate kept her head down and her eyes on the hem of the woman's dress. "There's plenty of hot water, tea and coffee. I'll make sure there's some soup with your dinner. Dinner's at six," she said cheerfully. Neither said a word.

The landlady stopped talking and left, closing the door behind her. Kate and Thunder stood in the room, making puddles on the carpet. There was a pile of newspapers. Kate pulled off her boots and put them on a few sheets. She looked at the beds with dismay. Thunder saw her look.

"It was all I could get. Single rooms would have meant questions. We're lucky to get two beds. She wanted to give us a double bed," he said.

"It will suffice," Kate said and took off her jacket. She was too tired to argue, she desperately wanted a cup of tea and a hot bath. She hung her jacket on the back of a chair. She stood looking round the room, silently flexing her hands which were white with cold.

"You'd better have a bath, you look shattered," Thunder said. He took off his jacket and dropped it onto a newspaper. He took the kettle and filled it. When he returned and plugged it in Kate hadn't moved although she'd stopped flexing her hands. "You look frozen," he said kindly.

"I'm not used to trudging through a wood all day in the rain knowing any minute might be my last!" she retorted.

Thunder felt sorry for her. This was normal for him, his way of life, danger, intrigue, death. "I'll run that bath," he said turning the kettle on.

Kate opened her bag and pulled out various things. When Thunder came back in Kate was sitting drinking a cup of tea. She went past him into the bathroom and shut the door. She pulled off her wet clothes and sank into the bath. The smell of food got her out. She came out in a robe with her hair wrapped in a towel. Clean with her hair off her face and no glasses she looked pretty. Thunder handed her a glass of wine.

"Compliments of the house," he said. He had eaten his dinner and went into the bathroom.

Kate attacked her dinner, not realising how hungry she was. She was beginning to feel more human now. She wasn't sure she liked this man, but she would have to trust his expertise. He was her only hope of getting out of this mess. He came out dressed in black trousers, white open neck shirt and burgundy jumper. He sat on the bed and put on some socks.

"What do we do now?" she asked.

"Sleep," he answered.

"I meant tomorrow," Kate said pointedly.

"I find us transport to Ryde and from there to Portsmouth. I have to get you to safety and find the right girl," he told her.

"I wonder where she went," Kate mused.

"I was told she was catching the half two train to Brighton from Victoria. I'll have to start there," he said.

"She could have taken a coach or stayed in London. Wouldn't be surprised if she wasn't at home, safe and sound," Kate said.

"I expect they're checking that," he said. Kate looked at him. She longed to get into bed. "I'll take a walk round and see what there is to this village," he said and went out.

Kate poured some more wine and got into bed. She sipped the wine and then rubbed her hair dry. This gave her time to think. Her thoughts chased round and round in her head as she combed her hair. She sighed, she could see no solution except to trust Thunder. At least he knew what he was doing and she didn't. She didn't even know where she was, although she guessed from his comments that it was the Isle of Wight. Finally she laid down and fell asleep, not hearing Thunder return. He looked at her sleeping, her hair spread out on the pillow. She looked peaceful. He went to bed and surprisingly slept.

The next morning Kate woke and turned over. She gave a start when she saw Thunder asleep in the next bed, on his stomach, his right arm thrown across the pillow. She sat up, hugged her knees and watched him. She could see weals across his back. She got up, pulled on the robe and looked out the window. It had stopped raining and the sun had come out. She watched the village come alive. There was a knock at the door. Kate turned and saw Thunder had woken up and was lying in bed watching her, hands behind his head.

"Mr Brown, are you awake? Early morning coffee," a voice called.

Kate threw a questioning look at Thunder. He dropped his arms and looked relaxed. As she crossed the room to the door she had the fleeting thought that he was anything but. A maid stood outside with a tray. Kate took it, thanked her and shut the door. She took it over to the bedside table between the beds and put it down. Thunder sat up. She sat on her bed.

His toned torso showed a few scars, signs that life had been hard and often bloody. He had a long scar on the right running along the bottom of the ribs disappearing around his side. The dark hair on his chest stopped short of a vivid scar on the left. It was about three or four inches long, puckered, white, clearly showing where it had been very crudely stitched and ran from his collar bone down to his breast. Kate's eyes became transfixed. He looked down at his chest and put a hand to it.

"Just a battle wound. A knife that nearly finished me off," he said lightly. The rest he waved off. "The others are life,"

"The surgeon wasn't too clever," Kate said.

He smiled. "Dan was drunk at the time," he said and gently probed it.

"And the weals on your back?" Kate asked. He looked at her sharply. "I saw them this morning," she explained.

"Scars from a jealous woman. Sharpened her nails into talons because she thought I was cheating on her," Thunder said with a smile.

"And were you?" Kate couldn't help asking.

He chuckled. "Not at the time. That was a few days later," She frowned at him. "Might as well be hung for a sheep as a lamb," he quoted.

He was taking this all so lightly, suddenly Kate felt helpless.

"What if they catch us?" she asked him quietly.

"Then I'll have to kill them," he said coldly. Kate looked at him. She believed him – and felt nothing.

"Coffee?" she asked in as normal a voice as possible.

At eight she got up, picked up some clothes and disappeared into the bathroom. By the time she emerged Thunder was up and dressed, same as last night. At half past eight they went down for breakfast. Halfway down he stopped.

"Here, you'd better wear this," he dropped a ring into her hand. "We are supposed to be Mr and Mrs Brown. Try not to call me Thunder,"

"What is your name?" she asked putting it on.

"Krysten. You do realise you are the only person I've ever told?"

"Oh I am honoured," she said sarcastically. She followed him downstairs. They had breakfast, talked about general things and then went out for a walk.

As they walked down the road Thunder pointed out things. "There isn't much. Mostly farmers. A pub. A post office and general store. The bus service doesn't run until Tuesday," Thunder said.

They carried on walking and came to the church. Against the wall was a seat. Thunder gestured to it. They sat down. People went past them without a glance.

"We'll have to stay here until tomorrow morning. The bus leaves about half ten," Thunder said. Kate had got used to him. His close proximity didn't bother her anymore. He faced her. "Why were you on a train going nowhere at Easter?" he asked putting his arm along the back of the seat.

Kate looked at him sideways. "I wanted to get away, that's all,"

"All? I think not,"

Kate sighed. She looked at him. He looked back, expectantly. "Nothing to write home about. Usual rubbish,"

"Ah huh? And?" he wasn't convinced.

Kate sighed again. "Okay," she gave in. "Boy meets girl. Boy cheats on girl. Many times. Girl finds out. Girl leaves. It's no big deal," Kate said defensively.

"So?" Thunder was intrigued.

"Well, this particular boy," she emphasised 'boy'. "When he cheated the first time and I didn't dump him, he started doing it more often. A friend, well now ex friend. My younger and much prettier sister. Finally my supposed best friend who is expecting his child. My sister took great pleasure in telling me, of course. Now he has decided that it's me he really wants so my parents are insisting that I marry the creep. It keeps him from my sister who they are pushing towards this rather good looking and rich solicitor they want as a son in law. My feelings don't come into it of course. Actually I don't have a lot of say in it at all. Bit medieval really but there you are, small minded people in small minded provincial town and all that. Now I have been given the ultimatum: marry the creep or get out. My friends, and I use that term loosely, are all encouraging me to do it because in their view it is the best offer I'm ever likely to get. Even my once best friend thinks it's a good idea! Gives her the chance to dump his child on his wife and bugger off!" she stopped. He didn't say anything. "So, to answer your question from... err... yesterday I think it was, no there is no one that will miss me!"

"I see. Where I grew up arranged marriages were the norm. So I have no idea. What do you want? Love, trust, romance?" he said.

"Hardly! Mind you mutual respect wouldn't go amiss. As for trust! Ha! I wouldn't trust that piece of shit as far as I could throw him with my hands tied behind my back!" He smiled. "Actually I don't know what I want. All I do know is that I don't want him,"

"Then leave," he said.

"Where to? I'm nothing more than a compliant door mat. I do what everyone tells me," Kate said harshly.

He leaned closer. "So why argue with me?" he asked softly.

She looked at him stricken for a few minutes. This close she could see his eyes very clearly. They were more green than grey, which was a surprise.

"Your eyes are quite green," she said changing the subject.

"I have my mother's eyes," he said, surprised. He never talked of his family.

She felt the sensation of someone walking over her grave and barely suppressed a shudder. "You can only see how grey/green they are close up," she said, more calmly than she felt.

"Just as well people don't get close too often," he said softly.

"They look blue from afar," she said calmly.

"And therefore very ordinary," he replied with a smile.

"Oh you're far from ordinary," she said. You certainly are, she mused to herself silently.

He smiled. Then put his hand to her face and, drawing her to him, kissed her. He released her, her face inches from his.

"Why did you do that?" she asked in a husky voice.

"Are you complaining?" he asked with a smile.

"No. I'll give you about half a hour to stop," she said jokingly.

"Only half a hour?" he asked mockingly.

"Okay, four half hours," she replied in the same tone.

Thunder kissed her again. The church bells suddenly started to peel, breaking the mood and them apart. They got to their feet laughing and walked back to the hotel. They sat in the lounge and read the papers. At six Thunder went out to check the time of the bus. Kate sat in a large chair in the corner reading a paper. Within minutes he was back.

"Kate, quick, go to the room," he said to her over the top of the paper.

She looked up. "Why?"

"I've just seen those two men from the train book in for the night. Luckily they didn't see me," he said.

Kate left quickly. Thunder took her place behind the paper. They came in with a map asking the landlady for directions. They took no notice of the few occupants of the lounge and left. Thunder folded the paper and thought for a few minutes. He got up and found the landlady in the hallway. He arranged for dinner to be served in their room and went upstairs.

Kate had been pacing but stopped when he came in. He threw the papers and magazines he had brought with him on her bed.

"We should stay here tonight," he told her.

She pulled a face. "A whole evening stuck in this room with no TV? Hardly my idea of fun," Kate said. "It's not as if I've got an interesting companion to talk to either," she added mischievously.

He looked at her sharply, saw her smile and relaxed. He turned on the radio. He picked up the paper and lay across his bed. Kate stood there and watched him. He looked totally unperturbed.

"Krysten, what if they find us?" she asked.

"I'll deal with them," he said without looking up. "Sit down, relax, read, listen to the radio, anything," he said. When he got no reply he looked up. "I can't go and slit their throats in the night, much as I'd like to. So relax," She started to pace again. He watched her. She reminded him of a large cat at a zoo pacing behind its bars. There was something about her that was appealing. He shook his head. No, he told himself, first rule: do not get involved with the victim. "Stop pacing! You're causing a draught. Sit down! Compliant my foot!" he said and returned to his paper.

Kate sat down. He looked so calm. She'd trusted him so far but suppose he was wrong? He'd been wrong about Sarah Palmerston-Smith, hadn't he? What if he was wrong about these men?

"What if they don't leave until after the bus? We'll miss it," she said.

"My guess is, they'll leave early so as to catch us out," he said. "I would, if I was them,"

"You'd go now," she said.

"True. Just as well they're not me," he said. He carried on reading. "Did you realise you called me Krysten without thinking?" he asked without looking up.

"Did I? I don't remember," Kate said.

He looked up at her. "Don't worry. We'll be fine. I'll deal with them if needs be," he smiled.

She smiled at him. She fiddled with the radio. She couldn't find a station. The music grated on her nerves whatever she found. He put the paper down with a sigh. He looked at her. He got up and found a channel with classical music, nice and soothing. He went back to his paper. She picked up a magazine and gradually relaxed.

At eight there was a knock on the door. He answered it, took the tray and shut the door. They ate in silence. The soothing music turned into brass bands. He turned it off. He suggested cards. She pulled a face.

"I could ask the landlady if she has a portable TV we can borrow," he suggested. He went off and came back with a portable TV. He set it up and they watched TV. There was nothing of particular interest on the news. A film came on. After about half a hour the TV started to play up. Thunder fiddled with the aerial. It didn't make any difference. Kate tried moving the TV. Eventually they found a position where there was a picture but it meant that Kate couldn't see it sat on her bed.

"Come and sit here," Thunder said and moved over so she could sit on his bed. She sat on the edge and watched.

At one point Kate burst out laughing and fell off the bed. Thunder started to laugh and pulled her back. She grabbed his arm and hauled herself back on the bed. They continued laughing. Thunder's was the first to die as he found his arms round her. Then Kate's laughter stopped as he pulled her close. Her arms went round him as he laid her down and kissed her, gently at first, then more demanding. Kate responded. Suddenly he stopped and looked down at her.

"This isn't what I planned," he said in that velvety voice.

"What did you plan?" Kate asked.

"Nothing like this. I have a strict rule, never get involved," he said.

"So this isn't a seduction then?" she asked.

"No," he said firmly.

"I see," Kate tried to move away. She couldn't go far without falling off the bed again. "So we'll watch the film and forget this happened?"

"Good idea," he said. He sat propped up against the pillows, one arm behind his head, the other round Kate. She lay within that arm and they watched the film. At the end she leaned over and kissed him on the cheek. His arm kept her from moving away.

"What was that for?" he asked.

"As a thank you," she said.

"For what?" he felt he hardly warranted it.

"For showing me what I'm missing and what I'll probably never have with Alan," he looked puzzled. "Respect," she said.

"Alan?" he asked.

"The man back home," she replied.

"Oh," he put his arms round her and kissed her.

She pushed him away. "Your rule?" she queried.

"I also remember you gave me two hours to stop kissing you. I worked it out. I've still got time left," he looked at his watch. "About one and half hours or more by my reckoning,"

She laughed and turned off the light. She ran her hand down his back. He sighed. As he started kissing her he hit the off button on the remote control and the room went black.

CHAPTER FOUR

At seven thirty Kate woke. She looked at Thunder sleeping, his arms around her. She remembered the night before and quietly slipped out of bed. Her own bed was cold so she went and ran a bath and didn't hear the door. The first thing she heard was Thunder knocking on the bathroom door. He sat on his bed in a robe reading the papers and drinking coffee. Kate stood at the door and watched him for a few seconds. He looked up.

"Morning," he said and put down the papers. He walked towards her. As he came level Kate smiled at him uncertainly. He stepped past her into the bathroom. Kate looked over her shoulder at the closing door.

She drank some tea while she got dressed in jeans and jumper. She pulled on one boot; it was still damp inside. She pulled on her trainers. She picked up the paper discarded by Thunder and started to read. Minutes later Thunder appeared dressed also in jeans and jumper. They looked like a holidaying couple. They quickly packed their bags and just before ten he left. Minutes later he returned.

"They have just left. It should take them about forty minutes to find the cottage. We leave in ten minutes," he told her.

They left the hotel and caught the bus with a few local people. Thunder bought two tickets and they sat at the back. The bus sped along country roads, bouncing and swaying. At a sharp bend the bus gave a lurch sending Kate into Thunder. He put his arm round her and held her to him.

"Will you help me find Sarah?" he asked quietly.

Kate didn't move her head. "Why do you need my help?"

"Because she will trust another girl,"

Kate looked sideways at him. "I'm sure you could wind her round your little finger, if you choose," she said sarcastically.

"I doubt that," Thunder knew he was good at his job, but not with people.

"Why bother?" Kate asked.

"Because she is in danger. I was hired to do a job and I always do what I was hired to do. Besides, those others are amateurs and will probably kill her," he said.

"Why her?" Kate asked.

"Because her father is a powerful man and his rivals need to bring him down. They are using her to get at him," he said calmly.

Kate looked round. The people sitting nearest were several seats away. No one was taking any notice of a couple sat on the back seat. She looked back at him. "But you were hired to kidnap her," she hissed at him.

"Yes," he said toneless. "But I would keep her safe and deliver her back to her father in one piece, untouched and alive,"

"Why the change?" Kate didn't put it down to her presence. She looked at his profile. The eyes that took in everything without appearing to do so; the lips that had kissed her so tenderly last night now drawn in a thin line; the strong jaw now set; his face grim, cold, determined. There were times when he didn't seem like the ruthless killer he portrayed. Today he looked like a ruthless killer; last night he had been the tender lover.

"No change. I never intended hurting her. I always return my victims unharmed. But that won't happen if I don't find her. Those two idiots will find the cottage empty and return to England to find us. They still believe you are Sarah," he said, his voice angry.

The bus lurched into Ryde and people got off. They took their bags and went to the ferry terminal. The next ferry would leave within the hour. They found a quiet corner on the ferry and sat silently looking out the window.

Kate was thankful when they docked at Portsmouth. They found the station. Kate led the way into the ticket hall. She suddenly spotted the girl in the mini skirt coming into the ticket hall. She immediately turned on her heel, pushing Thunder backwards. They ended up near the photo booths they had just walked past. Thunder put his arms round her and pulled her to

him. He watched Sue walk by over Kate's shoulder. She didn't
look into their direction, one more courting couple didn't interest
her. They followed her at a distance. She went through the ticket
barrier and onto a train. The barrier closed and they watched the
train pull out.

"Where's that train going to?" Thunder asked the guard.

"London,"

"Shit," Thunder swore quietly.

"Is there another way to get to London?" Kate asked.

"You can go via Brighton, but you'd be better waiting for the
next train," the guard said.

They went back to the ticket hall and Thunder bought two
tickets to London via Brighton. They found a corner in a carriage
on their own. The journey passed uneventfully and they spoke
very little. Kate looked out the window, Thunder read the paper.
The change at Brighton was uneventful. It was some hours later
when they pulled into East Grinstead.

"Let's get off and go to London Bridge," Thunder suddenly
said. Kate didn't argue.

On another platform they caught the train to London Bridge.
By now it was dark and Kate was tired. Once at London Bridge
Thunder bundled Kate into a taxi and gave his Wandsworth
address. Kate was too tired to take much notice.

Thunder helped Kate up the stairs and into the flat. She sank
into a chair and looked round. It was sparse, with only the bare
essentials and little furniture. Kate looked at the empty shelves
with interest, the dust told her that these had been recently
emptied, she didn't think he would live like this normally.

"Where are we?" she asked him.

"My flat. Do you want a drink?" he went to the only cupboard
left.

She shook her head. "Are we safe here?"

"No one knows where I live. We should be safe enough," he
poured himself a glass of whisky.

"I could sleep for a week," Kate groaned.

"You have the bed. I'll sleep in here," he showed her the
bedroom and closed the door behind her.

She looked round. It was very basic: double bed, bedside table, chest of drawers and built in wardrobe. There were no pictures. She got undressed, got into bed and slept.

Thunder sat in the chair and slowly drank his whisky. He started thinking about where Sarah could have gone; what she had done; how anyone could mix up Sarah and Kate. Only the clothes had been similar; and the bags; and the hair colour; and the fact that they both wore glasses. He sighed, perhaps they had been similar. He thought about Kate. He knew he shouldn't involve her, but she was involved whether he liked it or not, otherwise she would be dead and that bothered him. He would have to sort out the two men and Sue; find Sarah; get her and Kate to safety; sort out the hirers; return the girls to their lives. A tall order. He trusted her; not something that he did lightly; she had come into his life in the strangest of ways. On the one hand he felt comfortable with her; on the other having her with him unnerved him. He finished the whisky and went into the bedroom to get some blankets.

Kate was asleep in the bed. He stood by the window and looked out. London lights. Anonymous London. Here you could disappear and not be found. Could he find Sarah? Kate stirred. He looked over his shoulder. Slipping in with her would be so easy. Kate started to talk in her sleep, mumbling, then cried out but the words were indecipherable but he could guess what it was about. Alan. He thought he would like to meet this man; it might prove instructive - for him. He shook her shoulder; she fought his hand off; he grabbed her shoulders and shook her; she woke with a start and sat up. Thunder still held her shoulders.

"What?" she looked up, she couldn't make out his features. Why was he kneeling over her? And her shoulders hurt.

"You were having a nightmare," he said softly.

"I'm cold," she started to shiver.

He kicked off his shoes and lay down next to her. He put his arms round her, she didn't resist, just settled down, her head on his shoulder and went back to sleep.

Kate woke about eight. She turned over and saw Thunder asleep, his back to her, rolled up in a blanket. She went and made some coffee. She had to nudge him awake. He sat up and took the coffee. She got in bed and sat with her knees up and her cup balanced on top, watching him.

"What?" he asked.

"Nothing," she said. "What are we doing today?"

"I've been thinking. You'd be better at home. They don't know where you live. I'll find Sarah and sort out the mess," he said.

"That's not what you said yesterday,"

"I've thought sensibly about it since then," he replied coldly.

"I see," she got out of bed and went off to the bathroom. He watched her go. She had become a friend, someone he trusted. Then he turned cold; she had become someone who could be used against him and that usually meant one thing: she would die. He didn't want Kate to be sacrificed like his family or the other friends he had once had. He had to get Kate safely out of the way.

He got up, changed jumpers, went into the kitchen. Kate emerged dressed in ski pants and big baggy sweatshirt. They went to Leicester Square and then Chinatown. Thunder wanted to see Kit. After the fourth call he called it a day. Kit was nowhere to be found.

"He's obviously heard and gone to ground. Everyone knows he is my contact, he knows the places I go," Thunder said.

"Isn't that dangerous knowledge?" Kate asked.

"Kit knows how to look after himself. We'll go to Victoria, get some lunch and start the search for Sarah," he said.

They went up to the food hall at Victoria. Over lunch they discussed what they would do.

"I could go to Victoria coach station," Kate suggested. "Try to see if there are coaches that leave around the same time,"

Thunder nodded. "I could ask a few people," he said.

They finished lunch and left. They came down the escalators and at the bottom stopped. Kate watched other people coming down.

"Where shall we meet?" Thunder asked, expecting somewhere well known.

"The bottom of the steps at the bottom of Essex Street," she suggested.

"Where?" he thought he knew London.

"Essex Street, opposite the Law Courts, near St Clement Danes church, Fleet Street," Kate explained.

Thunder looked impressed. "What time?"

"Four?"

"Fine. See you later," Thunder turned away. He saw Sammy leaning against a wall watching them. Where had he come from? Sammy looked at them with interest. Kate walked away and disappeared into the crowd. Sammy looked from Thunder to her. He frowned, by the time he had realised she fitted the description she had disappeared. Thunder walked off towards the underground. Sammy looked once more where Kate had gone but she had disappeared. He pushed himself off the wall and started to follow Thunder. Thunder saw this and sauntered along seemingly unperturbed.

He went onto the Victoria line. Sammy followed a few yards behind. Thunder made sure he was being followed. Thunder sat in the middle of the carriage, Sammy stood at one end. Thunder looked out the window at Sammy's reflection looking at him. At Oxford Circus Thunder got off. He started towards the Central Line. Then he saw Sue. She was still in her red leather mini skirt, her long legs crossed at the ankles as she leaned against a wall. Her face registered Sammy and she followed him. Thunder now had both of them. He strode down the platform at a leisurely pace. The train left the platform and another approached soon after.

Thunder stood near the edge as though waiting. Sammy stood a few yards from Thunder. Sue followed Sammy. Suddenly Sammy looked to his left and saw Sue looking at the poster across the track. The train was getting closer and closer. People looked towards the train, expectantly.

Then it happened. Even people standing next to Sue saw nothing. Thunder watched helplessly as Sammy moved towards Sue still looking at the poster. He tried to move towards her. The train came into the station, people surged forward to meet the train. There was one scream followed by several others as Sue fell into the path of the oncoming train. She never stood a chance; no one could have saved her; there was no way Thunder would have got through the throng of people, no matter how he tried. As people surged forward and back Thunder took his chance and pushed his way through the crowd across the platform towards an exit.

Thunder walked quickly onto the other platform and down to the exit. He went up the stairs two at a time. People moved to and fro around him. He ignored them. He didn't look back. Sammy stood helpless among the crowd and watched him go; he started to push his way out of the crowd around him but by the time he got himself free of the people Thunder had disappeared. It took Sammy a couple of minutes to find out that a train had not come in on the other platform. Frantically he ran from the platform. A policeman blocked his way.

"And were are you going in such a hurry sir?" he asked.

"Some girl fell under a train. It was awful. I feel sick. I'm trying to get out but I'm lost," Sammy blurted out.

The policeman pointed up the corridor to an exit. Sammy quickly walked away and leapt up the stairs onto the street. Thunder was gone. Sammy got out his mobile phone and rang Joe. After a small conference they decided to try the pubs near the girl's home. It was exactly where Thunder was going.

Sammy flagged down a cab and met Joe outside the first pub. Together they toured the list of pubs they had been given. In the sixth one Sammy saw Thunder standing at the far end of the bar talking to the barmaid. He nudged Joe.

"There, at the end of the bar," Sammy said.

"Where?" Joe looked at the sea of people.

"At the end of the bar. Talking to the barmaid. Black jumper. Leather jacket," Sammy said pointing.

"So that is the great Thunder, you reckon," Joe jeered.

"Must be," Sammy said. "He was with the girl earlier,"

"Huh! Looks like nothing to me. Should be a piece of piss," Joe sneered.

Thunder suddenly looked at his watch, drank up, said goodbye and left. Sammy and Joe followed. Joe got the car and Sammy followed on foot. Thunder led Sammy into a chemist where he bought some batteries, then into a book shop where he looked at books, he asked the assistant something, then left. Joe sat in the car and fidgeted.

"Where's he going?" Sammy asked him through the window as they watched Thunder leave the book shop and walk down the road.

"How the fuck should I know. Just follow him," Joe snarled. "He'll lead us to the girl and then I'll take care of them both,"

Finally Thunder went inside a church. Sammy hung about outside. Joe slowly drove past just in time to see Thunder come out a back door and hail a cab. Joe banged the horn and sped off after the cab. He called Sammy on the mobile.

"I'm following him. I'll see you later," he snapped the mobile closed.

The cab turned into Essex Street and down to the end. Joe slowly followed. He parked on the corner of a road leading away and walked down the street where Thunder was paying off the cab. He watched the cab drive back up Essex Street and saw Thunder head towards the steps.

Thunder trotted down the steps and wandered how Kate knew about this place. It was certainly out of the way. She was stood at the bottom; back to a wall, foot beneath her, the sole against the wall. Her knee stuck out at an angle. She had her hands in her pockets.

"Did you have a successful day?" Thunder asked her. She looked at him coldly.

"Do you know how many coaches leave Victoria between two and three on Easter Saturday?" she was angry at the stupid girl.

"Lots?" Thunder said cheerfully. Kate muttered something.

Joe slowly side stepped down the steps, his back to the wall and stopped three quarters of the way down. If he sat on the step he had a good view of them both. It occurred to him that he could kill both now and no one would be the wiser. He slid his gun out and sat down. Thunder had his back to him. Joe had a clear view of his back and Sarah's head. It will be so easy Joe thought.

"Look out!" Kate yelled and leapt forward through a gateway opposite. She pulled at Thunder.

He turned, looked quickly over his shoulder and followed. As

Joe leapt down the steps he fired blindly, hitting Thunder in the thigh. Thunder held his leg and limped after Kate. Joe swore loudly and followed them. Ahead of him Kate was half dragging, half carrying Thunder up some steps into a courtyard with a fountain. Thunder had his hand to his thigh and was dragging the leg along. Kate dragged Thunder through a gate. Joe followed slowly, believing he had them trapped. He slowly screwed on the silencer as he walked.

Kate crossed the courtyard and went up an alleyway onto the Strand where she hailed a cab. Joe saw them disappear round a corner and started to hurry after them. He turned into the alleyway and started to run. He got to the street just in time to see them get into a cab and it speed away. He swore loudly. People walked round him. He put the gun back in his jacket and walked back to Essex Street for his car. He went back for Sammy. He did a lot of swearing as he drove along. They would have to work the pubs again.

Then it occurred to him that Thunder would need medical help and there wasn't many places to get it. He made a phone call and within minutes had it sorted. He whistled out of tune as he drove. Things were suddenly looking up.

In the cab Thunder gave his home address. The cabby moaned but drove. Kate wanted to take him to a hospital but Thunder refused. Kate didn't know what to do so sat with his leg across hers. He gave her a handkerchief to put over the wound. She sat holding the handkerchief to his leg trying to keep up the pressure.

As they approached the flat Thunder saw two men coming out of his building. He recognised both and one was not someone he would want to meet like this. He suddenly leaned forward and made a quick decision.

"Cabby, drive to the end and turn right. St Matthew's hospice, Kensington and be quick. There's an extra twenty quid for you," he called to the driver.

"Okay gov, whatever you say," the cabby drove, muttering. Kate threw a bewildered look at Thunder.

"Don't ask," he said and sat back in the seat.

She lifted the handkerchief and looked at his leg. It was still bleeding. The handkerchief was now red. She replaced it and put new pressure on it. As they neared the hospice Thunder took off his jacket and gave it to Kate. She looked at him quizzically.

"I don't want them to find something they shouldn't," he said. She felt the jacket and then nodded. "You'd better have this too. I don't want them going through it," He gave her his wallet.

She helped him out the taxi, paid the fare and helped him into the hospice. Two nurses appeared and took him. Kate followed. She was stopped at the last door but looked through the window. They cut off his jeans and start to prod his leg making him yell.

A woman doctor swept past Kate into the room. She looked at him briefly then sighed loudly. "Not another. Bloody thugs. Okay bind him up. Usual procedure. Get him out of my sight!" then she swept out the room past Kate and down the corridor.

The first nurse frowned. The second shrugged and pulled the first nurse away by the arm. "Forget it. The bitch is law," she said.

They discarded his clothes and shoes throwing them into the corner. A male doctor came through another door. He gave Thunder an injection in the leg, poked it a couple of times and then left.

"Clean him up" he told the nurses over his shoulder as he exited out the door he had come in.

The first nurse looked at the second. "Just do it," the second said.

"This is not what I trained to do, he needs decent help, not butchery," the first one snapped back.

"Whatever, it's your funeral," the second said. She started to clean up the leg.

The first nurse went out the other door and returned minutes later with the second doctor. He prodded Thunder who was now virtually unconscious. The doctor dug out the bullet, dropped it into a dish, gave Thunder another injection - this time in the arm and threw down the syringe in disgust.

"Now! Clean him up!" he emphasised every word. "Bind his leg and do as you are told! You are not paid to question my judgement!" he yelled at the first nurse. He swept out the room nearly knocking Kate over. She hastily stepped out of his way. She edged into the room this time.

"He's stable," the second nurse told her as she is leaving. "Now we wait," The first nurse gave the other nurse a withering look and followed her out, leaving Kate stood by the bed unsure as to what she should do.

Thunder came round briefly. He was extremely groggy, his eyes were hazy, unfocused. He peered at Kate standing next to his bed. "Get me out of here," he slurred.

"I can't. Not like this," Kate whispered back.

"Go, get some clothes, anything, I can't stay here," he whispered and then passed out.

Kate looked round. She left with his jacket and wallet. Outside a cab was dropping people off. She waited until the people moved away and then approached the cab.

"Where to love?" the cabby asked.

"Somewhere that sells clothes that's still open," Kate said.

The cabby drove to a little all purpose shop open late. She asked him to wait. She went into the shop and had a quick look round. They sold track suits and t-shirts. She bought two of each. The cabby took her back. She went back to the room at the end of the corridor. Thunder had gone. Kate's heart started to thump. A nurse went past.

"Excuse me, my friend was in this room earlier," she asked.

"He's moved to room 3B. I'll show you," the nurse said. Kate followed her upstairs. Thunder was trying to keep awake. He had been given more drugs before he was moved. He was partially covered by a sheet; only his waist and good leg really; his chest and the injured leg were uncovered. The thigh was now bandaged. There were monitor wires on his chest and a drip in his arm. Kate went over to him and touched his shoulder. He slowly opened his eyes. He was even more unfocused than before.

"Kate, stop the drugs," he slurred "They're killing me, I can't take any more," he lapsed into unconsciousness. A nurse came in. She checked the drip, took his temperature and was about to inject something into the drip.

"Can you please stop the drugs. He has had enough," Kate requested.

"It says here he is to have the injection every hour," the nurse consulted the chart.

"I don't care what the chart says, I'm telling you to stop!" Kate replied angrily.

"I'll speak to the doctor," the nurse said.

"I don't care what the doctor says. We are paying for this and if he dies you can kiss goodbye your money! Tell your quack that!" Kate retorted. The nurse left.

"Remind me not to get on the wrong side of you," Thunder croaked.

"Fucking arseholes!" Kate fumed.

"Language Katherine!" he mocked.

"Lie still and rest!" she told him. He closed his eyes. Kate sat in the corner and waited. The doctor didn't appear, but neither did the nurse. When it was obvious that they weren't going to appear Kate pulled the chair closer to the bed and laid her head down, effectively blocking access to the drip. Some time later she was woken by Thunder tossing and turning on the bed. She pulled the cover over him. He started to mumble; it was the description of Sarah.

"What have I got myself into?" Kate asked herself softly.

Thunder continued to mumble incoherently, only now he is swearing profusely. In several languages. Kate ran the towel under the tap and started to wipe him down. As she wiped his face he called out: "N'Gara!"

"Who's N'Gara?" Kate muttered. He fell silent so she sat down.

"N'Gara was my wife," his voice was suddenly clear.

"Wife? You're married?"

"Long time ago,"

"Where is she now?"

"Dead. Buried with the rest of my family in Kenya,"

"Is that where you were born?"

"No. We moved there when I was about 10. I don't remember earlier,"

"What happened to them?"

"The women were raped and killed. The men hacked and

hung up to bleed to death. The animals slaughter and burnt. I'd gone to market. I saw the smoke from the road. I've never run so fast in my life but I was too late. I was cut down and left for dead," he felt the scar running along his right ribs.

"What did you do?"

"I did nothing!" his voice was contemptuous, disgusted. "At first I hid and then when I tried... I was cut down... like... scything corn!"

"You must have done something," Kate reasoned.

"Built a bonfire and burnt the place, people and animals to the ground and left. Afterwards I found out who the murdering bastards were, hunted them down and killed them, one by one," he said tonelessly. "But that was after I'd learnt my 'trade'. Earned it," his voice was sarcastic.

"And you've been this... whatever... ever since?"

"Yes. A lifetime," Thunder said ironically.

"How old were you when...," Kate trailed off.

"Married? Widowed? Inducted into the killing profession?" his tone was harsh. Kate kept quiet. "Eighteen. I've been a mercenary for twenty long years," the last three words were drawn out.

Kate did a quick sum. Then changed the subject. "How do you know this place?"

"It used to be safe," his voice started to waver.

"Things have obviously changed," Kate said harshly. She looked round as she waited but he had lapsed back into unconsciousness. About five in the morning the female doctor returned with the second nurse.

"Get her out of here!" the doctor said pointing at Kate.

"I'm not leaving,"

"Get out!" the doctor screamed at her.

"We need to look after him," the nurse said pulling at Kate's arm. She yanked it away.

"I've seen your 'looking after', it's crap. I'm staying!" Kate said coldly. She faced up to the doctor across the bed. The doctor was the first to drop her eyes.

"Fine. Stay. Just get out of my way!" she snarled at her.

Kate moved away and watched. They unbound the leg and had another poke. The doctor checked the drip and the monitor. They didn't do another injection or add more to the drip.

"Fine. Give him a couple of hours. It's just what the doctor ordered," the doctor swept out. The nurse bandaged his leg again. Kate came closer.

"What did she mean?" Kate asked. The nurse looked at her and shrugged.

"Orders are orders and I follow mine," the nurse replied.

Kate realised what they meant. Suddenly she had the gun in her hand and pointed at the nurse. The nurse looked at her in surprise. Kate looked at Thunder and took a leap of faith.

"Take that drip out of his arm. Now! Do it! Properly! I don't want him bleeding on the floor!" Kate ordered curtly. The nurse looked frightened. "Don't even think of shouting for help. You'll be dead before you utter a sound," Kate snarled. The nurse removed the drip and put a dressing on. "Finish bandaging the leg. Where's the supplies?" The nurse pointed to a trolley. She finished the bandaging. "Put them in this bag and his clothes," the nurse did as she was told. Kate hit the nurse with the side of the gun. The nurse fell to the floor, her head bleeding. Kate put down the gun, put a wad to the girl's head and taped it.

"Thunder!" she shook him by the shoulder. "Thunder! For Christ's sake wake up!" she dragged him to a sitting position. "Jesus! Krysten, please wake up. I can't do this alone," she pleaded.

He opened his eyes slowly and looked at her. "What the hell have you done"?" he asked quietly sitting on the edge of the bed.

"Get up. You have to get dressed. Here," she rummaged in the bag, brought out the track suit and a t-shirt. She handed them to him. "We have to get out of here, before someone comes back," she urged him.

He got off the bed and nearly collapsed. She held him up and then dragged the chair over with her foot. He sat down. He pulled on the bottoms. Kate picked the girl up and laid her on the bed. Thunder watched her as she laid the nurse on the bed.

"What did you do?" he asked.

"Hit her with the gun. She's alive, but we won't be soon if we don't leave," Kate told him. She ripped open the nurse's uniform, removed the pads from his chest and stuck them on the nurse. He pulled on the t-shirt and then the jogging top. She checked that the corridor was clear, picked up the bag and helped him out. They didn't see anyone as they left.

"We'll never find a cab," he slurred.

"Let's get out of here and worry about that," Kate said, helping him out. The doors swished open.

"Don't faint on me now," Kate told him firmly as they stepped outside and the cold morning air hit him. He staggered, Kate tightened her grip on him. They got down the road and round the corner before she sit him down. She stood panting, thinking furiously what she should do. She put his jacket on him.

"Where are we going?" he still slurred.

"We need to get away from here," she replied. She suddenly spotted a cab and waved frantically at it. He pulled up at the kerb.

"Where to love?" he asked. He looked at Thunder. "Too much sauce?"

"Something like that," Kate heaved Thunder up, grabbed the bag and got him in the cab. She sat down with a huge sigh of relief. The driver looked at her through the window. "Farringdon Road, near the old market," Kate told the driver. She put his leg up on the seat opposite him.

"Where are we going?" Thunder asked. He put his head back against the seat and tried to focus at her.

"Somewhere that does breakfast at this unearthly hour," Kate told him.

Thunder was impressed. "You're a mine of information,"

"I used to work near there. We knew all the best places to eat. Even at this time of the day," Kate said looking out the window as the cab drove through London waking up. She looked at him. He had his eyes closed, his head back against the seat.

CHAPTER FIVE

The driver dropped them near Holborn Viaduct. They crossed the road and into a little cafe. Kate ordered breakfast, toast, a cup of tea and a large pot of black coffee. Thunder sat in a corner and put his leg up on the chair next to him. Even at this time there were some people about. He looked round, impressed.

Kate joined him, with a tray. On it were two mugs, one with tea in it and a pot of coffee. She sipped the tea. Thunder poured the coffee and sipped it in silence. Breakfast came with a large plate of toast. They started to eat. Thunder found he was ravenous. He finished off the toast, Kate ordered more. He ate whatever she put on his plate. When he had finished he pushed away the plate and sighed. He drank his coffee. Kate ordered another tea.

"How did they find the flat?" Kate asked.

"No idea," Thunder was now on his third coffee. "But it means we can't go back," Another cup of tea was put in front of Kate. She smiled up at the woman who returned to the counter.

"That hospice nearly killed you," Kate said quietly.

"It still could," Thunder replied, equally quietly.

"They kept pumping drugs into you," Kate stated.

He nodded and ran his fingers through his hair. He felt exhausted. "I need to rest, sleep off the drugs,"

"Where to now?" Kate asked.

"A hotel. I know of several that will do," he said. He lapsed into silence.

Kate sat quietly and thought. After a few minutes she looked at him. "Who were the men at the flat?" Kate asked. He looked back at her steadily.

"One was my contact at the Palmerston-Smith household," he said quietly. "So it wasn't a simple kidnapping," he drank some coffee and looked over the cup at her. "The other... doesn't matter. But if he's in the game, it's a trap for me to walk into," Thunder finished his cup.

"But I'm not Sarah," Kate said confused.

"The game's changed," he said bluntly. "We have to find Sarah," he poured yet another cup of coffee. Kate eyed him silently. He looked at her. "What? It keeps me awake," he protested.

"You'll be hyper," she said darkly.

"Better hyper than dead," he replied as darkly. He looked at her. She was eyeing him silently. "What?"

"Actually I was thinking how well you suited stubble," Kate said with a smile.

He stopped, the cup in mid air. He frowned and put down the cup. Then rubbed the stubble on his chin and grinned ruefully. "Surprising how quick it grows," he muttered. "How did you do at Victoria?" he asked brightly, changing the subject.

"Hum," Kate said and put down her cup. "Coaches went everywhere that afternoon," she said quietly. "She could be anywhere in the country,"

Thunder swore loudly. No one took any notice. He ran his fingers through his hair once more and leaned his head back. Then he looked at her.

"I need to sleep these drugs out of my system. Then I'll contact someone who might know where we should look for Sarah," he said finishing off his coffee.

"So where are we going?" she asked.

"Victoria," he thought of a nice little hotel tucked away down a back street, off the beaten track. It wasn't one tourists would use, you had to know it was there. And questions were never asked.

Kate paid the bill and they left going towards Farringdon tube station. Suddenly Thunder cried out in pain. He staggered against Kate, who dropped the bag and grabbed him. She staggered under his dead weight and sank to her knees, taking him down with her. He was out cold; she could hardly carry him and she didn't know where they were going.

"Need any help luv?" a voice above her head said. She looked up to see a porter from St Barts Hospital.

"My friend has a gashed leg and insists on walking. Now he's collapsed," she said without thinking.

"Hey Tom, give us a hand," the first one called to a friend nearby. He came over and they picked up Thunder. "We'll take him to the Doc at St Barts. He'll sort him out for you, no questions asked, if you know what I mean," the first one said.

They carried him up the road and round what had been Smithfield Market to the back of St Barts. Kate followed them meekly. The two men chatted away. Kate answered in mono tones, yes or no.

"How can you be so cheerful at this time of day?" she eventually asked.

"This is evening to us. We've just come off the night shift," the first said.

"In here," the second said and backed through a door. Behind the door was a corridor leading into the hospital. They went along this and through a fire door. There were several doors. At the second door they stopped and nodded at the door. Kate knocked.

"Come in," a deep voice said.

Kate opened the door. A man in a white coat sat behind a desk writing. He looked up as they came in.

"Patient for you Doc," the first one said as they carried Thunder in and laid him on the couch.

The doctor walked round his desk. The two men left. He looked at Thunder and then at Kate standing by the door.

"Why don't you sit down and tell me a version of what happened while I look at your friend," he suggested. He expertly stripped off the trousers and cut off the bandages. "Nasty," he commented. Kate looked up. The bandages were red.

"Oh bugger," Kate said.

He looked at her. "Still the wound is fairly clean, so it looks worse than it is," the doc said. Kate sat silently, lost for words. "Let me guess. Your friend ran into a spike. Wasn't shot by any chance? No, not a gun. You went somewhere who did such a good botch job that you left before it got worse. Then he collapsed. How's that?" the doctor said.

"Pretty good. We went to this hospice. They poked around in the wound, filled him with drugs," Kate admitted.

"Drugs? Don't know what?" the doctor asked.

"Pain killers in the leg. Others... God knows," Thunder said.

"Ahh, you're with us. Good. I'll inject the leg and then sew it up. They got the bullet out but that was all. They made a mess of it though. You would have bled to death," the doctor said.

"That's what they intended," Kate said. "They gave him two hours,"

"I'll give you some proper pain killers and show your friend how to dress the wound. Try not walking. I'd rather you stayed in bed, but somehow doubt you'll do that, in the circumstances," the doctor said.

Thunder looked up at the doctor. "What's your name doc?"

"Dr Swift, but most people just call me doc. I'm usually here first thing in the morning. I can attend to anything that turns up, catch up on my paperwork and that gives my secretary something to do when she comes in. So it works all round," he told him. "Right then young lady,"

"It's Kate,"

"Right Kate. The dressing," doc said. Kate watched him dress the leg and bandage it. Thunder lay looking at the ceiling, a resigned look on his face. "While you get dressed I'll write you a prescription. Come in and see me in about a week," the doc said to Thunder.

Kate helped Thunder off the couch and he pulled up the trousers. He put his foot to the floor gingerly. The leg felt numb but better.

"Plenty of rest. No running around, if you can," the doc said and handed over the prescription. "Come in the same way, it saves explanation,"

"Do you take payment?" Thunder asked.

The doc shook his head. "I presume you pay your taxes,"

"How about a donation to your favourite charity?" Kate suggested seeing Thunder's face. He wasn't used to getting things for free.

The doc raised an eyebrow. "You are used to dealing with

desperate types, aren't you?"

"I'm used to paying my way. Look, I'll write you a cheque and you can pay it to whoever you want," Thunder pulled his cheque book out of his pocket and wrote a cheque. He handed it to the doctor who hardly looked at it as he laid it on his desk.

He saw them out to the street. "If you can afford it, take cabs," he said and disappeared back inside. Once back inside he looked at the cheque.

"How much?" he exclaimed. He looked up and frowned. Surely not? They didn't look like they could afford the price of a bus fare.

"Where to?" Kate asked and spotted a cab. She hailed it. They got in.

"Victoria Burns Hotel," Thunder said.

They booked into the hotel. The hotel looked run down but at least it was fairly clean. Their room was on the first floor at the back and very quiet. Thunder made sure they had single beds this time. Kate's closeness bothered him. Kate didn't take any notice. She went and had a wash. By the time she returned he was asleep; laying across the bed, still clothed, a foot dangling off the end. Kate took his shoes off and wrapped the blankets around him. He didn't stir.

There was a kettle and two cups but nothing else. She went out and got some papers, groceries and his prescription. At least they had a TV. Thunder woke about one, ate some food, took his tablets and meekly went back to sleep. Kate read the papers, watched the TV and dozed from sheer boredom. Kate changed the dressing periodically but in the main Thunder slept.

Elsewhere people were looking for them. They had left the hospice before anyone had arrived to finish off the job. That evening Sammy and Joe took the list of pubs they had been given and started to ask questions. It became apparent by the third one that Thunder had not been in any of these pubs and even if he had no one was telling. Joe swore loudly.

"We'll try one more. The Nag's Head. That sounds like my sort of pub," he told Sammy.

The pub was a spit and saw dust type. It was quite crowded,

mainly students for the cheap beer. They stood at one end and talked to the barmaid. Their conversation was disjointed as she moved backwards and forwards behind the bar. Sammy soon lost interest in this and moved in on the students where he felt more at home and where he might get lucky. Joe persevered. By the end of the night he knew he was winning her round.

"What are you doing when you finish here?" he asked.

"Go home and sleep," she replied.

"Want some company?" he asked with a grin.

"Maybe," she went off to serve someone down the bar. She return ten minutes later.

"So, are we on for tonight?" he asked.

"Maybe. I don't know if I can trust you," she said.

"Oh you can trust me. I wouldn't hurt a fly," he said with a grin. She giggled.

"I'm not a fly," she replied.

"Just as well, I wouldn't know what to do with a fly, but you…" he winked at her. She giggled again.

Closing time came. Just before the students left Sammy returned to Joe.

"I've found nought out 'bout this guy," Sammy said.

"I may have struck lucky," Joe said nodding in the direction of the barmaid.

Sammy pulled a face. "Rather you than me,"

"You wouldn't know what to do with a woman," Joe said with a lecherous grin.

Sammy went off with some of the students. Joe curled a lip at him. Sammy's sexual preferences made him sick to his gut. He looked back at the barmaid. Mind you she was no oil painting!

The barmaid came over to him. "I'll be finished in about twenty minutes,"

"I'm in no hurry," he replied and finished his pint.

The last few people left and the lights turned off. The glasses were left stacked on the bar to be done in the morning. The barmaid left with Joe. They walked back to her flat which was just round the corner. She lived above a shop. They climbed the stairs. Her flat was sparse and dingy. She offered him a drink. He drank it down in one gulp. She got up to refill it. He grabbed her arm and pulled her down on him. He kissed her roughly. She responded. Soon they were rolling around the floor.

"Let's go to bed," he whispered.

She led the way. He kissed her again, undoing her blouse. He undid her bra, releasing her large breasts. Greedily he grabbed them. She moaned as he pushed her down on the bed, kneeling over her. She undid his shirt and pulled it off. He pulled up the tight skirt and ripped the scanty knickers off. He stood up and unbuckled his trousers, letting them fall to the ground, his pants followed.

He yanked her legs apart and entered her roughly. She gasped at the pain but it changed to gasps of delight as his movements quickened. She dug her nails in her back, moaning with pleasure. The more brutal he was the better she liked it and he knew how to be brutal. Soon it was over and he lay across her, spent, gasping for breath. He rolled off and lay on his back. She lay next to him and waited.

"Shall we get in the bed?" she suggested.

He pulled off his shoes and socks, kicked off his trousers and pants and climbed under the covers. Soon she joined him. He kissed her roughly. She kissed his neck, travelled down his chest and back up to one ear. He closed his eyes and grabbed a breast, then put his mouth to them, biting and sucking. She moaned and they started again.

After taking her twice more he fell asleep. At six he woke and took her while she was still half asleep. Afterwards he lay on his side and looked at her. She was a big woman, big boned, big busted, common and cheap. She lay looking at him.

"You remember my mate in the pub a couple of days ago?" he asked. Subtlety was not his strongest point.

"Which one? There are so many," she said.

"Dark hair, tall, wearing a black jumper and leather jacket," he said.

"Oh you mean Kit," she said. "He sometimes drops in,"

"Kit? Oh yes, Kit," Joe said. "I'm trying to find him. Got some business to sort out with him but the bastard's become invisible,"

"Oh you'll probably find him at the Victoria Burns," she said. "He lives there. Or works there,"

"Victoria Burns? Back street dive?"

"That's the one," she told him.

"I'll try him there. Now how's about some breakfast?" he said.

"Depends what you had in mind," she said.

"Oh I think you can guess what I want," he said with a dirty laugh.

"Again? You're exhausting me," she said.

"It's a hard life. Like me. Do your best luv," he pushed her head down and then lay back while she sucked. He grabbed her head and held her in place as he moved against her. When he had finished, he let out a deep sigh. "Now that's what I call a good breakfast,"

She got out of bed and went off. He could hear her being sick. He just grinned. She came back and pulled clothes out of drawers and got dressed. He lay back and watched. By the time she had finished and put on her 'war paint' she looked a right slag. He wasn't particular who he screwed but in the light of day she turned his stomach. She went off to work and he got up and got dressed. He used her phone to call his boss.

"I've found out where this guy is holed up with the girl. Piece of piss. I've plugged him once. Do I kill them both?" he said. The voice at the other end growled a negative reply.

"Do you want me to kill him then?" Joe asked a little disappointed. Again a negative reply.

"Take her, leave him," the voice said.

"I'll take her to the warehouse then," the phone went dead. Joe made some coffee and phoned Sammy who was still in bed and irritated at being woken up. The young student next to him didn't stir.

"I've found them. I'll pick you up at eleven and we'll go collect the girl," Joe said. Sammy grunted and put down the phone.

Joe looked round the flat but there was nothing of value or interest. It was a pokey flat with a slag for a tenant. He left at half ten and got his car, then drove to collect Sammy. He was sat on the wall outside waiting.

"Where to?" Sammy asked when he got in.

"Victoria Burns Hotel," Joe said.

"That dump? Thought he'd go somewhere with a bit of class," Sammy said disappointed.

"Makes no difference," Joe snarled.

"What's the matter with you? Didn't she come across," Sammy sneered.

"Oh she came across all right. God was she ugly by daylight," Joe said and shuddered. He drove to the hotel. He parked down the street and they walked to the entrance. Joe went in while Sammy waited outside.

"I'm looking for my friend. Dark hair, black leather jacket, limping, with a dark hair girl," Joe said to the receptionist.

"What's his name?" the girl asked.

"Which one do you want? I don't know which one he's using," Joe said.

"Well, if it's the one I think you mean, he's out," she said.

Joe cursed and left. He went outside to where Sammy was waiting.

"They're out. We'll wait," he said. They started walking down the street.

That morning Kate had decided that they would have to go out and buy a few essentials since they couldn't risk going back to the flat to pick up their stuff. Thunder agreed. He had slept all of the previous day and night. Now he was wide awake and restless. They went out for breakfast. As they walked back to the hotel they talked. Thunder wanted Kate to go home. Kate refused. He would need someone with him.

As they neared the hotel Thunder stopped. Kate carried on walking. He looked round but couldn't see what was making him suspicious. Years of living on the edge had given him a sixth sense and he sensed that something was wrong. By the time he decided that he was wrong Kate was at the corner. Suddenly she came running back.

"Those men are outside the hotel," she said and darted down a side road.

Thunder hid in a doorway and watched the two men run past after Kate. They didn't see him, they were intent on Kate. He thought quickly. The road Kate was running up curved round a car park into a dead end. He limped up a side road, stepped over a barrier and went up a ramp into a car park. He went across the car park and down some exit stairs in the far corner. Beneath him he could hear one of the men (Joe) shouting to the other, calling him by name, Sammy.

Cautiously he eased open the door at the end of the alleyway. He crept along it and peered round the corner. Kate was nearing it now, Sammy not far behind. Kate looked over one shoulder, saw Sammy was almost on her and side stepped. Sammy ran past her and then past Thunder in the alleyway. Joe approached Kate. She looked from one to the other and then frantically around. To one side of her was a pile of empty oil drums stacked against a wall. She kicked at a lone one and Joe went down trying to dodge it. He screamed obscenities at her.

Kate leaned back against the wall heaving, then started walking, breathing heavily, stepping sideways looking from Sammy to Joe and back again. Joe was still on the floor screaming at both of them. Sammy had stopped running and was walking back towards her, a sick grin on his face. Kate passed the alleyway. Suddenly a hand shot out and grabbed her round the throat, hauling her backwards. She screamed but was too frightened to fight. She was pulled back along the alleyway and through the door. Sammy stopped and stared.

"Get after them you fucking wanker!" Joe screamed at him.

"Keep quiet," Thunder whispered in her ear as he closed the door. Her scream died.

Sammy reached the alleyway and then the door. He thumped on the door, kicking it. It was one of those security doors that only opened from one side; the other side. Thunder looked at the door. It stayed shut. Kate spun away from him and stood bent over, hands on knees, heaving. Her heart was hammering against her ribs so hard, it hurt, and sounded very loud.

"You're not the only one who knows their way round obscure parts of London," he said dryly.

"Very funny," she heaved.

"This way," he said taking her arm. She stumbled after him as he limped up the stairs and across the car park. Kate had her free hand to her throat, it hurt like hell and her chest was still tight.

"You'd better stay here," he said. "I'll go and get our stuff," He found a corner and pushed her down. She sat down with a thump. "Stay down and keep quiet. I'll be back as soon as I can,"

He walked out the car park and back to the hotel. He saw Sammy and Joe standing at the other end of the road arguing; they didn't see him. He went to the hotel, collected their few belongings and checked out. Outside the hotel a cab was dropping someone off. Thunder waited until it was free.

"Where to mate?" the cabby asked.

"Into that car park. To start with," Thunder said. The cabby drove into the car park and round the bottom level. "Wait here,"

Thunder got out and walked off to the corner where he had left Kate, but she had gone. He groaned. He walked along the cars, looking. He heard a "pst" and walked back, gun in hand. As he passed a dark blue BMW Kate's head popped up.

"Krysten," she called. He walked between the BMW and a Jag. Kate climbed out of the back seat of the BMW. "Real careless of them to leave the car unlocked," she said and locked the door. "Wouldn't want it to get nicked," He looked puzzled. "I had to hide somewhere, they decided to search the place. They're up there somewhere," she pointed upwards.

"Let's get out of here," he said quietly and lead the way to the waiting cab. He gave the name of a hotel he knew of near Bloomsbury. It was a higher grade than the previous one. The receptionist looked suspiciously at him until he paid in advance in cash. They spent the rest of the day in their room. Thunder made a phone call from the telephone in reception.

That evening they went the Red Lion pub. It was a meandering walk, they strolled along slowly, Thunder limping. In the Red Lion Thunder was greeted as a regular by the barman. Thunder smiled at him.

"Is Ted in?" he asked the barman.

"Sure, Kit, pool room, out back," the barman said.

Thunder led the way through an arch to a room at the back of the pub. There was a pool table in the centre of the room and people playing. In one corner sat a large black man. Two other men sat with him. As Thunder approached the table the black man gestured to them to leave. They got up and walked away.

"Later, Ted," one said over his shoulder. Ted nodded. He gestured to the chairs. Thunder and Kate sat down.

"This is Kate," Thunder said. "Did you find the information I wanted?"

"Yeah," Ted drawled. An American, he had once been a marine but had settled in England - or been forced to. He was a force to be reckoned with. He looked with interest at Kate. She returned his gaze steadily, one eyebrow arched defiantly.

"She's got spirit," he said.

"And some," Thunder replied.

"There's been a couple of guys asking questions, gave a vague description of you," Ted said. "I didn't do anything about it. No one talked,"

"Someone did. They found the hotel I was in. They had to be tipped off," Thunder said.

"I'll ask around," Ted said. He drank his pint. The barman appeared. On the tray was another pint, a glass of whisky and a glass of white wine.

"I didn't know what you drank, love so I guessed white wine. If you want something else, just ask," the barman said and put the drinks down.

"Wine will do fine," Kate said. He took away the empties and left.

"This girl you're looking for. Some rich kid, right?" Ted started. Thunder nodded. "Thought as much. Some guy came in two nights ago asking questions. He didn't get any answers,"

"What did he look like?" Thunder asked.

"Tall. Crew cut. Wore black. Had a scar down his face," Ted said.

"Shit!" Thunder swore. Kate looked at him. He shook his head.

Ted looked at him astutely, head on one side. "This girl," he went on. "She has a secret boyfriend. Marcus Francis. Music student at Royal Academy. Very talented too and intelligent. Daddy doesn't approve of boyfriends, no one good enough,"

"You make him sound like a gangster," Kate said. Thunder threw her a look. She threw a withering look back at him. "You said he was a businessman, not Al bloody Capone!" she exclaimed.

Ted threw back his head and laughed; bellowed like a bull. "He is, sweetheart, they all are," he put his head near hers. She didn't flinch, just looked at him. He grinned at her.

Thunder found he was holding his breath. Then he exhaled. "Where does the boyfriend live? When he's not at college?"

Ted sat upright and looked at Thunder. He drank half his pint, put the glass down and wiped his mouth with the back of his hand. Thunder waited. Ted was ambivalent at the best of times; sometimes he was helpful, other times he wasn't. He could be your best friend one day and your worst enemy the next. Thunder liked his brashness and put up with his changing moods.

Ted eyed Thunder speculatively. He knew this man's reputation. He respected that. He knew he was good, they had worked together. He knew he could beat Thunder into a pulp but what would be the use, he'd probably blow him up later, when he'd recovered. And then there was the Chinaman. No one in their right mind killed him. Thunder had worked with Jimmy and Jack years ago and they had rated him; one of the best Jack had said. Well if he was good enough for Jack, he was good enough for him. No, Ted had decided long ago, this man was not the sort you made a foe of. You never knew when you might have need of Thunder's particular talent.

"Well, now," he began. "This kid lives on college campus but I believe he comes from Worthing,"

"Worthing?" Kate asked. "Oh shit,"

Ted stared at her and then roared with laughter. "I like this girl," he said. "She has balls," Kate gave him a withering look. Ted laughed all the more. She wasn't sure she liked this man, she wasn't sure she wanted him to like her either.

"Worthing. Marcus Francis. Shouldn't be too hard to find,"

Thunder said. "Does anyone else know this?"

Ted shrugged. "His college pals, I suppose. They've all gone home for the holidays. His thing with the girl has been kept real quiet like, so not many people know about it. Even some of his college pals probably don't know,"

"I'll settle with you next time," Thunder said. He swallowed his whisky in one gulp. Kate finished her wine. Thunder got slowly to his feet.

"See you around Kit. Take care, now," Ted called as they walked across the room. Thunder put up one hand in salute but didn't look back. Kate followed him out. They walked through the bar.

"See you John," Thunder called to the barman who waved to him. Thunder and Kate left the pub and went out into the night.

From his doorway Sammy finished his cigarette and slowly followed. They strolled away, Sammy followed at a distance. They chatted as they walked along, seemingly unaware that they were being followed. Sammy was careful not to be seen. He stood across the road and watched them go in the hotel. He waited a few minutes. They didn't appear. Sammy stood in a doorway, stubbed out another cigarette and called Joe on his mobile. They spoke briefly. Sammy lit another cigarette as he waited for Joe to arrive.

Once in their room Thunder sat on the bed and stared into space. Kate stood and waited. When it was obvious that he wasn't going to speak she put the kettle on and made tea for herself and coffee for him. He said nothing but accepted the cup. Kate sat down on her bed.

"You'll need a clean dressing," Kate said. She collected the bandages. Thunder pulled down the track suit bottoms. He inspected the bandage, then cut it off. Kate cleared and bandaged up his leg and he replaced the track suit bottoms.

Kate was in the bathroom washing her hands when there was a knock at the door. She came out holding a towel. She looked at Thunder. He looked back expressionless. He pulled out his gun and limped over to the door. There was another knock. He gestured to Kate to open it. She slowly opened the door. Standing in the corridor was a small Chinese man.

Thunder pulled open the door wide. The man stepped in past Kate. She eyed him as he passed her. She looked over to Thunder who was backing into the room, putting away the gun. Kate automatically shut the door and walked back into the room. The man and Thunder stood opposite each other. Thunder smiled at her. He gestured to the man.

"Kate, this is Kit Chan. Otherwise known as the Chinaman, my contact," Thunder said simply.

CHAPTER SIX

Kit Chan was a very atypical Chinese man. Small and compact, he came to Thunder's shoulder. His black hair gleamed in the light. He smiled a crooked smile which showed perfect white teeth. Thunder limped back to the bed and sank down with a sigh. Kate stood and leaned against the wall. Kit sat in the chair. He looked at Kate, a question hovered.

"Kit, this is Kate Bromham. I kidnapped her by mistake," Thunder said, his voice gave away no emotion; there was no anger; no regret or remorse, or even sadness; it was a voice without feeling. Kate frowned at Thunder.

"That was unfortunate," Kit said simply. He was Thunder's closest friend, there was no need for excess words.

"Someone has put two idiots on our trail. There was three but the girl was eliminated," he looked at Kate; she had a look of horror. She crossed to the other bed. "Oh it wasn't me,"

"I didn't say anything," Kate retorted.

"How did you find me?" he asked Kit.

"I have my ways," Kit said. "Your haunts have all been thoroughly checked out by someone,"

"They found the flat," Thunder said flatly.

"They must have put another tail on me. I probably led them to you when I visited last. My apologies," he said.

Thunder waved it away. "No matter," he said softly. "What I need to know is who is behind this. My contact in the Palmerston-Smith household must be getting his orders from someone," He sat on the end of the bed; his elbows on his knees; his leg was easing. The doc had done a good job. He hoped he paid the cheque to a worthy cause.

"The contract came from Bob Lowman. He appears to be giving the orders, but it could be whoever is behind him. He is allied to a large consortium, it could be anyone," Kit said.

"So who brought the others in on the act?" Kate asked.

"Lowman? To make sure the job is done?" Kit suggested.

"Sue knew the two men, but they didn't know her," Thunder said.

"Sue? You mean Mini Skirt Sue?" Kit asked. Thunder nodded. Kit frowned. "An old friend?" he whispered softly. Thunder gave him a withering look, one that should have stopped a rhino at 100 yards. Kit ignored it. Kate looked puzzled, then she remember what Ted had told them. Thunder had been annoyed.

"The man at the flat, with the contact," she stated rather than asked. "You mentioned him earlier,"

"You don't want to know about him," he said in his velvety voice. He turned back to Kit. "Find out what you can," they walked to the door.

"Are you sure about her?" Kit asked.

"No. But I trust her," Thunder replied. Kit looked impressed. He pointed at Thunder's leg. Thunder shrugged. "Par for the course,"

"I'll be in touch," Kit said. "If it gets too hot in the kitchen, you know where to cool down," he left. Thunder thoughtfully closed the door.

Kit walked down the corridor. He rounded a corner near the lifts and saw two men coming out of one lift. They stopped on the landing and looked at the signs on the wall which said which rooms were in which direction. Sammy pointed in the direction of Kit. They started walking towards him.

Kit looked over his shoulder and saw a door slightly open. He let himself in and peered through the crack. Sammy and Joe walked by without noticing. Sammy was looking at the door numbers, Joe followed. He pulled out his gun and checked it then put it back in his jacket. Kit watched them walk to the room he had just left.

"This is it," Sammy whispered to Joe. Joe nodded at Sammy, who kicked the door open. They rushed in.

Thunder was sitting on the end of the bed. Kate was changing in the bathroom. Thunder slowly got to his feet when they burst in. Joe pushed past Sammy and pointed the gun at Thunder.

"Now, don't be stupid," he said. Thunder sank back on the bed. "Find the girl," Joe said to Sammy over his shoulder.

Thunder looked concerned as Sammy pulled Kate out of the bathroom. She was dressed for bed in a nightshirt. She kneed Sammy in the side of the leg. He yelled in pain. Joe hit her once with the side of the gun and she slumped to the floor. Thunder took this opportunity to tackle Joe.

His first punch contacted with the side of Joe's jaw. Joe swore loudly. He staggered back, slightly off balance. He put the hand with the gun out and grabbed the unit behind him to stop himself falling over. Thunder advanced on him. He threw another punch. Joe ducked and kicked out at Thunder's bad leg. Thunder went down, both hands holding his leg.

Joe stood upright and wiped his mouth with the back of his hand; it had blood on it. "Shit!" he swore loudly. "Get her out of here. I'll finish him," he growled. Sammy picked up the unconscious Kate, put her over his shoulder and lumbered out the door.

"Right you bastard. I was lead to believe you were something special, but you're a right piece of shit. Time to say bye bye," Joe said. He stood over Thunder and aimed the gun at him. Thunder kicked with his good leg and caught Joe on the inside of the thigh. Joe staggered backwards. Thunder wiggled away across the floor. His gun was by the bed, out of reach, he had no hope of reaching it either. Joe advanced again. He held out the gun.

"This time I won't miss," he said coldly.

From his hiding place Kit watched Sammy carrying Kate down the corridor. He left the room, pulling the door closed behind him and quietly padded back to Thunder's room. Outside one of the doors was a tray. Kit picked up an empty wine bottle from it and silently stepped through the door. He hit Joe over the head, smashing the bottle and sending Joe unconscious to the floor. Thunder watched him fall and scrambled out of the way. He hauled himself on to the bed.

"That's one I owe you," he said to Kit.

"You've save my life enough times," Kit replied.

"Did you see where the other guy took Kate?"

"No. I came to see you," Kit replied.

Thunder got to his feet. The pain in his leg made him feel slightly sick, he swayed and sat on the bed. Kit came over.

"We're going to Chinatown," he said. He picked up the bag.

"Leave it. I'll be back," Thunder said. "Just find some track suit bottoms," Kit did as he was asked. Thunder pulled them on, picked up his gun and jacket and Kit helped him from the room. They left Joe on the floor. Outside the hotel Kit left Thunder leaning on a wall while he walked to the corner to flag down a cab. In the shadows a man stood. He watched as Kit and Thunder got in the cab and drove away.

Sammy put Kate on the back seat of the car. He drove off. He didn't wait for Joe, he would follow later when he'd finished with Thunder. Sammy didn't think much of this Thunder bloke, he had expected a big man who would knock six bags of shit out of them both. While obviously not small, Thunder hadn't put up much of a fight. Still Sammy had to admit that leg didn't look too healthy. He'd be a lot more unhealthy when Joe had finished with him Sadistic bastard Joe. He snickered to himself.

Joe came round and groaned. He crouched up and looked round, a hand to the back of his head. It came away wet and warm. He looked at his hand, there was blood on it. He swore and slowly got to his feet. Thunder was gone. He swore again and picked up his gun. He left, not noticing the man in the shadows.

Kit took Thunder to his home in Chinatown, a flat above a restaurant. Ling, his wife calmly looked at his leg. She cut off the bandage. There was blood coming from between the stitches. It looked red and angry. She got a bowl of warm water and started bathing it. Thunder gasped at first then lay resigned.

"Je-sus," he exclaimed,

"Sorry," Ling said.

"Sorry, Ling," Thunder said. "Just do the best you can. And bandaged it tight. I have to be able to walk,"

"You can't go anywhere tonight," Ling said.

"We have to find Kate," Kit said.

"A visit to Lowman might extract that information," Thunder

said. "Do you know where he can be found?"

"He's usually at his penthouse flat in Mayfair," Kit said.

Ling bandaged Thunder's leg as tightly as she could. He pulled on the tracksuit bottoms. Thunder stood up and walked a few paces. The pain was there but bearable. He threw some pain killers down his throat. It would have to do. He picked up his jacket and checked his gun. Kit handed him a spare clip. He tucked it in his jacket with the gun.

"Right," Thunder said. "Ready?"

Kit went into the kitchen and picked up a curved knife about eight inches long with a carved handle. He put it in a sheath and put it inside his jacket. Ling watched them in silence. She knew that it was useless protesting. They would go anyway. Thunder and Kit left. They took a cab to Mayfair and stopped outside the block of flats where Bob Lowman lived.

Thunder and Kit looked upwards. It had fifteen floors, the top one was Lowman's. They walked to the entrance. Thunder stopped. In the hallway sat three men in black suits. They scrutinised everyone coming in or out.

"They've been watching too many gangster films," Kit said quietly. "We'll use the back door,"

Kit led the way down the side of the block. A service door was ajar. Kit pushed it open and they entered the dark corridor. Kit went down the corridor to a door at the end. He opened it cautiously. It was a room where the heating was housed. They looked round. In one corner some stairs led up to the ground floor. At the top was a landing with two more doors. One lead off to the main hallway. The other to the stairs. Thunder tapped Kit's shoulder and gestured to the stairs. Kit looked at Thunder doubtfully.

Thunder started to climb. By the second landing he was struggling. By the third he was having to haul himself up with the help of the banister. Kit opened the door to the corridor. Thunder stood, breathing hard. He put a hand to his leg, it was throbbing and he was in pain. He gritted his teeth and followed. Kit went to the lifts and pressed the button. Thunder looked at him in surprise.

"We are wasting time. And you won't make it to the top floor," Kit hissed at him. "We take the lift,"

They took the lift to the fourteenth floor and got out. At the end of the corridor was a door. This led to the service lift. Kit levered the doors open and peered in. The lift was down near the bottom. He looked up and saw a ladder attached to the wall. He wedged the door open with a bin and started to climb. Thunder followed, his jaw set in a determined line, his face grim.

At the top Kit levered open the doors and climbed into the penthouse flat. He wedged the door with a spaghetti jar for Thunder to climb through. Thunder leaned on the kitchen unit and breathed heavily. His leg was now considerably painful and he was in a foul temper.

Kit pushed open the kitchen door. There was a hallway. Kit beckoned Thunder to follow. Thunder pulled out his gun and went past Kit into the hallway. This was more in his line than Kit's and he didn't want his friend leading them into a room full of men with guns.

The flat was in darkness, only a lamp in the hall near the door was lit. Thunder quietly limped into the sitting room. There was a pair of women's shoes discarded on the floor. Near some double doors was a blouse. Thunder tried the handle to the left door. It slid open. Thunder slipped through the gap. It was the bedroom and in the large bed was Lowman and a woman. They were making love. Thunder silently crossed to the bed.

"Move an inch and you're dead," he said in that deadly quiet voice. He had his gun to the back of Lowman's head.

Lowman froze. The girl beneath him opened her mouth to scream, a hand was put over it. Lowman moved to one side off the girl, all desire gone in an instant. Kit dragged the girl sideways, she grabbed the cover and pulled it with her as Kit dragged her off the bed and into the other room. Lowman looked sideways and up at Thunder.

"Sit up," Thunder told him. "And no tricks or it will be the last thing you will ever do,"

Lowman rolled over and sat up, pulling the remaining cover over his naked body. He put his hands in his lap and looked at

Thunder with interest. He interlocked his fingers, they were ringless.

"I presume you will tell me what this is about," he said gruffly. He silently cursed those fools downstairs. He would have their hides for this intrusion.

"You put a contract out on Palmerston-Smith to kidnap his girl. I was given it. Then you put two goons on it too. They have the girl and I have a hole in my leg. You could say I'm a little pissed off. So let's cut the crap. Where have they taken her?" Thunder said coldly.

Lowman looked at him in surprise. "So you're Thunder?"

"Obviously," Thunder said.

"You're not what I expected," Lowman said.

"That's what they all say," Thunder said. Then his voice dropped to a whisper. "Usually just before I kill them," Lowman heard the threat and knew better than to try something stupid.

"Those two arseholes weren't my idea," Lowman said. "I've heard how good you are. Lightman decided to bring them in,"

"Lightman? The man behind this, I presume?" Thunder asked. Lowman nodded. "Where have they taken the girl?"

"Why should you worry? Palmerston-Smith will do as he's told, now we have his kid," Lowman said.

"Don't you know?" Thunder said. Lowman looked puzzled. "That was the wrong girl. Sarah Palmerston-Smith is still free,"

"What?" Lowman nearly yelled. "I wasn't told. I'll kill the double crossing bastard!" he snarled.

"Lightman presumable?" Thunder asked.

"I'll pay you doubt to find the girl and get Lightman," Lowman pointed a finger at Thunder. He looked at the gun and dropped his hand to his lap.

"I want the girl those two bastards took tonight. Then I'll find Sarah," Thunder said coldly. "Then, if you're still interested, we'll talk money and I'll deal with Lightman," his velvety tone was back.

"Why? That girl isn't important," Lowman said.

"She is to me," Thunder said coldly. Lowman wasn't a fearful man but that voice sent shivers down his back. He shivered involuntarily. This man was one cold bastard!

"They've probably taken her to my warehouse, Express Deliveries, Wapping Road. Just don't blow it up. Take the girl, do what you like to those idiots, but find Palmerston-Smith's kid. I'll contact him," Lowman said.

"Not so fast. I'll contact Palmerston-Smith when I'm good and ready," Thunder said. "For now, you keep quiet, not even Lightman. If you don't, I'll come back and we won't talk business. I promise," Kit came in, two ties in his hand. He tied Lowman's hands behind his back and then his feet. He put a handkerchief in his mouth and they left him, tied up, lying on the bed wrapped in the cover.

The girl was tied up in the sitting room. Kit and Thunder went back to the kitchen. Thunder went down the ladder first and back to the floor beneath. Kit kicked the jar and followed. Kit put the bin back and the doors shut behind them. They took the lift to the first floor and got out. Thunder sent it to the ground floor. In the front hall the lift doors opened. One of the men got up to look and found an empty lift. He shrugged.

In the penthouse flat Lowman wiggled off the bed and on to the floor. He managed to kneel beside the bed and brought his head down on the alarm buzzer on the bedside table. The three men leapt up, got in the lift and went to investigate. They found their boss tied up and gagged. Whey they had untied him he let out a volley of curses, got dressed and then started laying into them with his fists. He picked up the phone and started to dial, then changed his mind and replaced it. If Thunder dealt with Sammy and Joe it would save him having to do it, but he was still angry that Thunder had managed to get into his flat so easily; at the same time he admired the man for doing so. His ruffled feelings were mollified by berating his men. Then, having dismissed them, taking the woman back to bed to finish what he had started.

Thunder and Kit hailed a cab. Thunder gave the address. Kit looked questioningly at him. Thunder said nothing. The pain in his leg had subsided a little but his anger hadn't. If those bastards had touched Kate... His anger flared. His thoughts were murderous, then cleared to sharp clarity; he knew what had to be done; he was at his most dangerous. His face was set grimly; Kit looked sideways at him, he had never seen him so angry; he looked like the cold ruthless killer of his reputation. If these people didn't think he was up to much, they were about to get one hell of a surprise.

Express Deliveries was a large distribution warehouse. Along one side was where the trucks backed up to be loaded and unloaded. Each bay had a roll door. There was a ramp at one end going up to the flooring. Above were the offices. There were a couple of lights on. Thunder limped up the ramp and found a door at one end. He carefully eased the door open. Near bay one were piles of parcels stacked on pallets wrapped in cling film. The rest was high stacks of paper on pallets making little corridors. Thunder edged round one of the stacks and listened. Behind him Kit stood waiting. Thunder could hear voices somewhere near the centre. To one side was a metal staircase leading to the offices. Thunder gestured to the stairs.

"You find Kate. I'll deal with them," he whispered. Kit nodded and padded off, his soft shoes silent on the concrete floor. Thunder edged along the stack towards the voices. He came to the end of a line and peered round. Seated in the middle was Sammy and four men. They were playing cards and Sammy was cheating. The men grumbled about it continuously.

"Where's Joe?" one man asked.

"Gone to see the girl," Sammy said and smirked. He knew what Joe had in mind, the randy bastard.

Thunder moved away. He went up the corridor opposite him. At the end he leaned against the stack and put a hand to his leg, it was starting to throb badly. He pushed himself away and gave the nearest stack a push. It wavered and fell. Thunder quickly moved up another corridor and waited. As he peered round the corner he took the silencer from his inside pocket and fitted it to the gun.

"What was that?" one of the men said.

"Go and see," Sammy said. The man went off in the direction of the noise. He walked up one corridor and found the fallen stack. He bent over and pushed the stack aside. He shook his head and looked up at the next stack. From his hiding place Thunder had the perfect view. He fired one shot. The man dropped silently to the floor. Thunder disappeared off down another avenue of paper.

Sammy heard the pop and jumped to his feet. "Joe? Joe? That you?" Sammy yelled.

Joe appeared at the door of the office. He leaned on the banister of the walk way and looked down. Thunder looked up. He hoped Kit would be all right.

"What?" Joe sounded extremely cross.

Sammy stood up in the middle. "Was that you?"

"Me what? Go and look," Joe yelled back and disappeared back into the office. He slammed the door shut.

Sammy looked at the three men. "Search the place," he said. He picked up his knife, a wicked looking thing, long and toothed. It did more damage coming out than going in.

The three men got to their feet. One picked up a rifle, checked it and walked off with it cradled in his arms; another picked up a crow bar; the third pulled a gun out of his jacket. They all went in different directions. Sammy wielded his knife in one hand and went off to investigate. The man with the rifle found the dead man, he yelled to the others.

Thunder stood with his back to the stack and watched them disperse. He quietly limped off down the corridor and looked round the corner. The man with the crow bar was coming his way. Thunder put his gun in his jacket. He waited until the man was level with him and then punched him in the side of the head. The man grunted and fell sideways. Thunder grabbed the crow bar and wrenched it out of the man's hands. He brought it down with all his might on the man's unprotected head. The man fell, face down, to the floor silently. He was dead. Thunder put the bar on the body and went off up another corridor.

Thunder could hear someone cursing. He pulled a bale hook out of the stack of wrappings. The man with the hand gun walked down the corridor looking each way, the gun in both hands. Thunder looked round the corner once. The man was getting nearer. As he came level Thunder swung the hook round and into the man's chest. He didn't make a sound as he slumped to the floor; he died gurgling blood. Thunder left the bale hook in his chest and limped away.

At the edge of the corridor he spotted Sammy walking round the wall of the warehouse opening doors. Thunder pulled out his gun. Opposite was a door. He waited until Sammy was level and opened it then silently closed in on Sammy's back. He hit him over the head with his gun. Sammy slumped forward and through the open door. Thunder kicked his feet in the door and closed it quietly. He looked round, no one was near. But somewhere was the fourth man with a rifle.

He walked down one corridor and stood at the corner of one stack near the centre. The fourth man had returned to the centre. He had found nothing, only the first dead man. He muttered to himself. He sat back in his chair, his back to Thunder, the rifle on his lap. Thunder smiled grimly.

He picked up some twine that was used to tie up the bundles and advanced silently on the man, twisting the twine round his hands. He slipped it over the man's head and pulled. The man struggled, he rose out of the chair and stepped sideways taking Thunder with him, the rifle clattered to the floor. They fell backwards with Thunder underneath. The pain shot up his leg, he bit back a cry and, using his anger, tightened his grip. The man suddenly stopped struggling and slumped. Thunder pushed him off and rolled to one side. He lay heaving and then got slowly to his feet. He righted the chair, put his arms under the man's arm pits and hauled him into the chair. He tossed the twine to the floor and limped away.

Kit padded silently up the stairs. A large stack hid his climb. He quickly glanced in the first office. It was in darkness and empty. Two offices along the light was on. Kit started to move towards it. He heard Sammy yell out and darted into the darkness of the second office. He watched Joe come out and yell at Sammy. He watched Joe return to the office. He waited a couple of minutes and then left the office. He looked over the banister. He could see the men moving about, but not Thunder.

In the third office Kate was tied to a chair. Joe sat on the edge of a small filing cabinet near the door. His gun was on the desk near Kate. He picked his nails with a knife. Kate watched him with distaste. He was an ugly brute of a man.

He put the knife down and crossed to where she was sitting. He ran a hand up her thigh, squeezing it roughly, pulling the nightshirt up. "Hum, nice bit of flesh," he said. Kate did not look at him and managed to keep hidden the revulsion she felt inside. She did not want him to think that his touch affected her at all.

"Never had a bit of class," he said rubbing her thigh. He pushed his hand between her legs. Kate bit her lip and blinked back the tears that threatened to fall. "I don't suppose you've had a bit of rough either, so it'll be a first for both of us. Have you had a man at all?" he said leaning towards her and leering. Involuntarily she moved her head away from him. He grinned, removed his hand and stood up. It added a bit of spice if the woman was unwilling.

He wiped his hand down his trousers, rubbing his groin and finding himself hard. He grinned. "Now, Sarah," he said. Kate did not put him right. There didn't seem any point. "We'll have a little fun. You'll please me and I'll give you a good seeing to and then you won't be killed," he said. He wound some of her hair round his finger. "I like beautiful women and you're not bad, not bad at all," he dropped the hair and titled her chin up. "But then all women are the same on their backs," he said gruffly.

He cut the ropes at her ankles and then the ones on her wrists. Kate rubbed one wrist. He pushed her off the chair to the floor; she lay in a heap with him standing over her. With one hand he slowly unbuckled his belt and then the button to his trousers. Before he had time to unzip them Kate leaned up and grabbed him by the bollocks and yanked downwards.

Joe screamed in pain. He held himself with both hands and sank to his knees. He looked at her and swung a punch. Kate ducked and rolled away. He tried to move forward but the pain was so intense he stopped and screamed again. Kit opened the door, picked up a crow bar just inside the door and brought it down on Joe's head. He toppled forward. Kate sat on the floor by the desk and watched him fall.

"Are you all right?" Kit asked her softly.

Kate looked up and nodded. Kit held out his hand. Kate took it gratefully and they went to the door. Kit closed the door after them and led the way down the stairs. Kate's legs went wobbly so Kit put his arm round her. They made it to the bottom and Kate's knees gave way.

"Come on," Kit hissed. "We have to get out of here,"

Kate pulled herself to her feet with the aid of the banisters. She put a hand to the wall and used that as support with Kit on the other side. He guided her to the side door. Standing there lounging against the frame stood Thunder. He had his hands in his pockets.

"What took you?" he asked with a grin. Kate felt relief floor through her. Joe had told her that he had killed Thunder. She should have known he was wrong.

Kit went out the door first. Kate started to follow. Thunder put his arm across the doorway barring her way. Kate looked at him. His eyes showed concern. He saw the torn nightshirt.

"Did he…?" he left it unsaid.

"He didn't have time," she said.

"Bastard! I'll kill him!" Thunder said. Kate didn't doubt that he would. He pulled her into his arms. The force made Kate stagger. Thunder fell back against the door frame, still holding Kate. He bent his head and kissed her. Kate was surprised at the force of feeling in that kiss; it was devouring. Thunder was even more surprised; he hadn't kissed anyone like that for a very long time. He suddenly released her.

"Sorry," he murmured. He pushed her through the door, the moment lost. Thunder looked into the warehouse and up toward the office. "Another time, bastards," he muttered.

Kit found Sammy's car and drove it round the corner. Thunder and Kate got in. Kit drove them back to their hotel, he and Thunder argued virtually the whole way there; Kit wanted to take them back to Chinatown; Thunder disagreed. The man in the shadows had gone. Thunder and Kate got out. Kit drove off and dumped the car, then returned to Chinatown.

Thunder and Kate went up to their room. Joe hadn't touched

anything. Thunder laid down on the bed. Kate sat on the other one and looked at him. He was breathing hard and looked a little grey around the mouth. He was obviously in a lot of pain. She got his pain killers and some water. Thunder took them without question. Neither said a word. Kate didn't trust herself to speak, she didn't quite understand Thunder's behaviour; she was just glad he had turned up with Kit. She knew what 'fun' Joe had meant. She felt dirty.

"I'm going to have a bath," she said in a small voice. Thunder watched her disappear into the bathroom. He stared at the empty space for a few minutes then looked at the ceiling. His anger was abating; it was being replaced by puzzlement. He lay there trying to analyse his feelings.

Kate got into the bath and scrubbed herself vigorously with the loofah and didn't stop until her skin was red and blotchy. She did the same to her hair, using the shampoo several times and scratching her head until it tingled. Satisfied she got out the bath and wrapped herself in towels. The she scrubbed the bath clean, removing every trace of the night's events. Then she put the nightshirt in the bin and dressed in knickers, t-shirt and robe.

Finally Kate came out the bathroom. Thunder was still staring at the ceiling, his analysing had gone nowhere, leaving more questions than answers. Kate went to bed and slept. Thunder did not move. He lay with his hands behind his head thinking. He didn't even see Kate. Eventually he turned on one side and fell asleep, his head on his arm.

At about three o'clock Joe entered their room. He had the biggest headache he had ever had, his bollocks still hurt and he was livid. Thunder did not sir as Joe crossed the room to his bed. It wasn't until Joe turned on the light and stood by the bed with his gun held at Thunder's temple that he woke.

"Get up you fucking bastard," Joe said in a menacing voice. As Thunder rolled off the bed, Joe backed away to the end of the bed. The pain in Thunder's leg had become a dull ache; it was bearable. Joe put his gun down on the unit. They faced each other at the end of the bed.

Joe punched Thunder in the face. Thunder stepped back one

pace, turning his head away. He put a hand to his mouth and tasted blood. Joe was surprised he didn't go down, most would have. Thunder brought his fist up and into Joe's stomach. Joe backed up a couple of steps. He punched towards Thunder's head again, Thunder blocked it with one hand and landed a punch under Joe's jaw with the other. Joe blinked with surprise. He punched Thunder in the stomach. Thunder grunted and leaned forward slightly. Joe grabbed his shoulders and pushed them down as he brought his knee up. Then Joe pushed Thunder into the unit. Thunder hit it with his shoulder but remained on his feet. He shook his head and turned to face Joe.

Kate had woken up soon after the light had gone on. She grabbed Thunder's gun from the side cabinet and managed to dodge past Joe to the bathroom door, from where she watched them fighting, wincing every time Thunder got hit.

Joe couldn't believe this man was still standing! Thunder's fist came up and smashed into Joe's face. Joe yelled in pain. Thunder followed with two more punches to the chest and stomach. Joe fell on Kate's bed. Joe kicked out at Thunder's leg and Thunder went down. Kate put a hand to her mouth as she saw him fall. He rolled, holding his leg. Joe kicked him in the back and then stood back. Thunder rolled onto his back. Joe picked up his gun.

"Now, you fucking bastard. This fucking time you will fucking die!" Joe said as he stood over Thunder. He aimed the gun. Thunder looked up. He heard a gun go off but felt nothing. He looked down and saw nothing. He looked up again and saw Joe toppling forward. He scrambled out of the way just in time as Joe fell to the floor with a thud. Behind them stood Kate; Thunder's gun in her outstretched hands.

Thunder got to his feet and approached Kate. He never took his eyes off her horrified face. He gently took the gun off her and laid it down on the unit. He put his arms around her. She leaned against him, his arms tightened. He kissed her head and stroked her hair. Kate's arms held him tightly. He could feel her tears on his chest and her heart thumping.

"It's all right, it's over now," he whispered to her. "I'll get rid of the body,"

He pushed Kate towards her bed and she sat down. He pulled Joe up and laid him over his shoulder. He staggered under the weight. He opened the door and peered out. Surprisingly there was no one about. He carried Joe to the fire escape door. On the landing outside he paused and tipped Joe's body off his shoulder and over the stairs to the ground. It made a reassuring thud as it hit the ground. Thunder went back to the room.

Kate was sitting on his bed. She looked up as he came in. "Has he gone?"

"Yes," he replied quietly, the velvety voice was back. It reassured her. He sat down next to her and put his arm round her. She leaned against him.

"Where?" she asked.

"The fire escape,"

With his right hand he brushed her hair from her left cheek. His hand fell to her throat and cupped the left side of her jaw. She leaned again his fingers and kissed the wrist. He pulled her face to his and kissed her. It felt so natural. They fell back on the bed, Thunder kissing her face and neck, his arms round her, holding her close, safe. Kate closed her eyes, the night's events were blurring. Suddenly she put a hand to his chest. He pulled away and looked at her.

"If this is revolting to you, I'll stop," he said softly.

"It's not that," Kate started.

"If he had touched you, I would have feed him his heart," Thunder said in a deadly voice, his hands gripped her arms like a vice. She didn't seem to notice.

"He didn't have chance," she whispered. "Can I sleep with you? I don't feel like sleeping alone,"

They got into bed. He held her and kissed her. Kate could feel the horror receding as his kisses became more passionate. Suddenly he stopped and rolled backwards.

"What's the matter?" Kate asked him anxiously.

"I can't do this. I keep seeing that bloody man," he said. They went to sleep in each other's arms, Kate's head on his shoulder. For some reason the pain in his leg eased.

CHAPTER SEVEN

Kate woke with a start; there was someone knocking on the door. Thunder stirred but did not wake. Kate gently slid out of his arms and got out of bed. She pulled on a robe as she went to the door.

"Who is it?" she asked through the door.

"Early morning tea," the voice said.

Kate opened the door a crack and saw the maid with a tray. She took it from her and shut the door. She put it down on the other bed and poured herself a cup, then sat on the bed. Thunder stirred and rolled over onto his back.

"Tea?" Kate asked. He pulled a face but sat up. The scar on his shoulder caught her eye. "How did you get that?" she asked pointing at it.

"A man tried to knife me and missed. He got my shoulder instead of my heart. Bad aim," Thunder said lightly.

"And the others?" she asked. She knew by touch and sight that his body had other scars, other battle wounds.

"Another time perhaps," he said quietly, his hands now in his lap.

Kate looked at him, his fingers linked together and then were still. He gave off an air of peace, but she knew this was deceptive. He was like a cobra curled up waiting to strike. She looked at his face; it was obvious from his expression that she would get no other explanation. She sighed and changed the subject.

"Where did Ted say Sarah's boyfriend comes from?" she asked as she poured him a cup of tea and handed it to him.

"Worthing," he said, sipped the tea and pulled a face. "I should have ordered coffee," he put the cup on the side.

"I could tell you that too much caffeine is bad for you," she said. He shrugged with a 'couldn't care less' look. She smiled.

"When do we go to Worthing?" she asked, putting his discarded cup on the tray.

He smiled. "As soon as we've had breakfast,"

Kate drank her tea in silence as she thought. He lay back against the pillows and watched her. Her forehead was furrowed; she was thinking what they would have to do and she worried that Joe's body would be found and linked to them. His gun still lay on the floor and Thunder's gun with silencer still attached was on the unit opposite.

"They won't link Joe to us unless someone saw or heard something. If they had, the police would have been here hours ago," Thunder said quietly, breaking into her thoughts. Kate threw him a look. He smiled. She thought how nice he looked when he smiled; how he didn't do it much. She smiled back without hesitation.

"I'll get dressed then," she said and went into the bathroom. Thunder got out of bed and looked at his leg. It ached but it appeared to have stopped bleeding, although the pain was still there. He sat waiting, quietly and very still.

When Kate came out she dressed his leg and he went into the bathroom. Soon they were both dressed and ready to go downstairs. Thunder put his and Joe's guns in their bag. They would leave as soon after breakfast as they could.

Kate put the tray outside the door. She watched Thunder pack the few things they had. It annoyed her that her belongings were still at his flat. She wasn't sure when she would get them back, if ever. Their shopping trip had bought essentials like toiletries, underwear and one nightshirt for Kate, which she would now have to replace after last night's events. Kate had bought a small holdall to carry their stuff in, but it still irritated her that they couldn't risk going back to the flat for the rest of their stuff. Until then she would have to buy more clothes and wash the few they had.

They went down to breakfast. The dining room was buzzing with the news that a man had been found in the alleyway shot dead. The police hovered in the background. Kate looked at Thunder. He looked back at her, unperturbed. The police were questioning people but getting no information at all. It had apparently happened in the middle of the night, no one knew which floor he had been on and no one had heard a thing. The police were baffled.

After a leisurely breakfast they checked out and went to Victoria. It was several hours later that the police decided to search the rooms. By the time they got to Thunder and Kate's room, discovered the blood stain on the carpet and the bloodied and torn nightshirt in the bin, they were long gone. However the blood stain was not Joe's but Thunder's and the nightshirt had Kate's blood on it. This only served to confuse things further and it was weeks later when it was concluded that Joe had been shot after breaking into one of the rooms, but no satisfactory explanation could be found for the blood stains, and they never found out who's it was. As no satisfactory explanation could be found the case was closed. Someone had rid the world of a piece of scum like Joe for which the police were grateful.

At Victoria Thunder bought two first class tickets to Worthing. The journey was uneventful until the ticket inspector turned up. Thunder was stretched out on one side asleep, Kate curled up on the other side looking out the window. The inspector came in and looked at them both. Kate looked round and saw his disapproving look.

"Tickets please," he said looking from her to Thunder.

Kate got Thunder's jacket down and handed him their tickets. He scrutinised them.

"Anything wrong?" she asked him.

"They've first class," he said surprised.

"Of course," she said with a haughty tone. "We always travel first class,"

He handed them back to her and moved away. He would have been willing to bet that these two would either have had second class tickets or no tickets. She returned the tickets to Thunder's jacket and sat back down. She looked at Thunder and then down at herself. She laughed out loud. They looked a right pair of scruffs. He was still wearing black tracksuit bottoms and a black polo neck jumper and she was still wearing the ski pants and jumper she had put on three days ago when they had left the flat. On one leg was a dried blood stain. Kate settled back in her seat, unconsciously hugging his jacket. Thunder hadn't stirred.

As the countryside sped past Kate thought about her life. Alan might be wondering where she was but she doubted it. They hadn't spoken for days before she had decided on her 'trip'. Her parents might think she had gone to see her friend in Brighton or gone away with Alan. Neither they or Alan would check, even when he appeared. Her friend in Brighton was actually in Cornwall so she wouldn't be worried either. Either way it didn't matter. Her boss believed her to be on holiday and would only start to miss her from Monday. No one was likely to be missing her and she certainly wasn't missing any of them. Without thinking she stroked the smooth leather.

She examined her feelings. She had to admit that Alan had bowled her over all those years ago; he had been so charming, so witty, so good looking. She couldn't believe her luck that he was interested in her. Now she saw him for the smarmy cheating creep that he was. No wonder her parents had said he wasn't good enough for her sister, the beautiful Elizabeth, the favourite. Tall, slim, beautiful, with dark blond hair and green eyes. A total contrast from Kate who was shorter with dark hair and eyes; short, dark and stumpy; "frumpy stumpy" Elizabeth called her. There were times when Kate wondered if she was adopted, so different was she from Elizabeth. She who had to have the best of everything while Kate got second best or less. The unfairness of it pricked Kate's feelings. Kate was always made to feel inadequate, stupid and ugly. With Thunder she was an equal partner. They were in this together.

Her eyes strayed to him asleep. The bandaged leg lying straight on the seat. The dirty tracksuit bottoms. The black polo neck showed off his broad shoulders. He was lying on his side, his back to her, his arms cradled in front of him. She had slept in those arms last night and had felt safe and secure. Now she wondered what they were getting into. Would they find Sarah? She hoped so, for their sakes as much as Sarah's. With a sigh she returned her gaze to the countryside. Perhaps if they found Sarah and returned her to her father this madness would be finished and they could return to their lives. She to her boring one with a family that belittled everything she did and him - to what? What did he do usually? Was it possible to return? Somehow Kate knew her life would never be the same again.

Kate's thoughts moved to home. What had she done to deserve such treatment? It wasn't as if her parents argued between themselves, they just joined forces against her, usually with Elizabeth. They had always made her feel unwelcome. Elizabeth took what few boyfriends she'd had in the past and friends too sometimes. What had she done to deserve their hatred? Her sister, though younger, had made it plain for years that she hated her, always made her feel inferior, that she tolerated Kate because she was family; like you would a poor relation. Elizabeth never wanted Kate around when she had friends round, which they did often. Their parents welcomed them. Any friends Kate had brought home soon danced to their tune leaving Kate out in the cold.

"I want you," a voice said quietly. Kate turned tear-filled eyes towards it. Thunder was sitting there. He had moved so quietly she hadn't heard or felt the movement. He put his arms round her and pulled her to him. Kate let the tears slid silently down her face.

"Whatever's ahead we'll fight it. Whatever was behind, move on from it. Whatever people had thought of you in the past, be it bad or belittling, they are wrong. You are stronger than you think. Perhaps they see it and it makes them feel inadequate so they belittle you, bring you down to their lowly level. Rise above it and leave them in their contemptible state. It's what they deserve," he said leaning his head on hers.

"You don't know them," she whispered.

"I can guess. Boyfriend? Parents? Sister? Friends?" he said.

Kate nodded. "They say I'm inadequate, useless, stupid, ugly," she sniffed. She heard Thunder draw in breath.

"It is them who are inadequate because they can't cope with your grasp of life. I wouldn't have come this far if you were useless. They are stupid to try and bring you down because you will never bend only appear to do so. Ugly? Beauty is in the eyes of the beholder. Each to their own. What beauty are you compared with?" he said

"Elizabeth. My sister. Tall, slim, fair hair, beautiful," Kate pulled a small photo album from her bag. She flicked through. There was one of Elizabeth laughing and posing.

He examined it and then sniffed. "She is too thin, like a clothes pole. All well and good for designer clothes, but hardly practical. Her hair looks mediocre; your hair shines with colour and life. She looks a tease," he said seriously.

He flicked through and came to one of Elizabeth with their parents. "Is this your parents?" Kate nodded. "So what's so special? They look like every other parent," He came to one of her with Alan. "Is this Alan?" Kate nodded. "Hum," was all he said and decided that he would have words with this cretin; make him see the error of his ways. He closed it and handed it back to Kate. He sat with his hands in his lap. His leg hurt so he put it on the seat opposite. He looked back at Kate.

"You have beautiful hair, which is shiny and clean," he examined the ends of a few strands. "Well looked after too. When the sun catches it there is gold and red in it. You have compassion, a graceful step and a quick brain. Most men like women with a bit of meat on them, not a bag of bones. And you know things. I've lived in London for years but I didn't know cafes that were open at that time of the morning and I never knew there was a maze of alleyways off Fleet Street," he told her seriously. "You're not as stupid as you make out, Kate Bromham,"

Kate laughed. "Why is it when you give me compliments they sound natural and flattering but when Alan does it they sound smarmy?"

"I say what I mean not because I'm after something," he replied.

Kate smiled and nodded. She knew what he meant. "Where are we going to look for Sarah?" she changed the subject so abruptly he smiled.

"Any other woman would have wanted to know more. You accept you are different and get back to the important things in life; living and surviving. We will book into a hotel, rest, do some checking and hopefully find Sarah safe and well and happy to go home," he said.

Thunder went back to his side of the compartment, made a pillow of his jacket and went back to sleep. That train journey changed Kate's life; she made decisions that effectively moved her life on and away from what it had been. She would tell Alan to get lost. She would tell her family the same. She would leave home and find somewhere to live, even if it was a grotty bedsit to start with. She would gain her independence. Even if she never saw Thunder again - and she had no reason to believe that she would - she knew that she deserved someone better than that smarmy bastard Alan. With that she fell asleep.

When the train pulled into Worthing they were both awake and ready to go. There was nothing suspicious; no one was following them. Now that Thunder had got rid of Sammy and Joe they expected no more trouble.

They booked into a hotel near the seafront. It was an old hotel that had been modernised but still retained some of its character. It had three floors and they were on the second. The main staircase was wide and swept down through the building making the climb easy enough. They had a twin bedded room with bathroom overlooking the sea. Kate looked out the window and sighed. They would be able to rest here for a few days. Thunder needed it. He was obviously in pain a lot as she noticed that the pain killers were never far away.

Kate turned back to the room and saw that Thunder had stretched out on one of the beds and was looking at her. She smiled at him. He put the two guns in the bedside drawer. As Kate pottered about the room she kept finding him watching her. Hanging their jackets in the wardrobe; putting their few clean clothes in drawers; toiletries in the bathroom; until he fell asleep. Kate decided to go for a walk. She took her purse intending to buy some clothes if she found any.

She found a shop selling tracksuits and t-shirts. Then she visited a chemist for more bandages. The streets were quiet, the seagulls noisy, the air brisk, she could smell the sea. After a little stroll on the prom she returned to the hotel. A few words with the receptionist and she found out where there was a laundrette so she washed their clothes.

When she returned to the room Thunder was sitting on the bed reading the papers. He looked up. "You've been busy I see," he said indicating the bags.

Kate had a shower. Thunder had cut off the bandage and was waiting for her to come out. His leg looked red and angry.

"Maybe a soak would help," Kate said looking at it. He went into the bathroom.

Kate rubbed her hair dry and looked at the paper he had discarded. There were no news of kidnaps or anything about Sarah. She didn't feel any safer for that. Thunder reappeared. He lay down while she redressed his leg.

"I looked Francis up in the phone directory while you were out," he said. "There are ten in it, I made a list,"

"At least you didn't tear the page out," Kate said dryly.

"I treat all books with respect," he said with mock indignation.

"I should think so," she said. "I didn't take you for a heathen,"

"Heathen?" he said loudly. "What do you think I am?" he asked in a normal voice. "As a matter of interest," he added in that velvety voice of his. Kate shivered. It was so deceptive, lulled you into a false sense of security, was so full of menace, yet could be soft and reassuring.

"Do you practise that voice?" she asked. He threw her a look. She looked back evenly. "Professional," she said.

"Oh thanks. You really know how to boost a man's ego," he said dryly.

Kate looked at him. "I'm no good at flowery compliments,"

"I've noticed," he said.

"If you want waffle, go else where," she said.

"Wouldn't get the honesty," he replied.

"On Monday we could look up the electoral roll. He should be there. And it's easier looking up roads then looking through the whole thing," Kate said. "And cheaper than making lots of phone calls,"

Thunder looked at her in wonder. How did she know these

things? Kate looked back at him without blinking. "I would never have thought of doing that," he said eventually.

They went down to dinner later. Thunder went first, holding on to the banister. A couple came up the bottom set of stairs. They stopped and kissed, totally absorbed in each other. They walked up a corridor, arms round each other, oblivious to their surroundings. Thunder waited on the landing for Kate. He gave them no more than a cursory look, then looked up back to Kate. She had stopped mid stair, a look of horror on her face which had gone a sickly white and was devoid of colour.

"Kate?" he called softly. "Kate?"

He started back up the stairs as fast as he could limp. Suddenly her face seem to crumple and she fell. He couldn't move quick enough to catch her so she fell to the floor with a thud and then rolled down the stairs coming to rest at his feet. He bellowed for help and two maids came running from the first floor and the manager and porter from the ground floor. He got her into a sitting position with the help of one of the maids. The porter picked her up and carried her to the manager's office where Kate came round.

"Where am I?" she asked quietly.

"The manager's office. Are you hurt?" Thunder said. He was leaning against the desk.

"My wrist feels like it's on fire," she said. The manager came over.

"Lets have a look," he said and knelt by her side. He gently felt the wrist and she let out a shriek. "Can you wiggle your fingers?" he asked. Kate couldn't. "It's probably broken. I'll get a cab to take you to hospital," he left.

"Looks like we're both in the wars," Thunder said and smiled. "Who was he?" he asked quietly. "Or was it she?"

"Alan. With yet another woman. I didn't know her," Kate said.

"Another addition to the harem?" he said dryly. Kate gave him a withering look.

They sat in silence until the manager came in to say the cab was here. They went out and got in. Neither said a word but the driver talked enough for all. When they got to the hospital Thunder got out his wallet.

"That's okay mate, the hotel's paid for it. When you're finished here there's a booth near the door, goes straight to our office," the driver said. Kate and Thunder got out and went into the hospital. They drew looks from the nurses.

"Would you like a wheelchair?" one asked him.

"No. It's her wrist," he said bluntly.

Kate was handed a card to fill in. "I can't, I'm right handed," she sounded distressed. Thunder took it and filled it in. She went off to x-ray.

"How did it happen?" a doctor asked Thunder.

"She fell down the stairs at the hotel. I think she probably fainted," he said honestly.

"And what about your leg?" the doctor asked.

"It's been stitched up. Kate dresses it when necessary. I have plenty of pain killers," Thunder said firmly. His tone of voice told the doctor not to pursue it.

"Here on holiday?" the doctor said.

"We came here for me to get some rest," Thunder said.

"Oh you two will get plenty of rest now," the doctor commented.

The doctor went away. Thunder sat and waited. Kate appeared with her arm in plaster and in a sling. They phoned for the cab and waited by the door. Neither said a word. Thunder thought about Kate's erstwhile boyfriend who goes away with another woman while his current girlfriend who he's asked to marry him is apparently visiting friends. He guessed rather than knew that Kate had not told anyone where she was. He wasn't a particularly curious man but this man's cavalier attitude towards Kate had now annoyed him; he would have to meet this man. As the cab turned up he put his arm round her shoulders.

"Lets go back to the hotel and see what dinner they have left for us. We'll be fine," he said lightly.

Kate smiled at him. Even if Alan had seen her, which she doubted, it wouldn't make any difference; it would have given them something to talk about at home. She looked sideways at

Thunder's profile, he had his stern expression, she knew he was more than a match for them! She smiled as she imagined the faces; first at meeting him, then as he started to take them apart - bit by bit. That would be one of those joyous moments other people had. When they got back to the hotel the porter was waiting to open the door and help them out. They went into the foyer where the manager was standing by reception.

"The dining room is still open," he told them and they walked over.

"Are you sure you want to sit in the dining room?" Thunder asked her.

She looked at him thoughtfully then turned to the receptionist. "You have Alan Barnard booked in. First floor? With a blond woman? Are they in the dining room?" she asked.

"Mrs Barnard was unwell, so they went to their room," the receptionist said.

"Huh! Likely story!" Kate said and marched into the dining room. Thunder followed, a thoughtful look on his face. He had seen that Alan was in room 10. He was tempted - but thought better of it. Time for that later.

They ate in silence. The waitress bought Kate's food already cut into pieces. Kate could feel her mood getting worse; her wrist ached and was becoming heavy in it's sling; she also had a headache coming on. This wasn't helped by her annoyance at Alan's latest cheating act. He thought she was away visiting friends.

"While the cat's away, the mice will play," Thunder said softly breaking into her thoughts. Not for the first time she was amazed that this man could tune into her thoughts and moods and say the thing she was feeling or thinking.

"How fortunate for him that the 'cat' is away," she said sarcastically. He smiled as she stabbed her food. She saw this and stopped. "I wonder how many times he done this," she mused.

"Do you care?" he asked.

"Not particularly," she replied, keeping her temper in check.

"You feel he's making a fool of you again and it annoys you," he said. She stabbed a piece of steak. It was what she felt like doing to Alan, but that wouldn't solve anything. The only way to hurt men like him was through his ego.

"Something like that," her voice was cold.

"The only fool is Alan. Now you will go home and finish with him. He will plead his case and you will know he is lying; and because you have conclusive evidence about him it will harden your resolve and he will find a brick wall. He has, in effect, cut the ties he had over you," Thunder said.

"Everything is much clearer now," she admitted. "Nothing I've ever done was as good as Elizabeth. Yet I left school with more exams then her and I've taken more since,"

"But you haven't told them?" he asked.

"No," Kate replied quickly.

"Sense of pride?" he asked.

"Or just that I know from bitter experience that it wouldn't make a jot of difference. I am not Elizabeth, the golden girl, the popular one. And most of my friends make better enemies," Kate sounded bitter. "I am not good enough for them. I never will be,"

"And the friend in Brighton?" he asked.

"I used to work with her. We got on. I never took her home or told her about it. Anyway she's in Cornwall with her boyfriend," Kate said. Thunder raised an eyebrow at her. He didn't ask what she would have done. He couldn't see her sleeping under the pier on the seafront though. She would have found some cheap and nasty hotel, to spend the time thinking, alone. Perhaps he had done her a favour; in a warped way.

"So now you can move on. I'll help, if you want," he said.

"Thank you,"

After coffee in the lounge they went back to the room about eleven. Both were tired by now. They slept well though. Kate put Alan firmly from her mind; she wasn't about to let him spoil her holiday. She even half hoped they would bump into them; the look on his face would be worth it.

They spent Sunday resting. They went for a leisurely walk along the seafront. Thunder discovered Kate's wicked sense of humour. They talked about things in general. They ended up in the arcade. Thunder did well at the rifles but Kate's driving won every time; even one handed she was far more reckless than him. They were competitive and ribbed each other ruthlessly on every point. They had a cream tea in a little cafe.

To the world they looked like a couple on holiday. Kate called him Krysten the whole time, she never once slipped. He relaxed; then realised he hadn't had so much fun in years; it made him realise what he had missed over the years of solitude - the companionship of a good friend. They returned to the hotel, both feeling and looking refreshed, relaxed and happy. They had enjoyed the afternoon and felt easy in each other's company. All thoughts of Alan were gone; all she thought about was here and now.

After dinner they watched a little TV. Alan had not appeared. Thunder felt cheated; but also relieved. On the one hand he would have liked Alan to see them together; on the other it might jeopardise the task in hand which was to find Sarah. So, for now, that would suffice. Tomorrow would tell if the trip had been worth it. He still had the feeling that he would have to sort out Lowman and even more so Lightman. After that what he did was his business; Alan would wait.

The next morning they went to the library. Kate got the electoral roll and Thunder produced his list. Two hours later and it was confirmed - he wasn't there.

"He must be ex-directory," Kate said. "Are you sure about his name?"

"You heard Ted as clearly as me. Marcus Francis. Lives in Worthing," Thunder was fed up.

"Not outside?" she asked.

"Worthing," Thunder was quite emphatic.

Kate looked up the local directories and found a few outside Worthing. Thunder was unimpressed. Kate looked up the addresses in the electoral roll. The last one was Marcus W Francis. Thunder was not amused.

"I'll take a cab and see if Sarah appears," he said tersely.

"I'd like to come too," Kate said. Thunder was about to argue the point but saw Kate's look of determination. Kate might be useful in convincing the girl.

The cab took them out of Worthing along winding roads to a small village where the houses all looked big and wealthy, Kate could almost smell the opulence of the area. The cab stopped outside a large set of gates. At the end of a long wide drive was a large red brick house sprawling over two storeys. On either side of the drive the lawns were set out with neat flower beds, bushes dotted here and there and in the middle of one lawn was a large oak tree. A high red brick wall ran around the outside of the property. Kate looked at Thunder who raised an eyebrow.

"I thought he wasn't good enough for her," Kate hissed.

"Daddy obviously hasn't done his homework," Thunder replied dryly. They got out and watched the cab drive away. "Lets go," he said and opened the gate.

As Kate followed him she looked round. "Nice place, small, but nice," Kate said sarcastically. She caught up with Thunder. "Do you think she is here?"

"Lets hope so, otherwise this has been a waste of time and effort," he said through gritted teeth. Walking on gravel jarred his leg.

They walked up the drive to the front of the house. Kate looked up, it was totally silent, no curtains moved. There was no car in the drive. No one appeared. There was not a sound coming from inside the house or around it. Not even a dog barked. The silence was deafening and eerie. It made Kate uneasy.

She went up the three steps to the front door. Thunder waited at the bottom. For a whole week Sarah and Marcus had been alone, unaware of outside events. Sarah had not contacted her home. No one knew Sarah was here and they expected no one to visit. They were about to be rudely awoken. Kate looked round once more, looked up at the building and sighed. Then she rang the bell and waited. Inside she could hear the bell resounding.

CHAPTER EIGHT

They stood on the doorstep and waited. Kate looked at Thunder. He climbed the steps carefully. After a few minutes the door opened. A young girl with dark hair in a pony tail stood there. She wore jeans and t-shirt and was bare foot.

"Are you Sarah Palmerston-Smith?" Kate asked.

"Who wants to know?" the girl looked at Thunder over Kate's shoulder.

Kate took a deep breath. "You don't know me but your life is in danger. Mine too. Can we come in?" Sarah just stared and stood squarely in the doorway.

"Who is it Sarah?" a young man appeared at her shoulder. This, presumably, was Marcus Frances. He was tall and slim, light coloured eyes in a chiselled face topped by black hair that tended to flop into his eyes, causing him to frequently push it back off his face. Kate had expected a Greek Adonis type, certainly not the earnest and sensitive looking young man looking at them with interest over Sarah's shoulder. He too wore jeans and t-shirt with bare feet.

Thunder decided it was time to prove a point. He pulled his gun and pointed it at Sarah over Kate's shoulder. "Just get inside," he said firmly.

Sarah turned pale. Any words Marcus was going to say died; his mouth opened and shut like a fish. Thunder gestured with the gun for them to back up. Kate stepped forward and into the house. Thunder followed. Sarah and Marcus backed away down the hallway.

"Lock the door Kate," Thunder said limping past her and down the hallway. Sarah and Marcus backed away from him. "Do you have a back room away from the road?" he asked Marcus.

Marcus nodded and led the way into the dining room. Sarah

followed, furious that her secret holiday was no more; and annoyed that Marcus hadn't resisted more, had just obeyed.

"Sit down and listen," Thunder ordered. Marcus sat on one of the mahogany chairs around the table. Sarah remained standing, arms folded, defiant, frowning. Kate came in and sat down.

"You'd better sit down Sarah, this is important," Kate said to the girl. Sarah looked from Thunder to Kate. Kate smiled and pointed to a chair. "Please," she murmured. Sarah abruptly pulled out the chair and sat down with a thump. She re-folded her arms and looked even more furious.

"The Aussie in your household? Did he suggest this break in Worthing?" Thunder asked. This was the first Kate had heard of an Aussie, but she presumed it must be one of the men they had come across - somewhere on their travels. She looked at her hand in her lap and fiddled with the sling.

"Bruce? Yes. He helped make it possible," Sarah said. "But I don't see…"

"He was my contact," Thunder interrupted her. "He told me what you were wearing the day you came here - jeans, white sweatshirt, boots, black leather jacket, black handbag, brown leather holdall," he ticked off the items on his fingers with the gun. He didn't take his eyes off Sarah. "And that you would catch the half two train from Victoria to Brighton," his voice dropped a little. Sarah just stared at him, her jaw fell. Marcus raised one eyebrow at Sarah.

"Only I caught that train and was also wearing jeans, white sweatshirt, boots and a black leather jacket carrying a black handbag and brown holdall," Kate interjected quietly looking up. Sarah's gaze moved to her. Her jaw stayed fallen.

"But I…" Sarah trailed off.

"You did something with your hair, caught a coach, even changed your clothes at Victoria," Thunder said.

"Then you…" the words died in her throat.

"I was to kidnap you and hold you until your father did whatever they wanted. If I'm right, I would then be told to kill you so that your father would put a contract out on me. Only no one knows what I look like, except for a couple of people who would never willingly betray me. They would have died and I would have gone after their killers. The people behind this probably believe they would then have me. However I don't kill my victims unless they deserve it. I would have held you and then returned you, except..." Thunder paused.

"He kidnapped me instead. And saved me from people who also knew you were due to be on that train and what you were wearing," Kate interrupted again.

"Right," he said softly. "Once I realised my mistake we came to find you before the others did. Others who were given the same instructions as me. Only they knew exactly where I would be holding you,"

A feeling of dread washed over Sarah. This was something that she knew her father had always feared. She had never questioned what her father did or the sort of people he dealt with. She didn't think him a gangster, just a businessman.

"So what do you propose to do now?" Sarah asked calmly.

"Take you home. Your father can protect you," Thunder replied.

"And Marcus?" Sarah asked. He had one elbow on the table and was leaning on his hand watching her. At his name he suddenly sat up straight, surprised.

"Can do what he likes. I doubt the others knew about him," Thunder said.

"Knew?" Marcus said looking at Thunder.

"They won't be bothering anyone now," Thunder said quietly. "And I doubt the men who hired them will know who you are," he added.

"Won't they? And what about Bruce?" Sarah asked savagely.

"What about Bruce?" Thunder asked warily.

"He knows about me and Marcus," Sarah said emphasising every word.

"He does?" Marcus said aghast, staring at Sarah who nodded but kept her eyes on Thunder. "How does he know about us?" Marcus asked her.

"Does he know where Marcus lives?" Thunder asked her.

"Possibly," Sarah replied vaguely.

Marcus frowned. "How does Bruce know about us?" he asked her again. She ignored him, concentrating instead on Thunder who was looking thoughtful. Marcus repeated his question again; Sarah continued to ignore him. He suddenly got to his feet, the chair toppled over, hitting the wall with a crash. "Sarah! How come Bruce knows about us?" he demand in a loud voice, leaning forward so that he was only inches from her head. He poked her in the arm.

"Ouch," she put her hand to her arm and looked at him over her shoulder. His face was very close to hers.

"Then stop bloody ignoring me and answer the question," he snarled at her.

"I had to tell him. He wanted to know why I needed the time away in secret. If it had been girl friends, it wouldn't have needed to be so secret," Sarah explained.

"Why didn't you say it was one of your friends?" Marcus asked.

Sarah faced him. "For Christ's sake Marcus, grow up!" she hissed at him.

"What?" Marcus was incredulous. He stared at her. Thunder moved to the window. Kate watched him.

"Marcus, sit down," Kate said quietly.

"What?" Marcus was distracted. He frowned at Kate and then at Sarah.

"Marcus, if Sarah had said it was one of her friends, that friend would have to have known the truth so that she could cover. If Sarah's father had rung her how would she explain why Sarah couldn't come to the phone?" Kate explained.

"Also Sarah's father doesn't approve of boyfriends and doesn't think she has one," Thunder said from the window.

Marcus looked at him over his shoulder, a frown on his face. "Why couldn't she have told me that?" he asked pointing at Sarah. "I would have understood," he said. He righted the chair and sat down, a hurt look on his face.

"Because Sarah is young and inexperienced. She lives in a different world to the rest of us. She doesn't know how to function in the real world," Kate said tersely.

Thunder looked at her sharply. This was hardly likely to get Sarah to trust them enough to take her home. He turned his attention back to Sarah. "Are you sure Bruce knows where to find Marcus?" he asked.

"Probably. You found us," Sarah said.

"I had the best help money can't buy," Thunder said with a hint of sarcasm.

Marcus looked alarmed. He didn't quite know what to make of all this. On the one hand he didn't believe any of it; but - and it was a big but - he hadn't believed Sarah could be so secretive or lie so convincingly. He'd heard talk about Sarah's father - who hadn't at college, but he hadn't paid much attention to it. He knew her father disapproved of Sarah having boyfriends; he felt hurt that her father had taken against him, particularly as they had never met. His father was a managing director and not exactly poor. He turned a quizzical look to the others.

"Why should anyone want Sarah dead? Or me?" he asked Thunder.

"They don't. They want Sarah's father to do something and are using Sarah to get him to do it. You are fall out - wrong place, wrong time, unlucky," he replied.

"But that's stupid. Don't go with them Sarah, how do we know they are who they say they are?" he said to Sarah.

"You don't but if I'm not telling the truth why do I have a hole in my leg and Kate a broken arm," Thunder told him.

"That could be fake," Marcus said stubbornly.

"I can assure you it's not. Check with the hospital. I went in Saturday night. And he can always show you the wound, if you want positive proof," Kate said indignantly. Sarah looked convinced. Marcus didn't.

Marcus looked at Sarah. This was all too far-fetched. Sarah's father wasn't a gangster, surely. "Could it be possible? Is your father that powerful that rivals are willing to kill to get at him? It sounds like gangster movie stuff. Why not kill him?"

"It doesn't suit their purposes," Thunder said.

"And if I'm kidnapped I'd like to believe that papa would move heaven and earth to save me. My brother would do nothing if papa was dead," Sarah said.

"And the deal would probably go through regardless, so they would have killed Sarah's father and still not achieved their goal. Which is to stop some deal," Thunder said. Sarah thought about what he said, it made sense to her but Marcus didn't look so convinced.

Kate listened without interest; most of it went over her head. Her wrist was beginning to ache and she felt tired. She wanted to sleep and let everything wash over her. She had felt shocked at actually seeing Alan with yet another woman. It left her with a feeling of indifference and a deep betrayal; now she could trust only Thunder.

"This all sounds very far fetched," Marcus said to Sarah.

"Not if you knew papa. He is always wheeling and dealing. It can be very cut-throat," she replied.

"Even so," he looked disbelieving. "What on earth processed you to tell Bruce about us? I thought we were supposed this great secret,"

"I've explained that," Sarah said with a tired voice.

"No. She explained it for you," he pointed at Kate. "You didn't explain anything. You never do and I'm expected to just go along with it. I can't believe you told Bruce about us,"

"I'm sorry, but I had to," Sarah said, her voice rising.

He gave her a stern look. "I haven't told anyone, not even my parents," he said coldly. "Who else have you told? Your college friends? The postman? Your dressmaker? The butcher? Baker? Candlestick maker?"

"Now you're being stupid," Sarah said.

"Me stupid? Yes, I've been stupid. Stupid to believe that anything we had was anything more than some stupid game! One word from daddy and I'd be history! This must be some ego trip you're on!" he ended up yelling at her. Sarah just stared. "Why don't you ring papa and ask him about these gangster types that are after you?" he asked sarcastically.

"He'd want to know where I was. And then he'd difficult," she said.

"Now I know where you get it from," he said coldly.

During this Thunder scrutinised of the back of the house. The green lawn seemed to stretch for miles in every direction. To one side was a shed and flower beds. A tree stood down the garden; a swing hung from it. There was a patio area just outside the French windows. On the other side of the lawn was more flower beds. A high hedge ran round the edge. It all looked immaculate, as only a garden with a professional gardener could look. This was a rich man's garden; there was no shortage of wealth here nor in the house which was beautifully decorated and furnished. He turned his attention back to the occupants of the room. Sarah and Marcus had subsided into an angry silence. Sarah was looking defiant with arms folded. Marcus had his hands on the table and his head down. Kate had a vacant look.

"We need to get going," Thunder said.

"Okay, I'll go back to my father, but Marcus comes too," Sarah said.

Marcus' head shot up. He was about to argue. Thunder threw him a look. Marcus shut his mouth. "Agreed," Thunder said. "Get packing," He turned to Marcus. "Do you have a car?"

"Yes," Marcus said.

"Good, we'll take that," Thunder said. "We're less likely to meet opposition,"

Sarah left the room. Marcus started to follow her. At the door he stopped and looked back at Thunder. "I still think this is far fetched, but Sarah doesn't and that will do for now," he said.

"Fine," Thunder didn't expect much more. Marcus left.

They all met in the hallway. Marcus got the car out of the garage. It was a five door automatic. Plenty of room for four. They went to the hotel first to pick up Thunder and Kate's meagre belongings. Within a hour they were on their way to London. After a couple of miles Thunder directed Marcus to a lay-by where a coffee bar was parked. All four got out. Kate bought some coffee and they stood drinking. At the other end of the lay-by a big black car pulled up. Only Thunder took any notice. Casually he flung away his coffee.

"Okay people, get in the car," he said quietly.

They looked round. Three men were walking towards them.

Sarah watched fascinated and horror-stricken together. Kate dropped her coffee, grabbed Sarah's arm and dragged her towards the car. Sarah resisted and they struggled. Kate was forced to let go. Suddenly one of the men took out a gun and fired at them. Marcus dropped his coffee, moved to push Sarah out of the way and got hit. Kate went to grab Sarah's arm again but Sarah became hysterical and started to scream.

"Get in the car!" Thunder yelled at her.

Kate grabbed Sarah firmly this time and dragged her to the car. She had to let go to open the door.

"You drive Kate," Thunder barked at her. He picked up Marcus and staggered under the weight.

Kate opened the front door and threw Sarah in and slammed the door shut. She raced round the front of the car and leapt into the driver's seat. She turned the key; it started first time. Thunder hauled Marcus into the back and slammed the door.

"Go!" he yelled.

Kate needed no second telling. She put her foot down and the car shot forward, tyres squealing, shale flying. The men dived out of the way as Kate drove at them. She swore quietly that she hadn't hit at least one of them. Thunder wound down the window and shot at the car's tyres as they drove past. He heard with satisfaction the hiss of tyres going down. Kate pulled out onto the London road and put her foot down once more. In the back Marcus groaned. Sarah tried to climb over the seat into the back. Thunder hit her and she slumped down. He leaned over, hauled her into a sitting position and fastened the seat belt. Marcus leaned back against the seat; one hand in his mouth; he closed his eyes; the pain was unbelievable. Thunder put a hand to his own leg and groaned; it felt like it was on fire.

Kate looked in the mirror. "How are the heroes?" she asked brightly.

Thunder threw her a filthy look. "Bloody wonderful!" he muttered. He looked at Marcus. "He's been hit in the leg, hip possibly. He's bleeding. I need something to stop the blood," he said. Kate took off her sling and tossed it over her shoulder. "Thanks. He needs a hospital,"

"I wonder if the doc is about," Kate said.

"Just drive," Thunder replied through clenched teeth. He leaned back.

Kate drove on. Occasionally she looked in the mirror at them or sideways at Sarah. They soon reached the outskirts of London. Sarah didn't stay unconscious for long. She sat very still in the front, blinked back tears but said nothing. She didn't dare look in the back, at Marcus nor that man. She went from anger to fear rapidly then descended into deep thought. Her father would hear of this and he would do something, she vowed, or else he would live to regret it! Kate found her way to the back of St Barts Hospital. They parked as close as possible to the entrance to the doc's office.

"Come on Sarah, we need to see if the doc is in," Kate said. They got out the car leaving Thunder and Marcus. They walked down the road to the door.

"I'm sorry about Marcus," Kate said.

"I'm sorry you were involved," Sarah said. "I've learnt today that my world isn't so safe after all. What's your friend's name?"

"Thunder," Kate replied.

"I think I've heard of him. Isn't he some big thug?" Sarah said.

"Appearances can be deceptive. He doesn't harm his victims and he always returns the innocent ones. Like us," Kate said. They reached the door. Kate opened the door. Sarah followed her in. Kate knocked on the doc's door. She hoped he was in. They went in when they heard his voice.

"Back so soon? What have you been up to?" the doc said, eyeing the plaster.

"I've broken my wrist. I'm afraid it will need patching," Kate said, the plaster looked battered. "It's my friend and Sarah's boyfriend that needs the help,"

The doc followed them to the car. He looked at Marcus first at Thunder's insistence.

"Help me get him to my office," he said to Sarah. Thunder, leaning heavily on Kate, followed. The doc and Sarah got Marcus on the couch, Thunder sat in one chair, Sarah sat in the other and Kate stood against the wall. The doc examined Marcus and then called for a nurse and a trolley.

"I'll admit him. He'll be anonymous and safe. Mark Kent will do. Now for you," he indicated Thunder.

Staying in the chair Thunder pulled off one leg of the tracksuit. The doc cut off the bandages, now red and threw them away. He tutted and gave Thunder an injection, then cleaned the wound and sewed him up, bandaging the leg. Sarah took one look at the bloody wound and looked away. Kate looked into space.

"Right, ladies, you next," he turned to Sarah. "That's a rare bruise you have coming there," he put something on a pad and put it on her face. She yelped in pain.

"That was me. Sorry Sarah, I didn't mean to hit you so hard," Thunder said. Sarah shrugged. The doc went over to Kate.

"I don't need to look too closely to see what you need," he said. "That will need a new cast," the nurse arrived with a trolley and two porters. They put Marcus on it. "Take Miss Bath to have her arm x-rayed and replastered," he said to one of the porters. "We will take Mr Kent to the ward," he said to the other porter and the nurse. "You two stay here," he said over his shoulder as they went out the door.

Thunder and Sarah sat in a chair each, in silence and waited. Just over a hour later Kate and the doc returned. They all left. Kate drove to Gerrard Street. They would be safe there for the remainder of the night. She parked in Whitcomb Street at one end of Gerrard Street. Thunder led them up Gerrard Street to a door. He rang the bell several times. Finally a pretty Chinese woman came to the door.

"Thunder? What are you doing here?" she asked.

"Ling, we need somewhere to sleep tonight," Thunder said. Ling opened the door. Thunder limped in followed by Kate and Sarah. Ling looked at each one as they passed. She said nothing and her face betrayed no surprise.

Thunder went up the stairs, Ling closed the door and followed. Kit jumped up as they came into the sitting room. He beamed a smile, pleased to see Thunder and Kate in one piece. He hadn't heard anything since Friday night. Ling found somewhere for the girls to sleep. They gratefully sank onto the beds, rolled up in the blankets and fell asleep. When Ling returned to the sitting room Kit and Thunder were talking, Thunder sat on the sofa with his leg up. She soon went to bed. Kit handed him a glass of whiskey. He sipped it and felt the warmth as the liquid went down his throat.

"After you left us at the hotel, the nastier one of the pair turned up, feeling sore," Thunder told him.

"After what Kate did to him, I'm not surprised," Kit said and laughed. Thunder looked mystified but Kit didn't elaborate.

"Anyway," he started again with a voice that would brook no more interruptions. "We had this little fight and Kate shot him,"

"Kate?" Kit yelled. "That's one feisty lady," Thunder threw him a look that normally would have stopped a rhino in its paces. "Sorry, go on," Kit said softly.

"Anyway," again the heavy sarcasm. "I had to dispose of him - he used the quick route down the fire escape. We checked out in the morning and went to Worthing, where we found Sarah with her boyfriend, Marcus,"

"So what went wrong?" Kit asked Thunder.

"Some goons turned up and the boy got hit," Thunder said.

Kit raised his eyebrows at his friend. "That was rather unfortunate," he said with more than a hint of irony. Thunder said nothing. His expression said he wasn't pleased. "So now what?" Kit asked.

"I'll return Sarah. Palmerston-Smith can protect his own daughter. Then a few more words with Lowman and hopefully that will be that," he swallowed the remains of the whisky. Kit refilled his glass.

"You think?" Kit was sceptical. There was more to this than met the eye, Thunder had said that all along and it looked like he was right. Thunder took another drink of whisky.

"I hope so. It's odd. They knew I had the wrong girl, yet still sent those two after us," Thunder mused.

"Perhaps they didn't know," Kit pointed out.

"Possibly. My contact at the cottage did. Lowman didn't know, that was sure. I get rid of Lowman's hired men. Men were sent to get Sarah. Lowman knew I wasn't giving up that easy,"

Thunder ran his fingers through his hair and leaned back. He felt tired and the whisky was starting to have a numbing effect. He suddenly leaned forward. "And they knew exactly where to find Sarah all the time, so why this charade?"

"Perhaps it was you they were after. You did say there was more to this," Kit suggested. Thunder lifted his head and looked thoughtfully at him. He shrugged.

"It's possible. Right now none of this makes sense," he said. He had another swig leaving just a covering in the bottom of the glass. Kit gestured the bottle. Thunder shook his head. "God, I'm tired,"

"What do you want to do?" Kit asked him.

"Sleep. Tomorrow I'll ring Sarah's father. She can return to him and I can find out who is behind this," Thunder said.

"Today," Kit amended. Thunder looked at him. "It's three in the morning," Kit pointed out.

Thunder looked at his watch. He groaned. "Oh shit, I could sleep for a week," he drained the rest of the whisky. He climbed the stairs to the loft where a bed was always kept for him. He lay in the dark, his leg throbbed, his thoughts chased around in his head. With a deep sigh he half turned over and fell asleep wrapped in blankets.

Sarah woke with a splitting headache. The bruise had come out, her face no longer looked quite so beautiful. The two girls sat in the kitchen with Ling drinking tea and coffee, waiting for Thunder to appear. He arrived, had his customary black coffee and sat opposite them. He looked at Sarah's face and winced. Her father wouldn't be happy about that.

"Ring your father, Sarah," he said handing over the phone.

Sarah rang her father's private number in his room. He had received the instructions from her kidnappers and was anxious and worried. She cut her father's questions short. "Listen papa. Please do as I ask and I'll explain later. No, never mind about that, papa. Just listen," something in her voice shut him up.

"We need to meet him. Tell him to go somewhere," Thunder said.

"I want you to drive. On your own. No one with you. Drive

to… where shall I say?" Sarah said.

"Where would be a good place?" Thunder asked Kate.

"Temple church," Kate suggested. "It's off Fleet Street and out of the way. Quiet too. Near where you got shot?" Thunder nodded, he vaguely knew where she meant, but had never been there.

"Tell him to take a cab to Fleet Street. Walk into the Temple and find the church in the middle. We'll meet him there in one hour," Kate told her.

Sarah relayed this to her father. "Never mind who I'm with, papa. Just do as I ask. And remember. Tell no one. Especially not Bruce. Understand? See you later," she put down the receiver and looked at them.

"I hope he doesn't tell anyone," Thunder said quietly. Kate looked at him speculatively. In one hour's time they would know whether it was all over and she could return to her normal life - or they could all be dead.

"Let's go," Thunder said in that velvet voice of his.

Kate and Sarah followed him out into Gerrard Street. They walked into Shaftesbury Avenue and hailed a cab. It took them to the Embankment where they got out and walked up one of the little roads into the Temple. The small church was open so they slipped in and waited. Thunder and Sarah sat in the circular part looking at the effigies on the floor. Kate had a look round, ending up near the altar. She sat in a pew and thought quietly. She wondered what Sarah's father would say, especially about her face. Why did Thunder have to hit her so hard? She watched people come in, there wasn't many visitors at that time of the morning.

She looked at her watch and saw she had been sat there nearly half a hour. Sarah's father should have arrived by now. Kate walked quietly back down the church. She saw Sarah in the arms of a man. Ray Palmerston-Smith was powerfully built, about six foot, with short brown hair. He had an aura about him. Power and toughness. His clothes were casual but expensive. Kate saw Thunder sitting next to a pillar watching the reunion so she went and sat the other side, keeping the pillar between them. Neither said a word. Thunder did not look sideways and gave no indication that he was aware of her presence. After a few minutes Sarah led her father over to them and made him sit down.

"You will have to be quiet and listen," she told him, sitting next to him and holding his hand. "After you went on your business trip I went to Worthing to stay with Marcus. You'll meet him later. He's in hospital right now, shot trying to protect me. This is Thunder and Kate. Listen to what Thunder has to say papa, it is very important,"

"And that?" Palmerston-Smith pointed at her face. Kate hadn't expected the blunt Yorkshire accent.

Sarah put her hand to her cheek and gently probed. It hit like hell. "It was necessary, I was endangering us all,"

Palmerston-Smith turned to Thunder sitting quietly, his back against the wall. He waggled a finger at him. "There had better be a good explanation for this," he said. "And why you hit my daughter," Kate noticed that his eyes were pale, green or blue, they seemed to change. Still he was not a man to cross.

"But not quite so hard," Thunder said dryly.

"Explain yourself," Palmerston-Smith said and settled back to listen. He was a fair man, listened to explanations and then made his decisions; no one pulled the wool over his eyes and he did not suffer fools gladly; he would know truth from lies. Only Sarah could wrap him round her little finger and get away with it.

Thunder told him about the contract that his rivals had taken out; that his contact was Bruce; what the arrangements had been; what had happened; that they had found Sarah and were bringing her home when more men turned up with guns. He didn't say about Sammy and Joe or their injuries; it wasn't necessary. He gave Palmerston-Smith the relevant bits; everything else was incidental.

"I have a feeling that there is more to this than meets the eye. Especially when I see Bruce coming out of my building with a man I have been avoiding for years. My guess is that after you had done whatever they wanted you to do I would have been ordered to kill Sarah so that you would put a contract out on me. As only a few people know what I look like they would have been killed to bring me out into the open. Once I had killed the killers or be killed it would be over. Someone seems to be weaving an awfully large web for me to fall into," Thunder said.

Palmerston-Smith listened intently, never interrupted once, his face became thoughtful. "This Marcus Francis? Could he be in on it?" he asked, not looking at Sarah and ignoring her protestations.

"Marcus Francis is a music student at the Royal Academy. He is a very talented and intelligent lad from a wealthy family. If he had been involved there would be no need for this elaborate charade. No. He is as innocent as Sarah," Thunder said cutting across Sarah. She subsided into silence once he started talking.

Palmerston-Smith saw this and mentally took note. He thought for a few minutes, Sarah sat silently. He looked at his daughter - it wouldn't be the first time someone had got close to a pretty girl as part of a larger plan. However what Thunder said made sense. He looked back at Thunder. "I agree," he said quietly. "You leave Bruce to me,"

"If you don't mind I would like the job of Bruce. I'm sure a little Chinese torture would have him singing like a bird. Failing that Kate's one handed driving would loosen his tongue," Thunder said and smiled. Kate looked daggers at him. "Only joking," he said softly.

"Okay. I'll leave Bruce to you. What do you propose to do now? I know a place you could go to. You can't stay here. I doubt those men would honour sanctuary," Palmerston-Smith said dryly.

"The two girls will go to somewhere I know. No offence, but I don't have time to check out your place and I know mine is safe," Thunder said. Palmerston-Smith nodded. He didn't like it but he accepted he didn't have a choice and it was obvious this man knew what he was doing. He would be a useful contact, especially when he found out who was behind this. He got to his feet.

"Right. Sarah will give you her key and tell you how to get in. She is obviously more adept at getting in and out without being seen than I thought," his sarcasm made Kate smile. "I will go home, keep Bruce with me and wait for your call," Thunder got up. Palmerston-Smith watched him struggle to his feet with a thoughtful look.

Sarah jumped to her feet and threw her arms round her father's neck. "I knew you'd understand once it was explained to you," she said to him.

He freed himself and held her at arms length. "I'm just glad you're safe. I'd been told you were kidnapped and to wait for my instructions. At least they hired a professional and not some cowboy," he told her.

"You got both," Thunder said quietly. "Fortunately the professional one got there first," He limped to the door with Palmerston-Smith. At the door they stopped. "I expected you to get mad. I'm glad you didn't," Thunder said.

Palmerston-Smith looked at him. "You held all the cards. Sarah means the world to me, just take care of her or you will answer to me,"

Thunder smiled. "That's what Bruce said,"

"Find out who's behind this. Leave Bruce to me. You'll get your money - and more. I've heard of you - on the grapevine - I didn't believe it, but the word is you're good," he said.

"I'm honoured," Thunder was sarcastic. He didn't tell him that he knew who was behind the contract, he wanted confirmation and more information. Palmerston-Smith left. Thunder returned to the girls. He stood next to Kate.

"Where are we going?" she asked.

"Back to Chinatown. I hope you like Chinese food," he said dryly.

CHAPTER NINE

They left the church, walked out to Fleet Street and hailed a cab. They got out near a restaurant near the end of Gerrard Street. Thunder walked straight through the restaurant, no one gave them a glance. Outside the kitchen was a metal staircase. He started to climb. It lead up to the kitchen in Kit's flat. Kit and Ling didn't look surprised when they stepped into the kitchen. Ling put the kettle on. Sarah and Kate sat at the table, Thunder went into the sitting room with Kit.

"Has anyone been around asking questions?" Thunder asked sitting down in the chair.

"Two men, two days ago, but they got nothing," Kit replied. He sat opposite.

"Anyone else? An old friend?" Thunder asked.

Kit shrugged. "He's been seen, fleetingly, with a blond man, Australian I think,"

"Talking of him. We have a little job to do," Thunder said. They went into the kitchen where Ling was making Jasmine tea. Sarah pulled a face and tried to pick out the leaves. Kate found it quite refreshing. Sarah couldn't believe that people actually lived like this.

"Kit and I are going out. Ling will look after you. Don't go out. Don't use the phone," Thunder told them. "First thing in the morning we'll go and see Marcus, but it will be early. About six," he said to Sarah.

"I'll be up," Sarah said quietly. She doubted that she'd sleep much anyway. Thunder and Kit went out leaving Kate and Sarah sat at the table.

"What if Thunder can't sort this out? What then? I can't stay here all my life!" Sarah said.

"I've only known Thunder for about a week, but if he says

he'll do something, he generally does. He'll sort it out and we can go back to our lives," Kate said to her.

"He's not afraid of anyone is he? The way he stood up to papa and back at the house. I hated it when Marcus just gave in but he knows when to give in and when to fight," Sarah's life had changed in just 24 hours; she had grown up.

"Marcus is very nice and sensible. That doesn't make him bad. There aren't that many like him. Most men I've come across are all mouth and no action, when it comes to the crunch they would save themselves long before you," Kate said.

"You have Thunder now," Sarah said.

"For now. Once he has sorted this out, he will be gone. At least I will have some pleasant memories and a marker though I doubt anyone will come up to his measure," Kate said sadly.

"I hope Marcus is all right," Sarah changed the subject; she hadn't quite changed; she still thought of herself and her interests before anyone else.

"The doc will look after him," Kate smiled. Sarah yawned. "Why don't you have a lie down,"

"In the middle of the day? I won't sleep a wink," Sarah looked worried. Kate took her firmly by the arm and lead her to the room they had slept in. Sarah curled up on the bed, Kate covered her with a blanket and left. Within minutes Sarah was asleep. Kate went back to the sitting room. There were two Chinese girls with Ling. They fell silent when she walked in.

"This is Sonja and Anna, Kit's sisters. This is Kate, Thunder's friend," Ling introduced them.

They spoke in English politely. They wanted to know what had happened. Anna and Sonja looked quite envious as Kate talked. It soon became obvious that all they wanted to know about was Thunder; whether it had been frightening or not was irrelevant. When Kate was asked the same question twice Ling tried to change the subject but one or other always brought it back to their favourite subject: Thunder. Kate wondered why he didn't choose one of them; they obviously loved him, wanted to be with him and Anna in particular was very beautiful. Eventually Ling gave them a mouthful in Chinese and they left.

Kit and Thunder left Chinatown by an alleyway. In Shaftesbury Avenue they hailed a cab. Thunder gave the Palmerston-Smith address. Kit sat back, a small canvas bag on his lap. He looked unperturbed. Thunder looked out the back window at the cars but none appeared to be following.

They got out and paid the driver. Thunder watched him drive off. Kit looked up at the houses. They were certainly expensive looking; large Victorian houses with a basement, three floors and an attic. Anywhere else these houses would have been converted into flats. Kit waited until Thunder decided it was safe to move. No one appeared at the windows and there didn't seem to be surveillance equipment although a burglar alarm was evident. They walked down the side of the house. Thunder put Sarah's key in the lock. It turned smoothly and silently, the lock obviously kept well oiled.

Inside was a narrow staircase. Thunder climbed this stiffly, his leg had been heavily strapped by the doc and not changed since. Kit followed, occasionally looking behind. No one followed them up. They came to a small landing on the first floor. There were three doors facing them and more stairs going upwards. Thunder took out his gun. He pushed open the first door, it was a bathroom. The second was a cupboard. The third was a short corridor. Thunder and Kit entered this. At the end were two doors. The first lead to a landing and the main house. At the second Thunder listened hard. He could hear voices. He slowly pushed open the door.

"Have you heard from the kidnappers?" Bruce asked Palmerston-Smith.

"Not yet, but I expect something any time now," Palmerston-Smith said.

Bruce looked worried. He should have received his instructions by now. "Is there anything else you want me to do?" Bruce asked. Palmerston-Smith saw the door opening behind him and knew the moment had come. Sat with his back to the door Bruce didn't see it.

"You can tell me again what happened that Saturday morning and what possessed Sarah to go off like that," Palmerston-Smith sounded annoyed.

"I've told you what I know. I don't know what possessed Sarah to leave," Bruce sounded irritated. He'd gone over this at least three times. His boss was becoming a pain. "She knows the rules," he added peevishly.

Thunder crept up behind Bruce and put the gun to his head. "Perhaps you'd like to tell us about the contract you set up," he said softly.

Bruce froze. His face went white. He looked sideways at Thunder and then at Palmerston-Smith who sat behind his massive desk and watched. He swallowed, pulled at his beard and looked back at Thunder.

"I don't know what you're talking about," he said at last, his voice nervous, the Australian accent vanished to be replaced by his native New Zealand one.

"Is there anything I can get you?" Palmerston-Smith asked.

"You know him?" Bruce's voice went up several decibels.

"Thunder and I are acquainted," Palmerston-Smith said quietly.

"Th... Th... Thunder? Oh shit," Bruce said.

Thunder looked at Palmerston-Smith. "Some hot water and a cup," he said. "For my friend,"

Palmerston-Smith went out and returned minutes later with a jug and a cup which he put down on the table at the back of the room. Kit put his bag down and took out a large knife, a chopping board and a roll of material. He unrolled this and put some of the herbs from the roll on the board. Palmerston-Smith went back to his desk, shuffled some papers and dropped them into a drawer. He looked at Thunder and Bruce and over them to Kit.

"I'll leave you gentlemen to it," he said. "Ring that buzzer when you have finished and we'll discuss your findings," he went to the door.

Bruce watched him go. "You're not leaving me with him?" his voice went high, like a girl's.

"Yes," and he left the room shutting the door firmly behind him.

"Now," Thunder said in his velvety voice. It sent shivers up

Bruce's spine.

"I'll talk. There's no need for violence," Bruce said, scared.

"Who said anything about violence," Thunder said.

"Well, that's what you're here for, isn't it?" Bruce said nervously.

"Whatever gave you that idea?" Thunder said in the velvety voice.

"That's what you do best, isn't it?" Bruce said looking up at Thunder.

Thunder walked round to face him. "Yes. That's what I do best,"

"That's why I said I'll talk. I'll tell you whatever you want to know," Bruce said, trying to be helpful.

"Oh you'll talk, but I thought we'd have a cup of tea first," he said looking over Bruce's shoulder at Kit.

"What?" Bruce was uncertain now.

Thunder looked at him. "Tea. You like tea, don't you Bruce?" Bruce looked over his shoulder at Kit who put some more herbs on the board and picked up the knife.

"It was Lowman," Bruce said before Kit lowered the knife.

"Lowman," Thunder said.

"Lowman put the contract out to you. He contacted me and I contacted the Chinaman. I did the arrangements, on Lowman's orders," Bruce said.

"Have I introduced my companion?" Thunder said and gestured at Kit. "This is the Chinaman," his voice dropped. Bruce looked at Kit, looked at the knife and swallowed, hard. "I know all this Bruce. You're not telling me anything I don't already know. Start chopping," Thunder said.

"I'll tell you, I'll tell you," Bruce cried out.

"I'm waiting," Thunder said softly. Kit held the knife in mid air and waited. Bruce looked at the knife and then back to Thunder.

"Lowman contacted me. Palmerston-Smith was in the way of some deal, he had to be edged out. Lowman told me to give you the contract," Bruce said.

Thunder leant forward, his face level with Bruce's. His voice dropped to just above a whisper. He stroked his cheek with his gun. Bruce looked at this mesmerised. "I know all this. You're repeating yourself. You're boring me, Bruce and then my finger starts to itch,"

Bruce started to shake. "What do you want to know?"

"Who put the two goons on the girl and me?" Kit put down the knife and folded his arms. Thunder straightened up. He went and sat in Palmerston-Smith's chair behind the desk. Bruce sighed briefly. Thunder heard it and raised an eyebrow. "Don't think about running. I am a good shot and my friend still has his knife. You'd never reach the door," his voice had a menacing tone.

Bruce blanched. "Sammy and Joe were hired to make sure the job was done. Lowman wasn't happy about it. I told Joe what she'd be wearing, the same as I told you,"

"And the girl?" Thunder asked.

"What girl?" Bruce asked.

"Mini Skirt Sue," Thunder said. "Tall, blond, wears red mini skirts,"

"I only told Joe what I told you," Bruce persisted.

Thunder thought he was lying. "Liar!" he growled. "You put her on the job. Who gave the order?"

"I'm telling you the truth!" Bruce cried. "I don't know of any girl," He started to sweat.

Thunder looked at him thoughtfully. Kit started to chop herbs. Bruce looked fearfully over his shoulder. He looked back at Thunder who was resting his chin on the barrel of his gun, elbows on the desk, looking thoughtful. Bruce swallowed and tried to stare him out but looked away.

"Why did Lowman contact you? What has he got on you?" Thunder asked.

"I used to work in one of his bars. He caught me fiddling the till. He got me the job here to keep an eye on the old man," Bruce said relieved that the subject had been changed.

"Is that how Cardol got in touch with you?" he asked softly. Kit stopped chopping. He looked round at Thunder. He had only ever heard Thunder talk of this man twice before. The last time they had nearly died because of him.

"Who?" Bruce was taken by surprise.

"Cardol," Thunder forced the name out between clenched teeth, he had never felt easy speaking the name, as if spoken too often he would appear.

"I've never met him," Bruce said, certain of it.

"You do know who I mean though. You went to my flat with him," Thunder's voice was deadly quiet. Kit waited. Bruce looked baffled.

"Your flat? I've never been to your flat. I don't know where you live. No one does," Bruce said.

"The flat in Wandsworth," Thunder said.

"I was sent to pick this man up in Wandsworth," Bruce said.

"So you do know him,"

"Lowman called me and told me to collect this man from Wandsworth and take him to this office. I didn't speak to him. He was silent," Bruce said.

Thunder thought about it. "How many tails were put on my friend here?"

"Lowman put one on him but lost him. I don't know of any others," Bruce said. He relaxed a bit. He felt better about this.

"Someone must know," Thunder said quietly. He sat and thought, occasionally rubbing his chin with the gun. The pieces were starting to fall into place. Another visit to Lowman was in order. A public one this time, no sneaking about. He looked at Bruce. Kit was leaning against the table, the knife in his hand. He stared grimly at Bruce. Bruce sat uncomfortably in his chair. He looked at Kit over his shoulder a couple of times, his eyes strayed to the knife. He swallowed several times. He looked back at Thunder. He wasn't what Bruce expected but the menace that emanated from this man was real and very deadly. Bruce fully expected to be killed once this was over. If not Thunder, then Lowman or Palmerston-Smith.

"Now what shall I do with you Bruce? Have you told us everything there is to tell? Hum? I wonder," Thunder said softly.

"Lowman put the contract out on Palmerston-Smith. He told me to give it to you. I did that. I arranged for Palmerston-Smith to go on a business trip, making it possible for Sarah to go away. I gave you the details I was given about the cottage. I told Joe the same as I told you. That is all. I don't know anything else," Bruce said fearfully.

"What about my contact at the cottage?" Thunder asked.

"Contact? I thought you were to contact me a week later," Bruce said surprised.

"I never got those instructions. And someone contacted me there, twice. I told them I had kidnapped the wrong girl. They warned me about Sammy and Joe. Now why would they do that? There are too many holes in this," Thunder said.

"I think the cottage belongs to a friend of Lowman. A man called Light… something, I think. I only part heard, but it was something like that," Bruce said. He swallowed. "What are you going to do with me?"

"Let's ask Palmerston-Smith, shall we?" Thunder said and pressed the buzzer on the desk.

"If he finds out I arranged for Sarah to be kidnapped, he'll kill me," Bruce said.

"Yes," Thunder's tone was uncaring.

Palmerston-Smith came in the room. He frowned at Thunder sitting in his chair. Thunder got up and gestured to him to sit. He walked forward, not looking at his employee. Kit started to clear up. Thunder walked over to Bruce.

"Have you the information you wanted?" Palmerston-Smith asked.

"Bruce has something to tell you," Thunder poked Bruce in the shoulder. Bruce looked appealingly up at Thunder. Thunder frowned and prodded him with the gun. Bruce looked at his boss and swallowed.

"Lowman put a contract out on you. The idea was to kidnap Sarah and make you pull out of the Ellis deal. I arranged it," he said unhappily.

"Tell him about this friend," Thunder prompted.

"Your friend?" Bruce asked looking up.

"No, Lowman's friend who owns the cottage," Thunder prompted.

"I only heard part of his name," Bruce started.

"But your boss might know who it is," Thunder said sharply.

"Oh. Light... something. He owns a cottage on the Isle of Wight," Bruce said.

"Lightman? Carl Lightman?" Palmerston-Smith asked. Bruce shrugged. Palmerston-Smith looked stricken. "But we are friends. We play golf together,"

"Some friend," Kit muttered.

"Could Lightman be behind Lowman? Bruce knew about Sammy and Joe but not about a girl. I expect my reputation for returning hostages unharmed has somewhat preceded me," Thunder said.

"Is that all?" Palmerston-Smith asked.

"The rest doesn't concern you, right now. Do you know Lowman?" Thunder said. Palmerston-Smith nodded. "Can you arrange a meeting between him and me? We have a little unfinished business. He'll understand,"

"Bruce will do it for you," Palmerston-Smith said. Bruce looked unhappy.

"Then we are out of here," Thunder said. Kit put the roll and board in his bag. "I'll give Sarah her key back,"

"You have Sarah?" Bruce asked.

Thunder nodded then had a thought. "Who sent the goons?"

"They were Lowman's men. When it looked like you weren't going to find Sarah I told him where to find her," Bruce said quietly and hung his head.

"You and me are going to have a very serious talk, Bruce," Palmerston-Smith said to him. He looked up at Thunder. "What will you do with Lowman and Lightman?"

"I haven't decided," Thunder said.

"Don't do anything final, if you know what I mean. I have an idea, something that will destroy them. Call it poetic justice," Palmerston-Smith said with a smile. "Call me later. Bruce will have set up that meeting,"

Thunder and Kit left the same way they came in. They got a cab and returned to Chinatown. Palmerston-Smith and Bruce settled down for their 'talk'.

It was about five when Thunder and Kit returned. Thunder

went and sat next to Kate, sitting in the window looking out at London's roof tops. He leaned his arm on her knees and looked at her. She absentmindedly put a hand on his arm. Thunder didn't find it odd; he felt they had grown close in the last few days; they were now good friends. What had happened between them had been pleasant but unspoken. He didn't think it would be repeated. He hoped Kate would now see that not all men were like Alan; or had their fleeting intimacy only reinforced her view? As for himself, any attraction he felt was being deliberately buried; people usually got hurt when he got involved.

"So what happened? Did he talk?" Kate asked.

"He took one look at Kit with that wicked knife he has and started talking. Most I already knew, but he filled in a few other gaps and confirmed most of what Lowman had said. I left Palmerston-Smith to mop up," Thunder told her cheerfully.

"Mop up?" Kate didn't understand.

"Bruce will be lucky if Palmerston-Smith doesn't bury him," Thunder said darkly. "He was not a happy man,"

Kate wasn't concerned about Bruce's fate. "So who is behind this?"

"A man call Carl Lightman. Apparently plays golf with Palmerston-Smith," Thunder said.

"I bet that hurt," Kate said.

"Lowman got Bruce to set up the kidnap and put those two amateurs on our tail. The cottage belongs to Lightman," Thunder didn't mention the flat. "For some reason his name rings a vague bell," he sighed. "Oh well, it will come to me,"

"So who hired the girl?" Kate asked.

"Don't know, yet. Perhaps Lowman can enlighten us," Thunder said.

"What about those men at the lay-by?" Kate asked.

"They were Lowman's men. When it looked like I wasn't going to find Sarah, Bruce told them exactly where to find her. That little shit knew all the time where she was going. Presumably after I told Lowman I didn't have Sarah, he got Bruce to tell his men where to go," Thunder thought about it. "I told Lowman to keep quiet. Neither knew I hadn't kidnapped Sarah. Bruce didn't know I had been contacted at the cottage," he sighed and ran his fingers through his hair.

"Are you tired?" Kate asked. He looked shattered.

"Deadly," he admitted. "You?"

Kate shrugged. "How's the leg?"

"Not too bad," he prodded it gently. "The doc bandaged it firmly,"

"Do you want me to change the dressing?" Kate asked. She suddenly felt an outsider. Thunder was at home here, she felt like a guest.

Thunder looked at her and raised one eyebrow. She looked disinterested. "If you like," he said quietly.

He took off a trouser leg and lay down on the sofa while she collected her 'medical kit'. She cut off the bandage and took off the dressing. It had stopped bleeding and was quite firmly stitched. Another battle scar to add to the tally. She put a new dressing on it and bandaged it. He helped but she still laboured. She sighed when it was finished, it was difficult with only one hand. Both were unaware that they were being watched from the kitchen.

Thunder pulled the tracksuit back on. She stood uncertainly. He pulled her down on the sofa and lay next to him. She lay rigidly against the back of the sofa. He put his arm round her and pulled her to him. She laid her head on his shoulder and her plastered arm across his chest. Within minutes they were asleep.

In the kitchen Ling and Kit talked quietly in Chinese, Ling told him about Sonja and Anna's visit. Kit tried to answer her questions and then fell quiet. Kit looked at Ling, recognised the look and smiled.

"I know what you are dying to ask, Ling. Are they lovers? I don't know. They've shared rooms but whether it goes any further, I don't know. He doesn't usually take advantage of his victims, he never gets involved but this is different," Kit said. Ling frowned at him. "You'll have to ask him,"

"They seem very… close," was all Ling commented.

"They have been thrown together since it happened. They've looked after each other. He could have dumped her," Kit said.

"That isn't Thunder's style," Ling said indignantly. "He looks after his victims," Sometimes Kit's cavalier attitude to life annoyed her.

"I suppose Anna and Sonja are feeling put out?" he asked.

"They can't forget they owe him their lives," Ling said.

"He isn't interested," Kit said bluntly. "She'd have to be something special to interest him,"

"Is Kate that special?" Ling asked.

He shrugged. "She's different. Amusing. Clever. But special? Possibly,"

"She doesn't think so. She doesn't think much of herself at all. She likes people but not herself," Ling commented. "Sarah is the opposite, she thinks a lot of herself and nothing of anyone else," she sighed.

"Thunder is moving Sarah tomorrow I think. Kate will stay with us for a while longer until it's safe to go home. Though Thunder doesn't think she wants to, he said it sounded pretty horrid," Kit said.

Ling started cooking. The smell woke Thunder. He eased off the sofa leaving Kate asleep. He limped into the kitchen. Kit sat chopping herbs with his 'wicked knife'. Ling was stirring soup.

"That smells good," Thunder said.

"Chicken noodle soup," Ling muttered.

"I'm sorry to dump Kate and Sarah on you but I had to take them somewhere," Thunder said.

"I would have been offended if you hadn't," Ling round on him brandishing a ladle.

He eyed the ladle. "And I wouldn't want to offend you, Ling,"

"Kate is nice," she said.

"Different. Not on the make," Kit added.

"Like Anna and Sonja?" Ling challenged.

"I saved their lives, I don't need payment from them," Thunder said bluntly.

"They need husbands," Kit said.

"Anna has a suitor, but she won't hear of it, he doesn't match up," Ling said.

"What?" Kit and Thunder both said, though in different ways.

"He doesn't match up to you, Thunder. You're a hard act to

follow," Ling said smugly. He looked shocked. "Surprised Thunder? You treat them like sisters but they love you and want to be so much more," she laughed at his discomfort. Kit just smirked. Thunder looked from one to the other.

"Tell us about Kate," Ling said and his relief was evident.

"She is… different. She's intelligent, funny. She says her family find her boring. I can't see why, she is hardly that," he said and then dried up. Perhaps this wasn't such a safe topic after all. He looked uncomfortable again. Kit smirked away. He had never seen his friend so uncomfortable - or confused.

"After living in each other's pockets for a week you get to know someone pretty good," Kit said. Thunder threw him a dark look.

"Go and see if they are awake," Ling said with a laugh.

Thunder looked thankful to escape. Sarah was still asleep. Kate was curled up on the sofa. She looked lost, carefully wrapping her arm close to her body.

"Does it hurt?" he asked.

"Yes. It feels heavy and aches," she looked up.

"Perhaps a sling would help," he suggested.

"Then my neck would hurt," she retorted. She could feel tears hovering.

Ling came in from the kitchen. She carried a cup. It looked clear but it smelt wonderful. "Some tea," she said to Kate. "I've put something in to help the pain,"

Sarah came in. They all sat in the kitchen. Sarah watched them eating with chopsticks. Her and Kate used a fork.

At ten Thunder rang Palmerston-Smith. "Did you set up a meeting with Lowman?"

"Tomorrow at his penthouse flat. He says you know where it is. He will meet you alone. I've assured him all you want to do is talk. I'll send a car, it will give his men something to look after," Palmerston-Smith ended with a sarcastic tone.

Thunder smiled. "Pick me up outside the Classic Cinema in the Haymarket. Half nine,"

"I'll send Bruce," Palmerston-Smith said. Thunder heard a protest that suddenly stopped. He passed him over to Sarah.

They watched TV for the rest of the evening until Kate said she wanted to go to bed. Thunder took her upstairs to a room with two beds. She didn't realise it wasn't the one she had shared with Sarah. She slept soundly until dawn.

Looking round the room when she woke she saw Thunder sprawled face down across the other bed, his left arm hung off the bed and he was naked except for shorts and the bandage. His gun was on the bedside table. The weals across his back could be plainly seen.

She got up and looked at the bandage. There was a spot of red. She carefully turned him over and cut off the bandage. It was weeping slightly. She cleaned it and put on a new dressing. Winding the bandage round his leg was difficult, she ended up putting his ankle on her shoulder. He didn't stir once. She threw a blanket over him and returned to her bed. When she woke again he was up and dressed.

"Did you change my dressing?" he asked her.

"You didn't stir," she said. "You must have been tired,"

"Anyone else I probably would have woken. I've got used to your presence," he said and stopped short.

"What will you do today?" she changed the subject.

"Get you some breakfast," he said with a smile.

"Don't fuss," she sounded irritated.

"Trip?" he asked.

"Fine," Kate wasn't bothered. He looked at her. She looked tired, or irritated, or both, he wasn't sure. She looked up. "I could do with a stiff drink and a decent book," she said irritable. "And stop being so bloody patronising!"

"I'll see what I can do," he went out. Kate sighed.

CHAPTER TEN

Downstairs Ling was cooking breakfast and talking to Sarah who looked much better. Kate came in. Thunder and Kit came in. Ling handed Thunder a cup of black coffee. Kate didn't look up. Sarah gave her some toast, which she ate without looking, it could have been anything.

After breakfast Kate retreated to the window seat in the sitting room. Sarah stayed in the kitchen with Ling. Kit and Thunder sat in the sitting room and quietly talked about the visit. Kit didn't want him to go alone.

"I have to go alone. I have to sort this out. Kate and Sarah have to be safe," Thunder argued.

"I still think you should take someone with you," Kit said stubbornly.

Thunder scowled. He looked across at Kate. "I'll take Kate. Happy?"

"That a good idea?" Kit asked.

"You want me to take someone," Thunder hissed at him. "It's Kate or no one,"

Kit shrugged. "Fine," he said. "I'll give her something handy," He went into the kitchen. Thunder stayed where he was and drunk his coffee. Kate was unaware of them, she was looking out at London rooftops and thinking about home.

Kit returned from the kitchen, in one hand was a short curved knife, in the other a sheath with a strap hanging from it. He crossed the room to Kate. She was still looking out of the window. Kit touched her shoulder. She slowly turned her head to face him. Her expression was one of acute sadness. It touched Kit's heart. He sat opposite her.

"You may have need of this," he said softly. He held out the knife.

"Why?" her voice was a whisper.

"You just might," he dropped the knife in her lap. Kate picked it up and looked at it, then up at Kit.

"Why should I need a knife? I don't know how to use it," she said.

"Use your instinct," he said to her. "You're going out,"

"Where?" she asked.

"To see Lowman," he replied.

Kate looked at him. "Why me?"

"I think he should take someone with him. He opted for you," Kit said.

Kate opened her mouth to ask another question, thought better of it and went to get ready. When Thunder returned to the sitting room Kate had her leather jacket on, the arm swung free. She was trying, unsuccessfully, to zip it up. He crossed over to her, zipped up the jacket and tucked the arm in the pocket.

"Why are you taking me?" Kate asked.

"Why not?" he asked.

"Kit springs to mind," her tone was sarcastic.

"Tough," his tone was curt. "Let's go,"

They went out onto the street and down Gerrard Street, turned into Whitcombe Street and up Orange Street. They stood outside the cinema in the Haymarket. Thunder stood with his back to the wall, hands in his pockets scrutinising the traffic. Kate stood aside and looked at the posters.

"We could go later," Thunder said without at her.

"I'm honoured, I'm sure," she replied sarcastically. She didn't look at him. They could have been strangers.

A black limo drove down the road slowly. It glided to a halt at the kerb. The back window unwound. Bruce looked out.

"Over here," he called.

"Keep your head down until we get in the car," Thunder said quietly. They got in the car. Bruce sat with his back to the driver. He tapped the window when they were in. The car pulled away.

"I thought you agreed to see Lowman alone," Bruce said looking at Kate. She looked up at him. He drew in breath. "For a minute I thought..." he trailed off.

"That's what I thought," Thunder said.

Bruce was silent for about ten minutes then he started to talk. Thunder ignored him and looked out the window. He was watching where they were going. Kate looked out the other window and pointedly refused to reply to Bruce's questions. Eventually he gave up. The car pulled into the drive of the block of flats where Lowman lived. The driver and the man in the front got out. The driver opened the door. Thunder got out and waited.

Kate looked at Bruce carefully. His hair had dark roots with blond ends. He looked like he'd been dipped in white paint. He had a dark beard and very blue eyes. "Are you sure you are Australian? Or are you just masquerading as one?" she asked him.

"Don't know what you mean Sheila," he said in an exaggerated accent.

"Oh I think you do. Bruce. You can drop the phoney over the top Ozzie accent with me. I'm willing to bet your name isn't even Bruce. You're about as Australian as I am," Kate said sharply.

His voice dropped to his normal voice. "You're right. I'm not Australian, I'm from New Zealand but it suited me to be from Oz," he said.

"I bet you're really glad you did it now, aren't you?" Kate asked.

"If I'd known one percent of the trouble I'm in right now, I'd have stayed at home," he admitted.

"Just stay out of any more trouble and you might get to see home again. What is your name?" Kate said.

He looked at her shrewdly. She smiled at him. "You won't tell?"

"Not even Thunder. Though I doubt he'd care," Kate replied.

"Joseph. Joey. And don't give me any jokes about bloody kangaroos. I've heard them all!" he said.

"Was it all for the money?" Kate asked.

"Yeah," he said heavily. "Had to get home somehow, wasn't going to manage it on the lousy pay I got tending bar,"

"I'm sure you could have come up with a better idea," Kate said and got out the car.

Thunder looked at her. She smiled at him then looked at the

two men. They stood at the front of the car, feet apart, hands together. They looked like gangsters from a movie, both wore black double breasted suits that looked bulky. He saw her disgusted look and smiled.

"Just your average every day bodyguards for high powered businessmen," Thunder murmured to her. She gave him an arched look.

"They've been watching too many American films. This is hardly Al bloody Capone," Kate hissed at him. Thunder smiled at her sarcasm.

"Stay with the car, Bruce. And don't think of doing anything stupid. I can deal with you later," Thunder said in that deadly cold voice of his. "Try not to rile Lowman's boys," he said to the two men, patting one of them on the arm as he passed. Kate followed him into the hallway.

A large man blocked their path. Thunder looked at him with mild annoyance. Another man appeared behind them. Kate looked over her shoulder and frowned at him. He stood behind her, folded his fingers together and rested them over his large stomach and looked forward over Kate's head.

"We have an appointment with Mr Lowman," Thunder said softly.

"We have to check you out," the large man in front of Thunder said with a growl. He started to pat down Thunder and found the gun straight away. "We'll look after that,"

"The hell you will," Thunder started.

The man behind Kate took her right arm to turn her round. All he got was an empty sleeve. He turned her round by the shoulders and unzipped her jacket. The larger man shoved Thunder to one side, crashing him into the wall. The man advanced on Kate.

"Check that arm," he ordered.

"Seems real enough to me," he said, tapping the plaster.

"Check it!" the large man said. The second man looked mystified. "Like this!" the large man grabbed Kate's arm and brought it down on his uplifted knee. The plaster broke in several places. Kate screamed with pain.

"You bastard," she muttered, tears welling up. She brought her knee up sharply into his groin. He groaned and keeled over. The second man grabbed her around the throat. Thunder quickly took his gun off the man rolling on the floor and put it to the man's temple.

"Unless you wish to have the shit that passes for brains spread over that wall, I suggest you let go of my friend and take us to Lowman. He is expecting me," Thunder said in his velvety voice. The man let go of Kate suddenly. She fell forward into Thunder. The man took this opportunity to pull his gun. Kate looked over her shoulder at him, saw the gun and kicked one leg out at him catching him squarely in the bollocks with her heel. He went down screaming. Thunder put her upright.

"That is another one I owe you," he said. He pressed the button and the lift doors opened.

Inside was a thin young man, he had dirty blond hair and thick dark rimmed glasses. Kate gave him a withering look. Thunder pointed the gun at him. The man backed away. They got in the lift, Kate nursing her wrist. This would mean another trip to the hospital. She was beginning to get a little fed up of this. The plaster wasn't even fully set yet.

"Which floor?" Kate asked.

"Top," Thunder replied. Kate hit the button. The doors shut and the lift descended.

"Shit for brains? Where did you hear that? A film? You're as bad as them," she said to Thunder as she leaned on the wall. He glared at her. She ignored him. The man cowered in the corner.

At the fifteenth floor the doors opened. Thunder gestured to the man to go first. He nervously walked out the lift. There was another man sitting there. He got to his feet when he saw them come out.

"We are here to see Lowman," Thunder said menacingly.

A door opened. Bob Lowman stood there. He was wearing a blue pinstriped suit. He frowned and gestured to the man to sit back down. Thunder pushed the young man away. He fell to the floor. Thunder kept the gun pointing at him.

"There is no need for the gun," Lowman said.

"Tell that to your shit for brains downstairs," Thunder said darkly.

Lowman frowned. "Get those arseholes up here," he told the man. "I'll deal with them later. Follow me," he said to Thunder, turned on his heel and walked into the flat.

Thunder watched the man pick up a phone and start speaking, he presumed it was to the men downstairs. Thunder put his gun back in his jacket, put his arm round Kate's shoulders and propelled her into the flat. They went into the sitting room. A pretty blond girl sat in one of the chairs, she was the same one that Thunder and Kit had seen here the time before. She smiled at Kate and looked at Thunder uncertain as to what he would do this time.

"Leave us," Lowman said to her. "And shut the door," she left closing the door after her.

Kate sat down on the sofa. Lowman looked at her. Then he looked at Thunder who had walked over to the window. He walked over to Thunder.

"That isn't Sarah, is it?" Lowman asked quietly.

"No. That is Kate. The girl we all mistook for Sarah. She has a broken wrist. Your chief... arsehole downstairs didn't believe it, so broke it for her again, just to make sure," Thunder said turning to face Lowman.

To give him his due Lowman looked furious. He moved away towards Kate. Thunder watched him.

"My apologies," Lowman said to Kate. "He will be dealt with, believe me," his voice had a menace to it that left Kate in no doubt of his sincerity.

"I've spoke to Bruce," Thunder said. He sat in a chair facing the door with his back to the window. He undid his jacket. Lowman could see the butt of the gun. Lowman sat in the other chair.

"And what did he tell you?" he asked quietly.

"He confirmed some of what you told me. I have a few unanswered questions though. I thought perhaps you could enlighten me," Thunder said. His voice was cold, contemptuous, deadly. Lowman could feel his hatred, taste it even. Thunder put his hands on the arms of the chair and spread his fingers. He could feel soft leather beneath them.

Lowman sat back in his chair. He put his elbows on the arms of the chair. Drawing his fingers together he looked at Thunder over them. Thunder looked back at him steadily. Kate sat on the end of the sofa and waited while these two men psyched each other out. It was obvious to her that each had the measure of each other. If anything Lowman, for all his massive build and unsavoury reputation, was more than a little afraid of Thunder. Thunder, on the other hand, feared no one.

"Oh for goodness sake. Grow up!" she muttered.

Both men looked at her sharply. Lowman smiled. Thunder turned his attention back to Lowman. He found Lowman looking at him steadily, his face was quite neutral, a slight smile was on his face.

"What sort of questions do you have?" Lowman asked slowly.

"Who put Mini Skirt Sue on the tail of the girl?" Thunder asked.

"Who?" Lowman was nonplussed.

"She was a hit girl. Got close to her victims and then killed them. She was quite good," Thunder said.

"Was?" Lowman asked before he could stop himself.

"Sammy pushed her under a tube," Thunder said and looked at Kate. He hadn't told her that. Kate looked unconcerned. Her wrist lay in her lap. "Have you any pain killers?" Thunder asked.

"Only alcohol," Lowman said with a laugh. He started to rise. "I'll get you a drink,"

Thunder waved him down. "No matter," he said. He got up and limped over to the bar. He poured a large whiskey for himself and brandy for Kate. He took the drinks and gave one to Kate. "Drink it," he ordered. Kate looked at it and then him with distaste. She hated brandy.

"Drink it," he repeated holding the glass out to her. Kate frowned and curled her lip in disgust. He gestured at her to take the drink. She took it and put it to her lips. She pulled a face at the initial taste, then tipped her head back and poured the lot down her throat. She coughed. Thunder took the glass and put it on the table. He sat back down opposite Lowman. Lowman watched him silently.

"I see your leg is improving," Lowman said quietly.

"Joe obviously couldn't hit a moving target that well," Thunder said contemptuously.

"Obviously," Lowman said. He picked up his drink off the side table but did not drink. A thought occurred to him. "Could it have been Lightman?" he asked.

Thunder shrugged. "Someone did and she knew the drill, the same as the rest of us. Bruce said it wasn't him. I have no reason to think he's lying. He also picked up a man for Lightman from Wandsworth. Do you know about him?" Thunder said sipping his drink.

Lowman thought about it while she sipped his drink. "What does he look like?" she asked.

"Tall, black clothes, black close cropped hair," Thunder said.

Lowman looked puzzled. "That description fits a lot of people," he said putting the glass back on the table.

"This one has a scar down his face," Thunder added.

"Oh, him," Lowman's voice lifted. "He works for Lightman," he was dismissive.

"He doesn't work for anyone except himself," Thunder said savagely. "Lightman is being used,"

"That's Lightman's problem. Mine is this deal with Palmerston-Smith," Lowman said.

"That's tough," Thunder said coldly.

"Look, we needed Palmerston-Smith to pull out of the deal with Ellis leaving the field open to us. Lightman came up with the idea of using his kid, personally I'd rather deal face to face with people, but that's Lightman for you. I set up the contract for you to kidnap Sarah and hold her to force her old man to cooperate. Once we had got the deal she was to be returned unharmed. Contrary to popular belief, I do not hurt women," Lowman sounded exasperated.

"Well, if Lightman has linked up with this man, you do now," Thunder was unimpressed.

"Not if I have anything to with it," Lowman said darkly.

"It is probably too late now anyway," Thunder told him softly.

Lowman picked up his glass, it was half empty. He drained the lot. Thunder could see his Adam's apple jump as he swallowed. Thunder slipped his whiskey. Kate sat staring into space. He saw she had the same expression that she had at the cottage when she had realised what had happened; it was one of no longer caring what happened to her. A thought occurred to him.

"Who contacted me at the cottage?" he suddenly asked.

"What cottage?" Lowman was beginning to feel he had only been told half a story.

"Lightman's cottage on the Isle of Wight. It was where I was to hold Sarah. Only someone told Sammy and Joe where to find me. We missed them by half a day, but only after I had been tipped off. By my contact there who knew I had Kate and not Sarah," Thunder said. He looked at Lowman, his eyes were cold and expressionless.

Lowman thought they were the eyes of a cold blooded killer. He thought he was cold but this man was more so. He didn't feel in danger though. It was obvious he wasn't the villain here. He would like to see Lightman dead and buried. Perhaps he would hire Thunder. That would give him something to muse on later. His attention returned to Thunder.

"I knew nothing about a cottage," he said flatly. "I assumed you would hold her somewhere you knew of and that you would contact Bruce who was to contact me," his voice lifted slightly. "I didn't want to hire Sammy and Joe, Lightman thought it would be insurance. Looks like Bruce has been working it from both ends. Not sensible,"

"Bruce is going to be lucky to still be alive next week. Palmerston-Smith is not a happy man," Thunder said.

"I'll bet," Lowman was being awfully calm about the whole thing.

"It would seem that a visit to Lightman is in order," Thunder said.

"He's difficult to get to. I've been trying for years," Lowman said. "He makes the appointment and the place," he thought of St

James' Park on a cold March morning.

"I have my methods," Thunder said.

"I'll bet," Lowman said. He thought about his "partner'. Something would have to be done about him. Lowman had a reputation to maintain, he did not need any other idiot believing they could pull the same trick. Lightman had caused him plenty of trouble already; he certainly didn't need more from other quarters.

Thunder watched him and sipped his drink. It was rather early in the day to be drinking but holding a glass gave his hands something to do. Better than strangling Lowman at any rate.

"We'll be going. I trust that I never have cause to visit you again," Thunder said. "There isn't anything else you want to add?" Lowman shook his head. "Good," Thunder's tone of voice was coldly indifferent. He drank the remainder of his whiskey and got to his feet.

Lowman also got up. Thunder helped Kate to her feet. By now she was in a lot of pain and cradled her arm to her body. The brandy had made her feel sick. Thunder put his arm round her shoulders and led her to the door. Lowman followed. On the landing sat the man reading a paper. He got to his feet when the door opened. The young man leaned on the wall by the lift door. He had his arms folded and was looking belligerent. He pushed himself away from the wall and stood straight, dropping his arms to his side. The other two were nowhere in sight.

Thunder turned to Lowman. "I suggest you teach those goons of yours some manners. Not everyone who comes here is like them. Some of us have a legitimate reason for being here," he said quietly. "We are not all out of some old film,"

Lowman nodded. The young man pressed the button to call the lift. The door opened seconds later. Thunder and Kate went into the lift and the doors shut. This time they were alone. Thunder looked around suspiciously. The lift descended quickly.

There was no one in the hallway. Thunder and Kate walked quickly out of the lift and through the front door. Palmerston-Smith's driver and man were standing near the front of the car waiting. They talked quietly, occasionally looking around. Bruce sat in the back of the car and waited. He felt little remorse for what he had done, the money had come in handy.

When Thunder and Kate appeared the driver nodded to the other man. He looked round at them and opened the door. Kate and Thunder climbed in. Bruce looked relieved that they were back. He looked at Kate questioningly. She was looking sickly white. Thunder did not explain. The two men got into the front. The driver pulled back the window.

"Where to?" he asked.

"St Bart's Hospital," Thunder said.

The driver looked mystified but didn't argue. He shut the window and drove away. Lowman watched them go from his window. His two men came in silently. Lowman turned to face them and unleashed his anger – and fists.

The driver expertly drove through the London traffic and pulled up at the front door of St Bart's hospital. Thunder and Kate got out. Bruce wound down the window.

"Do you want us to wait?" he asked. His orders had been specific. Pick up Thunder, take him to Lowman and take him back. Try and find out where he was staying.

"No, you can go back to Palmerston-Smith. Tell him we have business here. Sarah is not in hospital. But she will be if he tries to find her before I am ready," Thunder said coldly. He felt angry.

Bruce looked unhappy but wound up the window and tapped on the interconnecting window. The car pulled away. Thunder watched it disappear into the traffic. Kate stood next to him and waited. Thunder looked up and down the road, the traffic passed continuously. Kate got fed up of waiting and turned on her heel. She walked down the road to the back of the hospital. After a couple of minutes Thunder followed.

Kate found the door and went in. She knocked on the doc's door. The sound of his deep voice bidding her enter was a welcome sound. Kate thankfully pushed open the door.

"Well, Kate. This is a nice surprise," the doc said. He looked at her critically. She looked sickly white and in great pain. She held her arm to her body to protect it. Her jacket flapped and hang off her shoulders. He moved round his desk. "Back so soon? What is wrong now?" Thunder slipped into the room.

The doc had got as far as the corner of his desk. He stopped and looked at Thunder. "You seem to be walking a lot better," was all he said and moved to Kate who stood between the chairs.

"We went to visit someone and one of his entrance men got carried away," Kate said bitterly. "They've broken the plaster and it feels like the rest of my arm,"

The doc took off her jacket and guided her to the chair. He examined her wrist, feeling with his fingers, murmuring softly. Kate didn't cry out this time. The doc looked up. Kate was chewing her lip, the tears silently slid down her face. The doc got to his feet. Thunder was leaning against the wall near the door, a look of concern on his face.

"I'll have someone look at your arm. It will have to be x-rayed again," the doc said. He picked up the phone and spoke rapidly to someone. "You'd better come with me," he said to them both.

Thunder and Kate followed the doc out and into the hospital. Kate's arm was x-rayed and it was discovered that Lowman's goon had indeed broken another bone in her wrist. Thunder swore silently. That would mean another trip to Lowman's flat. Most of Kate's arm was plastered and put in a sling. About mid afternoon they left. Thunder took Kate out the front door this time and hailed a cab.

"Piccadilly Circus," he told the drive and they settled back. Thunder didn't say anything, his expression was now as black as his mood. Kate took one look at his face and sat huddled in the corner, silent, as far away from him as she could get.

CHAPTER ELEVEN

They got out near Eros. Kate saw a burger bar and crossed the road. Thunder followed, he wasn't about to argue where she was going.

Kate ordered burger, fries and a drink. Thunder ordered the same. Kate tucked the drink in her sling, picked up the bag, and walked away leaving Thunder to pay. He smiled ruefully and paid up. He followed her upstairs. Kate sat by the window and unpacked the bag. Thunder sat next to her. They started eating in silence.

"I'm sorry about your arm," he started in a soft voice. Kate looked at him coldly. Why didn't he just go away and let her go home? She decided to change the subject in her head. She didn't want to go home really and bitter recriminations wasn't going to help matters.

"Did you get all the answers you needed?" she asked him instead.

Thunder looked at her. "You were there, what do you think?" he said tersely.

"I wasn't taking a great deal of notice," Kate said, slightly sarcastic. "I heard you mention Lightman and Sue, describe some man with a scar but not much else. Was there anything else I missed?" she put some fries in her moth.

Thunder sighed deeply. He put his burger down and wiped his fingers, then moved in his seat so that he was half facing her. "Okay. To recap. Lightman ordered Lowman to give me the contact to kidnap Sarah to make Palmerston-Smith play ball with Bruce the contact," first finger. "Sammy and Joe were hired by Bruce on the orders of a reluctant Lowman on the orders of Lightman," Second finger. "Bruce told me and then Sammy and Joe what Sarah would be wearing and doing," third finger. "The helicopter and cottage were probably organised by Lightman as they were his. Bruce knew about the cottage but thought I would contact him," fourth finger. "Lowman knew nothing about the cottage so I presume it was Lightman who contacted me," fifth point, a thumb. "Which means that it was Lightman or his men who contact me at the cottage and who tipped me off about Sammy and Joe. Lowman and Bruce didn't," first finger, other hand. "Whoever this contact was they knew I didn't have Sarah, Lowman and Bruce didn't," he looked at his fingers. "What else is there?" he looked at Kate who had been eating fries while he talked.

"Who put Sue on to us," Kate put up her thumb. Thunder nodded. "Who sent those men to find Sarah at Worthing," first finger.

"That was Bruce. They were Lowman's men," Thunder said. Kate put down the finger. Thunder put up one of his.

"Why did they try to kill us?" Kate asked.

"They were sent to get Sarah from Worthing. They were trying to kill me and take Sarah. They didn't know about you," Thunder said. "Or Marcus,"

"Why are they trying to kill you?" Kate asked. Her finger pointed at him.

"Because they thought I had Sarah," Thunder said slowly. Kate looked at him and chewed thoughtfully.

"But didn't they know you didn't have Sarah?" he shook his head. "So why send men to Worthing?" Kate said. Thunder frowned. "And if they knew where Sarah was, why the elaborate charade?"

He frowned. "Someone else is behind this," he said.

Kate bit into her burger and thought. "The man with the scar?"

"But where does Cardol come into this?" Thunder asked. Himself more than Kate. "Lowman thinks he works for Lightman,"

Kate shrugged and put another chip in her mouth. Thunder picked up his burger and took a bite. He chewed and thought about it. Kate continued eating fries. People around them came and went. Kate drank some of her drink. They ate in silence while they both thought. The situation had become complicated and rather muddled.

"The problem is we don't know what Sammy and Joe's orders were," Kate said. Thunder threw her a look. "I mean, why would they go to the cottage to get Sarah if they had the same orders as you? As far as everyone was aware you already had Sarah, so why send them as well? It doesn't make sense," Kate continued. She ate another fry thoughtfully.

Thunder looked at her. "Maybe they aren't working for Lightman or Lowman after all," he said slowly.

"They got their orders from Bruce, the same as you," Kate pointed out.

"They may have got other orders from someone else. Bruce said Lowman reluctantly hired them. Lowman says they were hired for insurance. He knew about the warehouse though," he took a mouth of burger.

"What about Sue?" Kate asked. "Who was she working for?"

Thunder shook his head. They had just managed to complicate it again, and he was certain he had sorted it out in his mind. "Lightman ordered Lowman to put a contact out to me to get at Palmerston-Smith. Lightman orders Lowman to put Sammy and Joe on the same job. Someone put Sue on the same job. There has to another player in this game that we don't know about," Thunder explained.

"The man with the scar?" Kate suggested.

"Cardol? I hope not," Thunder said sincerely.

"Who else could it be?" Kate said.

"But how did he find out the details of the contact?" Thunder asked.

"Lightman?" Kate suggested.

Thunder shook his head. "It can't be Cardol," he said. "He does his own dirty work," Thunder said unconvinced.

"Why? It would explain the holes," Kate said.

Thunder looked at her. "He is after me, not Sarah or her father. I doubt he even knows or cares who they are," Thunder said softly.

"But, if he heard you were put on the contact, wouldn't that be a good opportunity to get at you?" Kate asked. She looked at him.

Thunder slowly shook his head. "He has promised to get me personally, not by a couple of cowboy killers like Sammy and Joe," Thunder said firmly.

"What about Sue?" Kate asked. "You said she was quite good,"

"She was. Very good. But that isn't Cardol's style either. Well, no that's not strictly true. It is Cardol's style, but not for me. He wants to turn the knife himself," Thunder said quietly.

"It's a bit macho bullshit, isn't it? Sounds like Terminator stuff to me," Kate said doubtfully.

Thunder smiled. He put his face close to Kate's and looked into her eyes. "I killed his family. Every last one. And a lot of his father's men. I gave him the scar that reminds him of me every time he looks in the mirror. Cardol has every reason to want to kill me, himself, face to face. I threaten his existence, his honour. He can't allow me to live," Thunder said in his deadly quiet voice. It sounded velvety, like fine material on glass.

She looked into his eyes and saw a deadly coldness there. They were quite without expression or feeling, just two grey/green eyes like flint looking into hers. He wasn't smiling, his face was as expressionless as his voice. His whole being was one of cold indifference. Yet there lurked beneath this cold exterior a warm and passionate man, who was capable of great tenderness and humour. Again he reminded Kate of a ruthless cat, killer instinct without feeling, protective of her young, playful and gentle. Thunder's claws were tucked away safely; but within a second they could be out and around someone's throat. Kate sat perfectly still. She could feel her heart beating, pounding, hammering against her ribs. His nearness was unnerving.

"We saw this Cardol being picked up from your flat by Bruce. Right?" Kate said quietly. Thunder nodded. His face remained inches from hers. "Lowman says that Cardol is working for Lightman. Right?"

"You were listening," Thunder said barely above a whisper. Kate ignored this.

"What's to say that Lightman is really working for Cardol? Perhaps Cardol and Lightman arranged it between them? Lightman to get Palmerston-Smith, Cardol to get you," Kate didn't look away once although she felt his eyes were overpowering. They drew you in like magnets. Or a spider to its web. She shivered involuntarily.

"That's possible," Thunder said slowly. He looked away and thought about it for a minute or two. It certainly answered a few questions. Then the penny dropped. "And I've just realised why his name was familiar. Lightman is American, I've come across him before, so that's the connection," he said softly.

"If that's the case," Kate said and took a deep breath. "What do we do now? Lightman knows I am not Sarah. He must know by now that you have Sarah," She looked at Thunder. "What is he likely to do now?"

"He can't back out. He needs that deal too much to give it up now. He has to bring me out into the open so that he can get Sarah," Thunder said. "Perhaps I could contact him asking for his terms,"

"What good would that do us?" Kate said. "He must realise that Palmerston-Smith knows about this,"

"It would help Palmerston-Smith to nail him," Thunder said.

"But what about us?" Kate asked.

"We will cross that bridge when we get to it," Thunder said.

"You have to have some sort of plan," Kate hissed at him. Thunder looked at her sharply. There was a faint rebuke in her voice.

"Where would be the last place to look for Sarah?" he asked. Kate shrugged. "How about safely back at home with daddy?"

"What about Marcus?" Kate hissed at him. "Sarah wouldn't let him be thrown to the wolves. By you or her father,"

"He is safe enough," Thunder said.

"Sarah wants to see him some time," Kate replied. "If she's at home, what's to stop her just going?"

"I'm sure it could be arranged," Thunder replied, a touch of sarcasm in his voice. "Palmerston-Smith isn't totally useless,"

"He couldn't protect his daughter," Kate retorted.

"That was because he didn't know she was in danger. I think now he will never let her out of his sight," Thunder said.

"And what about me? Am I to stay in hiding for the rest of my life?" Kate asked.

"You could go home and act normally," Thunder said. "It is me Cardol is after. He will find me eventually but I will be waiting for him. I can do it better if I am not worrying about you,"

"Thank you very much," Kate said bitterly. She finished her food. "Can I go and collect my stuff from your flat? Or is that too dangerous?" she asked darkly.

Thunder sighed. "I suppose it won't hurt," he said.

Kate got up. She threw her rubbish in the bin and started down the stairs. Thunder frowned and followed suit. They walked silently back to Gerrard Street.

Ling and Sarah were in the sitting room chatting. Once over her initial shock Sarah was quite enjoying herself. It wasn't quite how she imagined people lived, but it was proving to be an education. Both looked up as Kate stomped in and sat heavily in a chair. The sling caught their eyes. They looked at each other.

"What happened Kate?" Sarah asked, concerned.

"One of Lowman's bozos decided to check if my wrist was really broken. So he broke it again just to make sure," Kate said, now in a bad mood as well as in pain, tired and irritable. "We went to see the doc, but we didn't see Marcus," she added.

"I was wondering if I might be able to go and see him soon," Sarah said.

"You'd better ask boy wonder," Kate said, heavily sarcastic.

Ling and Sarah exchanged looks. Thunder came in. He looked in as foul a mood as Kate. He walked though and out the door to the upstairs without looking at any of them. His heavy footsteps up the stairs could be plainly heard. Kate sat and started into space, apparently unhearing.

"Perhaps later," Ling murmured. Sarah nodded her head in agreement. She had admitted to Ling that she was frightened of Thunder. In his present mood, all the more so. It made her realise just how dangerous he was, even with a limp. They heard his footsteps returning. He came and stood in front of them.

"I understand you want to see Marcus," he said to Sarah.

"If it's okay," she said timidly looking up at him.

"We'll go later. Be ready," Thunder replied. He walked out. They heard the door slam.

"Fine," Sarah muttered.

Ling looked at Kate. "Have you two had an argument?"

"No. He intends getting rid of me and Sarah though. Soon," Kate replied. "I think I'd like a lie down," She went up to the room Sarah was using and lay down on one of the beds. Soon she was asleep.

Some time later Thunder returned. Ling and Sarah were still in the sitting room. Thunder looked at them from the door. He folded his arms and leaned on the door post.

"Sarah, we're leaving," he said gruffly.

"I'll get my coat," Sarah jumped up and ran out of the room.

"Well Thunder?" Ling asked. She got up and faced him.

"Well what?" he asked, still leaning.

"You are in a rare mood. Have you been arguing with Kate by any chance?" Ling said.

"No," he replied.

"No? It looks like you have," she said.

"So?" he challenged.

"Kate thinks a lot of you, you know," Ling changed tactics.

"Huh! After today, I doubt that," he said coldly.

"That changes nothing," Ling replied softly.

"She goes home soon anyway," he said abruptly.

"And?" Ling left it hanging.

"And? And what?" he demanded.

"Anything to add?" Ling asked.

"No," Thunder became defensive.

"You can be so stubborn sometimes," Ling said with a sigh.

"Can I?" Thunder's tone softened slightly.

"Yes! Stop being a pain in the arse, Thunder. It doesn't suit you!" Ling retorted.

Sarah appeared. Thunder looked at Ling who stared back defiantly. He shrugged and turned to leave. Sarah walked towards the door. Suddenly he turned back to Ling. Sarah stopped so abruptly she nearly bumped into him.

"I'll think abut it," he said to Ling and left the room. Sarah looked mystified at Ling and followed. At the bottom of the stairs before the front door Thunder stopped. He pulled a scarf from his pocket.

"Put this on. It will disguise you a little. Enough to get by," he said. Sarah tied it round her head. Thunder looked at her critically. It would have to do. They left, went along Gerrard Street and into Shaftesbury Avenue. Thunder hailed a cab.

The cab pulled up at the front entrance of St Bart's. Sarah followed Thunder into the hospital and up to the desk where Thunder asked which ward Marcus was on, remembering the assumed name the doc had given him. The receptionist pointed the way and Thunder limped off, Sarah following.

Marcus was in a ward with older men. He looked bored and thoroughly fed up. He lay in bed reading some tatty magazines left by other patients. His face lit up when he saw Sarah coming towards him pulling off the scarf. Thunder followed her to the bedside.

"Sarah," Marcus said. She kissed him on the cheek. She held his hand as she sat down. Thunder stood at the end of the bed and looked at him.

"So how goes it?" he asked.

"It will be better when I can get out of this ward. It is so depressing," Marcus said looking at Thunder for the first time. "I should have believe you. My apologies," he added.

Thunder waved it away. "No problem. I'm glad it wasn't worse," he said. He looked at them. "I'll leave you two alone and wait outside," Thunder turned on his heel and left.

The door swung behind him. He looked though the small window once and saw Marcus pull Sarah into his arms. Thunder turned away sadly, a feeling of longing inside. Not him, never him.

He stood with his back to the wall and his left foot up under him. His hand lay across his bandaged thigh. He looked up and down the corridor, people passed him but he took no notice of them. While he waited he thought.

On the ward Sarah and Marcus talked. Sarah wouldn't tell Marcus where she was. At first he was annoyed but then realised that as long as she was safe it didn't matter where she was.

"I just wish I was with you," he said bitterly. "Instead of being cooped up in here,"

"Thunder says it won't be for long. He's talking about me going back to my father," Sarah said.

"And I can just see your dad agreeing to me being there," Marcus said.

"We'll see," Sarah said.

"How's Kate?" Marcus asked.

"She got her wrist broken again this morning. I think she and Thunder have argued. They aren't speaking. They seem very close one day and remote the next," Sarah said, glad they had changed the subject.

"Thunder has to be careful who he gets involved with," Marcus said. "He doesn't want her to get hurt,"

"She already has," Sarah pointed out.

"Exactly," Marcus said.

They talked of other things, their time together at Worthing, college, friends, general things that didn't matter. The nurse came over and spoke to them, telling Sarah that 'Mark' was doing well and would soon be able to leave. Sarah was politeness itself and surprised Marcus. The events had changed her for the better, she was much less self-centred and selfish. Marcus liked the new Sarah better than the old one.

"I'd better go," Sarah said reluctantly. "I've been here over a hour. I don't want to annoy Thunder. He frightens me enough already,"

"Yes," Marcus mused. "He has that feeling of menace. Just be careful. Come and see me again,"

"When I can," Sarah wasn't sure when she would see Marcus again. He looked a lot better than the last time. "I'm glad you didn't fight him. He would have killed you," she said.

"Sensible is my middle name," he joked. Sarah kissed him and left. She found Thunder outside the door still leaning against the wall. He was looking forward, seeing no one. She stood next to him and tied the scarf back on.

"I'm ready to go back," she said quietly. He looked at her and heaved himself off the wall. His leg felt stiff. He hobbled for a few yards until the feeling returned.

They returned to Gerrard Street in silence. Neither wanted to make conversation and neither had any questions. Both sat in the cab lost in their own thoughts. Sarah was determined that if she had to go back to her father's for safety, Marcus was going too, if possible.

Dinner was a quiet affair that evening. Ling and Kit didn't talk much and if they did it was mostly in Chinese. Sarah ate her food, her thoughts were miles away. Kate did not appear and Ling did not seem perturbed. Afterwards they settled down to watch TV. Kit went down to the restaurant.

Later that night Thunder rang Palmerston-Smith. He sounded pleased to hear from him. Thunder came straight to the point and did not bother with pleasantries. Palmerston-Smith found he liked him more for it.

"You are friends with Lightman, can you get me close to him so that I can ask him some questions?" Thunder asked.

"Is that wise? Perhaps I could ask him. I'm due to see him soon for a meeting," Palmerston-Smith said.

Thunder thought about it quickly. "I suppose so. I need to know if a man called Cardol approached him or whether he approached Cardol. He is taller than me, has black closely cropped hair, dark eyes and a scar running down one side of his face. He may have said that he lives in Wandsworth. Bruce picked him up from there once. I have a feeling that Cardol is using Lightman to get me. I am fairly sure that Lightman or one of his men contacted me at his cottage on the Isle of Wight. I'm not sure why Sammy and Joe were sent to kill us though. That could be Lightman making sure the job was done or it could be Cardol. I think either Lightman or Cardol hired Sue," Thunder told him. Palmerston-Smith made notes.

"I'll see what I can find out. Will you give me a couple of days?" he said.

"Okay. See what you can get out of the creep," Thunder said.

Palmerston-Smith needed no reminder.

"Can I talk to Sarah?" he asked. Thunder handed the phone to Sarah. She chatter for a few minutes and then hung up.

"My father is becoming more insistent abut where I am. I try not to give away any clues but soon he will catch me out," she told him.

"You'll be back with your father soon enough. Once he has seen Lightman. I hope he finds the answers I am looking for. Then I can decide which course of action to take," Thunder told her.

"Marcus too?" she asked hopefully.

"Possibly," he replied. "I'll talk to the doc,"

The rest of the evening passed pleasantly enough. Thunder looked round several times. Ling did not volunteer any information. Thunder did not ask. Kate did not appear at all.

At eleven Sarah went to bed. Ling followed soon after. Kit came in from the restaurant. He found Thunder sitting with a glass of whiskey. He joined him. Kit turned off the TV. Thunder sat in the chair, his elbows on the arms, his glass held with both hands just under his nose, he stared ahead over the rim of the glass without seeing or hearing. Kit watched him.

"When will Palmerston-Smith see Lightman?" Kit asked.

"What?" Thunder was jerked out of his trance. "Oh, I don't know. Soon I expect. I have an uneasy feeling about this, Kit. There is more to this than meets the eye," Thunder said. He drained his glass. "And I don't like surprises," his voice as deep and menacing. Kit refilled the glass.

"I could ask around," Kit suggested. "See if anyone knows anything,"

Yes, that might be a good idea," Thunder said, distracted. "What happened to Kate tonight?" he asked in an even tone.

Kit looked at his friend with raised eyebrows. Thunder had fidgeted all night but hadn't asked. His curiosity must have been burning. "She went to bed this afternoon and hasn't been up since. Ling looked in on her earlier but she was asleep. Do you think she will be okay? Ling said she seemed pretty upset when she came back," Kit said sipping his whiskey.

"I'm not surprised. I don't suppose having her arm broken

again today helped. I'd like to break that goon in half. We had an appointment to see Lowman and his idiots treated us like criminals. They've been watching too much of the Godfather. This is not the Mafia, just London businessmen," he sounded like he was on a soapbox. Any minute now Kit expected him to start thumping the chair arm. Thunder saw his friend's look and grinned ruefully. "I'm getting too old for this game. That goon just knocked me over like a feather. And he took my gun off me like candy off a baby," Thunder ran his fingers though his hair. He leaned back in the chair and rested his head on the back. "I feel so tired. This is the very last time," he said in weary voice. For the first time Kit actually believed him.

At about one, after more discussion, they finished drinking and went to bed. Thunder looked at the empty bed in his room and shrugged. Kate was sleeping in Sarah's room. He put his gun on the table and got into bed stiffly, leaving his shorts on. He was soon sleep.

Just after five he woke. He sensed someone was in the room. He looked at the table and edged his hand out towards his gun. Silently he slipped it off the table and laid it on top of the covers. He put his head up slowly and looked round the room. In one corner someone was going through his and Kate's belongings. He quietly pulled the covers back slowly edging out the bed. The figure didn't take any notice of him.

Thunder padded silently cross the floor, the gun in his hand. He stood behind the figure who was bent over. Thunder slowly brought the gun up the person's back until it was near the back of the head. He prodded the person in the back of the head with the barrel of the gun.

"Don't move," Thunder said very softly. The figure stiffened. "Stand up slowly. Don't do anything that you'll regret," The figure straighten up slowly, the gun stayed up against their head. "Right, step backwards, slowly," he ordered, his voice still low and quiet.

"If this is your idea to frighten me, you've succeeded," the figure said.

"Kate?" Thunder was astounded. He pulled the gun away and

with the other hand pulled her round by her left shoulder.

Standing before him in a black coat was Kate. She held the coat together with her plastered hand, the sling discarded. She looked at him with a slight smile on her face.

"And I thought you'd forgotten what I looked like," she said softly but vaguely sarcastically.

"Hardly," he replied softly.

"Is this how you planned to get rid of me? Shoot me in the back of the head? What would you do with the body? Dump it like Joe's?" Kate sounded disgruntled.

"No. No!" Thunder said horrified. They had gone through too much in such a short space of time, he would never do that.

"Why not? I've served my purpose," Kate said bitterly.

"Kate, you know better," he sounded hurt.

"Do I?" Kate's voice was soft. "Sometimes I wonder," this was barely a whisper.

Thunder looked at her appalled. He put his hands on her shoulders. She looked at the gun on her left shoulder. He moved his hands down her arm and round her back, pulling her to him roughly. His lips sought hers with a hunger. Her arms went round him as his embrace tightened. The coat feel off one shoulder. Kate shivered.

"You're cold," he said softly. He pulled her over to the beds. He took off the coat and threw it down on the other bed. "Come in with me," he whispered and put the gun on the table. He pushed her into his warm bed and slid in next to her. She lay there stiffly, her plaster arm across her chest. He lay on his right side and pulled the covers over her. He put his arm under her neck and round her shoulders.

"How's the arm?" he asked in a quiet voice, looking at him.

"It aches," she retorted. "It had better remain plastered this time,"

"Perhaps I'd better give you the gun next time," he said with a smile. Kate heard the laughter in his voice and elbowed him in the ribs. He grunted.

"There isn't going to be a next time," she hissed at him.

"No," he murmured and kissed her check.

"I mean it, Krysten," Kate said firmly.

"No," Thunder murmured again kissing her on the mouth. Kate pushed him away and looked into his eyes.

"There… is… not… going… to… be… a… next… time," she said firmly emphasising each word.

Thunder smiled. "I believe you," he whispered and pulled her to him. He kissed her again, still she didn't respond, still she was annoyed with him. He smiled and kissed her mouth, then her cheek, travelling down to her throat.

"Krysten," Kate's voice warned him.

"Hum," he muttered still kissing her. He kissed the base of her throat, pulling the night shirt neckline away. His hand moved down her back and held her body tightly to his. He continued kissing her and she slowly relaxed. His lips brushed her cheek en route for her mouth. This time she responded, matching his mounting passion. He relaxed his hand on her back and slowly pulled the night shirt up and over her head. She did not resist. His shorts were next. They continued kissing and slowly made love.

Their passion spent, they lay in each other's arms as the dawn came up. Kate had her head on his shoulder and could hear his heart beat steadily. She felt reassured.

"What happens now?" she asked in a whisper.

"I don't know," Thunder admitted. "I am running out of ideas and things are getting confused,"

"That's not like you," Kate replied.

"I have a feeling that Cardol is behind this somehow but I'm not sure how exactly," Thunder said.

"He wants you badly, doesn't he?" Kate asked.

"He has done ever since I killed his family," Thunder replied.

"Should I go home?" Kate asked.

"Not yet," Thunder said. He didn't want her to go. Despite his best endeavours he was getting involved. Kate looked at him.

"You would be better off without me," she said quietly.

"No," he said firmly, but his voice wobbled slightly.

Kate said nothing, just sighed. He kissed the top of her head. Kate closed her eyes and fell asleep. Thunder stayed awake and thought of their time together. It had been short and full of adventure. He suddenly longed for peace and tranquillity. He wanted this to be over. Once he had dealt with Lightman, then it would be finished and he could take Kate home. He wanted to see this family of hers, he wanted to get her way from them. Suddenly a longing to stay with Kate welled up inside. It caught him unawares and his eyes filled with tears. He raised his face to the ceiling and fought his feelings. Kate stirred in his arms. He looked down at her and smiled. Resting his head against hers he closed his eyes.

CHAPTER TWELVE

At about nine Kate and Thunder appeared in the kitchen. Both looked relaxed. Ling put a cup of coffee in front of Thunder. He drank it without a word. Kate slipped a cup of tea and ate some toast. Sarah looked from one to the other and then at Ling. Ling shrugged. Whatever had happened, she wasn't about to ask questions.

"What are you doing today?" Ling asked Thunder.

"Not a lot," he replied. "I have to wait until Palmerston-Smith has seen Lightman. Hopefully he will get the answers, otherwise we could be here indefinitely and I don't think you would like that,"

"We could visit the flat," Kate suggested.

Thunder looked at her. He frowned as he thought about it.

"We need the clothes," Kate persisted.

"I'll check it out first," Thunder said. "Where's Kit?"

"In the restaurant," Ling said.

Thunder finished his coffee and left. The three girls sat chatting and leisurely finished their breakfast. Sarah was getting used to tea and toast in the morning. She had even taken to drinking Jasmine tea and eating Chinese food with chopsticks. Life for Sarah was never going to be the same again. They went into the sitting room. Thunder and Kit came in. Kit went into the kitchen. He returned frowning.

"What happened to my knife?" he asked Ling.

"Oh I still have that," Kate said. "I didn't use it," she rushed upstairs and came down with the knife in its sheath. She pulled it out. Sarah looked at it with horror.

"Kate, you had that?" she was shocked.

"For her own protection," Kit said. "I could teach you,"

"No. No. Thank you, Kit. I will do without," Sarah curled up in the chair in horror. Kit grinned.

He took the knife and followed Thunder out. In Shaftesbury Avenue they got a cab. Thunder gave his old address with trepidation. He didn't want to walk into Cardol. He needed to get his leg better first. He would have to be 100% fit to face his old adversary.

The cab stopped a couple of houses away from the flat. Thunder and Kit got out the cab cautiously. It looked like normal. Kit went down an alleyway and round the back of the houses. He peered over the walls into the gardens and saw nothing out of the ordinary. He returned to Thunder sat on a wall.

"It looks safe enough," Kit said.

"That's what I'm afraid of," Thunder said.

"You were never afraid," Kit said.

Thunder walked up the path to his old home and put the key in the lock. The door was communal so Thunder knew it wouldn't be bobby trapped. He climbed the stairs to the first landing and his flat. It looked like normal. He pulled out his gun and slowly walked to the door. He searched the door for any tampering but found nothing.

"Try the key," Kit suggested, standing behind him.

"Easy for you to say, you're not standing in front of the door," Thunder hissed at him over his shoulder.

He put the key in the lock, closed his eyes and turned it. The door shuddered and opened. Just like normal. Thunder's hair on the back of his neck stood on end. He stepped back and toed the door open. It swung open and stopped.

Thunder stepped to the other side of the door frame and peered in. He could see that the few bits of furniture were scattered. He looked round the door frame. Nothing. He put his head though the door space and looked inside. Nothing. He peered through the crack between door and frame. Nothing.

"Most odd," he muttered and walked into the flat. Kit followed.

Kit whistled at the mess. Thunder's belongings were everywhere. The flat had been very thoroughly turned over. Thunder picked his way through the debris. Kit looked round the other side of the room.

"Whatever you do, don't touch anything," Thunder warned. He put his gun back in his jacket and put his hands on his hips. "Shit. They made some mess,"

"Could have been worse," Kit said.

"Could have been?" Thunder queried.

"Your good stuff could have been here," he pointed out. Thunder nodded. Kit poked about in a pile by his feet.

Thunder made his way into the bedroom. "Oh shit," he muttered. The room had clothes strewn every where. His and Kate's. They had upended her bag over the bed and gone though it with a fine toothed comb. He picked up a couple of t-shirts and put them on the bed. He went back into the lounge. Kit was putting books back on the shelves.

"Leave it," Thunder said. "It's not worth doing now. We'll do it another time," Kit dropped the books to the floor with clatter.

"Where have you been, mate?" an Irish voice said from the door.

Thunder turned and saw Liam, the mad cap Irishman from the upstairs flat. At over 6 foot tall, as broad as Thunder, if not more, he leant against the door frame with a nonchalant air, looking with concern at the debris on the floor. He wore his usual jeans and t-shirt, his unruly red hair tied back in a pony tail that only got some of the hair. He looked like some wild Celt from an Irish bog. Thunder had often gone drinking with Liam, he was one of the few people who knew Thunder as Kit, and he was one of the few people Thunder trusted.

"Boy did they have fun," Liam said.

"When did it happen?" Thunder asked.

"A few nights ago. Old bag downstairs called the cops. By the time they got their arses round here they'd gone. None of us had a key so they did nothing. You should phone them or something," Liam said. "The old bag thought you'd been murdered in your bed. It was twenty minutes before she stopped demanding they break the door down," he chuckled.

"Oh wonderful," Thunder said sarcastically.

"Have they taken anything?" Liam asked.

"No idea," Thunder admitted. "They've scattered my friend's clothes round a bit though. There might be something missing there, I suppose,"

"I thought I saw you with a girl. A few days back. Thought I was dreaming," Liam laughed. "Kit with a woman, that's a laugh," Liam went off, his laughter could be heard down the passageway as he returned upstairs to his flat.

"Kit? Does anyone know your real name?" Kit asked.

"Only Kate," Thunder admitted.

"Even I don't use it," Kit said.

"Do you know it?" Thunder asked.

Kit thought about it. "No. Come to think of it, I don't," Kit said. He indicated the mess with a wave of his hand. "What do you want to do about this?" he asked. "Police?"

"Certainly not! I don't need them poking about in my affairs. No. We'll collect Kate's stuff and some of mine and leave. Another day I'll clear up and get out," Thunder said.

"Likely story," Kit scoffed. "Where do we start?"

"Close the front door. I don't want the old girl downstairs turning up. She's a right pain," Thunder said.

Kit shut the door. He followed Thunder into the bedroom. Thunder started picking up Kate's clothes and stuffing them into her bag. Kit picked up several items and put them on the bed. When Thunder had finished he dumped his bag on the bed and started putting his belongings in it. Within a hour they had finished.

Thunder had a last look round the flat. He picked up one or two things and thrust them into the bags. Satisfied he had collected everything he needed he dumped the bags by the door. Then he heard voices, one of which was loud, high and shrill.

"Oh shit, that bloody woman downstairs," he muttered. "And PC Plod. That's all I need,"

There was a knock on the door. "Mr Brown? This is the police,"

Thunder swore and opened the door a couple of inches. Two policemen in uniform stood there. Behind then stood Mrs Cornish from downstairs. She looked anxiously between them and then through the crack in the door but she could see nothing.

"I thought I heard someone in here," she said in her high pitched voice. "I thought it was the burglars come back,"

"Why don't you leave well alone, you interfering old busybody," Liam said in the background.

"I was doing my neighbourly duty," she screeched at him. "More than you've ever done,"

"I don't interfere with my neighbour's privacy," Liam replied acidly.

"That will do," one of the policemen said.

"Mr Brown?" the other asked Thunder.

"Yes," Thunder replied. Kit turned away with a smile. All his secrets were coming out now.

"Is there much damage?" the second policeman asked.

"Enough," Thunder replied. "I was about to leave,"

"Mrs Cornish phoned us the evening it happened," the first one said. "Aren't you bothered?"

"Not really. Most of the good stuff went before Easter. I was in the process of moving. So whoever did the flat over got nothing of value," Thunder said.

"We have to make a report of this, naturally," the second said.

"Naturally," Thunder replied. "But can I do this some other time? I really don't want to deal with this right now. I'm not living here at the moment. I don't know what is missing, if anything and quite honestly the rubbish that was here, they're welcome to,"

"I see. Of course it's up to you, but if we are to catch the culprits it would be helpful for us to know what they took," the first policeman said.

Thunder remained at the door. He had not let them in and deliberately kept his foot behind the door so it wouldn't open any wider. He didn't want Mrs Cornish getting a look either. She was a nosy old bag at the best of times. He certainly did not need her spreading rumours about him in the road.

"Leave me a number where I can contact you and in a day or so when I've sorted out what's left I'll give you a ring," Thunder said.

The second policeman handed over a card to Thunder. He

looked at it and put it in his pocket. He smiled at the policemen.

"Thank you so much for your help. I will be in touch," he said and closed the door. Then leaned on it and sighed.

"I thought Mr Brown was being murdered in his bed that night," Mrs Cornish was heard to squawk. The policemen ushered her down the stairs talking soothingly as they got her away. It was obvious to them Mr Brown didn't want her seeing his flat.

"You wouldn't have time to call the police if we were all being murdered in our beds, you old bag, you'd be too busy listening through the walls and ceilings!" Liam shouted at her.

"One day you'll thank me for keeping an eye on this place," Mrs Cornish screamed back at him, her voice going up several octaves and more than a few decibels.

"Nosy old bag," Liam shouted once more and slammed his flat door.

Thunder smiled. "It is so wonderful to be home," he said.

"I'm surprised you want to leave all this," Kit said.

"Quick, lets go before she is back up here offering tea and sympathy," Thunder said.

They picked up a bag each and left the flat, literally tiptoeing down the stairs to the ground floor. Near the bottom of the stairs Thunder could hear Mrs Cornish's voice. He stopped and listened, much against his will. Kit stood behind him, grinning.

"Mr Brown is such a nice man. Quiet too. No bother at all. Never any trouble," Mrs Cornish was telling the policemen who had been persuaded to enter her flat. "I've never seen him with a lady friend either, except a few days ago. Most surprised I was, I can tell you," she continued.

"Oh Gawd," Thunder muttered. He spoke to Kit over his shoulder. "That means the entire bloody street knows by now that Kate was here," he hissed. "For one night! I ask you, one night!" Kit grinned at him.

The policemen made some comment too quiet for Thunder and Kit to hear. This obviously didn't mollify Ms Cornish as she continued in her shrill voice.

"Not like that Irish heathen in the top flat. Wouldn't be at all surprised if he didn't have Irish connections," she said loudly in a disgusted voice. She lowered her voice. "If you know what I mean," Then her voice went back to normal. "Always having parties too. Not that you'd find Mr Brown at one of those,"

"Liam gives very good parties. I've had some of the best times of my life at his parties," he said. "Let's go before she gives a tour," Kit just ginned.

They hurried out the door before Mrs Cornish spotted them and turned down the road. At the end Thunder saw a cab and stuck out his hand.

"Piccadilly Circus," he said. It sped away just as the two policemen managed to escape also.

"Poor bugger. No wonder he wants to move. She's enough to make the entire population of London move," they got into their car. "To another country!" he added with feeling. The other policeman laughed.

That same morning Palmerston-Smith was having a business meeting with Lightman. For twenty minutes they sat discussing general topics and mutual business interests over coffee. Lightman brought up the subject of Sarah's disappearance; Palmerston-Smith had said nothing and acted as if nothing had happened.

"I hear on the grapevine that Sarah is missing," Lightman said casually.

"Yes," Palmerston-Smith said, not enlightening him further. He was pleased that Lightman had brought it up, he wasn't quite sure how to bring up the subject and ask the questions that Thunder wanted answers to. In fact he wasn't entirely sure just how he was going to ask the questions at all, never mind get the right answers.

"Is it serious?" Lightman asked.

Palmerston-Smith looked at him steadily for a few seconds before replying. "Serious enough," the Yorkshire accent was soft.

"Boyfriend trouble I expect. Girls that age, it's nearly always boys," Lightman said, a confirmed bachelor, pretending to be knowledgeable.

"No. It's nothing to do with a boyfriend, although she does have one," Palmerston-Smith said, his voice was still soft.

"Oh?" Lightman raised his eyebrows. He didn't know that. He would have to talk to Lowman, it might be useful. Gratified that the man was suffering distress, it was of little concern that Sarah was the apple of his eye. Lightman felt no fatherly emotion. In fact he felt no emotion at all.

"He doesn't know where she is either," Palmerston-Smith replied, seeing where Lightman's train of thought was going. Thunder didn't need to worry about protecting Marcus as well.

"You've spoken to him then?" Lightman asked.

"No. Not directly," Palmerston-Smith answered slowly. "But he told my contact that he doesn't know and I have no reason to doubt it. I hardly think he would lie," he added brightening up.

"Ohh," Lightman sounded intrigued.

"To be quite honest I don't know what possessed the girl to leave the house. Some errand, I expect," Palmerston-Smith said giving the impression of bafflement.

"Have you heard from the people who have her?" Lightman asked.

"How do you know she is being held by someone?" Palmerston-Smith asked, this time the voice was hard, brittle.

Lightman opened and shut his mouth a couple of times while he thought furiously for something to say. "I think I was told that," he waved his hand vaguely. "Bob Lowman possibly, the last time we met," he finally said.

Very good, Palmerston-Smith thought. You covered yourself there, throwing the blame onto someone else. "Actually I have reason to believe that it is a plot against me and not about Sarah at all," he said quietly, looking at Lightman steadily.

Lightman stared at him. "Really?" he said.

"Though why is beyond me," Palmerston-Smith said. Lightman managed to keep an innocent expression. "There was a time when I thought Lowman might be the culprit, but I doubt that now," Palmerston-Smith said. "There is no evidence,"

"Oh? Who do you think is behind it then?" Lightman asked in spite of himself.

"I don't know," he sounded vague, but kept looking at Lightman. "Bruce told me about some scarred man, but I'm not sure if he's covering his tracks or not," Palmerston-Smith watched Lightman for a reaction.

Lightman swallowed slowly. "Scarred man?" he asked, his voice higher than usual. He cleared his throat. "It could be anyone," he pointed out and laughed nervously. "Half of London for that matter," he added.

"Oh this was a particular man. Tall, very short hair, distinctive scar down his face. So I'm told. Not by Bruce of course. He doesn't know his arse from his elbow, Aussie twit," Palmerston-Smith said.

Lightman let out a slow breath. He thought he might have to sort Bruce out. "So is Bruce behind it?" he asked and managed an incredulous voice.

"No, he's an idiot," Palmerston-Smith said with a laugh. "Much bigger fish is behind this,"

"This other man then?" Lightman spoke like a man who was thick.

"Possibly," Palmerston-Smith said. Lightman was acting his socks off, but it was obvious he was only acting ignorance.

"Does this walking corpse have a name?" Lightman asked and attempted a jovial voice. "I'll keep my eye out for him,"

"Now what did he tell me? I'm sure he told me what his name was," Palmerston-Smith scratched his head. "No it's gone," he said after a couple of minutes of pretending to think.

"Well, never mind," Lightman said soothingly.

"But you know him don't you?" Palmerston-Smith suddenly said. "Goes round with a tall blond girl,"

"Me? Girl?" Lightman all but squeaked. "Why should I know them?"

"He thought you might," Palmerston-Smith said.

"He?" Lightman asked quickly.

"My friend," Palmerston-Smith said. "He supplies my information, all sorts of information, about all sorts of people," he added, his voice had a quiet menace to it. Lightman inhaled quickly and then tried to exhale slowly but it came out in short bursts. "You okay old boy? You seem a little breathless today," Palmerston-Smith said friendly.

"Just coming down with a cold or something," Lightman passed it off with a wave of his hand.

"How's your bid for the Ellis deal?" Palmerston-Smith asked bluntly.

Lightman stared at him in disbelief. How did he find out about that? He pulled at his collar, the room had suddenly become unbearably hot. He stood up and walked to the cabinet and poured himself some Perrier. He looked at Palmerston-Smith over his shoulder. "Want some?" he asked, waving the bottle. Palmerston-Smith shook his head. Lightman returned to his seat, bringing the bottle. "Must be a bug or something," he said. "Came over funny then," he drank the cold liquid.

Palmerston-Smith waited. He had received the response he had been waiting for – confirmation. His mind suddenly became clear, he knew exactly what to do, how he was going to exact revenge on this merciless man. Using his daughter to manipulate him. Him! Palmerston-Smith! It was unthinkable. Unacceptable. Something would have to be done, so that no one ever had the idea to do it again.

While Palmerston-Smith thought about this, Lightman drank the glass dry and then refilled it. Palmerston-Smith had shaken him. How had he found out about his interest in the Ellis deal? Lowman? He pulled a face. No, Lowman stood to lose as well if Palmerston-Smith got that deal. It had to be Bruce who had split the beans. Something would definitely have to be done about that boy. And soon.

"The Ellis deal?" Lightman managed to keep his voice light and vague.

"Tom Ellis is selling his entire empire. To the highest bidder. Would be good business for you. Me too, for that matter," Palmerston-Smith filled him in.

"Really," Lightman sounded superficially surprised. "Are you bidding then?" Lightman asked. Palmerston-Smith was ready for him.

"Wasn't interested before. Might be now though. Don't expect to get it, of course. It will probably go to some big group. I'm surprised you aren't in on that race," Palmerston-Smith said lightly.

"First I know of it, old boy, first I know of it. Shall have to give my chaps a rocket for not being quicker off the mark," Lightman was relaxing. He tried to sound old English, and failed. He sounded absurd. Palmerston-Smith found his assumption of close friendship grating.

Bloody hypocrite, he thought savagely. Must keep my temper, it would soil everything to lose it now and he wanted Sarah back safe and sound, now and in the future. With that thought he kept his voice under control. "That's why Sarah was taken," Palmerston-Smith said quietly looking through narrowed eyes at Lightman.

Lightman looked at Palmerston-Smith unblinkingly. He suddenly felt cold. He pulled himself together mentally. "No," he said in a disgusted voice. "Well I never,"

"Surprised you hadn't heard about it – on the grapevine," Palmerston-Smith said savagely.

Lightman laughed, a high hollow laugh that was obviously forced. "The grapevine isn't infallible, old boy," he said.

"No?" Palmerston-Smith's voice was low and disbelieving.

Lightman thought it politic to change the subject and he started talking about something else. Palmerston-Smith answered questions, asked his own and they talked for a further hour before Palmerston-Smith could make his excuses and leave.

He walked to the lift and pressed the button. The lift arrived and Palmerston-Smith stepped in. It was empty. He put his briefcase down on the floor and pressed the button. As the lift descended he leaned back against the wall. He felt sick. Betrayed by his own friend. The lift shuddered to a halt. Palmerston-Smith pushed himself away from the wall, picked up his briefcase and strode out. Once out on the pavement he stopped and looked up and down the street. Across the road was a cafe. He crossed the road and entered.

He ordered a coffee and sat down in the corner by the window. He stared out of the window at the passing traffic until the waitress brought the coffee. He took a note pad from his briefcase and as he sipped the coffee he jotted down a list of things to do. They would have to be done in secret. And about the only person he could trust not to leak this list was his secretary, Janice. He finished his coffee, paid and went back out onto the street. He hailed a cob.

"Cheapside, near St Pauls tube," he said to the driver.

He walked to the restaurant in the centre and called Janice on his mobile. He gestured to the waiter for a coffee while he waited for her to answer the phone. He hoped his hunch about this young woman was right, a lot was riding on this, if this leaked out he would be dead, business wise speaking. She answered the phone in her usual efficient manner.

"Janice, I want you to make some excuse to leave the office now and meet me in the Italian restaurant in the centre. You know the one I mean?" Palmerston-Smith told her quietly. She answered in the affirmative. "Good. I'll see you in fifteen minutes,"

Janice replaced the phone with a slight frown. She put some papers into a file with some items of post then picked up her handbag. Sally, the other secretary looked at her with interest. Janice looked at her. "I'm just going out to the post office for Mr Palmerston-Smith. I'll be back in a while," Janice said in answer to Sally's unspoken question.

Sally nodded and continued typing. Janice tucked her pad and pen in her bag and quickly left the room. She had to repeat the same reason for her errand to the doorman before walking calmly out of the building and down the road.

In the restaurant Palmerston-Smith sat waiting. He watched her come in and waved. She came over and stood looking at him.

"There's nothing wrong, Janice. What I have to say I want kept strictly between us. No one, absolutely no one, must know about this. This is between you and me," he said leaving Janice in no doubt that this was something very special. She sat down. He looked at her and took a leap of faith. "Quite honestly my daughter's life may depend on it," he added.

"Have you heard from the people who have her?" Janice asked for the first time. "I didn't like to ask before," she added quietly.

Palmerston-Smith looked at her. Janice had been working for

him for three years. She wasn't one of these feather-brained females they usually got. Janice Whittaker was a plain woman in her early thirties. She liked her job. She liked her boss, even if he could be a little odd at times, but on the whole she had no complaints. She was level-headed and not easily flattered. She knew she was no beauty and found men suspicious that said otherwise. She dressed smartly, conservatively even, her hair was always neatly tied back, she wore little or no make up and didn't spend her time chatting idly in the office. She was efficient, tidy, methodical. She knew where everything was and was always one step ahead of his meetings. Her work was always neat and clean and all the papers were kept together.

She shared her office with Sally, a dizzy, leggy blond who drove her boss to distraction with her chaotic work and haphazard filing, but she looked good round the office and she was popular with the men. Their office was called the beauty and the brains. Janice knew this and didn't care, she would rather be the brains any day. Palmerston-Smith thanked his lucky stars that he had the somewhat plain Janice to depend on. Sally would have blabbed his entire secrets to all and sundry within the hour.

"Between you and me," he started in a low voice. "I've seen and spoken to Sarah. She is fine and well protected from the real people behind the kidnap,"

Janice looked pleased. "You must be so glad," she said simply and quite sincerely. Palmerston-Smith felt his trust was well placed. "So what do you want me to do?" she said becoming businesslike.

"Good girl," he muttered quietly. He pushed the list he had made towards her. "Can you manage to organise this for me?" he asked. Janice looked at the list and asked a few questions, made a couple of notes, put the list in her pad and shut it firmly.

"If you think of anything else, ask me," Palmerston-Smith said.

"Okay. You will be meeting all these people at their offices so there is no need to organise anything at work. Less notice that way," she said.

"Fine. I don't want anyone at our office getting wind of what

I'm doing," his voice dropped to a low level. "I don't need this leaked to Lightman,"

"I understand," Janice said. "I'd better get back to the office. Sally will wonder where I've got to. And don't worry, she won't know a thing," Janice knew exactly how to organise it - during one of the many times that Sally went walkabout.

Janice got up and left. Palmerston-Smith sat for a few minutes more and finished his coffee thoughtfully. If he pulled this off, there would be bonuses all round. A change was as good as a rest, he thought and left the restaurant. The day wore on.

CHAPTER THIRTEEN

Just as expected, Sally went off for one of her walkabouts soon after Janice returned. She rang Bill Jones' secretary, Anne.

"Hi Anne. How's you?" Janice said naturally. They spoke often. Bill Jones and Ray Palmerston-Smith were old friends. Janice listened while Anne gave a run down on her hassles with work. Janice sympathised with her. Bill Jones' firm was in trouble and in danger of going to the wall. Anne finished her moan.

"How's full is Bill's diary?" Janice asked.

"Empty. It's getting worse. People know and stay away. Bill is not happy," Anne said.

Janice consulted Palmerston-Smith's diary. He had said that he would move anything to accommodate this plan of his. Janice knew which meetings she could re-arrange. "How about 10am tomorrow?" she asked.

"Fine," Anne said. "Anything important?"

"You know Palmerston-Smith. Everything is important," Janice said with a laugh. She was enjoying this subterfuge.

"At your office?" Anne asked.

"No, yours. He likes to escape this office once in a while," Janice said lightly.

"Don't blame him. I'd love to escape this office right now," Anne said.

"Palmerston-Smith will bring any papers with him. He hasn't given them to me yet," Janice said.

"Typical," Anne commented and they rang off.

Janice then rang his personal solicitor and made an appointment for tomorrow afternoon. She gave no reason why and his secretary didn't have the brains to push the point. Sally wandered back in then and Janice had to stop. She took an armful of post and went off to Palmerston-Smith's office. He was out.

Janice changed his diary and only put the number from his list to replace the cancellations. She left the diary open at that page so that he would see what she had done. If anyone happened to see his diary it would not be clear what he was doing. Janice smiled and returned to her office. Sally was being chatted up by the office Romeo, Geoff. Janice disliked him intensively. He was always hanging about for a morsel of scandal or gossip.

"Janice," he said as she sat down at her desk. "I swear you look lovelier everyday,"

Janice looked at him suspiciously. He smiled his winning smile. Janice concealed her dislike and turned her back. She shuffled papers and ignored him. Geoff frowned. He sidled over to her and sat on the end of her desk.

"Janice, Palmerston-Smith works you too hard," he gushed.

"Ohh Janice, I do believe Geoff is chatting you up," Sally trilled from across the office and giggled, her girlish giggle grated on Janice's nerves.

"Guilty as charged, I'm afraid," Geoff gushed. Sally giggled again.

"Janice, in my office, now," Palmerston-Smith stood at the door. He glared at Geoff who jumped off the desk. Palmerston-Smith glared at Sally, strangling her giggling immediately.

Janice picked up her pad and got up. "Thanks, Geoff," she muttered as she passed him. He smiled sympathetically at her.

"I'll make it up to you," he whispered.

"Don't bother," Janice said in a 'drop dead' voice.

She followed Palmerston-Smith down the corridor and into his office where he shut the door loudly and then sat down. Janice stood in front of his desk and waited.

"Well done Janice," he said. "I see tomorrow is fixed. I might need to see the bank manager at short notice, can you speak to him tomorrow morning? Use my office if necessary,"

"Okay," she said. "I don't encourage Geoff," she added.

"I know all about Geoff. If this deal comes off there will be a few changes round here. Some will be good, some won't. We'll have to see, won't we?" Palmerston-Smith said. He didn't like Geoff, he was too oily, too open, too suspect. He gave her some work and Janice returned to her office. Geoff was gone. Sally looked concerned.

"Was he all right?" She asked.

"Fine," Janice said curtly. She sat down and looked at Sally who was looking suitably sympathetic. "Sally, why do you encourage Geoff? He is such a creep. He isn't sincere at all. He's just out for what he can get or how far he can get in this office," Janice said to Sally.

"But he's lovely, Janice. If you bothered to talk to him, you'd find out," Sally retorted.

"I doubt that very much!" Janice looked at the girl's face and saw she was wasting her time. She frowned slightly. "Oh well, never mind," she murmured quietly.

Sally looked at her. "Did Geoff drop you in it with Palmerston-Smith?" she asked sympathetically.

"No. Mr Palmerston-Smith doesn't like the secretaries being bothered by creeps like him. And he's always hanging around here, trying to sniff out information that he can use elsewhere to further his career. At the expense of yours! Sally, you should be more careful of him!" Janice said.

"Oh Janice, you're so stiff. You should chill out!" Sally tried to make her voice light and girlish and was unsuccessful. She sounded trite instead.

"Please yourself, Sally. I've said my piece, let's forget it," Janice said quietly.

Sally started typing furiously. Her cheeks were a little pink. She frowned and pursed her lips together, giving her a tight stern face. Janice silently sighed and returned to her work. Sally was a lost case. She would never see that Geoff was only using her to get ahead. And if push came to shove he would throw her to the wolves quick enough to save his own skin.

The following morning Palmerston-Smith went to see Bill Jones. Their meeting started with a statement of how business was – or rather wasn't. Bill Jones had lost a large contract which was damaging his business, badly. If something didn't happen soon he would be going belly up in a major way. So Palmerston-Smith's suggestion came as something of a surprise.

"If you put a bid in for the Ellis deal, I will finance it on the quiet for a share in the business. A sleeping partner if you like," Palmerston-Smith said bluntly.

Bill was totally lost for words. They talked about the Ellis deal at length. Bill could see it would be a wonderful opportunity for his firm but he knew he didn't have the capital or the clout to get the deal. He was more surprised at the generosity of his friend who he knew from past experience never did anything without there being a catch.

"My creditors will swallow what money you put into this firm before I can clinch the deal with Ellis," he said.

"Not if it's handled right," Palmerston-Smith said.

Bill decided to that the bull by the horns, so to speak. "This isn't like you, Ray. You don't usually bail out firms in trouble even for friends," Bill said. "What's the catch?"

"What I have to tell you must stay within this office and between you and me. Not even Vivian must know or your secretary," Palmerston-Smith said. Vivian, Bill's wife, lovely though she was, was also a terrible gossip, and this would make juicy telling.

Bill raised his eyebrows. It must be serious if he couldn't even tell his wife. He nodded. "You have my word," he said.

Palmerston-Smith told him about the attempted kidnap of Sarah. "Now, you can tell Vivian that Sarah has been kidnapped, what you mustn't tell her is that I have seen and spoken to Sarah and she is fine," Palmerston-Smith said. He went on to tell Bill about Thunder and Kate and Marcus, and what Thunder had told him, and what he had found out from Lightman. In fact he told the entire story to his old friend. When he had finished he felt as if a load had been taken off his shoulders.

"Bloody hell, Ray. I'd kill him!" Bill said.

"I will do better than that, Bill," he said, then stabbed at the desk with his finger to emphasise the points. "I intend to ruin Lightman. He badly needs this deal. His board of supporters, financial people and the rest are depending on him and Lowman getting this deal. They kidnapped my Sarah to force me into withdrawing from a deal I wasn't even interested in, leaving the field open for them. Well, Thunder has better morals than that. And I have an alternative plan. You get the Ellis deal, I get a share, you get to keep your business, get the creditors off your back, and most importantly of all, I get my revenge on that bastard! We all win, expect Lightman," Palmerston-Smith ended on a savage note.

Bill whistled in admiration and shook his head. "I would love to be a fly on the wall when they discover the Ellis deal has gone to an unknown," he said "But how will you get me the deal? Without my creditors knowing?"

"Ellis has virtually agreed to sell to me anyway. So he sells to you and I put up the money. We draw up the papers between us before the papers for the deal. As it is secret negotiation your creditors need never know how you got the money or the deal as long as they get their money. We'll look on it as a loan, between old friends," Palmerston-Smith said waving a hand as if dismissing the problems involved.

"Some friend," Bill said sarcastically.

"That's what I thought about Carl Lightman. I've known him since he came here from America. I got him started, for Christ sake! And this is how he repays me, by stabbing me in the back! So, I trust my old friends," Palmerston-Smith sounded quite hurt.

"How do you know you can trust me?" Bill asked quietly.

"I don't, totally, but what do you have to lose?" he said.

Bill nodded. "Fair enough," he said. "Americans aren't like us Brits anyway," he muttered.

"I often wondered why Lightman had to leave America. He never said. But two can play at his game," Palmerston-Smith said softly. Bill shuddered, he wouldn't want to be on the wrong side of Ray Palmerston-Smith, good friend or not.

They discussed a few points in detail. By the end of the morning Bill had agreed. In fact he didn't have much choice but to agree. Palmerston-Smith knew this. He found he disliked treating his old friend in this manner but it was necessary and it helped Bill out in the long run. In fact Palmerston-Smith had undergone something of a change in the last few days. His world was showing cracks and he didn't like it.

Palmerston-Smith returned to his office and called in Janice.

"The deal is in motion. I need to see my solicitor and the bank manager this afternoon. Can you arrange that? Also call Tom Ellis and see if I can see him this evening. I want this thing agreed in principle. Today. Tomorrow we'll sign the deals. Tomorrow I need a meeting with Bill Jones, Tom Ellis, my solicitor and the bank manager in one place. Book a room somewhere we don't usually use. I'll leave the details to you to sort out," he quickly briefed Janice. "Any problems here?" he asked.

"Mr Maxwell was nosing around earlier. I said you had some business to sort out and wasn't sure when you would be back. I expect he's on his way here now. Word spreads fast in this place. Mr Lowman phoned this morning. I put him off. He wants you to ring him in a couple of days. Mr Francis wants a meeting with you to discuss the Ellis deal," Janice read the messages off the pad in her hand.

"I'll speak to Maxwell when he turns up. Make an appointment with Francis for a couple of days time. If Lowman rings again, see if you can find out what he wants. Anyone wants to know where I am, keep to the vague business story. That's very good, Janice. I'm very pleased," Palmerston-Smith said.

"Thank you Mr Palmerston-Smith. I do my best," Janice was nonplussed.

"Your best is better than that," Palmerston-Smith said sincerely.

Janice left to make the other arrangements and passed Maxwell in the corridor. Palmerston-Smith listened to Maxwell with patience and warily answered his questions. Suddenly he viewed everyone with suspicion; suddenly everyone seemed to be asking some very unusual questions; and suddenly people who normally got on and did their job were bringing little problems to him to sort out. It wasn't usual; there were too many spokes being put into this wheel; he could feel too many under currents. He shook his head.

"I'm getting paranoid," he told himself.

On Sally's next walkabout Janice consulted her list of telephone calls and dialled the first one – the bank manager, who agreed to see Palmerston-Smith soon after his visit to the solicitor.

Next on the list was Tom Ellis. He agreed to see Palmerston-Smith later that afternoon. Next was the Grosvenor House Hotel for the major meeting. Item four was Bill Jones. Anne was mystified and tried to question Janice but she admitted nothing and was totally vague about the whole thing. Then Janice went to see Palmerston-Smith to tell him the times of the meeting. Maxwell had just left.

Palmerston-Smith looked tired. Janice felt sorry that he was being hassled so much. It was common knowledge that Sarah had been kidnapped. That sort of information didn't stay confidential for long in this place.

"Would you like a cup of tea?" Janice asked him.

"No, thank you, Janice. I'm about to leave. God, Maxwell is an old woman, some old rubbish that he should handle and not bother me about," Palmerston-Smith rubbed his chin and sighed. "Oh well, time to go," he left.

Janice returned to her office to find Geoff quizzing Sally. As she entered the room she heard the tail end of their conversation.

"He's been in and out of the office today, Janice has been up and down, like a yo-yo, backwards and forwards to his office," Sally was telling Geoff who listened, agog, and eager for more information.

"Really? There must be something going on," Geoff replied. He was sitting on her desk. They both looked up as Janice entered.

"Here's Janice. She'll tell us what's going on," Geoff said.

Janice sat at her own desk. Geoff walked cross the room and leaned casually on her desk. She looked at him disapprovingly. "I know nothing," Janice said firmly. Geoff looked unconvinced. "And even if I did, I most certainly wouldn't tell you. Now go away and let me get on with my work, Geoff. I don't know why everybody is being so nosy all of a sudden. If there is anything going on, I'm sure Mr Palmerston-Smith will tell you in his own good time! Now buzz off!"

She turned her back on Sally and Geoff. After a couple of minutes she heard Sally typing. Looking over her shoulder she saw that Geoff had gone. She felt relived. She would be glad when this was over, but at the same time she was enjoying this too.

At Lincoln Inn Fields Palmerston-Smith was shown into his

solicitor's office. A talented solicitor, Mark Wray was tall and fair with grey eyes that belied the ruthlessness that had made him a partner in his early thirties with this older established firm. A couple of years ago Palmerston-Smith had needed a ruthless solicitor to fight off a take-over bid and Mark Wray had been put on the case. His success had impressed Palmerston-Smith so much that he had kept his business with him.

The two men had a healthy respect for each other and enjoyed a good working relationship. Mark sat behind his huge leather topped desk and looked at his client with a quizzical air. It wasn't often that Palmerston-Smith visited Mark's office, it was usually the other way round.

"Well, Ray, to what do I owe this privilege?" Mark asked when Palmerston-Smith had sat down and tea had been served.

"I have some private business that must be kept confidential or the whole deal will be blown. I could let the firm's solicitors handle it but I don't want my entire office knowing about it before it is signed," he said.

Mark raised one eyebrow. "So how can I help?" he asked getting straight to the point.

Palmerston-Smith briefly told Mark about the attempted kidnap and the information he had received from Thunder. He didn't mention Thunder, it wasn't particularly necessary, and he found himself wanting to keep the man's identify secret. He continued with the deal with Tom Ellis and Bill Jones and what he wanted setting up. Mark listened carefully, made a few notes but didn't interrupt. Once Palmerston-Smith had finished he asked a few questions mainly about the deal and offered no opinion or comments on what had happened or on Lightman.

"Obviously, this has to be kept absolutely secret, No one, but no one must know, except those involved in the deal," Palmerston-Smith finished.

"You know I know Lightman? Who doesn't? He doesn't come here though, so that will work for us. Do you want me to draw up the agreement today or leave it until tomorrow when you've seen everyone?" Mark said.

"I see the bank manager after you and Tom Ellis later. Can you draw up the papers tomorrow morning after our meeting?" Palmerston-Smith asked.

"No problem. Let me take some details and you can let me know the final copy," Mark said. He wrote down the points and Palmerston-Smith agreed or changed them one by one until a draft had been hand written. Mark personally went and photocopied it and gave the copy to Palmerston-Smith. It would make things easier to finalise. Mark took note of the meeting. Then Palmerston-Smith left to see his bank manager.

The bank manager was pleased to see him. They sat in his office and Palmerston-Smith outlined what he wanted to do, told him that he didn't want to openly get the deal but wanted to put it the way of a friend with a share for him. As he had already earmarked the money for the deal he couldn't see any problems. The bank manager agreed. Palmerston-Smith requested his presence at the meeting the next day and returned to his office. He told Janice what had happened that afternoon. She was pleased it was going so well. She passed on the few messages and was about to leave.

"Janice, I would like you to come to this meeting tomorrow. There will be some arrangements to make after. I want this to be signed and sealed within hours. You'd better arrange with the hotel to have a computer for your use. Just tell Sally you have the day off," he said as she reached the door. Janice looked totally surprised.

"I have a lap top at home," she said. "I'll bring that,"

Palmerston-Smith nodded pleased. "Oh, and another thing, can you arrange for an office planner to come in. Next week some time. I want to rearrange the office. You can do that quite openly, it will give the gossips something to talk about," he said.

Janice left, a smile on her face. His sense of humour could be very dry at times. She could imagine what Sally would make of this titbit.

As Janice spoke on the phone Sally continued typing but Janice noticed that the typing got quieter and quieter and then stopped. By the end of her conversation Sally was sat listening openly, her mouth open. Janice put down the phone, looked over

Thunder

at Sally quickly and turned her attention to something else on her desk. Minutes later Sally picked up some papers and announced she had to deliver them.

"Oh Sally. I won't be in tomorrow. I'm having a day off. Mr Palmerston-Smith is out all day at meetings so it won't matter," Janice said.

Sally stopped so suddenly she collided with the door frame. She looked back, her mouth hanging open. "You are taking a day off? Just like that?"

Janice looked up. "Yes. Mr Palmerston-Smith knows, so it's okay,"

"But you never take days off! Not at short notice," Sally said surprised.

"Well, I'm taking tomorrow off. I have some things to do. I might go shopping. I might go out with my mother," Janice said.

"You might... Janice, is there something going on? Have you got an interview somewhere? Is that what this is all about?" Sally ventured back into the office.

"No. Nothing like that. I just feel like taking a day off. There's nothing suspicious about it. This is no big deal, Sally," Janice said.

Sally looked at Janice, looked at the papers in her arms and then fled out of the room. Janice smiled at her disappearing back. That would really give the gossips something to chew on!

The next morning was grey and overcast. Janice made her way to the hotel in good time. She had difficulty explaining to her mother why she wasn't going into the office that morning. The desk clerk directed her to the room and she set up her lap top. While she waited for the people to arrive, she drank some coffee.

Mark Wray was first to arrive. While she poured him a coffee he went over the agreement that would need to be typed after the meeting. Janice assured him she would be able to do this while they had lunch so they could sign it that afternoon. He relaxed, smiled broadly and took the coffee to the table. He reviewed his notes while he waited.

Next to arrive was Tom Ellis. Janice poured more coffee and introduced him to Mark. They sat chatting. Then Bill Jones arrived and Janice did the coffee and introductions routine. A few minutes later and she was repeating this for Mr Brown, the bank manager. Finally Palmerston-Smith arrived, apologised for being late, he had been caught up in traffic.

"Don't worry about it, Ray. Janice has been the perfect hostess," Bill Jones said. "I wish my secretary was as competent," the others murmured agreement. Palmerston-Smith smiled.

"Janice will make any notes and will type the agreements after the meeting. I've arranged for us to have lunch here. I would like this signed and sealed before we leave, if that is possible," Palmerston-Smith said.

The men all agreed. They sat round the table. Janice sat next to Palmerston-Smith at one end. They all knew why they were there so there was no need to go through explanations. Palmerston-Smith had outlined the points with each, now he pulled the different points together.

Coffee was brought in after a hour. By mid morning the meeting was nearing its conclusion. Janice had made a few notes and altered the draft agreement slightly.

"Janice, can you read out the agreement again please. If we are all agreed, it can be typed and signed," Palmerston-Smith said.

Janice read out the agreement. Tom Ellis was to sell his business to Bill Jones, financed with Palmerston-Smith's money. In return Palmerston-Smith would have a large share in the firm, keeping Bill in control, Palmerston-Smith would be a sleeping partner, but would attend board meetings and would be on the list of partners, his name would also appear on the Company records and be lodged at Company's House. The money put up would be solely for the purchase of Tom Ellis' business and not used for bailing out Bill Jones' current firm with his creditors, although it was believed that the new business would create money to pay off the creditors and put the firm back in the black and therefore in profit. Janice read the agreements clearly and slowly, but there were no interruptions or questions. All angles had been covered and all were very happy.

Tom Ellis and Bill Jones announced they were happy with that and would sign as soon as the agreements were drawn up. Mr Brown would arrange the transfer of funds. Mark Way would draw up the legal documents with Janice as soon as the meeting was finished. Palmerston-Smith smiled broadly. It was all going to plan.

"Splendid," he said. "We'll leave Janice and Mark to put the finishing touches to this. Knowing Janice it wouldn't be long so Bill, Tom, Mr Brown and I will adjourn to the lounge for fresh coffee before lunch,"

Janice moved to the other smaller table to start typing the agreement, Mark poured two cups of coffee while the others went into the lounge. Half a hour later Janice and Mark emerged with the agreements. This was read, agreed, and signed. Then they all went in for lunch. The talk was now general. Janice found herself sitting between Palmerston-Smith and Mark Wray, who she found amusing company. He neither flattered nor patronised her.

"If you ever want to leave Palmerston-Smith, I would give you a job straight away. You are better than my secretary. She can be so thick at times," Mark said to Janice.

Janice laughed. "No thank you. I am quite happy with my job. He is a very good boss," Janice replied.

"He is a good man to know. He gave me a break. The old boys in my firm found me a little hard to handle, but Ray gave me a chance and now the old boys don't want to lose me," Mark laughed. He told an amusing story about one of the oldest partners. Janice laughed.

When lunch was over, Palmerston-Smith, Tom Elliot and Bill Jones sat smoking cigars, drinking brandy and talking. Mr Brown went back to the bank. Janice returned to the room to pack up her lap top. Mark appeared to collect his briefcase.

"Look, I don't usual do this, but would you have dinner with me one evening?" he asked her as they were about to leave.

Janice looked at him sharply. He returned the stare steadily and waited while she weighed up the situation. "I don't usually say yes, but I will," she replied.

He arranged to meet her in a few days time, then they both left, Mark disappeared out the door into a waiting cab. Palmerston-Smith appeared in the foyer.

"Ahh Janice. My car is outside. I insist that it takes you home. I

will return to the office and try not to look so pleased with myself.
I'll see you tomorrow. You have the papers?" Janice nodded.
"Good. We'll talk tomorrow, then," he said. He escorted her out to
his car where his driver was waiting. "Take Janice home, Frank.
She will give you the address. Pick me up from the office about
six," he went back to the front of the hotel where a porter hailed a
cab for him.

Janice climbed into the car and gave Frank her address. She
had some explaining to do when she arrived home. She wasn't
sure her mother entirely believed her either.

The next morning Sally asked her about her day off.

"Oh, I didn't do much. Just a few bits and pieces, pottered
around the house, mainly. It was a nice relaxing day really,"
Janice said. She took the mail into Palmerston-Smith's office.

"I have been thinking about the office," Palmerston-Smith told
her. "I would prefer you sat near my office instead of down the
corridor sharing with Sally. It will give the Geoff's of this world
less chance to chat. It won't stop the gossiping but it should cut
down on the pestering of the secretaries," he said.

Janice looked at him in surprise. "I don't mind sharing with
Sally,"

"But as the senior secretary you shouldn't have to share a
room with some scatter brained bimbo when your work is more
important than her social life," Palmerston-Smith said firmly.
Janice suppressed a smile.

"But I'm not the senior secretary," she said. "I'm just a
secretary, one of many,"

"You are the senior secretary and my assistant, as of now," he
told her. She opened and shut her mouth. "Of course, this means
you will get a pay rise in line with your position. I don't expect
you to work for peanuts,"

"Oh," was all Janice could say. She was totally surprised.

He went on to outline what he wanted changing in the office
generally and a few in particular. The secretaries would be graded
depending on their bosses and their work performance. It would
mean that girls like Sally who spent most of her time idling would
not earn as much as others who worked hard. Janice thought that

was fair and pointed out a few of the secretaries who had lower grade bosses than Sally but worked twice as hard. Palmerston-Smith made a few notes.

"I also want to give you projects to do or oversee," he said. "Collect information and give it to me in a cohesive form instead of the bumff I get now from the likes of Maxwell who couldn't give a straight answer to a simple question if he tried. It will mean you having to sit through endless chat while he waffles around the houses,"

"When will this all happen?" she asked.

"Pretty immediate," he replied. "The office move may take time but I want the structure to be in place within a month. People won't like it, but they can always leave," he said. Janice smiled. She knew a couple of people straight off who would complain – Sally and Geoff.

Palmerston-Smith outlined a few other duties he wanted Janice to take on. Mostly to do with the work he did out of work, like charity functions, social things. She would be a sort of social secretary. She thought she could cope with this. They discussed some other points and then Janice returned to her office. Sally looked up.

"You've been a long time," she said.

"Actually he was outlining my new duties," Janice said.

"New duties? That sounds grand," Sally said.

"It is. His whole plan is grand," Janice replied and sat down at her desk. Sally looked hopefully at her but Janice got on with her work and after a couple of minutes Sally followed suit. After fifteen minutes of furious typing Sally announced that she had to go and see someone and off she went on one of her walkabouts. Janice could hear the buzz of gossip already and smiled to herself. Wait until they find out what it really entailed, then there will be plenty to talk about!

CHAPTER FOURTEEN

As it was obvious Sarah and Kate would be here for a while Ling started to teach them how to use chopsticks. Kate, being naturally right handed, found using her left hand difficult. Sarah picked it up quite easily, much to her delight. Kate soon retired to her window seat with a book.

Kit and Thunder came in from the street. They dropped the bags on the floor. Kit went into the kitchen, Thunder sat down and looked at Kate. There were dark shoulders under her eyes and she looked too pale.

"Do you want to ring home?" he asked her.

She looked up. "And say what? Having a wonderful time. Can't tell you where I am but someone is trying to kill me because they think I'm some rich man's kid? They'd love that, I'd get so much stick, I'd think it was my birthday," sarcasm dripped.

"What about your boss? Won't he wonder where you are?" Thunder asked.

"I've rang him. Told him about my broken wrist. Ling has already sent off the sick note," Kate said.

"Wasn't he worried?" he asked.

"A bit. He's nice. Could do with giving me a pay rise, but hey you can't have everything, can you?" Thunder just stared. He didn't have to worry about money. She frowned at him. "Course you over there are different, Moneybags Malone,"

"How about a trip?" he changed the subject.

"Where? A sun drenched island where no one will bother me?" Kate asked.

"Seriously," Thunder said with a smile.

"I was being serious," Kate replied darkly. "Wouldn't paradise suit you?"

"Where would you like to go in London?" he asked.

"Oh London," she thought. "The Planetarium,"

"Okay," he got up.

She looked at him over her glasses. "Very funny. We might bump into someone we shouldn't,"

"They won't know. I'm bored and you need the air," he said.

"You won't know boredom if it bit you in the bum," she returned to her book.

Ling came in. Thunder turned to her. "I've just asked Kate to come out with me and she refused. I'm hurt," he put on a dejected air. Ling laughed.

"You don't know the meaning of hurt," Kate said darkly not looking up.

"You could do with some air Kate. Sarah will be fine here. She wants to try on some Chinese clothes so Kit's gone to get some," Ling told her.

Sarah came in all excited. "Kate, I get to do some shopping and don't have to go out. I could get to like this," Kate gave her a withering look. "Oh don't look like that. I can't help it," Sarah said crestfallen.

"Have fun Sarah," Kate said and got up. "Looks like I'm going out. Under protest," Sarah and Ling started talking about clothes.

Kate found she actually enjoyed the afternoon out and returned to Chinatown with a renewed air. Sarah told her all about the clothes, showing her the suitcase full that Kit had brought. Kate picked up a vivid red satin dress with embroidery on. She liked the feel. Ling suggested she put it on.

"I don't wear red," Kate said flatly.

"Well you should! Pastel clothes drag the colour out of your face. You should wear vibrant colours instead of hiding behind those dull colours you wear," Ling said.

"Yes Kate. You don't suit brown at all. When this is all over, we will go shopping and get you a decent wardrobe, full of colour and styles, not the dowdy stuff you have," Sarah said.

"I like the clothes I have," Kate said flatly.

"But they don't suit you," Sarah said. Kate looked defiant.

"Sarah may not be the most tactful of people Kate, but she is right," Thunder said from his chair across the room.

"I like my colours," Kate said firmly.

"You like them because you have a bad opinion of yourself and that is what you have been told you should wear. You should wear what suits you, not what some petty-mind jealous bitch told you!" he replied just as firmly.

Ling and Sarah looked at each other and held their breath. The air had suddenly turned cold. Sarah looked from one to the other and waited for the explosion of temper. To Kate's horror she started to cry, her face crumpled as she sobbed uncontrollably. Sarah and Ling quickly left the room. Thunder went over to her. He pulled her into his arms and she cried into his shoulder.

"I'm sorry Kate, but it had to be said," he whispered above her head. "Sarah is right. Your wardrobe is terrible. Colours that don't suit you, styles that are totally wrong. Why hid behind an illusion someone else has created? If you want to cut the ties, then start with your wardrobe and show the world the real you,"

"I don't know how," Kate sobbed. "I don't have a clue about clothes,"

"I'll speak to Ling and Sarah, they'll know. And they won't be petty and vindictive, just honest. Sarah especially," he laughed. He held her until she stopped crying, then while she washed her face he spoke to Ling and Sarah.

The next morning Sonja and Anna arrived with large suitcases each. The girls all went upstairs and all that could be heard was female chatter and laughter. Kit disappeared into the restaurant. Thunder picked up Kate's discarded book and sat in a chair. He hadn't read a book in years and found it surprisingly good.

It was later that afternoon when Ling appeared at the sitting room door. "Well Thunder what do you think?" Ling suddenly asked. He looked up and saw Kate standing with Ling. But this was a transformed Kate. She was wearing a burgundy shirt and black fitted trousers. Thunder just stared. Ling laughed. "Told you," she said triumphantly to Kate.

"Do you like it?" Kate asked.

"Yes," he said and swallow nervously. She looked so different. "Very much," he added, he could feel his heart beating a little faster.

"Shame you have nowhere to go," Ling said, her hint wasn't very subtle.

"Well..." he started falling into the trap. He suddenly realised. "Oh very good Ling. Kate, would you like to go out tonight?"

"Where to?" Kate was unsure.

"Well, how about a decent meal?" Thunder looked pointedly at Ling. She sniffed disdainfully.

"Okay," Kate smiled. Ling swept out. "I think you've offended her,"

"I doubt that very much," he came over to her and pulled her into his arms and kissed her. Someone coughed behind them. He looked over Kate's head and saw Sonja and Anna looking stony faced and Sarah and Ling smiling. "I think I'd better go and book that meal," he muttered and quickly left.

Ling ushered them into the sitting room. Kate sat in the chair he vacated. Sonja and Anna sat together on the sofa and talked quietly in Chinese. Sarah and Ling sat elsewhere. After a few minutes of pointed stares Anna and Sonja left.

Sarah looked at Kate and then at Ling. "Is there something Kate should know?" she asked.

"Thunder saved Kit and his sisters and brought them to England. They are very grateful but ever since they believe they have a right to his affection, even believing that one day he will pick one of them. Thunder has always acted like a brother towards them. It's about time they got on with their lives," Ling said. "Without him,"

"Thunder and Kit have been good friends a long time?" Sarah asked.

"Yes. I soon realised that Thunder went with the territory," Ling said.

"What happened?" Sarah was curious.

"Kit never told me the details, too painful I suppose. Thunder brought them to England and a new life," Ling said. Sarah looked put out.

Kate had tried ignoring them by reading her book but when she had read the same sentence too many times she gave up with a sigh. "Okay, okay. I give up. I know about Thunder. I don't know the details about Kit but I do know he never gets involved with his work. When this is over he will disappear to some other job and I'll return to my life,"

"I don't want you to get the wrong idea," Ling said.

"Tell me something I don't already know," Kate said, her voice hard. "Look, all my life I've had to put up with whatever piece of shit someone kindly threw me. If you think for one minute that I'm about to lose my head over someone who treats me with any degree of respect, then you are very mistaken. I know exactly what Thunder does. I have no illusions about him,"

Ling was about to argue the point. Sarah put her hand on Ling's wrist. "I think Sarah knows what she is doing," she said softly. She looked at Kate. "I know I'm just some rich kid who doesn't live in the real world but this has taught me. I will never take anything for granted again. Kate has faced that all her life,"

"How the mighty have fallen," Thunder's voice came from the doorway, sardonic, menacing. "Kate shouldn't just accept what shit she is thrown. I hope I have shown her that, if nothing else. I should hate to think that my presence has been a waste," his voice dripped with sarcasm.

"I'm sure you both know what you're doing," Ling began.

"And if we don't it isn't your place to tell us. We are both adults," he retorted.

Kate got up, the book fell to the floor unheeded. "Don't speak to Ling like that! She is concerned," she said angrily.

"There is no need. I haven't failed yet, and I don't intend to this time,"

"I know that,"

"So why question it?"

"I'm not," they faced each other across the room.

"Sure?" he challenged.

"Of course," Kate replied calmly.

"Good," his voice dropped.

"I know that this is just an interlude in your chequered career. When it is over you will disappear into some hellhole to put something else right!" Kate retorted.

He looked startled. "I see," was all he could say.

"I doubt that," Kate replied coldly.

He recoiled as if he had been slapped. He had the fleeting thought that before she would have backed down. Now she faced up to him. "I'm sure you weren't like this with Alan," he said quietly.

It was Kate's turn to recoil as the barb hit home. She inhaled sharply. "I face my mistakes. I don't run and hide!"

"No, you just put up with them and don't change anything,"

"Not. Any. More," she said slowly.

"And when I have 'disappeared', what will you do then? Go home? To your loving family who treat you like shit?" he asked coldly.

"At least I have a family to go home to!" she blazed at him and immediately regretted it. She covered her mouth with her hand but couldn't take back the words. Thunder hardly reacted but she heard the sharp intake of breath and saw a haunted look appear in his eyes for barely a second to be replaced by a hard stare.

"Very good," he said quietly. "At least you're fighting now,"

Kate's hand dropped. "I've learnt my lesson well,"

"Obviously," he said softly.

"But then I had the best teacher," her tone was also soft.

"Yes you did," he muttered. "The table is booked for 8.30, be ready to leave by 8 on the dot, or I'll go alone,"

"I'm surprised you still want to go," Kate replied.

"I keep my promises," he said.

"Then I'll be ready," she promised.

"Good," he looked at his watch. "You have nearly three hours to get ready. Should be long enough for most women,"

"Miracles take time, the impossible much longer," Kate retorted.

He frowned. "Then I'll expect a miracle,"

"Don't worry, I won't turn up wearing my usual drab clothes," she retaliated.

"Good. I don't want to be seen out with a drudge," he retorted and walked across the floor and upstairs, slamming the door behind him.

"Bastard!" Kate sat down.

All through the argument Sarah and Ling had watched; Sarah with fear, Ling with concern. It was obvious to her that Thunder had met his match. He had the ability to hurt people with his words but Kate had hurt him right back. It was also obvious to Ling that Thunder had told Kate something of his past otherwise her comment about her having a family would not have hurt him quite so deeply. Ling went off into the kitchen. Kate and Sarah sat in stoned silence for a few minutes before Sarah had the courage to speak.

"Kate, why do you annoy Thunder?" Sarah asked. She was fearful of being left to fend for herself.

"He baits me, I bait him. It keeps us amused," Kate replied looking at her. "Sarah, try not to be so afraid of him. He is only a man,"

Sarah looked at Kate in wonder. She may have changed for the better from a spoilt arrogant brat but she was still afraid of the unknown. And that included Thunder.

"But a man who has my life in his hands," she said.

Kate picked up her book. Sarah picked up a magazine and flicked through it. She soon got bored and went into the kitchen to talk to Ling.

Upstairs Thunder stood by the window in his room staring at London rooftops. He leaned against the wall with one arm, both hands were clenched. He breathed slowly and deeply, his anger subsiding not at all. He pulled his free hand roughly through his hair, raking his skull with his nails until it hurt.

"Bloody woman," he snarled. "Damn her. Damn her,"

He pushed himself away from the wall and stalked out to the bathroom. He still felt angry when he had ran a bath and lowered himself into the warm water. His leg stung slightly but felt better. Kate's administering had done it good. That only annoyed him further. He got out the bath and towelled himself dry. He shaved, making sure he did not cut himself. Back in his room he tried to bandage the leg. He didn't want to have to call Kate to do it but no matter how tight he tried to wrap the bandage it fell down.

"Shit," he said loudly.

"You called," Kate said acidly from the door.

"I can't bandaged this bloody leg," he said irritated.

Kate crossed to him and shoved him in the chest. He fell on the bed. He swore. She bandaged his leg without looking at his face. When she had finished she looked down at him sprawled across the bed, a towel wrapped round him.

"I hope you are wearing something more appropriate tonight," she said before she stalked out the room, slamming the door behind her.

"Appropriate? Appropriate? What do you think I am? A bloody idiot?" he yelled at her.

"No," came the reply.

"Bloody woman!" he started to get dressed, choosing with care what he was wearing. Aftershave. He wrinkled his nose. He would smell like a whore's boudoir. He pulled his clothes out the wardrobe. White wing collar shirt, thin black leather tie, pale grey double breasted suit and black shoes. He put his cuff links in and then the expensive gold watch he kept at Kit's for safety. It said ten to eight. He checked his wallet and put it in his pocket. Then he went downstairs. Kate was nowhere to be seen but Kit was.

"I suppose Kate is coming tonight?" he said to Kit sat in the chair. "Or have I dressed for nothing?"

"She is upstairs with Sarah and Ling. Pooh, what is that smell?" Kit wrinkled up his nose.

"Don't start!" Thunder warned.

"Well, you certainly scrub up good," Kate said from the door.

"Ready?" Thunder asked over his shoulder.

"Obviously, or I wouldn't have a coat on," she replied. "See you later, Kit," They went out.

"I'd love to be a fly on that wall," Kit said.

"You wait till he sees what she's wearing," Ling said.

Thunder and Kate walked down to Piccadilly Circus. Thunder turned towards Regent Street.

"Don't tell me we're going for a burger," Kate said.

"No," Thunder lead the way to the Cafe Royal. Kate looked up at the doorway and then back at him.

"I am impressed," she said. "But won't they throw criminals like you out?"

"Not when I'm dressed appropriately and paying," he said going in. The maitre'd approached. "Table for Abe,"

"This way. Can I take the lady's coat?" he took Kate's coat. Thunder looked round. They were shown to their table, Kate was seated. "Would you care for a drink?"

"Gin and tonic. Kate?" Thunder looked at Kate for the first time. She was wearing a soft velvet dress in deep blue. Her hair was simply clipped back. She wore enough make up to emphasis her dark eyes and earrings dangled from her ears. She wore no glasses. He looked astonished.

"Rum and coke," she said. The waiter disappeared. She looked at Thunder. "Don't you like it?"

"It...," he swallowed. "You look wonderful," he said simply.

"Thank you. I wasn't sure but Sarah persuaded me," she said.

"You should blue more often," he said.

Kate waved this away. "You look very smart Krysten. Quite a change from the usual," He inclined his head.

"Perhaps we should wear clothes like this more often," he said.

"We'd have to behave civilly then," Kate replied.

"That's no bad thing," Thunder replied softly. The waiter brought their drinks and produced menus. As the meal progressed they talked generally, like old friends. Over coffee Thunder brought up the scene that afternoon.

"I stand by what I said, Kate. You don't have to accept the old anymore," he said.

"Ling is worried I'll get hurt," Kate said.

"She is probably right, she usually is. She is right about me not getting involved," he replied.

"I know that," Kate sounded impatient. "When this is over we will go back to our lives and not see each other again,"

"If that what you want?" he asked softly.

She looked at him sharply. "What I want doesn't matter. That's what will happen,"

"But is that what you want?" he persisted.

"It doesn't matter," she repeated firmly.

"It does to me," he said softly.

"Tough!" Kate hissed at him. She drank her coffee.

"Sometimes you can be so infuriating," he said.

She gave him a withering look. "Pot. Kettle. Black,"

They returned to Chinatown. Everyone had gone to bed. Thunder poured them both a whisky. Kate sat on the sofa.

"I'm sorry about the comment about your family. It was unforgivable," Kate said.

"It doesn't matter," he said.

"I shouldn't have said it," Kate replied.

"Kate, lets not fight, lets go to bed," he changed the subject.

"Man's answer to everything. Bed. Sex. As if it solves anything," she sounded bitter.

"You know me better than that,"

"No, I don't," Kate picked up the coat and went upstairs. Thunder took the bottle to the sofa and poured himself a very large measure.

At half past seven Ling got up and went downstairs. She found Thunder asleep on the sofa cuddling the bottle of whiskey. She smiled and made some coffee. A cup of strong black coffee wafted under his nose was enough to wake him. He put the bottle on the floor, sat up and took the cup from Ling.

"Thanks. What time is it?" he said bleary eyed and yawning.

"Nearly eight," Ling answered, picked up the bottle and returned it to the cabinet. "Did you have a good evening?" she asked looking at him.

Thunder sipped the coffee and looked at Ling over the cup. He shrugged. "Pleasant enough," he said. "Considering," he added quietly.

"Considering? Considering what?" Ling folded her arms and leaned back against the cabinet.

"Kate believes I will disappear from her life when this is over. Nothing I say will convince her otherwise," he said.

"So? It's true, isn't it?" Ling said.

"It used to be, but not this time. This time is different," Thunder admitted.

"Oh. Tricky," Ling was at a bit of a loss what to say. This was quite a departure for Thunder. She thought about it for a few minutes. Thunder sipped his coffee. "It's not like you to fall for your victims," Ling said eventually. She couldn't think of anything else. The situation was so new.

"I know," Thunder smiled. "Kate is different, somehow," he ended lamely.

"The great Thunder has fallen in love and the lucky girl doesn't believe him?" Kit was standing at the door, his voice sarcastic. "I never thought I'd see the day," he chuckled.

"Do you have to take quite so much pleasure out of this?" Thunder blazed at him. He shifted uncomfortably. "I'm going out, he said and got up.

"Just as well the rumpled look is in at the moment," Ling said as he got to the door. Thunder looked down at himself. He was still in his suit and it was indeed rumpled.

"I'll change first," he muttered and went across the floor, past Kit, through the door, Kit's laughter ringing in his ears.

Ling went into the kitchen. Kit stayed lounging against the door frame. Within minutes Thunder reappeared in jeans, jumper and black leather jacket. He glared at Kit as he passed him.

"I need to ring Palmerston-Smith," Thunder said. Kit handed him the phone with a grin. Thunder glared at him but rang the number. It took a few minutes for Palmerston-Smith to come to the phone. He sounded happy.

"I wondered when you would ring," he said.

"Did you get the information we need?" Thunder asked.

"Yes. Retribution is in place," Palmerston-Smith replied.

"Retribution?" Thunder queried. Palmerston-Smith's voice sounded almost smug.

"Why don't you come over to the house and I'll fill you in," Palmerston-Smith suggested. "You might have some suggestions as to how we proceed further,"

"I'll be there within thirty minutes," Thunder replied.

"I'll be waiting," Palmerston-Smith said.

Thunder went up to Shaftesbury Avenue and flagged down a taxi. As they drove to Palmerston-Smith's address Thunder thought on what sort of retribution Palmerston-Smith could have organised. Thunder thought of some people he wanted to dish out retribution to. Alan, definitely. Cardol, certainly. Lightman, maybe not. Lowman, no need. Bruce? He shook his head. The taxi pulled up outside the house. Thunder got out and paid the driver. He looked up at the house and walked up the drive. No need to sneak in through the back door this time.

A man answered the door and gestured for Thunder to enter. He wore the black attire of a butler. No heavy weight goons here Thunder thought. He was shown into a small sitting room just off the main hallway. Thunder looked round the room. It had cream walls with carpet, furniture and curtains in tones of green. The picture over the fireplace was a print of London. The other pictures were of similar taste. Thunder nodded; this man had taste; no semi naked women on his walls.

Palmerston-Smith came in followed by the butler carrying a tray which he put down and then left. Palmerston-Smith gestured to one of the chairs and Thunder sat warily.

"You are an extremely exclusive man to find. Do I call you Mister Thunder or just Thunder?" Palmerston-Smith asked. He poured two cups of coffee. The smell of real coffee wafted across the room. He offered one to Thunder, taking the second, helping himself to milk and sugar.

"Just Thunder will do," Thunder replied. He found that he quite liked this man. He was straight forward, to the point and broad minded. He put the cup beneath his nose and breathed in the heavenly smell.

"I've had men all over London looking for you and a possible hiding place for Sarah but they can't find you. Mind you they are hampered by the fact that no one seems to know what you look like. Am I privileged seeing you like this? Or will I become your next victim?" Palmerston-Smith asked.

"A chosen few know what I look like but they don't all necessarily know it's me. Or what I do," Thunder told him.

"That's very clever," Palmerston-Smith stated. He was impressed with the coolness and professionalism of this man.

"You spoke of retribution. I have a few things I want to put right myself. Shall we swop ideas?" Thunder said.

"Very well," Palmerston-Smith put his coffee down. He told

Thunder about the meeting with Lightman and the information or confirmation he had managed to get. Thunder nodded but didn't interrupt. He then spoke about the deal he had set up.

"Do these people know who else is involved?" Thunder asked.

"No. As far as they are concerned I am helping out an old friend, stitching that bastard up in the process. They know Sarah has been kidnapped to make me pull out of the deal. My personal solicitor has drawn up the documentation, my personal bank manager has sorted out the funds. My secretary is the only one who knows the whole story and I trust her implicitly. If my son wasn't such a little shit I might have told him," he sniffed in disgust and continued telling Thunder about the deal. "When Lightman hears I have officially pulled out of the deal he will wet himself in anticipation. Just wait until he finds out who has got the deal," Palmerston-Smith chuckled.

"Can it be traced to you?" Thunder asked.

"If they dig deep enough. I am a sleeping partner of the firm who has got the deal," he said. He leaned forward. "Now what happens about Sarah?"

Thunder sipped his coffee and thought about it. "A public showing would be fitting," Thunder suggested. "Something that Lightman would attend. He might bring Cardol with him, but I doubt it,"

"There is a charity function in three weeks time. I am due to go but was considering staying away," Palmerston-Smith said. "Makes it difficult giving a good enough reason for not going without telling the whole world that my daughter has been kidnapped,"

"Make the necessary arrangements to go, include Sarah. Act as if nothing has happened. It will give Lightman something to think about and I have no doubt that he knows what is going on without Bruce reporting back to Lowman," Thunder said.

"You mean I might still have a spy in the house?" Palmerston-Smith was horrified. "But who? I trust everyone,"

"No, I don't think that. I just think that whatever you do, someone sees it and tells Lightman. Someone must have seen Sarah leave the house to tell Sue what she was wearing. Bruce's orders were to tell me and Joe. Lowman knew nothing about Sue or where I was holed up. Which means that Joe and Sammy were told by Lightman where I was. It could have been Cardol. It was Lightman or his men I spoke to at the cottage and Bruce who sent Lowman's men to Worthing. Bruce knew exactly where to find Sarah so why the charade? He might have been playing all ends or working on someone else's orders. Or he might not know at all," Thunder told him, the pieces were starting to fall into place.

Palmerston-Smith considered this. He looked at Thunder. "Will you attend this charity ball?" Palmerston-Smith asked him.

"I have a better idea," Thunder said. "Get three extra tickets beside Sarah,"

"Three?" he was mystified.

"Yes. Lets give Lightman something to really wonder about," Thunder had a wicked grin on his face.

"Who were you thinking of bringing? Beside yourself?" Palmerston-Smith asked.

"Kate and Marcus. That should give Lightman a headache," Thunder gave a wicked laugh. "It will also cheer Sarah up, she's missing Marcus,"

"Is Sarah unhappy then?" Palmerston-Smith looked worried.

Thunder waved away his doubt. "She is happy enough, but she is missing her family and Marcus," Thunder said.

Palmerston-Smith looked slightly relieved. "And three weeks should give Sarah enough time to organise her outfit," he chuckled.

"It also gives Marcus enough time to get on his feet," Thunder said.

"This Marcus, is he a sound person? I mean, he's not after Sarah's money is he?" Palmerston-Smith sounded unsure as only an over protective father could.

"Marcus Francis lives in a large house in Sussex that is probably bigger than yours. His family is not short of a bob or two, believe me. He is a student but from what I've heard, an extremely clever one. He loves Sarah for herself: spoilt, arrogant, frivolous. Who could ask for more?" Thunder said coldly.

Palmerston-Smith thought about it. "When does Sarah come

home?" he asked.

"How about three days? That should give you enough time to organise some protection. She will have to stay here but if you brought Marcus here too that would give her an added incentive to stay put," Thunder said.

"Three days?" he said stunned. "Done. Bring the lad here too. Why not. It will put Ben's nose of out joint good and proper,"

"I would suggest not telling the entire household just yet. Just those you can really trust not to blab. I'll leave the details to you," Thunder said cautiously. "You don't want this place raided,"

"Very sensible. I'll make the arrangements," he said nodding. "How do I contact you?"

Thunder handed over a card. "It's my contact. Leave a message on the answer phone and I'll pick it up,"

Both had finished their coffee. Thunder saw no reason to sit and chat so he got up to leave. Palmerston-Smith saw Thunder to the door. He was looking forward to seeing Sarah again. He missed his feisty daughter. He called in the butler and gave him instructions. He knew he would tell no one.

CHAPTER FIFTEEN

Thunder returned to Chinatown. He found Anna in one of the shops and suggested they go for a walk. They walked down Shaftesbury Avenue talking. Thunder noticed that Anna walked close to him and acted like a lover not a friend. There was a feeling of intimacy that Thunder disliked. He saw Anna as a sister only. He decided to charge in and say what he had to say. He could tell from her behaviour that she wasn't going to like it, but he needed to sort this out, once and for all.

"Do you remember when I rescued your family?" Thunder started.

"Oh yes. It was the happiest day of my life," Anna gushed, putting a hand on his arm.

He frowned at this but she didn't remove it. He took her hand off his arm. "I wanted nothing in return. I was glad to take you out of that hell hole alive, some friends didn't make it. You friendship is the only reward I have ever wanted," he said.

"Well, we are friends, Thunder," Anna said putting her hand back on his arm.

"No Anna, I can't be the sort of 'friend' you want me to be," he removed her hand again. "You have to get on with your own life. Without me in it," he said firmly.

"But you will always be part of my life," Anna said.

"No I won't. I flit in and out but I can't be part of your life," this was difficult. "I don't 'fit' in your life,"

"You fit in with Kate," Anna said accusingly.

"No. Kate fits in with me. She believes that when this is all over I will disappear and she will return to her old life," he said.

"That would be best," Anna said firmly.

"It's not what I want though," Thunder said softly. "I want to give up this life,"

"Good. It's dangerous," Anna said smiling. Thunder stopped and faced Anna. They stood to one side of the pavement near a building. People passed them without a glance.

"But that does not mean I am going to be part of your life. I have to have my own life. So do you. And that does not include me. Marry that nice Chinese boy. Forget me," he said.

"He means nothing to me. He's just a boy. I want a man. A man like you," Anna said.

"You're not old and that boy will become a man. You don't want a man like me. You can't have a man like me," Thunder said. He ran his fingers through his hair. This was hard work!

"But you are all I've ever wanted," Anna whined.

"Oh shit," he whispered. He grabbed her by the shoulders. "Anna, get a grip on yourself. You sound like a love sick school girl!" he said angrily. "You ceased being that a long time ago. I see you as a sister, nothing more," he said coldly.

"But it could grow into love," Anna whined.

"Don't be stupid! You know life isn't like that. You have to give up this childish idea!" he said grimly.

"I can't," Anna said in a small voice.

He looked at her without pity. "Then you will get hurt," he said softly. His hands dropped by his sides. "Because I am in love with Kate," he had said it and it hadn't been so hard after all. Now to tell Kate. Anna looked at him, pleadingly. He looked away, over her shoulder, to the traffic driving past them. He looked down at her and then walked away, not once looking back.

Anna stayed where she was, watching him go, believing her heart was broken. In a darkened doorway across the road Cardol watched, his face almost concealed by the pulled up collar of his long black leather coat and the pulled down trilby on his head. His hands were thrust deep into his pockets. He was a handsome man in an unconventional way. He had closely cropped black hair and dark almost black eyes, high cheek bones, sensual lips and two days stubble. The scar on the left side of his face ran from the forehead across one eye and down the cheek ending at the jaw. It was a clean cut, not puckered, and it didn't distort his features.

He stood in the doorway and watched and waited. He saw

Thunder limping away and remembered Joe boasting that he had shot him. He knew that Kit was his contact and that Anna was Kit's sister. Perhaps a visit to Anna would extract the whereabouts of Thunder. He mulled this over, then looked again and saw that Anna had gone, disappearing into the crowd. No matter, he would be able to find her again. Although he knew that if Thunder had gone to Kit it would impossible to get to him. He would have to do this some other way. He left the doorway and walked off into the crowd, disappearing up a side road. Thunder had not seen him and he hadn't seen where Thunder had gone. It wasn't important right now.

Thunder returned to the flat. Kit was out. Ling was busy in the kitchen. Sarah sat watching TV. Kate was curled up in the window reading a book. He stood in the doorway and watched them. How could anyone get them mixed up? They were as different as chalk and cheese. Only the dark hair was similar – but different lengths. Thunder shook his head. He slowly stepped into the room. Sarah looked up, fearfully. Thunder regretted that look at once. He didn't want her to be afraid of him. He smiled at her.

"You'll get square eyes, Sarah," he said gently. Sarah smiled at him uncertainly. He crossed to Kate and stood next to her. She didn't look up. He bent down. "I need to talk to you," he whispered.

"That's nice but as you can see, I'm busy," Kate said.

"The book can wait," he said harshly. Kate sighed and put it down. She looked at him and frowned.

"What?" she said wearily.

"Not here," he said and straightened up. Kate saw his determined look and got to her feet. She followed him out and up the stairs. He went to his room at the top.

"Did you sleep in your bed last night?" she asked.

"No. I fell asleep on the sofa," he admitted.

She picked up his discarded suit. "So I see," she hung the jacket over the back of the chair, folded the trousers and lay them on the chair also.

"You're not the cleaner," he said defensively.

"No," Kate looked at him. "You needed to say something?"

"Yes," he walked to the window and looked out. "I saw Anna today," he started.

"That must have been nice for her. She thinks you're the bee's knees. Can't see why, myself," Kate sounded peevish.

"I told her to marry that Chinese boy,"

"I bet that pleased her,"

"I told her she's not for me,"

"How charitable of you,"

Thunder turned to face her. "I told her I was in love with someone else," he said quietly.

"That wasn't nice," Kate commented. "How did she take it?"

"Badly," he started to pace, with a limp. "I can't help it. I can't pretend to feel something I don't. I don't want her body in payment for something I did years ago,"

"How's the leg?" Kate watched him. He was limping worse. "You should try and rest. It won't get better if you keep pacing like something demented. Take you jeans off and sit down, I'll change the dressing," Kate disappeared.

Thunder sighed and ran his hands through his hair. "Oh shit. This is more difficult than I thought," he muttered and took his jeans off. The bandage looked scruffy. Kate reappeared. She tutted at the state of it, cut it off, cleaned the wound and rebandaged it.

"It is getting better," she said. "But it would get better a lot quicker if you stopped running here, there and everywhere,"

"Yes nurse," he said with a grin.

"Behave," Kate told him firmly. She put things away in the box she used.

Thunder took her by the shoulders. Kate looked up. "I told Anna that I wanted to give up this life," he said quietly. Kate didn't speak, she didn't look convinced at this statement. "I want to retire, live a normal life," he said.

"With the girl you love? Does she know?" Kate said coldly.

"Not yet," he replied.

"Don't you think you ought to tell her?" Kate said. She felt cold. Despite her good intentions she felt betrayed.

"I've tried. She doesn't believe me," he said.

"I'm not surprised. You never say what you mean," Kate said.

"I promised to help Ling," she got up. Thunder didn't stop her.

"Another time perhaps," he muttered.

"Perhaps," Kate replied. She put the box on the bedside cabinet. "Perhaps if you didn't play games, Thunder, people would believe you," she said and left.

"Well that certainly told her," he muttered and pulled his jeans on.

At dinner that night Thunder sat talking quietly with Kit. Sarah and Ling talked across Kate who was struggling with her food. She felt tired. She wanted to go home. Even that would be preferable to this. Ling looked at her concerned as she spoke to Sarah. Kate's wrist wasn't getting a chance to heal and she looked drawn and pale most of the time. Thunder looked across the table at Kate. He leaned over, took her plate and cut up the food, returning the plate. Kate didn't say a word.

"Sarah, I'm told there is a charity ball in three weeks time. Will you be ready for it?" Thunder suddenly asked. The table went silent.

"What charity ball?" Sarah asked.

"The one your father is taking you to," Thunder replied.

"He is?" Sarah's face lit up.

"You go home in three days time. It gives your father time to make arrangements for your safety," Thunder told her.

"You've spoken to him then?" Sarah asked.

"This morning. He is looking forward to having you home," Thunder said.

"Three weeks. Now what shall I wear?" Sarah mused. She talked to Ling about it while Thunder and Kit returned to their conversation. Kate longed to go home more than ever.

"Can Kate come?" Kate heard Sarah say to Thunder among the chatter. She looked up.

"I expect so," Thunder replied.

"Oh good. I shall have to think about this," Sarah said.

"I might not want to go," Kate said in a quiet voice.

"It will be fun, Kate," Sarah said.

"I want to go home," Kate said.

"You will, Kate, after the ball. I promise," Thunder said.

"Your promises are like the crust of a pie," Kate said stabbing at her food. "Made to be broken. Sorry Ling, I'm not hungry. I think I'll go to bed," Kate got up and left.

"Have you told her yet?" Kit asked.

"I haven't had the opportunity. Or the words," Thunder said.

They finished their meal in silence. Thunder left the kitchen.

"What's going on?" Sarah asked.

"Sonja told me that Anna saw Thunder this afternoon and that she has been crying ever since," Kit said quietly.

"He's told Anna then?" Ling asked.

"Told her what?" Sarah demanded.

"Thunder told Anna that he loves someone else. I don't suppose Anna took it very well," Kit said.

"Oh poor Anna," Sarah said.

"I also think he tried to tell Kate," Ling said.

"Oh no. Poor Kate," Sarah said. "She'll be so hurt,"

"I doubt it," Kit said.

"But Kate thinks an awful lot of Thunder," Sarah said.

"You don't understand, Sarah. It is Kate that Thunder loves, but he can't tell her," Ling said gently.

"Oh," Sarah was lost for words.

They went into the sitting room. Sarah and Ling watched TV. Kit went out. Thunder sat in the chair staring into space. When they had gone to bed Thunder got a glass and the whiskey bottle from the cabinet. Then he turned the lights down and lay on the sofa.

Kate listened to a clock chime midnight. She couldn't sleep. She couldn't get comfortable. She was cold. Her wrist ached and felt heavy. She lay in bed listening to the various night noises and the sounds of the city. It didn't help. Her thoughts were incoherent and chased around in her brain as she tried to make sense of things. Her feelings were in turmoil and she couldn't make sense of them. Finally she gave up and got up silently. She didn't want to wake Sarah asleep in the other bed. Perhaps a drink would help.

The sitting room was in semi darkness. She found the cabinet easily enough. A light came on when she opened the cupboard so she could see what she was doing. She poured a glass and knocked it back in one. She left the glass on the side and shut the cupboard. Finding her way back across the room proved to be difficult. She walked into the chair and then the sofa. She swore each time.

"Do you have to be so noisy?" a voice said. She recognised Thunder's low and velvety voice. His trademark. His arms pulled her onto the sofa.

"Sneaking around in the dark stealing drinks is hardly your style," he said quietly.

"You smell of whisky," she replied.

"I bet you taste of port," he replied.

"At least it's only one glass, not an entire bottle," she retorted. "Were you going to bed sometime?"

"Sometime," he whispered. He lay back on the sofa. She lay next to him. "I needed to think," he held his glass on his chest, it rose and fell with his breathing.

"When did you decide to retire?" she asked.

"Before this job. But for definite the other day when I discovered I'd rather be with the person I was with. I'm getting too old for this lark. Arseholes like Lowman's men wouldn't have bothered me before, even injured," he said.

"When will I go home?" she asked.

"After this charity thing," he said. "Palmerston-Smith has done some deal. When Lightman finds out it will be over. Or I will kill him. Either way,"

"I'm glad for Sarah. She misses her father," Kate said.

"And you?"

"I couldn't care either way. I can't be a prisoner for ever. I have to go back to work at some point. Pick up the pieces and get on with my life," she said.

"You still intend leaving home?"

"Yes. You've taught me independence,"

"I'm glad I taught you something," he muttered.

"So little time," Kate mused.

"It feels like an eternity. I'm tired. Will you come to bed with me?"

"To sleep," Kate said. He put the glass and the bottle on the floor. He lead her upstairs to bed. With her head on his shoulder, his arm round her, the pain receded, as did the turmoil in her brain.

"I didn't mean you to get hurt," he whispered.

"Too late," she whispered back. "Will you tell her about us?"

"She already knows,"

"You're told her? When? How?"

"She knows every intimate detail," he teased. "She lived it, she was there, she experienced every pain and every pleasure,"

"How?" her mind felt numb.

"It's you," he said softly.

"Me? I don't understand,"

"Kate, it's you I love. There is no one else," he said simply, his voice velvet.

"I wish you wouldn't use that voice, it gives me goose bumps," Kate said.

"Which voice," he said in the same tone.

"That one! Sometimes you are such a bastard!" Kate said.

"I don't feel any goose bumps," he whispered and started to kiss her.

"Oh no you don't. You're not getting round me like that. Go to sleep," she said. They lay there silently for a few minutes.

"Don't you believe me?" he asked.

"No. I think you've had too much whisky,"

"I've had just enough," he kissed her forehead. "This is what I want,"

"You wouldn't know what you wanted if it fell on you," Kate replied.

A few minutes more of silence. "Kate, I love you,"

"Liar!"

"It is the truth, I swear," his voice was normal.

"I still don't believe you," she replied.

"I'm not leaving," he said.

"Until the next job,"

"There will be no next job," he said. "Once Sarah is safe and this is over we can go home and start a new life together,"

"I still don't believe you," she said stubbornly.

"You will,"

"I doubt it,"

He kissed her before they started an argument.

"Bastard!" Kate whispered. He just chuckled.

Thunder and Kate slept late. Ling and Sarah were sitting in the kitchen talking when Thunder finally wandered in. Ling poured him a black coffee. He sat down at the table and drank it.

"Is Kate coming down?" Sarah asked him.

"Any minute," he said and smiled. Sarah looked at him with a worried look. "I won't eat you Sarah, I promise," he smiled lazily at her uncertainty. Kate had far more courage; he wished she had some of Sarah's self assurance.

"Of course you won't," Sarah said nervously.

"He only gives the impression that he might," Ling said. "Ah the other guest has arisen," she added as Kate walked in.

"Pardon?" Kate said startled and looked at her.

"Forget it Kate," Thunder said. "Ling is trying to be funny,"

"Oh," Kate couldn't see what was funny.

"I wondered if Kate and I could do some shopping," Sarah said. "From here of course," she added quickly.

"For what?" Kate asked. She sat down. Ling put down a plate of toast.

"Our dresses for the charity ball," Sarah said, quickly getting in her stride. "We have to plan it, otherwise there will be no impact and I want to make such a big impact that certain people won't forget this in a hurry," she poked the table with her finger to emphasise her point. She meant business.

"Like who?" Kate started eating the toast.

Thunder sat at the end of the table and watched them. They were so different it was ridiculous. Sarah - alive and vibrant - was a conceited, vain, spoilt rich kid with little intelligence and not a shred of common sense. Kate, on the other hand, was intelligent and possessed common sense in abundance, yet she appeared withdrawn and introverted in comparison and was so lacking in self confidence it annoyed him. She had plenty of courage but seemed afraid of life. If only she would believe in herself she would come across just as vibrant as Sarah. Sarah chatted away, he wasn't really listening, just watched Kate listening intently. Ling quietly worked away in the background but he knew she was listening also.

"And I thought that would be a brilliant idea," Sarah finished. Thunder realised he had missed something.

"What would?" he asked.

"I think that's a good idea Sarah," Ling said giving him a hard stare.

"What is?" he demanded.

"You weren't listening, were you?" Kate said. "You'll have to wait and see,"

"Is Kit in the restaurant?" he asked Ling who nodded. He took a piece of toast and left. He found Kit talking to two Chinese men. His Chinese was limited so he didn't understand much of what was said. After a few minutes the two men went off in opposite directions.

"There was a message on the machine this morning," Kit said. Thunder looked interested. "From Ted. Said there was someone looking for you,"

"I'll go and see him," Thunder said.

"Want some company?" Kit asked.

"Ted doesn't take too kindly to foreigners in his pub. He barely tolerates Irish, he certainly won't Chinese. I'll go alone," Thunder said. Kit grunted. Thunder smiled. "See you later," and he turned to go.

"You're doing that a lot lately," Kit said. Thunder looked back over his shoulder. "Smiling. It's a bad sign - for you," Thunder smiled once more and left.

When he went in the pub John, the barman gestured to the back room. Thunder nodded and went through the arch to the billiard room. He found Ted sitting at his usual table in the corner with two men. They were laughing. When Ted saw Thunder he gestured for the men to leave. John brought a couple of beers. Thunder sat down.

"You left a message for me," Thunder said.

"Didn't know you were involved with the yellow peril," Ted

said.

"The Chinaman is my contact," Thunder explained.

"Is he?" Ted stored that. "Found out who grassed you up,"

"Oh?" then he remembered that he had asked Ted to found out how Sammy and Joe had found him. "Anyone I know?"

"Barmaid at Nag's Head. Sally. Ugly cow. Got picked up by some ugly bloke. He gave her a good seeing to and told her he was a friend so she told him where to find you. What d'you want doing with her? I've given her one meself a couple of times. Right goer but a slag. Comes across for anything in trousers," Ted said.

"Oh give her a stiff talking to, nothing too violent, if she's that ugly she has to get her jollies somewhere," Thunder said with a hint of sarcasm.

Ted roared with laughter. "You're too kind. Aye I'll give her a stiff talking to," Thunder had no doubt that his huge carcass would be heaving itself on top of the unfortunate girl as punishment.

"Your message said someone was looking for me?" Thunder said.

"Oh yes," Ted took a mouthful of beer, belched loudly and wiped his mouth with the back of his hand. "Had a paddy in here last night, looking for Kit Brown. By the description I thought it might be you,"

"Did he have a name?" Thunder asked, though he thought he knew.

"Liam. Red hair. Drank enough ale to sink a battleship," Ted said.

"That sounds like Liam. Good man to have in your corner," Thunder said.

"Don't hold with foreigners," Ted snarled. "Unless he's putting money across my bar,"

"And Liam spent a lot of money last night?" Thunder already knew the answer.

"Like I said, drank enough to sink a battleship. Man after me own heart," Ted said obviously converted on this 'foreigner'.

"Is he coming back or do I contact him?" Thunder asked.

"Said you'd know where to find him," Ted said. "Strange

friends you have pal. How's the lass?"

"She is fine," Thunder said.

"Bring her in again. I liked her. Can't stand weak willies," Ted said.

"I'll tell her. She'll be…" Thunder searched for the right word. "Flattered,"

Ted roared with laughter at his sarcasm. "Aye, she will that,"

Thunder got up. "Which pub did you say this girl worked in?"

"Not to your liking, if that lass is anything to go by," Ted said.

"I was thinking of my Irish friend," Thunder said.

Ted roared again. "He'd have to be blind drunk to give that slag one. Don't know what you'd catch,"

Thunder smiled and left. He took a cab to his flat. Unfortunately Mrs Cornish saw the cab draw up and was waiting for him on the doorstep.

"Mr Brown, I thought you'd gone for good," she screeched at him before he got through the door. He braced himself for the torrent that followed. "That Irish… person on the top floor. Huh, don't think much to him, or his friends," she dropped her voice. "If you ask me I think he has 'connections' if you know what I mean," she nodded knowingly at him.

"Very likely," he told her quietly. "I've just come back to see what damage has been done to my flat," he said in a normal voice. He quickly fled up the stairs. He waited to see if she followed him but heard her door shut. He went up to Liam's door and was about to knock when the door opened. Liam stood there looking as wild as ever, his hair all over the place. He looked very hung over.

"Good night was it?" Thunder said lightly.

Liam groaned. "Bloody man. Had to show him my money before he'd let me in! Thought I could put it away but he left me standing,"

"He speaks highly of you too. Considering he hates foreigners, I think you've converted him," Thunder said

"I'm honoured, I'm sure," Liam opened the door wide. Thunder went in and up the stairs. He had gone to a few parties in Liam's flat and slept on the sofa more than once. The flat was its usual untidy state; glasses, cans and bottles littered the floor among the clothes.

"I see you've had a party recently. And you didn't invite me. I'm hurt," Thunder said looking round.

Liam looked sheepish. "Well you know how it is. A few people round for a late drink and it turns into a party," his smile became a leer.

"I hope you protected your assets," Thunder said with a grin.

"But of course," Liam said, a wicked grin on his face. He went into the kitchen. Thunder heard the fridge being opened.

"I'll have coffee," he called.

Liam's head appeared. "Did I hear right? Coffee?"

"Black, no sugar," Thunder replied and found somewhere to sit down.

Liam disappeared back into the kitchen shaking his head in disbelief. He returned with two mugs of black coffee.

Thunder looked at his friend speculatively. "I got your message," he started.

"Ah yes. Well no. Well yes, I suppose," he dried up.

"That beer's addled your brains," Thunder said.

"That guy came back. The man that did over your flat," Liam said.

"Oh? Did he see you?"

"No, but I saw and heard him,"

"Good. Let me give you a piece of free advice Liam. If he ever comes again, avoid him, like the plague, he's dangerous,"

"I can handle myself, you know. I'm not a total innocent," Liam sounded almost hurt. He pushed his unruly locks back and tried to capture all of his hair in a hair band. The front sprang forward almost immediately giving him the wild look. He pushed his hair back with a sigh.

"You need to get your hair cut,"

"You always say that. Get a haircut like yours? The ladies like my hair wild and free,"

Thunder ran his fingers through his hair, it was getting long. Left too long it curled like Liam's. "You always say that," he said. "The ladies like my hair like they like me - wild and unruly," he took off Liam's Irish accent wickedly.

"Now, you wouldn't be taking the piss, would you now. Of me accent, like?" Liam exaggerated his accent.

"To be sure, I wouldn't," Thunder said in another exaggerated Irish accent. They both laughed. "Certainly not," he became serious. "Oh by the way if you're ever near the Nag's Head you might fancy a quick one with Sally. She dropped me in it, without realising. She needs a stiff talking to. Although she has a face like the backend of a bus,"

"Nothing a paper bag won't solve," Liam said wickedly. "I'll take a look,"

"Comes across for anything in trousers," Thunder said. "You might be an education for her, or the other way round,"

"Bit of a dog eh?"

"Understatement," Thunder said. "Depends on your point of view,"

"And my point of view is always horizontal,"

"The old bag downstairs thinks you have connections," Thunder became serious.

"Now what sort of connections would that be?" Liam asked equally serious.

"The sort from across the sea, as in emerald isle sort of connections," Thunder said.

"Oh," Liam's face fell. "Those sort of connections," he muttered. They laughed. "Stupid bag. She'd have ears to every wall and floor if it meant she'd get the gossip first. She knows everything that goes on here. She knows my every move and reports to her neighbour who's silly enough to believe her,"

"That's never stopped you in the past," Thunder said. "Makes interesting gossip. So what did this man do?"

"He poked around in your flat, swore a lot, spoke in a foreign language,"

"Probably Afrikaans," Thunder said.

Liam looked at him. "Then left. He was here before with a blond man," Liam said.

Thunder nodded. "Did you see him?" Liam nodded. "Scar down his face?" Liam nodded again.

"Black leather coat. Very expensive. Black hat," Liam added. "I take it you know him?"

Thunder nodded. "Oh yes. We are... old friends... from way back," Liam drank his coffee in silent thought. "Look, you can reach me faster on this number," Thunder handed him a card. "And stay away from that man. I don't want another friend being killed because they are my friend,"

"With my connections?" Liam said lightly and laughed. Thunder didn't laugh. Liam's laughter died.

"Sometimes I wonder Liam, sometimes I wonder," Thunder said quietly.

"Next time bring the girl with you. I'd like to meet her," Liam said as they both got to their feet.

"You think I'd let you near Kate? I'd have to watch your every move," Thunder joked.

"Kate, so that's her name, is it? I'd be on my best behaviour, well best for me," Liam said.

"Yeah right," Thunder left and returned to Chinatown, a happier man.

In the taxi on the way back he mused about Liam. He suddenly realised he actually missed him, their friendship and their banter. Perhaps he would introduce Kate to Liam, one day. It would be interesting to see how she'd take to him.

CHAPTER SIXTEEN

Thunder told Kit about his visit with Liam. Kit wiggled his nose and screwed up his mouth thoughtfully. "So Cardol is looking for you,"

"Looks like it. I just hope he doesn't find me. I don't want you and Ling involved," Thunder said.

"And Kate?" Kit asked. Thunder frowned.

"Sarah wants to see Marcus," Ling said behind him.

"She'll see him soon enough," he replied.

The evening was spent quietly. Sarah looked at Thunder sadly. He ignored it.

"You could have taken her to see Marcus," Kate hissed at him when Sarah had finally gone to bed.

"She will see him soon enough," he replied firmly.

"You are one mean bastard!" Kate hissed at him. He looked at her sharply. She looked at him steadily with a cold look. He was about to talk to her when she turned her back on him. He shrugged.

The next day dragged by interminably slowly. Thunder went out the next morning and when he returned in the afternoon told Sarah to pack her bag. Kate sat on the other bed while she did so and they talked.

"You'll be going home soon, won't you?" Sarah said to Kate.

"I suppose so. Now your dad's done this deal there is no danger to us," Kate said.

"I hope so. I'd like to get back to normality," Sarah said.

"Do you know normality?" now good friends Sarah didn't mind Kate's occasional dig about her background.

"Well my kind of normal," she smiled. They both laughed.

"Will life ever be normal again?" Kate asked. "Have you asked Thunder about Marcus?"

"No," she answered quickly. "I didn't like to,"

"He won't bite," Kate said.

"I know but he still frightens me,"

"You're daft. He's only human,"

"The humans I know don't carry guns," Sarah said.

"Do you know Lowman?" Kate asked.

"I've heard of him," Sarah said thoughtfully.

"Well he has bodyguards and they carry guns. Like the Godfather. Too much watching gangster movies," They laughed.

"I hope Marcus does come to my house. I'm dying to introduce him to papa. He doesn't think Marcus is good enough for me," Sarah said seriously.

"How good is good enough?" Kate asked.

"I dread to think," Sarah's voice was sarcastic.

Kate smiled. Sarah had grown up somewhat in the last week. Was her father going to be in for a shock. "We're back to the movies again,"

"Which one?" Sarah asked.

"Romeo and Juliet, I think," Kate said.

"Romeo, Romeo wherefore art thou Romeo?" Sarah quoted dramatically.

"In the garden you silly mare," Kate replied. They laughed again.

"What do you think to my idea for the charity ball?" Sarah asked.

"I haven't given it any thought," Kate admitted.

"But people think we are one and the same," Sarah started.

"How they possibly get us mixed up is beyond me,"

"So, let's confuse them!"

"How?"

"We'll dress the same but different,"

"And how do you purpose to organise this?"

"Maxine will make two dresses, same colour different styles,"

"You've obviously thought about this,"

"Oh I have," Sarah came and sat next to Kate and they whispered together.

Later that day Ling explained to Kate about make up and

mixing colours and styles together. It certainly showed Kate that Thunder was right. Her colours and styles had been chosen for her, a trend she had continued, even though they were totally wrong for her. It had been a deliberate act. Kate promised Ling that she would change her wardrobe.

"Ask Thunder. He will tell you truthfully if something doesn't suit you, without malice. Some people like you for you, not scoring points or putting you down," Ling told her firmly.

Mid morning the next day Thunder suddenly announced to Sarah that it was time to go. Suddenly Sarah was reluctant. There were tearful goodbyes with Sarah thanking Kit and Ling very politely for putting up with her. Ling gave her a little bag and told her to open it at home. A reminder of her time.

Sarah hugged Kate. "I'll see you at the ball,"

"What will Thunder be wearing?" Kate whispered.

"A monkey suit just like everyone else," Sarah replied with satisfaction. Thunder looked at her blankly. She smiled. Thunder took her to the end of the road where a cab was waiting.

"You don't have to take me home, I can go on my own from here," Sarah said.

"Precaution," was all he said. They got in. As Sarah got nearer home she was eager to be there. They drove in the drive and past the front door.

"I can use the front door," Sarah protested.

"Not this time. We sneak in the side door. It's all part of the game," Thunder said.

"Oh," her face dropped. "Don't they know I'm coming home?"

"No. They still think you're kidnapped. Even Bruce doesn't know and we want to keep it that way,"

"I didn't tell Marcus it was Bruce who set the kidnapping up. They were friends,"

"He knows. He was told the whole story last night,"

"You saw him? You didn't take me?" tears welled up.

"You'll see him soon enough," he got out the cab, telling him to wait. Sarah followed, head down so that he couldn't see her tears. "Do you still have the key?"

"There's no need," a gruff voice said above them. Standing at the side door was Palmerston-Smith.

"Oh papa," Sarah threw herself into his arms nearly knocking him over, tears flowing unheeded.

Palmerston-Smith looked at Thunder, one eyebrow raised. "She's pleased to be home," Thunder said softly.

"Lets go," Palmerston-Smith said. "It's all arranged. You have the attic to yourself," They went up the stairs in silence, punctuated only by the occasional sniff from Sarah. She held her father's hand tightly. Behind her came Thunder. At the top of the house the stairs opened onto a landing with one door. They went into a little sitting room. Sarah sat down. Palmerston-Smith took her bags into the bedroom.

"I'm still a prisoner," Sarah muttered tearfully.

"You can keep me company then," a voice said from the doorway.

Sarah looked up. Marcus stood at the door with Palmerston-Smith standing behind him. Sarah was up and across the room into his arms, knocking him against the wall. Palmerston-Smith put out a steadying hand. Marcus laughed at her. Palmerston-Smith left them and went over to Thunder.

"How is he?" Thunder asked.

"Better now I think," he said looking over at them. "My little girl is growing up. Once she only wanted me,"

"Things change," Thunder said dryly.

"You were right about him. He's a good lad. Clever. We had a chat last night. I see a great future for that boy, if he works at it, and he will. Better than my son, Ben," Palmerston-Smith said.

"So what's the plan? When does the news break?" Thunder asked.

"At the ball I think. They can't do much there,"

"Sarah and Kate are cooking up something, God knows what. Something to do with clothes is all I can make out,"

Palmerston-Smith laughed. "Typical women. Sort out the important things in life - what they are going to wear. Everything else sorts itself out,"

"Are we all going to the ball?" Sarah asked at his elbow.

"I've told her but she won't believe me," Marcus said.

"Bad start that, when women won't believe what you tell them," Thunder said.

"We are all going to the ball. Me, Ben, you, Marcus, Thunder and Kate," Palmerston-Smith said. "Plus a few friends. There will be a whole table just for us,"

"I'd better order some more suits," Sarah said.

"Already done," Palmerston-Smith told her.

"We sorted that out last night when I brought Marcus here," Thunder said.

"Marcus was here? Last night? On his own? With papa?" Sarah looked incredulous.

"And still alive," her father said. "I won't eat him Sarah. Marcus and I have a chat over dinner. We understand each other perfectly," he smiled at Marcus who smiled back.

Sarah looked at her father with wide eyes. She wasn't the only one who had changed. Suddenly her father looked different.

"We are fine," Marcus said softly.

"This is the first time I've seen my daughter speechless," Palmerston-Smith said.

"I'll leave you to it then. I'll bring Kate over before then so you two can create whatever it is you're creating," Thunder said. Sarah's face radiated happiness. He hoped that one day Kate would look like that.

Palmerston-Smith went with him to the door. "Sarah will be safe after this?" he asked uncertain.

"If it's the person I think behind this, it's me he wants. Lightman's kidnap plan was a handy pawn to bring me out into the open," Thunder said.

"Makes life difficult for you,"

"Nothing I can't handle,"

"If you need anything, call me,"

"Keep her safe," Thunder said and left.

He went back to his flat. Mrs Cornish wasn't in nor was Liam. The flat was the same as before, there wasn't much left for Cardol to destroy. He spent some time tidying up, made a few calls, left Liam a note and returned to Chinatown. It was the end of an era.

During the time until the charity ball Thunder went off for a couple of days. He didn't talk about it and Kate didn't ask him. She still didn't believe his declaration. She believed that when this was all over she would return home and he would go to the next job wherever it took him. She hoped he could avoid this man looking for him until he was ready. She hoped that he would succeed when he did meet him. And she wished that she could help him, but knew that he was quite capable of looking after himself without her. Suddenly home looked quite welcoming. Especially as now she had things to do.

A week before the charity ball Thunder took Kate to see Sarah to sort out their dresses. They sneaked in through the side door. No one knew that Sarah was at home now. Palmerston-Smith still acted as if she was kidnapped and gave Bruce a hard time about it every day. Bruce wished he had never come to Britain. There had to be an easier way of earning money than this continual nightmare. Even Lowman gave him a hard time on the few occasions that he rang Bruce for news of Sarah.

Sarah was pleased to see her and they went off together with the dressmaker to create 'the right impression' as Sarah called it. Thunder sat and talked to Marcus. He was feeling much better and both men were limping less than before.

On the morning of the charity ball, Thunder and Kate packed overnight bags, they were staying at the Palmerston-Smith household. They left Chinatown after lunch and got a cab to Sarah's home. Thunder knocked on the front door. The butler opened the door and looked at them with disdain.

"Tell Palmerston-Smith Kate and Kit are here," Thunder told him walking into the hall. Kate followed.

The butler directed them to a room off the hallway. Thunder recognised it and sank into a chair. Kate looked round.

"Why don't you sit down?" Thunder asked her.

"I might crease the covers," Kate replied sarcastically.

"Ah Kate, you're here," Palmerston-Smith walked into the room. "This way," he gestured to them to follow him. They went to his office. Bruce came in with the tea. He put it down on the desk and then stopped when he saw Thunder. He was about to say something when he saw Kate. He looked at the plaster and clamped his mouth firmly shut.

"Nothing to say Bruce? You surprise me," Kate said acidly.

"How are you?" Bruce managed to sound smooth.

Kate gave him a distasteful look. "Fine. Considering. You set Sarah up to be kidnapped and when they got me instead you didn't stop to think what would happen did you?" Bruce backed away as Kate advanced on him. Palmerston-Smith sat in his chair and smiled, his fingers pressed together making an arch. Thunder stood leaning against the wall, his arms folded.

"I... I... didn't mean you any harm..." Bruce started.

"No? And what do you call this?" she held up her arm. He looked at it and swallowed hard. Thunder shoved him in the back. He looked at him over his shoulder. Kate advanced on him again. He tried to back out of the way but found Thunder's very solid form keeping him there. He threw an appealing look at Palmerston-Smith. He stared back steadily and said nothing.

"I've owned up to my part in Sarah's kidnap," he said to him.

"Have you?" Kate blazed at him. He looked uncomfortable and started to hop from foot to foot. "And how many times do I have to get my arm broken before you and your friends get the message?" she asked him harshly. He looked at her miserably. "Two, three, four times?" Her voice dropped to a whisper. "And what about Sarah? What would they have done to her?"

"They wouldn't have hurt Sarah," he said.

"From some creep like Joe? I doubt that. His idea of 'safe' isn't mine," Kate said no more, what had happened at the warehouse didn't need to be said.

"I've called it off. I've stopped it," Bruce whined.

"Have you? Are you sure? I don't think so! Not by a long chalk! I'm still in danger. So is Thunder. So that means so is Sarah!" Kate was relentless.

He looked over his shoulder at Thunder. "You said she was safe," he said accusingly.

"She is... for now," Thunder told him. Bruce looked stricken.

"You're pathetic, a stupid little cretin. You think those men are going to just let you go? Think again!" Kate said harshly.

"Bruce, I think you should take the rest of the day off," Palmerston-Smith said quietly from across the room.

"Thank you, sir," Bruce said with relief and made a move towards the door.

"Oh and Bruce?" Thunder's voice froze him. "Don't think of leaving this house today. Or making any phone calls you will regret,"

"And just to make sure," Kate said and raised her knee, hard. Bruce's eyes filled with tears as he crumpled to the floor holding his groin. Thunder hauled him up and out through the door. Bruce stumbled away.

Thunder turned to her. Just behind her he could see Palmerston-Smith's startled face. Before he had been trying not to laugh, pressing his hand over his mouth. Now it was pressed there with shock. Thunder looked at Kate.

"That wasn't very nice," he stated.

"That pathetic little shit!" she looked defiantly at him. "He deserved more!"

"You should have come that day we spoke to him. You frightened him more than me or Kit did," Thunder said.

"I doubt that very much," Kate retorted.

"We'd better go and see Sarah before she wears the carpet out," Palmerston-Smith said recovering his senses.

They all went upstairs. Sarah jumped to her feet and flung her arms round Kate. Marcus got to his feet, stiffly. Thunder had stopped limping altogether. It was just another scar to add to the tally. The men sat and chatted. Suddenly Sarah looked at her watch.

"Teresa will be here soon. She will ask for Kate," she said.

"That's our cue to leave," Marcus told Thunder. "I have no wish to have my hair fluffed up like a tart, thank you all the same,"

A small woman came in. She kissed Sarah on both cheeks. Palmerston-Smith got up. The three men left. Teresa worked on them. Same hair style: swept up into an elegant pleat at the back. To Sarah's surprise Kate picked out the make up she wanted and started to apply it.

"You've been having lessons," she said.

"Ling's been teaching me about colours, make up, hair, styles. It's been an education," Kate said. Sarah looked pleased.

They sat around until half seven when Palmerston-Smith came to tell them it was time to leave. He looked very handsome in his evening suit. His face dropped when he saw them both dressed in the same deep blue. Sarah's dress was tightly fitted, the front cut across the throat, the back low cut with criss cross straps across the back, tight sleeves. It emphasised every curve. Kate looked at her with envy; she didn't have the tall slim figure to carry it off; nor the confidence.

Kate's dress was straight to the knees, then billowed out, shorter at the front, long at the back. It was strapless with a little bolero jacket with long sleeves shaped to cover the backs of her hands. It covered the plaster perfectly. They both wore blue jewellery. Palmerston-Smith grinned at them.

"Shall we go ladies?" he offered both arms. They went downstairs where Thunder and Marcus was waiting. Both looked up.

"Oh my God," Marcus said first

"My thought exactly," Thunder replied. "So that was the scheme, very good,"

Kate went over to Thunder. "Now make sure you have the right girl with you or you might get your face slapped," she told him.

"I wouldn't dare!" Sarah said behind her.

"Coward!" Kate hissed at her.

A young man came downstairs. He looked in a bad mood. He frowned at his father. "I think this is in very bad taste father," he snarled.

"This is my son, Ben. Marcus, Kate," he stopped as he realised he didn't know what to call Thunder.

"Kit," Thunder volunteered.

"Ah yes. And you remember your sister, Sarah," Palmerston-Smith added.

Sarah stepped out from behind Marcus. Ben's face dropped a mile.

"But... you're... you've been..." he floundered.

"I think the word is kidnapped," Kate said quietly near him. He looked at her, then his eyes widened. Kate smiled at him.

"Ho... ly... sh... it," he stuttered. "They could be sisters. Father, what's going on? Is there something you haven't told us!" he turned to his father.

"Nothing. Put your jaw back into place and we'll go," he said smoothly.

They left. From a window Bruce watched. His eyes bulged when he saw first Kate and then Sarah step out and get into the car. He picked up the phone but his hand shook so much that he couldn't dial. He dropped the phone, fell into a chair, put his head in his hands and started to moan.

At the Grosvenor House Hotel the car came to a halt. The doorman opened the door and helped the girls out. He looked at them briefly and then looked again. Palmerston-Smith swept inside appearing not to notice the stares. They followed.

At the bar the rest of the party are waiting. Palmerston-Smith introduced them all: Janice Whittaker, his secretary; Tom and Cathy Ellis, Bill and Vivian Jones, his friends; Mark Wray, his solicitor. They made their way to their table, ignoring the looks from others.

Palmerston-Smith had arranged the table for maximum affect. He sat with Kate and Sarah either side of him. Kit (Thunder) sat the other side of Kate with Janice and Mark to his side. Marcus sat next to Sarah with the Ellis's the other side. The Jones' and Ben sat on the other side of the table. Ben looked across the table at his father and grinned. His father was certainly in his element tonight. Father and son looked at each other across the table and smiled.

"Mr Palmerston-Smith told me about you, Kate," Janice said leaning across Thunder. "I'm glad you and Sarah are safe,"

"I must say, you look very like Sarah, until you get close, and then you look different. Gave me quite a turn, seeing you two together," Mark said.

"That's the general idea," Thunder told him.

"I'd say it's working, judging by the attention we're getting,"

Mark said. Thunder looked round. People were looking once and then a second time with a stunned look.

"I see what you mean," he mused. "I doubt there's a man in the place that hasn't noticed,"

"Women too," Mark said.

"You haven't seen anything yet," Kate said. "Sarah has a few tricks up her sleeve,"

"In that dress? Where does she keep them?" Mark quipped. They all laughed.

After the meal Sarah decided to talk to some people she had seen. She took Kate with her. They walked around the tables. Occasionally a friend of Palmerston-Smith would stop and talk. Sarah did not introduce Kate and she didn't speak unless spoken to and then it was single words. Kate spotted Bob Lowman. She lead Sarah over to his table. She leaned over his shoulder.

"Hello Mr Lowman. How are your goons? Still breaking arms?" she said in his ear. He looked up at her and then at Sarah standing just behind her. "Do you know Sarah Palmerston-Smith? Sarah, this is Mr Lowman,"

He got to his feet and smiled. He looked from one girl to the other then kissed their hands. "Very nice ladies. Very nice indeed. My compliments to your father, Sarah," he said. "And your friend," he added.

"Which table is Carl Lightman on?" Sarah asked him.

"Table 5. On your way to the ladies. Good hunting," he said and smiled.

Sarah and Kate smiled and thanked him. They moved off in unison. Bob Lowman watched them go and smiled. Although he thought Kate looked different he could see why people would get them mixed up, especially dressed the same. He wished he was a fly on the wall when Lightman saw them.

Sarah and Kate approached table 5. They slowed down as they walked, causing maximum effect. Carl Lightman looked up, looked away and then looked back sharply. He started to breath quickly.

"I do hope papa finds whoever is responsible for my kidnap," Sarah said in a loud voice as they walked round the table.

"His friend will find him and I don't fancy being in his shoes when he does. I hear he blows things up," Kate said. Lightman had gone very white.

"That man looked very ill," Sarah said.

"Drunk probably. Some men don't know when to stop," Kate replied.

Lightman opened and shut his mouth like a demented fish out of water. He drank a glass of water and then got up. He staggered off across the room towards Palmerston-Smith who saw him coming and got up.

"I say, old man, you look like you're seen a ghost," Palmerston-Smith said and helped Lightman into the chair vacated by Sarah. "Do you know Tom Ellis?"

Lightman shook Tom's hand and looked wildly at Palmerston-Smith. "Was that your daughter I've just seen? In blue?" he blurted out.

"Possibly," Palmerston-smith said. "Let me introduce you to Bill Jones, an old friend of mine," Bill Jones shook his hand.

"She was with another girl. Sister maybe?" Lightman

"I only have one daughter," Palmerston-Smith said.

Tom and Bill sat down, their wives had gone off to chat. "If you come over to my office on Monday, we can go through the outstanding tenders," Tom said to Bill as if they were continuing a conversation. "I'm sure you and Ray will have no problem taking over my business,"

"It's nice to keep things within the circle of old friends," Bill said.

"Yes. Best to keep out the foreigners, especially the Yanks," Tom said.

"Nothing like the old boy network to work out problems," Bill said.

"Ellis? Did you say your name was Ellis?" Lightman suddenly said.

"Yes. Tom Ellis of Ellis Construction Ltd. I've just sold my business to Bill here," Tom Ellis replied.

"What about the other bids?" Lightman asked.

Ellis waved them away. "Bunch of no good hopers," he said.

"Bill's was the best offer by far,"

Lightman opened and shut his mouth, his colour now a sickly green. Palmerston-Smith looked at him with concern.

"Carl, are you all right? You've gone an awful colour, old boy," he said.

"Don't you old boy me," he hissed. "You've got that deal,"

"No. Bill's got the deal. I just happen to be a shareholder,"

Lightman gave a strangled sound and staggered to his feet. Thunder suddenly appeared. Lightman looked at him. He didn't recognise him, he didn't know who he was. He was about to be enlightened.

"Let me take you back to your table," Thunder said smoothly. "We can talk on the way," he took Lightman firmly by the arm and led him away. Lightman looked over his shoulder once and then with horror at Thunder as he started to talk to him. No one ever knew what he said. Thunder wouldn't tell and Lightman looked too stricken to tell a soul.

Thunder returned after a few minutes. "He kept muttering that he was finished. He didn't look too well when I left him," Thunder said in a pleasant tone.

Palmerston-Smith danced with Kate and caused all sorts of comments. Thunder asked Sarah to dance. She looked horrified.

"Come on Sarah, I won't eat you," he said and pulled her to her feet. To Sarah's horror Marcus fell about with laughter as Thunder propelled her to the dance floor. Kate danced with Thunder and then she went over to Bob Lowman and asked him to dance. She didn't care what people thought. Lightman watched, horror crept up his back and he broke out in a cold sweat. Then it was Sarah's turn to dance with Bob Lowman. Lightman was helped outside with a suspected heart attack. Palmerston-Smith looked unperturbed through the whole proceedings. Sarah and Kate were causing such a stir, it would be the talk for many weeks to come.

"Are you sure they aren't in danger? They are causing a lot of comments," Marcus asked Thunder.

He looked round thoughtfully then smiled. "I doubt it. This evening is about revenge and I think that's been achieved. The man behind this is after me and neither girl can be said to be linked with me. Don't worry Marcus, after tonight Sarah is safe,"

"And you and Kate?" Marcus asked concerned.

"Ah," Thunder said, smiling. "That's different. That has yet to be sorted out. But no worries. I'll sort it. I just haven't worked out how,"

Marcus looked at his new found friend with a slight frown but Thunder was so unperturbed about it all that Marcus relaxed. If Thunder thought he could sort it out, then he could and there was no cause for concern.

When Marcus and Sarah danced it was very obvious they were an item. Kate danced with various people and treated them all the same, including Thunder. He marvelled at her composure but then she'd had a lifetime of pretending. Being polite to people she didn't like, treating everyone with the same neutrality. She didn't relax for one minute, only in the ladies away from watching eyes could she relax. It didn't bother her that she could drop and pick it up at will.

Finally Palmerston-Smith took his party home. He saw Marcus was starting to wilt. Best to leave the company wanting more than to over play their hand. He had achieved what he wanted. That Lightman had suffered a heart attack into the bargain he saw as poetic justice, although he would have loved to know what Thunder told him. For once Ben had enjoyed himself and he and Sarah had actually got on.

CHAPTER SEVENTEEN

Back at the house everyone soon went to bed, everyone was more tired than they would admit. Tomorrow would be time enough to analysis the evening. Sarah and Kate had breakfast together in the attic. This was the last time Sarah would have to hide. Downstairs Thunder, Marcus and Ben were having breakfast with Ray.

"Well I think that has sorted out Lightman," Marcus was saying.

"Oh I don't think you'll have any more problems with Mr Lightman," Thunder said wryly.

"What did you say to him? He looked scared to death," Ben said.

"I think that will stay between myself and Lightman. I doubt he will ever tell anyone," Thunder said calmly. Ben sensibly shut up.

"What about the man in partnership with him?" Marcus asked.

Palmerston-Smith looked puzzled, then realised who he was talking about. "Oh Bob Lowman. I doubt he will bother me. He was a small fish in this,"

"The look from certain quarters when first Kate and then Sarah danced with him, it was worth it just for that. I shouldn't be surprised if you don't get business from him in the future," Thunder said.

"The big man? That was Bob Lowman? His jaw dropped when Sarah went up to him," Ben chuckled.

"Not him. The other one," Marcus said.

"The other one?" Ray looked confused.

"He wants me," Thunder said.

"Why?" Ben asked.

"Because I killed his family because they killed mine," Thunder said with ease, it surprised him.

"That's a bit drastic. Why not tell the police?" Ben said. Marcus and Ray exchanged looks. His son was naive at times.

"It doesn't work that way," Thunder said quietly.

"What happens now?" Ray changed the subject quickly.

"Sarah can go back to her life. So can Marcus. You have your revenge. I will deal with my friend, in my own way," Thunder said.

"And Kate?" Marcus asked.

"I will take Kate home," Thunder replied. Sarah and Kate joined them at that point so the subject was dropped. Kate was holding her wrist.

"I think Kate should go and see the doc today to see if her arm has healed," Sarah said to Thunder. He nodded.

She looked at him coldly. She was in pain. He recognised that look. She shrugged. A hour later they left by the front door. Bruce still hadn't made an appearance. At St Bart's the doc had the arm x-rayed. It wasn't good news. They eventually went to Chinatown, Thunder in a foul mood, Kate near to tears. Ling took her off to hear about the evening, Kit and Thunder sat in the kitchen. Kit put a black coffee in front of him.

"Kate has tendon damage that probably won't heal sufficiently well. She won't be going back to typing that's for sure. Lowman's men need a lesson in control," he said angrily.

"I wouldn't waste your talents on them. I'm sure a word in Lowman's ear would be enough. You have to stay out of Cardol's clutches. He will do a lot worse if he finds Kate," Kit said.

"Any news?" Thunder asked.

"Liam rang. Cardol visited your home again and half killed the old lady. Liam wasn't there. He keeps finding Cardol only to find that he's just moved on. He's certainly not staying in one place for long," Kit said.

"I'm beginning to think that Liam is leading a double life too," Thunder said.

"Don't be so surprised," Kit said. Thunder looked at him.

"What do you know about Liam?"

"Nothing that you don't already know or suspect,"

"You're being evasive,"

"It's my nature," Kit said. "Will you take Kate home now?"

"You've changed the subject," Thunder said accusingly. Kit looked at him steadily. He sighed. "Yes, I'll take Kate home now, but not tonight, I'm too tired for family dynamics,"

They spent a quiet night in the flat. Kate stared at the television without seeing. Eventually Thunder suggested she go to bed. She went without a word. Ling looked worried. Kit and Thunder exchanged looks. Kate looked withdrawn.

The journey back to Kate's home was made in silence. She wouldn't talk and anything she did say was monosyllables. It unnerved him slightly. He could feel her withdrawing, he could almost smell her dread of home and the nearer they got they worse she got. He could feel what little confidence she had draining away. He put his arms round her, she leant her head against his reassuringly solid chest, heard his steady heart beat.

"It will be fine," he whispered. "We'll go in, take what you want and go. We can stay in a hotel if you like,"

"Why did you make me ring home? Why couldn't we just turn up?" she asked.

"You caused a sensation the other night. Now it's my turn," he replied.

They took a cab from the station. Thunder asked it to stop a few houses away from her home. As they got out she could feel the curtains twitching. As they walked up the road and through the gate you could almost hear the cracking of bones as necks were cricked. When they got to the front door Kate was shaking. He hugged her and kissed her on the cheek. She gave him a strained smile.

"Call me Krysten. Krysten Abe. Let's start as we mean to go on," he said to her. She nodded and opened the door. He followed her in.

Upstairs Elizabeth was waiting, dressed ready to make her grand entrance. She looked out the window. She watched the cab pull up and watched with disinterest as a couple got out. The man drew her attention, the woman not at all. She turned away bored.

Downstairs her parents waited in the sitting room.

"She is late," her mother muttered. "So typical. I expect she'll be in those disgusting jeans. No refinement. I have no idea where she gets it from," she threw her husband a withering look which he returned with the same venom.

As Kate closed the front door behind her the door to the sitting room opened. Her father stood there. To his surprise she was wearing a burgundy suit and high heels. Her hair was swept back and twisted up. For a moment she reminded him so sharply of his mother and aunt Kitty that it hurt.

"Ask them in then, dear," her mother called. He gestured them in.

Kate's mother stood in the middle of the room like royalty receiving guests. Krysten looked at her critically. She had a faded beauty look like an overblown rose and her face had a pinched look as if her life had not turned out as she expected. The saying 'face like a slapped arse' rose unbidden to his mind. He smiled.

"So you're Kate's friend," her mother said. Her voice wasn't booming or shrill but still grated. "You'd better sit down. Elizabeth will be down in a minute,"

They sat down. Mr Bromham was an angular man with thinning hair swept across a balding head and a cold forbidding air. Here was a man who had never been happy in his entire life and made sure that others suffered for it. This was not a happy marriage; both bitterly disappointed in each other.

They sat in silence. Krysten said nothing. Kate looked at her hands in her lap. She looked desperately unhappy. He wanted to reach out but the atmosphere stopped him. Suddenly the door flew open and there stood Elizabeth in a clingy dress that was so inappropriate it was absurd. Krysten stifled a laugh.

"Hi, I'm Elizabeth," she said with a provocative drawl. It obviously made an impact on the local lads but he was of a different world. Elizabeth looked at him in wonder: where had her stupid sister found this gem? She sat on the arm of a chair in what she thought was a provocative pose. Krysten tried hard not to laugh again. It turned into a cough.

"You're putting on weight, Kate," Elizabeth said.

"You'll never be as slim as Elizabeth if you keep eating those sweets," her mother added.

"I'm surprised she has any teeth left," her father said.

"Oh I don't know," Krysten started. "I prefer women with a bit of meat on them. Clothes horses are too bony for comfort," he looked at Mrs Bromham. Hardly a 'buxom' woman. She glared at him.

"But she always looks so frumpy," Elizabeth whined.

"Only in the wrong clothes," Krysten said quietly.

"We'll have that cup of tea now," Mrs Bromham said sweetly.

"I'd rather have coffee, black, no sugar," Krysten said.

"I suppose you want yours with your usual ton of sugar," Mrs Bromham said to Kate.

"No thank you. Nothing thanks," Kate replied.

"No Jasmine tea?" Krysten asked her with a smile.

"Jasmine tea? That's foreign isn't it?" Elizabeth said. She felt annoyed. He only had eyes for Kate, he wasn't taking any notice of her at all. She sauntered past, so close he had to sit back, and sat on the arm of the sofa, close to him. He could smell her cloying scent, it made him feel sick. Kate closed her eyes as the familiar scenario started to play out.

"It's Chinese," Krysten told her.

"Oh really. That's interesting," Elizabeth felt a shiver go down her shine. He would be worth taking. She might keep him for a while. It would make her friends jealous. Her mind wandered.

"Foreign muck. Wouldn't catch our Elizabeth wasting her time on it," Mrs Bromham said archly.

"When I first had it I tried to remove the leaves. You're supposed to leave them in," Kate said and laughed.

"Well you always were stupid," her father's voice cut across her laughter, killing it dead. "Now Elizabeth, she'll go far,"

"Oh you're leaving?" Krysten said to Elizabeth.

"No. I work locally. I won't commute like Kate. God what a waste of money," Elizabeth said. "I have better things to spend my money on,"

"Like clothes?" he asked her.

"Yes," Elizabeth sat forward so that the front of her dress fell open. All he saw was bony ribs. Mrs Bromham got up. She beamed a smile. Elizabeth was getting on well with Kate's friend.

"I'll go and make that tea. Coffee," and she swept out the door. Elizabeth smiled at him in what she believed an alluring manner. He clenched his teeth before he'd gag. He sat back against the sofa and put his hands in his lap.

"Clothes are a necessity, nothing else," he said in an off hand manner. "It's the person inside that is far more interesting. My friend's wife buys mine,"

"She has very good taste," Elizabeth gushed. She ran a finger over his sleeve.

"She's Chinese. She picked Kate's suit," he told her. Elizabeth's face fell.

"Yes, well, a bit loose, but then Kate prefers clothes like that, covers all that fat," she sneered. "Not that she has any interest in clothes, of course,"

Krysten's eyes narrowed. Mr Bromham suddenly got up, muttered something about his car and left the room. Kate's spirits sank like a stone. She knew what was coming next. Any minute now her mother would reappear demanding she help her, leaving Elizabeth with Krysten. Kate went tense, waiting for the inevitable. Sitting next to her she could feel that Krysten was just as tense. Although he could feel her tension he was actually trying to keep his temper. He gritted his teeth to stop himself getting up and leaving.

Then, as if on cue, Mrs Bromham reappeared. "Kate, dear, can you come and help me with the tea," she said. "Make the coffee for your friend,"

Kate looked at Krysten. He saw the resigned look and heard her mutter something rude as she got to her feet. It was obviously an old scenario. They must have done this a thousand times. Kate followed her mother out the door.

"Did you have a nice holiday?" Elizabeth asked him.

"Excuse me?" that took him off guard.

"Well I presume you met Kate on holiday. At least we thought she was going on holiday but we didn't receive a postcard. At least you look well. I expect she stayed in doors," Elizabeth said and sniffed her disapproval.

"I'm always well. We did meet on holiday and we went out when it was fine but usually we stayed in bed," he said.

"Kate's always in bed, such a lazy cow," she was snide now. "What do you do for a living?"

"Oh this and that, travelling mostly, killing time," his irony was lost on her.

Elizabeth slid off the arm onto the sofa and sidled up to him, cuddled up next to him, she laid her hand on his sleeve and looked at him with her most alluring expression. He almost burst out laughing. It was so absurd.

"Tell me," she breathed. "What do you see in Kate? She is the most boring person I know. I would think someone like you would need someone much more exciting than her,"

"Would you? You should get out more. Kate isn't boring, she's alive and fun with a spirit of adventure, willing to try anything," Krysten told her.

"Willing? Oh yes, she willing all right. Willing to have most of the men in the street. And then Alan. Positively threw herself at him. Didn't stand a chance," Elizabeth said in a scathing tone.

"Like you're doing now?" he asked.

"Pardon?" Elizabeth was thrown.

"Throwing yourself at people," he explained.

"I don't know what you mean," she became indignant and then coy.

He removed her hand and virtually threw it at her. "Oh don't play the innocent with me. I've been kicking around this world for far too long to be taken in by a woman on the make. Most have more subtlety,"

"Why you... what has she been saying? I bet she's spun you some line about us. She brings shame onto this family and we have to put up with it!" she spat out the words, relishing her role. "I never bring my friends home, I'm too ashamed,"

"You should be! This pathetic seduction act? You're transparent Elizabeth, like ice and twice as cold!" he said coldly.

"Well of all the... You come here, you make eyes at me and then when we're alone you insult me," Elizabeth started.

"I haven't even started on the insults. But even if I was blind I wouldn't make eyes at you. You're as alluring as a crocodile!" he retorted.

"How dare you!" she snarled. He grabbed her wrist before she slapped his face.

"Oh I dare. I've met your sort too often. Make very good prostitutes actually," he threw her hand back at her. She heaved herself off the sofa and flounced out the room, her heavy stomping up the stairs clearly heard. He sat in silence waiting for someone to return.

After about half a hour Kate came in. She looked round in surprise. He sat on the sofa, hands in his lap, looking into space. Elizabeth was nowhere to be seen.

"Where's Elizabeth?" she asked handing him a cup of black coffee.

"Upstairs. Dented ego," he said. She looked at him with a questioning look. He stared back innocently. Kate sat down next to him.

"What did you do?" she asked with a sigh.

"Nothing," he replied and sipped the coffee.

Her mother came in with cake. She too looked round for Elizabeth. She looked at Thunder and then at Kate with a frown.

"Gone upstairs," Kate said. Mrs Bromham sat in her chair. She ate her cake and drank her tea in silence looking at the door. The clock ticked ominously loud on the mantelpiece. Eventually she turned to Krysten.

"What do you do for a living?" she asked.

"Travelling, selling mostly," he replied.

"Which firm do you work for?" she asked.

"I'm freelance. I work for they who pay," he said. Kate smiled at this.

"Sounds interesting,"

"Deathly boring," he replied.

"Being with Kate must be a change for you then," she replied tartly.

"Oh Kate can be exciting when the situation warrants," he replied.

"Really? I'd never have guessed," she lapsed into silence.

Krysten could see why Kate withdrew. Being an intelligent person unable to communicate with morons would be enough to make anyone retreat. Mr Bromham came in. Mrs Bromham gestured to Kate to follow her out to the kitchen. Kate went with a sigh.

"Why do you insult your daughter?" Krysten asked him.

"Pardon?" he was taken aback.

Mrs Bromham came in with a cup of tea and plonked it on the table, slopping it in the saucer. Mr Bromham looked irritated but said nothing. Perhaps, in a household of women, he had retreated behind a wall of insults. Krysten looked at him without pity. All he saw was a spineless man trapped in a miserable existence. Kate came in with cake on a plate which she handed to her father with a smile. He looked up at her, a suspicious look on his face and then snatched it out of her hand. She returned to her place next to Thunder with a resigned look and sat in silence, arms across her waist defensively. Thunder narrowed his eyes as he sipped his coffee. He suddenly felt oppressed, the air had chilled. Mr Bromham ate his cake noisily and slurped his tea. Mrs Bromham looked at him with ill concealed loathing.

"Krysten is a traveller," Mrs Bromham him. "He sells things,"

"Really? Where have you travelled to? Scotland? Manchester?" Mr Bromham said, the sneer clearly visible.

Kate turned her head away and closed her eyes against the threatening tears. She had never felt such humiliation; they really were the pits today. Oh dear god why did I do this? she asked herself. This is purgatory.

"Australia, New Zealand, Africa, South America, China, Egypt, America, Japan, Europe, Canada. I've been to every continent. I was in Cairo recently killing time before coming back to England," Krysten said ticking them off on one hand. He looked at Mr Bromham steadily. To his surprise the man suddenly looked interested.

"I've always wanted to travel but mother doesn't like flying or foreign food or foreigners," he said wistfully. Kate suddenly felt sorry for her father.

"Nasty smelling places. And the heat. Disgusting," Mrs Bromham said and ate some cake.

"Did you take any photos?" Mr Bromham asked him.

"Didn't have the time," Krysten said. Kate smiled. He could hardly take photos of his latest victim or the building he was about to blow up!

"That's a shame. I would have liked to have seen some photos. Perhaps, if you came again, to see..." his voice died as Mrs Bromham sniffed loudly with disdain. His belligerent look returned.

"Oh I'll come and see Kate again," Krysten said.

"Oh yes, Kate. Travelling. Always wanted to travel," Mr Bromham lapsed into silence.

Mrs Bromham gave her husband a filthy look and then turned to Thunder with a smile. It reminded him of Elizabeth. "Where will you go tonight?" she asked. "Kate doesn't know any night clubs. You'd do better asking Elizabeth. Kate doesn't dance. Too clumsy,"

"Kate and I are going for a meal," he said. "We'd better be going, Kate, you promised to show me round,"

They quickly left the room. He waited in the hallway while Kate got their coats. Elizabeth suddenly appeared on the stairs. She was dressed in tight ski pants and a black polo neck jumper designed to show off her slimness. She reminded Thunder of a stick insect.

"Going so soon? Kate bored you already?" Elizabeth said draping herself over the banister.

"No. Only empty people like you bore me," Krysten retorted.

"You must be very boring then, no one finds me boring," Elizabeth replied

"Even prostitutes get boring if you visit them enough, so I'm told," he replied.

Kate returned with the coats, smiled at Elizabeth who scowled back.

"Lets go, the air has turned suffocating," he said to her.

"If I run into Alan, shall I give him your love?" Elizabeth asked. Kate smiled in a smug way. It perturbed Elizabeth. She had never seen her sister look so smug.

"Oh, yes. Why not. Bring him home too. Krysten would love to meet him," Kate said and went out the door.

"Yes, him I'd really like to meet!" Krysten told her and followed Kate.

Elizabeth went back up the stairs, a worried look on her face. Now what could they mean? She would have to hatch something with Alan. Or her mother. Or both. She wanted to hurt Kate so badly, it gave her a pain. She wanted to make him eat his words as well. No one treated her like that and got away with it.

As they walked up the road Kate was acutely aware of the flickering curtains. Krysten, on the other hand, walked with ease and confidence caring little for the stares. He tucked her hand under his arm.

"Is your family like that all the time or was I being honoured today?" Thunder asked.

"I've never seen them so bad. Oh Elizabeth was her normal self but my parents were on truly bad form. God only knows what's going on," Kate said.

"You should have left a long time ago, Kate. But now, you will do," he held her hand and together they walked away.

Kate started talking about her family, those she knew. "Great Aunt Kitty was different. She and my grandmother were twins. Apparently they didn't like my mother and my parents had to wait until grandmother died before getting married,"

"Sounds like your aunt had taste at least," he muttered.

Kate threw him a sideways look but he looked innocent enough. "Aunt Kitty always said my mother killed grandmother. The dates tell me that my mother was pregnant when she got married and I guess that killed grandmother. I was named after aunt Kitty, the society belle but I'm hardly that," Kate said.

"Try looking from my angle," he replied quietly.

Kate stood next to him and looked in the same direction. "No, all I see is the gas works," she said finally. He laughed and put his arms round her. A couple walked past and then stopped.

"I thought that was you, Kate. You look different," the woman said.

"Hello Mrs Goodman. How are you?" Kate suddenly went coldly polite. Thunder could feel her coldness. He dropped his arms. Suddenly she looked at her watch. "Is that the time? We must be off," She marched Krysten off without a word. He marched along until they were virtually out of sight then he stopped, abruptly.

"Are you ashamed to be seen out with me?" he asked.

"No. That's my mother's friend. It will be out on the grapevine quicker than rain. Her and Elizabeth could blab for the world," Kate replied. "I have no doubt that Elizabeth is planning even now how to wrestle you away from me,"

"She'll fail," he muttered.

"But there are others," Kate pointed out.

"Would they carry me through back streets with a bullet in my leg? Let me bleed all over their trousers? Find breakfast at 6.30 in the morning? Kick some goon in the balls to protect me? Hardly!" he said seriously.

Kate looked at him steadily. "Probably not," she admitted

"I trust you not to put a knife in my back, verbally or for real, or desert me at the first sign of trouble. You don't care if you break a finger nail or whether you've been living in one pair of trousers for days because your clothes are stuck in a flat somewhere,"

"I don't have nails to break," Kate started. Thunder threw her a look.

"Where's the nearest pub, I want to be on show," he laughed.

"Bloody exhibitionist!" and she lead the way to a pub.

The barman recognised Kate. They went and sat in a corner so that they could see the bar. After a while a noisy group came in, Elizabeth among them. Someone noticed Kate and pointed her out to Elizabeth. Elizabeth laughed out loud, the group went silent. It was so obviously stage managed, Krysten had to smile.

"That's my sister's latest exploit. Mind you he is a hunk, can't think what he's doing with her," Elizabeth said loudly. Someone made a comment that made them laugh. Kate looked away. Krysten looked from one to the other and wondered if they really were sisters; they were so different.

When he went to the bar one of the men in the group came up to him, turning him round by his shoulder. "What are you doing with our Kate?" he asked.

Krysten looked coldly at him and then at the hand on his shoulder. The man removed his hand. "Your Kate? Is she? Yours I mean? I don't think so!"

He looked Thunder up and down in disgust. "You think you're so smart with your designer clothes and your money but Kate always returns to where she belongs,"

"In the gutter with the likes of you?" Krysten said coldly. The man blinked rapidly at the menace hidden there. "I don't think so!" the voice suddenly dropped in volume, the menace barely hidden. The man backed away and returned to Elizabeth's side. Krysten curled a lip in disdain and returned to Kate. They would have to do better than that!

"What did Mike want?" Kate asked him.

"Doing Elizabeth's dirty work. Hiding the real whore," his voice was cold. He felt angry. He looked at Elizabeth, draping herself over one man and then another. "If she hasn't had every one of them I'm going senile in my old age,"

Kate looked at the group, one by one. She looked at Krysten, her face had gone white. She looked sick. "Can we go? I feel sick," she said in a small voice.

"Where to?" he asked.

"Anywhere. Away from this shit hole," she said acidly. They drank their drinks and left. At the door Kate turned back. "Elizabeth try not to be late home. You know what mother says: if you're not in bed by ten, go home!" she said loudly. The pub fell silent. A few people snickered. Elizabeth looked daggers at her as they left the pub.

They went for a meal returning to the house about eleven. As they walked up the road Alan came out of the alleyway. He'd been tipped off by Elizabeth and had been waiting in the alleyway for them. He stepped out in front of them, frowned at Thunder as a vague memory stirred and then looked at Kate. She looked so different, so relaxed and happy, he was stunned.

"I want to speak to Kate," he finally said.

"I thought Kate had told you to get lost," Thunder said.

"I don't know who you think you are pal, but Kate is MY girlfriend," Alan tried to appear threatening by standing close to Thunder. He failed. Thunder looked unperturbed.

"I have nothing to say to you Alan. I've told you it's over," Kate said.

Alan swung round to Kate. "You was going away to think about it,"

"Well I've thought. Get lost!" Kate started to walk away.

Alan grabbed her arm. "Not so fast. I deserve some kind of explanation," he said, stepping away from Thunder, now forgotten. No one dumped him without a good explanation and another man wasn't a good enough excuse.

Kate wrenched her arm out of his grasp. "I would have thought Worthing was a good enough reason!" she snapped at him. He blinked several times, opened his mouth but nothing came out. "Don't bother to deny it. So who was she? This time? You really are a piece of shit Alan. Well I've had enough. Get lost! Is that clear enough? Or perhaps you'd like me to write it across the sky!" Kate blazed at him and then briskly walked away.

Alan looked at her stunned. How did she know about Worthing? She'd gone to Brighton. He started to follow her. Thunder's hand on his chest stopped him. He took Alan by the arm and propelled him down the alleyway.

"Now. Lets make this very clear. I don't want to have to repeat myself. Kate has made her decision. Get. Over. It!" Thunder's voice was very precise. "Move on to the next woman who's stupid enough to believe your lies. Just stay away from Kate," Thunder pushed him away.

Alan took a step back and looked at Thunder. "Or what?" he retorted. "You'll do what?" he sneered. He laughed. "You? What will you do with your designer suit? You wouldn't want to get it dirty," he taunted contemptuously.

"This designer suit will still kick your arse without getting it creased," Thunder muttered through clenched teeth.

"Yeah right!" Alan sneered.

Thunder suddenly took him by the throat and slammed him

against a wall. Alan's eyes bulged, his back exploded in pain. Thunder's face was very close to his. Alan looked at him, saw the deadly expression and felt his knees start to sag. The fear was suddenly very real, Thunder could smell it, his nose twitched.

"Now," Thunder started very softly. "I really don't like repeating myself. Kate knows about your little trip to Worthing with the blond tart. She has told you her decision, given you the latest reason why. She could give you a whole catalogue of reasons. She hasn't! Do yourself a very, big, favour and piss off! She isn't going to change her mind, take you back or put up with this fucking crap any longer!" his voice gradually rose until the last sentence punctured Alan's consciousness like a hammer. Thunder let go of his throat and took a step backwards. He looked at Alan with an icy expression so that he was left in no doubt. "If I have to come back to this... conversation," he said the word with distaste "I promise I will not be so... accommodating," he paused. "Now. Do you understand? Is that clear enough?"

Alan held his throat, his eyes never left Thunder, he was mesmerised by the man, his presence, his supreme self containment.

"Well?" Thunder's voice sounded loud in the quiet of the night.

"Yes," Alan said nervously. "I understand,"

"Get this very clear. If you even think about bothering Kate. Contacting her. Or going anywhere near her. I will be back. And next time we won't talk. And I won't be wearing a suit, designer or otherwise," Thunder said concisely. The point rammed home, he turned on his heel and walked away.

Alan leaned against the wall and then slid down, his knees finally giving way. Never, in all his life, had he ever been so scared, by anyone, by so much menace. And he knew that he never, ever, wanted to be so scared, ever again. Once he had recovered his composure he quickly made his way home, through the alleyway from Kate's road, resolving to forget her. Just swallowing, doing up his top button or tying his tie a bit too tight reminded him of that resolve. Then he would put a hand to his throat and hear Thunder's voice in his ear.

CHAPTER EIGHTEEN

Thunder walked up the road. Kate was waiting at the gate for him. She looked annoyed. He smiled at her. Her eyes narrowed, thoughtfully and then she turned up the path to the front door. There was no need to speak about it. Both had achieved what they had wanted to achieve. When they got into the hall Mrs Bromham was waiting.

"Did you see Elizabeth?" she asked.

"She was with the usual crowd," Kate replied.

"Oh that's good, they'll look after her," she replied and went upstairs.

"I'll bet," Krysten muttered and followed Kate up the stairs to her room.

The room was spartan, white walls, no pictures, cream carpet, white furniture, shelves filled with books. A kettle, tea and cups in one corner and TV in another. There were no toiletries on the dressing table. Krysten looked in the wardrobe. There were several pairs of jeans, a couple of skirts, some sensible blouses, a coat, some flat shoes and not much else. The chest of drawers was much the same. Everything was in drab browns and dull greens with oddments of black or navy. He slammed the last drawer shut.

Kate was sat on the bed watching him. "As Elizabeth rightly said I have no interest in clothes," she said. He said nothing.

"This reminds me of the Isle of Wight," he said. "Only it's me who's nervous,"

Kate looked at him with a withering look and mouthed something he couldn't make out. They had some coffee, watched some TV and then went to bed. Thunder slept on the spare from under the bed.

At one o'clock Elizabeth did her usual returning home routine and woke the entire household. Mr Bromham stood on the landing and shouted down the stairs at Elizabeth who shouted back. Mrs Bromham came on to the landing and started shouting at Mr Bromham who shouted at her. He returned to the bedroom, slamming the door. Mrs Bromham thumped downstairs. Her and Elizabeth could be heard laughing in the kitchen. Thunder sighed and counted - loudly - to ten. Suddenly he put on the light.

"Right that's it. Pack a bag, we are leaving. I can't stand this anymore," he said.

"We can't leave now. Where will we go?" Kate hissed at him.

"A hotel would be preferable to this!" he hissed back.

"You won't find a hotel open to take guests at this hour! We're not in London. You'll have to put up with it until the morning," Kate told him. She turned off the light.

He grunted and lay there muttering obscenities in every language he knew. "I can hear you," Kate said quietly. He lowered his voice but continued to mutter. Kate smiled in the darkness.

The next day, after they had breakfast, and back in her room, he told her to pack a bag while he rang for a taxi. Elizabeth met him on the landing.

"Look Krysten, we got off to a bad start. Let me make it up to you. Come into my room, I don't want Kate to get the wrong idea," she said. He threw her a withering look. "Well suit yourself. You don't know what you're missing. Better than that fat cow any day,"

Suddenly he grabbed her arm. She giggled. When he put a hand to her throat and she hit the wall the giggling died. She thrilled at his strength and shivered in anticipation. She licked her lips and felt aroused. His face hardened to cold hatred.

"I'm getting a little tired of this crap, so I'll keep it simple so you'll understand. You're a cheap whore Elizabeth, flaunting your wares like some of the prostitutes I've seen on my travels. Only they were more welcoming. And they cost money. You should charge your customers, not give it away! Fucking you would be like fucking a copse, you're all bones," his voice was cold, hard, hurtful.

She looked at him furious. "I'm better than her! She's ..."

"Worth ten of you. She has something you never will - integrity. And she has morals. You have the morals of an alley cat. You've had more pricks than a dartboard! You keep to your kind and don't aspire to something you can't have!" he stepped away from her.

"You bastard!" Elizabeth screeched at him as he went down the stairs.

"Are you finished Elizabeth?" Kate's voice came from behind her. Elizabeth whirled round.

"He started it. Coming on to me. Tried to rape me. Against the wall," Elizabeth said putting her hands to her throat.

"But that's how you like it Elizabeth. Bit of rough treatment. Up against a wall. Wasn't it an alley last time?" Kate said.

Elizabeth looked at her wide eyed. Thunder crept up a couple of stairs to watch. Kate looked calm; Elizabeth fraught, her confidence was shaken.

"That's when Mike won the best fuck with Elizabeth contest," Kate said. "You're called the bike for a good reason,"

Elizabeth looked furious. "Very funny," she muttered. "Course you..."

Kate cut her off. "You think that someone like Krysten would dirty his hands on a little slut like you? Think again! He has better taste,"

"Is that why he's with you?" Elizabeth sneered and then laughed, a cackle, leaning towards Kate, her face a jeer.

"You fucking bitch!" Kate's voice was low. Suddenly her fist shot out and hit Elizabeth full in the face. Elizabeth's hand flew to her face as her body flew backwards. She hit the wall and bounced. Kate's fist connected with her face again and back she went towards the wall. Again she bounced back. Kate grabbed her by the hair with one hand and the throat with the other. She pulled her forward. Elizabeth let out a scream. Blood was pouring from her nose and one eye was going to have a nasty bruise by tea time. Thunder got to his feet, ready to break it up. Kate twisted the hair round until it was taunt, Elizabeth started to whimper.

"If you ever speak to me again I'll rip out every nail and puck out every hair on your body! With a pair of tweezers!" Kate said coldly. "Now get lost Elizabeth. I don't want to see your ugly skinny carcass again!"

She pushed her sister away forcefully. Elizabeth fell with a sob to the floor in a heap looking up at Kate with fear. This was a different person. She would never be the underdog again. Kate stood over her.

"Are you still here?" she asked quietly. Elizabeth scrambled away into the bathroom.

Thunder stood near her and tentatively put his hand out. At his touch she whipped round. He recoiled. Her fists were ready. Not fleeing, now she was fighting. She saw him and relaxed. He put his arms round her and she slumped against him, suddenly shaking.

"Go and get packed. I'll get a taxi," he said. She nodded and went into her room. He went downstairs and rang for a taxi. Within fifteen minutes they were gone.

They went to a hotel out of town. Kate couldn't face meeting anyone she knew. Thunder booked them in as Mr and Mrs Brown. Kate curled up on the bed, she noticed nothing. After a while she fell asleep. Thunder spent time on the phone, making various arrangements.

The following day they returned to the house. It was silent. There was a note on her bedroom door. Mr Bromham had gone out for the day. Mrs Bromham and Elizabeth had gone shopping. Thunder refused to say why they were returning to the house. They went into her bedroom.

"Why are we here?" Kate asked for the umpteenth time.

"You are moving out. Today. I'll help you pack. A van will be here about lunchtime. Get some black sacks. I'm going through your clothes. No more crap," he told her. She looked at him stunned but did as he said.

He went through her clothes and most went into the black sacks. She packed her books and other belongings into carrier bags. About two o'clock someone banged on the door. Thunder went downstairs. Kate could hear him talking to someone and then they came upstairs. He was followed into the room by a large man with wild red hair, who filled the door frame.

"This is Liam," Thunder said. "He's a good friend,"

"So this is Kate," Liam said. Kate found herself in a bear hug that felt strangely reassuring.

"Okay, put her down," Thunder said. "I knew this was a bad idea,"

"I'd have been well pissed if you hadn't rung," Liam said. "Where have you been man? That old bag downstairs has been giving me grief about you leaving. She thinks it's my fault. It isn't is it?" Kate liked his accent.

"No. Time to move on," Thunder said.

"I can see why," Liam grinned at Kate. "I found where your friend was staying but by the time I got there he'd gone. I left word with the Chinaman,"

"Kate knows about Cardol. I got the message from Kit. The situation with Palmerston-Smith is sorted. That just leaves me," Thunder said. "You heard of Lowman?"

"Old London heavy. Thug that worked his way up," Liam replied.

"He employs idiots," Kate said acidly and held up her strapped wrist.

"Ah. Didn't think Kit had started hitting women," Liam said.

"That reminds me…," Thunder started.

Kate looked at him sharply. He tried to look innocent. "I know what you meant! I'm not totally stupid!" she retorted.

"Got you sussed pal," Liam said.

"Too clever by half," Thunder said.

Kate looked at them both. Thunder gave Liam some bags of books which he took downstairs. Thunder started moving bags to the landing. Kate stood and watched. After a couple of trips he looked at her still standing there.

"What?" he asked.

"You are so…," she sighed. "Where did you find him?"

"Flat upstairs," Krysten said.

"Shame Elizabeth isn't here," she grinned wickedly "She'd love him!"

"What?" he looked horrified, then started to smile. "Liam'd

give her an education and some," he shook his head. "Doesn't bear thinking about. Lets get out of here. Just tell us what you want to take. You can take this if you like," he indicated the furniture. "Will go in the second bedroom,"

"Second bedroom? Where are we going?" Kate was mystified.

"Somewhere better," was all he would reply.

He continued moving things out onto the landing. Liam appeared and took them downstairs to the van. Once Kate had finished in her room, she went through the house, ending up in the loft where she found old photo albums and a painting of Aunt Kitty.

It took only a couple of hours to pack up the van, including the bags of clothes that Thunder has discarded. Kate had one last walk around the house. Three hours and she was gone; no goodbyes; no notes; no forwarding address; nothing. She felt nothing, there was nothing. Before leaving she dropped her keys on the kitchen table and then she walked out slamming the front door with great satisfaction.

When she got to the van Thunder and Liam were discussing where they are going. Kate directed Liam to some charity shops where Thunder dumped the black sacks. Once this had been done Liam drove out of the town and away. Thunder gave him directions him to a village where he picked up some keys and then down a little country lane to a cottage.

Thunder showed them round. It had been gutted and done up. There was new wiring, central heating, kitchen, bathroom, carpets, shelving, fitted bedrooms and the chimney had been swept so a fire could be lit safely. Thunder was pleased with his new home.

They unpacked the van into the empty cottage and went to the pub. That night they slept in the sleeping bags Liam had brought with him. The next morning a removal van arrived with Thunder's belongings from storage. They spend a week arranging and rearranging furniture and doing all those little things that need doing. As well as spending many hours in the pub. Then Liam returned to London leaving Thunder and Kate to get used to life in the country. A new life together.

Unknown to Krysten and Kate, Kit and Ling, even Sonya, Anna had met Max Cardol. His plan was unfolding nicely. Now to tighten the net.

After Thunder had spoken to Anna in Shaftesbury Avenue she stayed away from her family and Gerrard Street. She spoke little to Sonya even though they shared a flat. She didn't blame anyone but herself. She didn't blame Thunder for not wanting her; she understood all too well that she was not good enough for him. She didn't hate Thunder or even Kate. When Sonya told her about the charity ball she found herself enthralled. She was silent when Sonya told her that Thunder had taken Kate home and had not returned, although he had spoken to Kit. Kit expected him back in London soon. So she didn't know about the cottage or where they had gone.

After moping around the flat for a few days Anna was pleased to get a call from her friend Shelley. They had worked together since Anna first came to London. Shelley had been her first friend outside the family, even the Chinese community. Shelley was a Londoner, tall, willowy thin, with wispy blond hair and a look of fragility that hid a hard heart. She was a mercenary, a fair weather friend who only wanted people who could do things for her, make her look good, further her career, make her dreams come true. Anna was a perfect foil for Shelley's looks. Blond and jet black hair, tall and short, both slim. They complemented each other perfectly and Shelley made sure they were seen in the right places to maximum effect.

So when Shelley phoned to invite Anna to one of her parties, Anna pulled out all the stops. She arrived fashionably late - to maximise the impact. She was met by one of the catering staff who took her coat and handed her a glass of champagne. She drifted about, chatting to this person and that group. There were quite a lot of people she knew. She spotted Shelley with a group on a landing and made her way up the stairs.

She could see that there were a couple of people in the group that she knew. Shelley waved and came over to her. They met at the top of the stairs where they kissed each other on the cheek and exchanged pleasantries. Shelley knew that standing together at the top of the stairs they would make a sensational impact. Anna looked stunning in a scarlet Chinese dress, her long hair twisted back and hanging loose down her back. Shelley was dressed in a long black dress which showed more skin than it actually covered, her blond hair clipped up with a few curls hanging down. Heads turned to stare at them. Only one man in the group Shelley was with seemed oblivious to their effect. He kept his back to them. Shelley took her by the arm and lead her over to the group.

"You must meet my very special guest, Anna. He is simply THE most gorgeous man you will ever meet," she told her. She put Anna at the man's side. "Anna, this is Max,"

He slowly turned round. He was as tall and broad as Thunder but there the similarity ended. His eyes were dark and very intense. You could almost drown in them. He had closely cropped dark hair and looked gorgeous in a tux, bowtie and whiter than white shirt. Down the left side of his face ran a scar from his forehead through his eyebrow across his eye and down his cheek ending at his jaw line. It was a smooth scar and if anything enhanced his looks than detracted from them. He smiled slowly with a coldness that reached out and grabbed her; she was mesmerised, captivated. And suddenly nothing else mattered.

"See? Wasn't I right?" Shelley whispered in her ear.

"You were right," Anna whispered back. Shelley beamed a smile at Max.

Shelley left them together and went off to talk to someone else. For a minute everything stopped and fell silent for Anna as she looked at Max smiling down at her. All thoughts of Thunder were gone. The sounds of the party drifted back.

"Would you like another drink?" he asked. It brought Anna out of her stupor.

"Sorry? Oh yes, I'd like that," she managed to say.

"What would you like?" he asked. His voice was deep, had a slight accent which Anna couldn't place. American? Or something similar? Who cares she thought. A familiar thrill at meeting good looking men went through her. He handed her a glass of champagne. She took it and smiled.

"How do you know Shelley?" she asked.

"Through a mutual friend," he replied.

"Do you live in London?" she asked hopefully.

"For now," he replied.

Safe questions but she could think of nothing else to say. They stood for a few minutes in silence. It felt like hours. She frantically thought of things to say; witty, funny things that would keep him at her side.

"What do you do?" he asked.

"Do?"

"Work,"

"Oh, not a lot. I'm not qualified to do much. I work with Shelley when she needs an extra pair of hands and I sometimes help out in a friend's restaurant," Anna said and then regretted it. It made her look so stupid and useless. A few people went past them, one knocked her in the back, she pitched forward. He caught her and held her close. She looked up at him and shivered. "I was put in service," she said simply and quietly with a hint of irony that was lost on him.

"Service?" he had to bend to hear her.

"Back home. A man put me on the streets to be of service," she said softly.

"You were a prostitute?"

"My family were brought to London by this man," she said.

"Did you have to pay him a lot of money?"

"Nothing,"

"Nothing? That was kind of him,"

"He only wanted my brother's friendship,"

"That must have been painful for you," he said softly.

"We would have given him much more," she admitted bitterly. "But he wanted none of it,"

"Perhaps I can help to ease the pain," he said softly.

Anna smiled at him. "I would like that,"

They found a corner to sit down. Max got a bottle of champagne and kept filling her glass. He drank little, a few sips at most. By the end of the evening he knew everything about her, she knew nothing of him. However she didn't tell him anything about Thunder nor his name. Something kept her silent. At the end of the night he took her home in a cab. They arranged to meet again the following day. Anna went home considerably happier than before.

The next day she dressed with care and made her way to Piccadilly Circus where they had arranged to meet. She stood near the statute of Eros and waited. From a doorway Max watched. He knew he couldn't get to Thunder through the Chinaman, it would have to be through Anna. He hadn't known about the rescue, he assumed Kit and Thunder had worked together years ago. She hadn't spoken much about him last night, but he could wait. He would make use of Anna for now until he got the information he wanted or something else turned up. He walked over to her.

She spun round and her jaw dropped. Last night he had looked gorgeous in a tux, today he wore black - jumper, jeans, leather jacket. Anna wished Thunder could see her with this man, it would make him think twice about rejecting her. And then she forgot about Thunder.

They spent the day at Chessington zoo, returned to London for a meal in the evening. Once over her initial shyness Anna relaxed and enjoyed the day out. Max treated her like a queen.

He got the measure of her that day. She was insecure about herself and when shown even the smallest affection she transferred all her attention, her affection, everything to that person - to the exclusion of everyone else. What he liked, she liked. What he hated, she hated. With a consuming passion. She discarded old favourites, old habits, would even discard her culture if he'd asked, without a thought. Anna was incapable of having an original thought or action. That was why Shelley stayed friends with her; she was so easy to manipulate, to mould. Every thought, every action, every decision had to be created, devised by someone else. Thunder had saved her from squalor; he was a hero, her saviour. He could do no wrong. Until he had rejected her and someone else had picked her up.

Max knew when he looked into her eyes, when he kissed her, that she was his for the taking. She would betray Thunder without a qualm and cheer him on while he destroyed her former all-consuming love. The thought of destroying Thunder thrilled Max more than anything else. It was going to be so easy. This time. Thunder had walked right into it. By rejecting Anna's love he had made himself vulnerable. Max was going to make sure that he had the advantage this time.

He took her home in a cab, his arm round her. She was just the sort of girl he liked: pretty, petite, brainless, obliging. He kissed her briefly.

"We could have lunch," he suggested. Her face fell. "Or we could have a meal at my flat. If you like," he added. Her face lit up. "I'll pick you up at Marble Arch near the cinema, at six thirty," He kissed her again, taking time.

She stood on the pavement and waved at the receding taxi. He waved once and then turned away. Anna went into the flat feeling elated. In the sitting room Sonya sat waiting. Lee, the Chinese boy that had been chasing Anna for months was also waiting. He had been there for hours, moaning about Anna to Sonya. Sonya was therefore not in a very good mood.

"Where have you been?" he demanded before Sonya could say a word.

"Somewhere nice," Anna replied smiling sweetly.

"Who with?" he demanded. Sonya watched him advance on Anna who was far too wrapped up in her own world to notice. He stood in front of her. She looked at him with a frown. He was spoiling her day.

"Someone far nicer than you!" Anna yelled at him.

"I've a right to know," he shouted back at her.

"Right? You have no rights. You never did and you never will! Just get lost!" and she flounced off to her room.

Sonya folded her arms and put on her most annoyed look. Lee looked at her. "I did tell you. Several times," she told him. "Go home Lee," she said with a sigh.

"She's messing me about," he moaned.

Sonya sighed. Stupid boy. "She will never look on you favourably if all you do is shout at her," she said firmly.

"It's that bloody man!" he said.

"This is a new man," Sonya said. "Someone who doesn't shout at her or try to make her do what she doesn't want to,"

"Couldn't you talk to her?" he suddenly asked in a little boy voice.

Sonya cursed in Chinese. He looked startled. "You're pathetic. Get lost. Grow up. Piss off!" Sonya started sarcastically and ended up yelling at him. He left looking miserable and dejected. Sonya swore some more.

The next evening Anna went to Marble Arch. Max arrived in a cab. He had been playing squash. They went to his flat. It was the top floor of a converted Victorian house in a street full of the same houses. Anna could almost smell the wealth here. She looked at the houses with interest as they pulled up. He led her in and left her in the sitting room while he went for a shower. He came back dressed in just a towelling robe. She was looking at the ornaments and books on the unit.

"Now what do you want to do? We could have dinner here or go out somewhere," he asked her. He stroked her arm.

"Whatever you want to do," Anna said turning to him.

"I know what I'd like to do, but it's early," he said quietly. She smiled up at him. He kissed her, putting his arms around her and holding her tight. She virtually melted into him. He lead her to the sofa and pulled her down. She didn't resist. He kissed her, she responded. He started to undress her, she didn't stop him. They continued kissing, he held her against him.

Suddenly she wiggled away from him and sat on the floor between his knees. She pulled open the robe and started kissing his chest. He didn't touch her, laid his hands on the sofa as she worked her way down his chest to his stomach. She undid the tie, pulled open the robe and started kissing him again working down from his stomach. He put his head back against the top of the sofa and closed his eyes as she kissed and caressed him.

She pulled off her trousers and climbed onto his lap. He groaned softly as he entered her. She put her hands behind his head and pulled him to her. He pulled off her top and started kissing her breasts. He put his arms round her hips, pinning her to him. Suddenly he moved forwards, falling to his knees, lowering her to the floor. They made love wildly, rolling across the floor, clinging to each other. Anna sank her nails in his back making him gasp, with pleasure more than pain. She wound her legs around him, he thrust deeper and deeper, the sweat poured off them until they collapsed into a heap.

He lay across her, pinning her to the floor. Her hair was spread out on the floor. He groaned as she stroked his back. Immediately she put her hands on the floor. He leaned up on one elbow and looked down at her. She looked afraid.

"I don't mind," he said quietly. "I enjoyed it,"

"But I hurt you," she said in a timid voice.

"It was a pleasurable pain," he said.

"I didn't mean to hurt you," she said.

"You didn't. I need another shower," he got up. She curled up in a ball on the floor. "Why don't you come and wash my back," She followed him into the bathroom.

She carefully washed his back with a sponge and then his chest. He stood letting the water pour over him while she washed him. Then he washed her. He put the robe on and gave her one to wear too. They returned to the sofa. Whatever he suggested she did. He suggested tea, she jumped up and went into the kitchen returning later with a tray with tea things on it. He found something to cook and they ate in silence. She washed up, poured him a brandy and then snuggled up against him, before falling asleep.

He watched her sleep, like a child, and marvelled at the innocence there, particularly after her earlier actions. She was a child of the street still. Old habits were hard to break. He carried her to bed. She woke as he got in beside her. She stroked his chest, his shoulders, she kissed his neck and then his cheek.

"How did you get this scar?" she asked.

"In a fight. It was a long time ago," he said without thinking.

"My friend has many scars. He has had many fights," suddenly she clamped her hand over her mouth and looked at him in horror. It was the first time she had thought of Thunder. "I haven't thought of him for days," she cried.

"Good!" he pulled her to him kissing her. She melted against him, ever willing, ever pliant. He pulled her onto him. She straddled him. He lay back with a smug look of satisfaction. As she kissed him, moved on top of him, giving him pleasure, he knew he had her right where he wanted her. The sex being good was a bonus. He had to admit that she aroused him like no one ever had. Later, as she lay in his arms he thought again of Thunder. It wouldn't be long before she would betray him. In the meantime he would enjoy her body and ever-ready desire.

Max treated Anna like royalty. He was always kind to her, never shouted at her, took her to expensive restaurants, gave her presents. It wasn't very long before she was spending all her time at his flat. She cooked his meals; washed and cleaned the flat; waited on him hand and foot. She had become a very willing slave, who put him first and foremost.

Plus. She was always ready for sex no matter what the time or place. He could take her at any time, day or night, she woke at his touch, or would wake him. She was as willing in the flat as outside, the danger of being caught only added to the enjoyment; like when he had her against a wall in an alleyway just yards from a busy street. He felt very satisfied with this life.

CHAPTER NINETEEN

Two months later Anna simply disappeared. She had virtually stopped living at the flat for the last two weeks and left only a few clothes. Sonya and Shelley hadn't seen or heard from her in days. When she had been gone two weeks Shelley started to worry. She couldn't find Max either and was now ringing Sonya daily. Sonya tried not to worry but something niggled her.

One day Sonya met Kit in Gerrard Street. He dragged her up to the flat. Sonya's heart sank as this meant an interrogation. Ling sat in one chair. Sonya made herself comfortable on the sofa. Kit paced the floor like a caged animal. Suddenly he stopped and stood in front of her.

"Who the hell is this man?" he demanded.

"You're been talking to Lee," Sonya replied and then turned to Ling. "That's how he is. All demands. No polite conversation. No normal speaking. Just screaming and shouting and demands. It gives me a headache,"

"What's his name Sonya?" Ling asked.

"Max. That's all I know. I know nothing else about him. Anna wasn't exactly forthcoming," Sonya replied.

"Max? Max who?" Kit demanded.

Sonya looked at him. Ling sighed. He had been like this for days and getting worse.

"Sonya's just said she doesn't know," Ling said to Kit.

"Anna met him at a party. One of those Shelley specials. Lots of people, no one knows who they are," Sonya said.

"Where's he from?" Ling asked.

"America, I believe," Sonya said.

"Where does he live?" Kit asked.

"London," Sonya replied.

"Can't you be more specific?" Kit asked with a sarcastic tone.

"No. Somewhere in London. Victorian houses converted into flats. Lots of money. And before you get jumpy that's all Anna said. Somewhere in London where it's rich," Sonya said.

Kit looked exasperated. Ling looked up at the ceiling. She felt tired. "Kit, Anna can look after herself. She is a big girl now,"

"Anna will come back when he returns to America," Sonya said.

"She might go with him," Kit said.

"Doubtful. Anna is a whore. He won't take her back with him," Sonya stated.

"She is not a whore!" Kit's voice went up several decibels. Ling winced. Sonya could be so blunt sometimes, but she was right.

Sonya gave her brother a withering look. "Kit, Anna has always been a whore. That nice man who took her for a holiday on his yacht? That nice old man who bought her diamonds and pearls? That nice man who wanted to buy her a flat? You think they did this out of the goodness of their hearts? They did it for sex. They give her nice things and they get to fuck her! Nice young Chinese girl who will do anything for money. That's being a whore! I may not have been on the street but I know a whore when I see one!" Sonya said brutally.

"My sister is not a whore," Kit said hollowly.

"Suit yourself. You always was blind when it came to Anna. You should have left her in that whore house in China," Sonya and Kit stared at each other, neither wanted to back down.

"What if Anna doesn't return, Sonya? What then?" Ling asked quietly. "I know you're worried Sonya, you have that look about you,"

"You and that bloody all seeing eye," Sonya said bitterly. She looked at Ling who didn't flinch. "Good luck to her. If he takes her back with him, all well and good. It would be the making of her,"

"We'll see," Kit said and slammed out the door downstairs to the street.

Sonya folded her arms and looked belligerent. Ling stayed calm for a few minutes and then her temper snapped. She leapt up and let out a tirade of Chinese at Sonya. Sonya leapt to her feet and answered her. Ling let loose a string of accusations and recriminations. Sonya answered likewise. Soon both were arguing, screaming and shouting at each other, you could hear it in the street. Kit returned and soon he was joining in. The three of them screamed at each other for several minutes and then suddenly they stopped. Ling stormed into the kitchen, Sonya out the door to the street, Kit sat down and picked up the paper. He shook it several times, folding and unfolding it several times, but he read not a word.

A week later Anna still had not contacted Sonya or Shelley or reappeared. Shelley was now ringing twice a day. She was calling all her contacts to try and find Max. Even the 'mutual friend' who had introduced them didn't know where he was. Perhaps he'd gone back to America? So where was Anna? Sonya tried to give an air of nonchalance, as if she wasn't worried but she didn't fool Ling. Kit was virtually climbing the walls and driving Ling to distraction. Even if he went out to work all day he would ring two or three times to see if Ling had heard.

One day Liam rang Kit. Ling started to listen to the answer machine and then on impulse picked up the phone. Liam was struck dumb.

"Hello Liam, this is Ling. I've been listening to your message. Thank you for trying to find Thunder's friend. We have a bit of a crisis here. Anna has disappeared with an American man. You don't think they could be one and the same man, do you? Or am I being paranoid? Anna's boyfriend, Max comes from America and people think he has gone back," she told him. There was silence. "Liam? Are you still there? I'm sorry to bother you, but could you speak to Thunder? Kit is being pig headed about contacting him. Hello?"

"I'm sorry, you took me by surprise. I didn't expect anyone to answer. I'm sorry but I don't know who you are," Liam said.

"I'm Ling, Kit is my husband. He's Thunder's contact," she explained.

"Oh you mean the Chinaman. That makes sense. I suppose. I'm confused. Who's Anna?" Liam said.

"Kit's sister. Thunder knows her," Ling replied.

"Oh. Right. I don't know Thunder," Liam said.

"Thunder is... Thunder," Ling trailed off. She didn't know Thunder's various names or even his real name.

Suddenly it dawned on him. "Oh you mean Krysten. Dear God. How many names has that man got? If I find his friend I'll ring. I don't know if he's the same man as Anna's boyfriend. I'll speak to Krysten," he rang off and then grinned. "Your secrets are all coming out pal," He rang Krysten.

They talked for a few seconds. "Well you didn't ring to pass the time of day. So what's up?" Krysten said.

"I was leaving a message on the Chinaman's answer machine when Ling answered. Took me by surprise, I can tell you. Your secret's out. That's where you were hiding. Thunder. I've heard of him. One nasty dude, not to be tangled with. If I'd known it was you I would have offered my talents," Liam said and laughed.

"Oh," Krysten was speechless. "Shit!" Liam laughed louder. "What did Ling tell you?"

"Apparently Anna's disappeared with some American by the name of Max. They're worried sick but Kit won't contact you," Liam said becoming serious.

"What?" Krysten yelled. "Oh fucking hell! Shit! I don't believe it! Oh Christ!"

"Now you're used all the usual words, what do you want me to do?" Liam said with a grin.

"Nothing. I'll ring Kit. Shit!" he was furious.

"Ling wonders if your friend is the same as Anna's man," Liam said.

"What? Oh..." he trailed off. He thought furiously. "What did she say his name was?" he suddenly asked in a small voice.

"Max. American. They think he's gone back to America," Liam replied.

"No way. He came to do a job, he won't turn tail just because he can't find me. Oh shit! I can't believe he would stoop so low. Actually I can believe it. Oh Christ. I'd better ring Kit. Thanks for the call Liam," Krysten said.

"Give my love to Kate," Liam said in a wicked voice.

"What? You bastard!"

Liam gave a wicked laugh and the line went dead.

Krysten phoned Kit but got the answer machine. He tried the restaurant but Kit was out. He left a message for him to ring. Kate had come to the door when she heard him yell and stayed there. She watched him as he cradled the phone in his lap, a thoughtful look on his face, and her heart sank. It could only mean another job. He looked up, saw her watching him, put the phone back on the table and smiled at her.

"Don't come the innocent look with me, it won't wash," she told him.

"Anna's done a runner. She's done it before but this time they are worried. Her new man is called Max," Krysten told her.

"So? Good luck to her. Poor kid. About time she got a break," Kate said.

"Cardol's first name is Max," Krysten said quietly.

"What? Oh. You don't think..." Kate trailed off.

"Ling has the suspicion that they are one and the same and I have to agree it sounds suspiciously like it," Krysten said.

"Well you'd better pack a bag and go and find her then," Kate replied.

"Liam's already trying to find him without success. Why would I be any more successful?" Krysten asked.

"Because you know him better than Liam," Kate replied.

"Liam sends his love," Krysten said with a smile.

"That's nice. He's such a nice man. I keep wondering what would have happened if I'd met him first. Oh well, never mind," she went out leaving him staring and then he started to swear quietly – in several languages.

Kit rang later. Krysten tried to be up beat about things but Kit wasn't having it. He had heard Liam's message and that it had finished abruptly, followed by Krysten's message to ring him. It wasn't hard to work out what had happened.

"So when was she last seen Kit? And who by?" Krysten asked.

"Sonya probably. Her friend keeps ringing Sonya. Sonya is being...,"

"Sonya and pretending nothing's happened," Krysten

interrupted.

Kit didn't answer for a few minutes. "Yes. I'm worried, Thunder. I know Anna's gone off before but this time it feels different,"

"Your trouble is Anna keeps slipping back to old habits. You can't accept it, but she does," Krysten said.

"She is not a whore!" Kit yelled. Krysten jerked the phone from his ear. He swopped ears.

"Fine, you believe that. The rest of us knows different. Where is this friend?" Krysten said.

"I don't know. Sonya would be able to tell you. She's not speaking to me," Kit said and sounded dejected.

"You do surprise me. Sonya not speaking to you. How strange," his sarcasm wasn't lost on Kit who started to curse him in Chinese. "You know I don't know what you're saying, although I can guess. I'll get Liam to talk to her," he said. "As only Liam can," he added in a low voice.

Liam was more than pleased to go and see this girl. He visited Sonya first, behaved impeccably and then went off to see Shelley. A cheap meal, a bottle of wine, some honeyed words as only Liam could speak and Shelley was eager to tell him everything. Liam got what he wanted - in more ways than one - and Shelley got what she wanted - as only a slut would. About midnight Liam left her in bed.

The next day he rang Kit. Got the answer machine. He rang Krysten and got Kate. After several minutes of talk Kate handed the phone over to Krysten.

"Oh you want to talk to me now?" Krysten said.

"You know I like talking to Kate but I thought you might like to know what I found out," Liam said smugly.

"What did you find out?" Thunder said in a tired voice.

"Shelley organised the party for a client to impress his business associates. Basically whore's paradise, lots of willing men and money. Her client asked if she knew an oriental girl for a friend of his who was partial to them. She set up Anna. The 'friend' turned out to be this Max. Shelley is only just short of being a madam, in the whore sense of the word. She sets up girls with rich men for money. She gets a cut, the girl gets well paid, the man gets a beautiful girl. Everyone's happy," Liam said. "If I had money my womanising days would be over,"

"Just as well you don't," Krysten said. "What else?"

"This Max took Anna, spent lots of time and money on her and now she's disappeared. Shelley hopes he's taken her to America. Got all romantic and misty eyed. Load of cobblers," Liam replied. "Now what?"

"Try and find her. Them. Know anyone who can check flights? No on second thoughts forget that. He has his own private jet, if I remember rightly. I'd better come to London. Shit! I promised Kate no more of this," Krysten said and ran his fingers through his hair.

"Kate understands," Liam stated.

"Yeah right. See you," Krysten put down the phone.

Kate dropped a bag at his feet. He looked at her with a quizzical look.

"Well I presume you're going to London," she said. "So I packed a bag,"

"Bit premature," he said.

"Rubbish. You're going, don't deny it," Kate said.

"I hate it when you're right. It makes me feel guilty," Krysten smiled.

"Just find the stupid girl, give her a good slapping, hand her over to Liam to keep amused and come home!" Kate retorted.

"Yes ma'am," Krysten said in his politest voice.

He got to London late afternoon and made his way to Chinatown. Kit was in. He was still annoyed but pleased to see Thunder. They sat down and talked about things. Ling sat in the chair and listened.

"This is no coincidence," Thunder said. "This was set up,"

"That bloody little bitch Shelley no doubt," Kit was annoyed.

"Actually not directly. Cardol was pulling the strings, Shelley was just the puppet," Thunder said calmly.

"I've talked to people. Apparently there was the same man hanging around Chinatown for weeks, when you first appeared but he hasn't been seen for a while," Ling said. Kit threw her a look which she calmly returned. "You've been too annoyed to think straight. Someone had to ask,"

"Any descriptions?" Thunder asked.

"Tall, dressed all in black. Long black leather coat, hat pulled down over his face. One person thought he had a scar on his cheek. He stood in doorways, wandered up and down the streets, didn't buy anything, doesn't seem to take his hands out his pockets even. Did a lot of watching," Ling replied.

"Cardol. It has to be him. I thought I was being paranoid but I felt watched. I should have done some checking," Thunder said.

"You can't check every doorway on every street, you had more important things to do," Ling replied.

"I'll need help this time. I can't do this alone," Thunder said.

"Well I never. The great Thunder needs help," Ling was surprised.

"Very funny. Kate isn't here, I'll make do with Liam," he said.

"Anna has found herself a boyfriend that can appear and disappear at will. A Thunder if you like," Ling said. Thunder frowned at her. "Don't give me that look. It crossed your mind,"

"But you said it," Thunder pointed out.

"It had to be said," Ling said calmly.

Thunder looked at her in silence. Ling returned his stare without hesitation. Kit found himself looking from one to the other waiting for them to look away. When it became obvious that they weren't his patience ran out.

"When you two are quite finished eyeing each other, we have to find Anna," he said.

"I'll contact Liam," Thunder said and moved away.

Unknown to Liam a figure had watched him visit Shelley. He saw Liam go in. He saw them come out. He followed them down the road to the restaurant. He returned to his car parked outside Shelley's bedsit to await their return. He waited while Liam was inside. He saw Liam leave about midnight and walk off down the road. He waited until the lights had gone out in the building and then got out the car. He took a knife from his pocket and easily prised open the front door. He closed it quietly behind himself. He knew which room Shelley lived in. He slowly stepped up the side of the stairs to the first floor and along the landing keeping to the wall. Shelley's door was also easy to prise open. No one stirred, the house remained silent. He removed his coat and hat and crossed to the bed. Shelley had thrown the covers off and was sprawled across it wearing a short nightie. He rolled her over. She moaned and then woke.

"I didn't hear you come in," she muttered.

"That was the general idea," he said quietly. Even through her drunken haze she knew it wasn't Liam but Max.

"Max, this is unexpected," she half sat up, the thin straps fell off her shoulders. She stretched her long legs out down the bed. She could just about make him out in the gloom. "Bored with Anna and come for some superior company?"

"You had a visitor. I had to wait. I don't like waiting," he said.

"You should have rung me. I would have put Paddy off," she said. "I can't see you, I'll put the light on," she got up and crossed to the light switch.

He followed her and as she reached out for the switch grabbed her arm bringing it up behind her back. He pushed her against the wall. He leaned against her. She wiggled against him.

"What did you tell him?" he asked, his voice very low in her ear.

"Nothing," she said quickly. "I know nothing,"

"Just as a reminder, so you don't forget," he kept her pinned to the wall and undid his trousers. She heard the zip.

"Two gorgeous men in one night, it must be my birthday," she muttered.

"Must be," he said. He took her roughly without care. His thrusting pushed her against the wall, harder and harder until she cried out in pain. He ignored her cries, thrusted harder and then finished. She was crying.

"That's a good girl," he said as he kissed her shoulder while doing up his trousers. He let her go. She fell to the floor. He dragged her up by the arm and across the floor. She crawled on to the bed and lay there sniffling.

"What did you tell him?" he asked again.

"Nothing," Shelley said.

He slapped her face and turned her over. Shelley lay waiting. He pulled out his knife and slit the nightie up the back. He pulled out the belt from his trousers.

"What did you tell him?" he repeated.

"Nothing," Shelley repeated.

He brought the belt down across her buttocks. She cried out in surprise. He repeated the question. Shelley kept to her stock reply. He beat her again. He repeated the question. Shelley stayed silent. He beat her again. She cried out in pain. He leaned over her.

"You will tell me," he said. "I don't have time for games,"

"I didn't tell him anything," Shelley cried out.

"Like hell," he said. "You're a slut. A man, a bottle of wine and you'd open your mouth almost as fast as your legs,"

"I don't know anything," she cried.

"Then this will be a little reminder to keep it that way," he stuffed some of the sheet in her mouth and started to beat her in earnest. She tried to squirm away, he held her down by kneeling on her legs. When he stopped he removed the gag. She was crying. Her back and buttocks were cut to ribbons.

He felt an erection and undid his trousers once more. He pulled her to the edge of the bed, knelt down and took her once more. Her fingers curled round some of the sheet. He thrust deeper, she moaned in pleasure. He suddenly felt disgusted that this slut could arouse him. He put his hand against the back of her head and held her head down, her face into the mattress. As he was climaxing she started to struggle so he pushed down harder. Then he heard a little crack and she went limp. He finished, got to his feet and washed himself in the sink. As he passed the bed on the way out he threw the sheet over her, picked up his coat and hat and left. He paused outside the door. The house was still silent. No one stirred, no one heard and if anyone did they would put it down to her normal behaviour. Her sex antics were well known.

It wasn't until later in the day that one of the girls noticed that the curtains were still closed, they hadn't seen Shelley, they hadn't heard Shelley and knocking on her door got no response. The girl called the police. They broke in and found her. In her purse was

Sonya's phone number. The next day the police contacted her and that evening she went to Kit in hysterics. Ling managed to calm Sonya down. Kit phoned the policeman who had left his number with Sonya to find out what had happened. He looked shocked as he put the phone down. Ling and Thunder waited.

"Well? What's happened? Is it Anna?" Ling asked him. Kit slumped against the wall. Ling spoke to him in Chinese. Still he didn't answer.

"For Christ's sake Kit, tell us what's happened," Thunder shook him.

"Shelley's been killed. Broken neck. They don't know if it was rape or just violent sex. They found a used condom but the semen inside her doesn't match," he said in a shocked voice. Thunder stared at him.

"Oh shit," was all Thunder could say.

"Is that it? What if he does that to Anna? This is your fault! You should have faced the bastard years ago!" Kit suddenly blazed at him.

"Kit! That isn't fair," Ling said quietly. "You know why,"

"No I don't!" Kit rounded on his wife. "He never said! He never says anything! He just does things and we have to put up with it. No explanations. No reasons why. He just does what he likes!"

"Kit is right. This is my fault. I should have dealt with Cardol a long time ago. I didn't," Thunder said.

"They want to know who the men were. One of the girls fingered your friend, the Irishman," Kit said.

"I'd better find him before they do," Thunder left.

He arrived at his old address. The place was in darkness. He climbed the stairs to Liam's flat. Thunder knocked on the door and rang the bell. No answer. After a couple of minutes Thunder started to pound on the door. Several minutes later Liam opened the door.

"Why didn't you just break the door down?" he asked.

"I was about to," Thunder went past him up the stairs. He stood in the sitting room. It looked cleaner than it had in a long time. After a few hours in Shelley's hovel Liam had come home and tidied up.

Liam made some coffee. By now Thunder was pacing the floor. Liam watched him and then handed him a cup. Liam sat down and sipped his. Thunder sat down and put his down on the table. Liam looked at him.

"Okay, tell me what's happened. Your face is giving me a headache," Liam said in his normal good natured voice.

"Shelley has been found dead," Thunder stated.

"Oh! And?" he wasn't particularly bothered.

"They found a condom," Thunder started.

"Oh well that puts a different light on things. I'd better give myself up, guilty as charged, use of a condom," Liam said with a laugh.

"This isn't funny Liam. Shelley was killed last night. The girl downstairs has fingered you," Thunder said.

"She never touched me!" Liam laughed and then stopped. Thunder's face was still serious. "Okay. Serious now. I went to see her, took her for a cheap meal, tipped a bottle of wine down her throat, she told me what I wanted to know, I fucked her and came home. I felt so dirty I washed myself and the flat. See?"

"That's all?" Thunder asked.

"You always tell me to protect myself. I did when I fucked her. She wasn't so fussy, if you know what I mean," Liam said and grinned wickedly. Thunder had to smile in spite of himself. "That wasn't too hard, was it?" Liam asked.

"It would seem our Shelley had another visitor after you. What time did you leave?" Thunder asked.

"Midnight. Must have been a late caller or an early bird. What happened?" Liam said.

"Broke her neck during violent sex," Thunder replied calmly.

"Ah well, won't be me. I'm not violent, well not during sex anyway," Liam said with a grin.

"The police have spooked Sonya anyway. She's at Kit's in a right state. Sonya is still convinced that Anna will come walking back with stories of her adventure," Thunder shook his head.

"But you and I know different. Look if he did that to Shelley, what would he do to Anna?" Thunder shrugged. "Shelley said the party was set up by her boss for a client. He had a friend who liked oriental girls, could Shelley line him up with one. Now call me cynical but that sounds just a little too pat. Shelley and Anna have been doing these parties for a long time, they are well known. These girls are whores. No, they're prostitutes, they got paid for these jobs and they got paid well. I was surprised Shelley didn't live in a better pad but hey, who cares. She obviously spent her money on other things. And Shelley had no scruples about telling me about some of the things they got up to. Whatever Kit might think about his sister, she is no sweet angel. Put me off sandwiches, I can tell you!"

"Sandwiches?" Thunder queried.

"Shelley asked me if I had a friend so we could all have a sex sandwich and she didn't mean bread and butter, pal. It was something that Anna had done with two brothers. Shelley wanted to try it," Liam said. Thunder looked stony faced. "Look, Shelley isn't...," Liam stopped and mentally changed tense. "Shelley wasn't worried about Anna. She was pissed off because she wasn't there as well! Shelley didn't care two hoots for Anna. She just wanted some of the fun as well. She used Anna to get what she wanted,"

"So who killed Shelley?" Thunder asked.

Liam threw him a filthy look. "Are you being deliberately dense or what? It's obvious. It has to be this chap. What's his name? Max,"

"Cardol. How does he know where to find Shelley?" Thunder asked.

"Shelley's boss? He's the pimp here. He sets up these little parties. Shelley just provides the girls," Liam suggested.

"We need to speak to the boss then," Thunder said.

"Why not let the police deal with him? I'll go to them, tell them some of the things that she told me and drop him in it. It's the least I could do for Shelley. She wasn't bad as dogs go. Or are you worried they'll arrest me?" Liam said.

"Oh no I doubt they'll arrest you. The semen inside her wasn't the same as that in the condom, so you're off the hook there," Thunder said with a smile.

"Why you bastard!" Liam retorted.

"Well I had to be sure you weren't tying up loose ends for me," Thunder said seriously.

"I'd tell you if I was, but Shelley wasn't a loose end, well not for you anyway, but she obviously was for someone," Liam said.

"Obviously. I couldn't care less about Shelley. I have to find Anna. And then deal with that bastard Cardol," he lapsed into silence. He drank his coffee, Liam drank his. "Oh I nearly forgot. I got a photo of Anna from Kit," he handed it over to Liam. "It's a bit old but she hasn't changed much,"

Liam looked at it quickly and put it in his wallet. Thunder went home after that. Liam promised to ring him at Kit's flat if he came up with anything.

The next morning Liam went to the police and made a statement. He also told them some of the things that Shelley had told him. As he walked away he saw the policemen he had spoken to leaving in a car at speed. He grinned to himself as he walked off, he'd bet his beer money that Shelley's boss would be getting a visit any minute soon.

He spent the afternoon visiting some of his contacts but none of them had come up with anything. His mate Ron thought he had found the location of the Victorian houses but none of them had been rented out in four months, had been sold recently or were up for sale. That meant Cardol must have a base in London or had borrowed one from someone. Liam felt fed up and found himself outside his favourite Irish pub, the Coachmakers, off Marylebone Lane. It took less than a second to go inside.

He greeted Neeve the barmaid who poured him a Murphys. As he stood at the bar waiting he looked round. The pub wasn't very busy, most were regulars, but sat in the corner was a young man and a young Chinese girl. They looked so out of place. Liam went to the gents and took out the photo.

He just stared at it. "I don't bloody believe it," he muttered.

He returned to the bar. Using the mirror running along the back of the bar he watched them. They both looked miserable, hardly spoke to each other, she sat as far away from the man as she could without moving to another table. The young man looked like a greasy spoon; he had greasy hair, earrings and dirty clothes. He looked very uncomfortable and fiddled with a packet of cigarettes continuously. At half past ten they left.

"I'll be back," Liam said quietly to Neeve. She left his pint where it was.

As soon as they were outside he lit a cigarette. They crossed Wigmore Street and went down Marylebone Lane, then down a small alley. Liam slowed down as he walked past. Looking quickly over his shoulder he saw them climbing fire escape stairs. He stopped and watched them disappear into the darkness. Thoughtfully he returned to the pub to finish his pint.

The next day he dressed in scruffy clothes and took up residence on the road opposite the alleyway. About noon the young man came walking up Marylebone Lane from Oxford Street still dressed in the same dirty jeans and t-shirt. He turned into the alley and slowly climbed the fire escape stairs to the top of the building.

Fifteen minutes later he came back down and went back towards Oxford Street. He returned with a McDonalds bag in his hand. He stayed in the building for half a hour, left and did not return. At five Liam went home.

CHAPTER TWENTY

The next day Liam was back. The man did exactly the same. He turned up at noon, climbed the stairs, returned to the street, went off to Oxford Street, returned with McDonalds, and left after half a hour. About three o'clock Liam climbed the stairs quietly, looking up, down and around. At the top was a locked door.

Liam looked at the building. The fire escape gangway ran along the top floor to both sides. He tried one way first, peered through a couple of windows but the inside was empty. He went the other way. The first window was a kitchen, the second a sitting room where Anna sat flicking through a magazine. A portable TV was on. She looked bored and miserable. As far as he could see there was no telephone. He guessed the next window was a bedroom and the end one with the frosted windows a bathroom. It looked very basic, very barren, and basically a prison.

Liam returned to the street keeping watch all the time. He stood at the corner and carefully looked round. The streets were deserted. He returned home and rang Thunder, leaving a message. Then he had a soak in the bath. He had only just got out when he heard the pounding on the door. Swearing, he went to the door, a towel round his middle, his hair dripping. Thunder looked at him, one eyebrow raised.

"Not interrupting anything, was I?" Thunder asked.

Liam threw him a filthy look. "Come in, bastard," Thunder followed him in. "Get yourself a drink. I'll get dressed,"

He disappeared. Thunder went over to the unit where there was the usual assortment of bottles: gin, rum, vodka, brandy. At the back was a selection of whisky. A bottle of Irish whisky caught Thunder's eye. He poured two large glasses and sat down to wait.

Liam reappeared dressed in jeans and jumper, feet bare,

vigorously rubbing his hair. It was wilder than usual. He tried to drag a comb through it. After much tugging and several swear words he gave up. He dropped into a chair and picked up the glass.

"Cheers," he said and poured the entire contents down his throat. "Ahh, I needed that," Liam got the bottle and poured himself another glass. Thunder sat still, the glass in one hand, the other resting on the arm. Liam sat back down and dangled a leg over the arm. He sighed deeply. "Clean at last,"

"Clean? That never bothered you before," Thunder said calmly, his voice did not betray the impatience that was growing. He knew it was pointless rushing this man. Liam lived at Irish time, a slower pace than anyone else.

"Must be Kate's influence," he eyed Thunder who looked at him stony faced. Liam tactfully changed the subject. "About Anna,"

"Yes," Thunder dragged out the word. He was fed up with the girl. Kit was impossible to live with. Ling had the patience of a saint to put up with him.

"I've found her," Liam said simply.

"What?" Thunder almost jumped off the sofa. "Where?"

"Just off Marylebone Lane. This little weasel took her to my pub. My pub!" he poked himself in the chest. "The bloody cheeky little shit! So I followed them home," he said with annoyance. His voice dropped. "Didn't have far to go so I went back for my pint,"

Thunder put down the glass with a thump. He ran his fingers through his hair, his elbows on his knees. He started to swear in a foreign language that Liam didn't know. Then he looked up.

"Kit and I have been running our arses off all over London looking for the stupid bitch and all the time she was near your pub?" Liam nodded with a grin. "Shit! I'll kill her myself!" he poured himself another drink and started to swear in the foreign language again. "I am getting too fucking old for this shit," he muttered.

"Nonsense man. You just don't have the Irish luck," Liam said.

Thunder scowled at him. "When do we go and get the bitch?"

"Tomorrow afternoon after the weasel gets her McDonalds," Liam said.

"What weasel?" Thunder asked.

"The weasel that took her to my pub. They didn't look too happy about the arrangement either. He gets her a McDonalds every day," Liam said patiently.

Thunder suddenly had a thought. "Skinny guy, greasy hair, dirty jeans and t-shirt, probably heavy metal. Earrings. Smokes,"

"That's him. Know him?" Liam looked impressed.

"Oh yes," Thunder said with a laugh.

Liam wagged a finger at him. "Tie up loose ends,"

"Yes, I should. I should do a lot of things. Retire for one," Thunder said.

"We'll take the girl, hide her and if he's been less than a prefect jailer he'll get worried and lead us to Scarface," Liam said.

Thunder looked at his watched. "I ought to go back to Chinatown,"

"You don't sound too enthusiastic about it," Liam said.

"Sonya and Kit argue virtually the whole time, each blames the other. Ling plays referee and every so often I get to be ball. I've learnt more Chinese swear words in these last few days than I know Chinese," he said.

"Stay here, get pissed, without a ball they can't play," Liam suggested.

"They'd play without," Thunder said gloomily.

Liam ordered food in, got the beers out and they sat talking into the early hours. About three Thunder fell asleep on the sofa. Liam looked at his friend. This was taking it's toil on him. He wasn't his old self. Perhaps it was time for both to retire.

At half eleven the next morning they were on Marylebone Lane looking in shop windows. Just before noon along came Sammy, whistling tunelessly as usual. Thunder recognised him straight away. He nudged Liam.

"That's him," Liam said.

"That's Sammy. You'd think he'd learnt his lesson last time. Obviously not. Time to put it right. This is something I have to do alone," Thunder said.

"Just don't get carried away. This is very public," Liam looked round. Today there were lots of people walking about.

Thunder went off after Sammy. He caught him at the bottom of the stairs. Sammy didn't hear him. Thunder grabbed him and shoved him against a wall.

"Give me the keys," Thunder said. Sammy handed over the keys. Thunder knocked him out with his gun and left him in a corner. He climbed the stairs quickly and opened the door at the top. It lead into a small hallway with four doors off it. He could hear Anna in the first room.

"I suppose you want a cup of tea before you get lunch," Anna called.

Thunder stood at the doorway. "I wouldn't say no to a cup if you're making one, but I'd prefer coffee,"

Anna spun round and her face dropped. "What are you doing here?" she snarled. "If Max finds you here, you'll regret it,"

"I hope Max does find out. I want to meet this mysterious man," Thunder said with a smile.

"Jealous?" Anna challenged.

"Not at all. I want to make sure he's good enough for my old friend," he replied calmly.

"You aren't my friend," her voice had a hardness that Thunder had never noticed before. "You never were my friend," she spat at him. "I know that now,"

"I will always be your friend Anna," he said softly. "How have you been?"

"Better than before," she retorted.

"In a prison," he looked round.

"This isn't a prison," Anna scoffed.

"Isn't it? Locked in. Sammy your only visitor. What would you call it?" Thunder said.

"This is protection," Anna said with a haughty air. "It's better than Chinatown,"

"I thought you like Chinatown," he said.

"Except for certain people, like my brother and sister, who treat me like a slave and pay me less, order my life as if I'm nothing," Anna retorted.

"Then you should have told them to butt out," Thunder said.

"Oh yeah? Like they'd listen," she retorted. "I had more freedom on the streets in China," her voice was contemptuous, hard, cold.

Thunder looked at her. Was this the same Anna that he had rescued; scared, crying, pitiful, drugged from the squalor of a Chinese whore house? How could he take this hate filled person home? Anna trotted out every grievance, every excuse, every slight. They all sounded petty, the complaints of a spoilt brat. Thunder answered her patiently but this only irritated her more. She turned on him with a vengeance. He was patronising her, treating her like a child, like an idiot. She knew him for what he was. She deserved better than his sort.

Downstairs Liam looked at his watch, it was gone half past, for a rescue mission this was taking a long time. He hoped Thunder had got rid of Sammy at the bottom of the stairs, permanently this time, otherwise he'd be waking up and sounding the alarm. Liam crossed the road, found Sammy unconscious in the corner and tied him up to the stairs. Then he climbed the stairs quickly.

Instead of going in the door he climbed out on to the balcony. The kitchen window was open so he could hear what was going on. Anna's voice got louder as she denounced everything: her family, Thunder, her life. Thunder replied patiently, quietly. He could see Anna as she paced back and forth, her back to the window. Thunder was obviously on the other side of the room by the door. Liam edged the window open a little more, sat on the balcony and waited.

"Max told me what you did to his family. How could you? Hunted them down like animals," Anna said, her voice was harsh.

"Did he tell you how his father massacred my family?" his voice was detached, there was a pause. "No? Raped and gutted my young wife who was six months pregnant? I'm not surprised,"

"You were never married!" Anna was scornful.

"I was when I was young, younger than you are now," his voice was soft.

"Max has told me how you've hunted him for years," Anna

said defiantly.

"As he has hunted me," Thunder's voice was patient.

"You scarred his face," Anna said coldly.

"As his father's men did me," Thunder replied.

"You've murdered lots of people," Anna accused him.

"Yes. His count is less," Thunder said. "But I saved your family,"

"I don't know why you bothered. We were better off there," Anna's voice dipped venom.

"I promised your father," Thunder said softly.

Anna's face softened for a minute. "Max will be a father soon," she boasted proudly.

"You'll never live that long," Thunder told her.

"Max is taking me to America," Anna told him proudly.

"He's already gone," Thunder lied.

"No he hasn't, he's going to kill you and then we're going to America," Anna said confidently.

"He killed Shelley," Thunder said.

"Shelley was a cheap whore," Anna sounded hypercritical.

"Like you?" Thunder countered.

"Max loves me," Anna screamed at him.

"Max loves no one," Thunder replied.

"Like you!" Anna snarled at him.

"Love is a commodity I didn't have room for," Thunder admitted.

"You're a cold hearted killer. Max is gentle and kind!" Anna said.

"Max isn't coming back to take you to America. He will kill you like he did Shelley. Unless I stop him," Thunder said.

"You can't stop him. He has the advantage," Anna said.

"He will kill you like he killed Shelley," Thunder repeated.

"No he won't! I love Max, he loves me," Anna said.

Anna moved into Liam's eye line. She leaned on the worktop briefly and then started across the room. Liam moved. He could see Thunder standing near the door. He had put his gun down on the nearest worktop. He looked harassed but unperturbed. He felt no danger. Liam could plainly see the knife in Anna's hand behind her back. He took his own knife from the sheath strapped to his calf. He opened the window wider still. Thunder looked at her as Anna advanced on him.

"I hate you," she screamed as she got closer to Thunder. Her hand dropped to her side. Liam threw his knife. With a cry Anna fell forwards into Thunder's arms. He looked at her, at the knife in her back and then up at the window.

Liam climbed through. Thunder laid her on the floor and stepped over her towards Liam. "What the fucking hell are you doing?" he shouted at him.

"She had a knife in her hand," Liam said quietly.

"What? Are you mad?" Thunder yelled at him. Liam grabbed his arm before he could throw a punch. They fell against the worktop. Their faces were inches apart. Thunder looked furious. Liam remained calm.

"Look at her!" Liam said firmly. He pushed Thunder away.

Thunder threw off his hands and stepped away. Liam stayed still. Thunder half turned and then whipped round and punched Liam on the jaw. Liam staggered back against the work units, a hand to his face.

Thunder picked up Anna and pulled out the knife, it clattered as he threw it across the floor, coming to rest near Liam's feet. As he bent to retrieve it, a second sound of metal against the floor was heard as the knife fell from Anna's right hand. Thunder looked at her hand and then at her face. The malicious expression was still there. A look of hate. Thunder felt tears welling and put a hand to his face. Liam crossed to his friend and put a hand on his shoulder.

"I can't believe she'd do it," Thunder whispered.

"I'm sorry my friend but I couldn't take that chance. It was you or her, there was no question for me," Liam said. He knelt down. He pulled a towel down and wiped his knife on it and put it back in the sheath.

"How do I tell Kit?" Thunder whispered.

"You don't, I will. I did it, I will tell him," Liam said calmly.

Thunder let Anna fall to the floor, his legs suddenly going from under him. He fell against the cupboards, a look of horror on his face. "I was supposed to bring her home alive, not dead," he whispered.

"We have to get out of here," Liam said. He got up and stepped passed him into the hallway. He found a blanket and returned. He wrapped Anna in the blanket, put Thunder's gun in his pocket and pulled Thunder to his feet. He was sitting staring into space.

"Come on," Liam said dragging him out. He pushed him down the stairs, stumbling and falling a couple of steps. Liam put Thunder's arm round his shoulders and took him to the pub. The landlord and barmaid didn't bat an eyelid.

"Two drinks," he ordered.

Neeve came over with two brandies. "Looks like you've had a shock,"

"Two more in five minutes," Liam said. She nodded and left.

Thunder drank his without hesitation. The second one arrived and he downed that too. Liam drank his slightly slower.

"I can't go back to Chinatown. Kit will kill me for sure," Thunder said. "Dear God, what am I going to tell him?"

"Leave that to me," Liam said. "Pat, call me a cab will you," he called over. The cab arrived minutes later. Liam shoved Thunder in it and they went back to his flat. He put Thunder in the spare room and then rang Kate.

"Get on the first train. Come to my flat," Liam said to her.

"What's happened?" Kate asked.

"You'll find out when you get here," Liam said.

"Is Krysten okay?" Kate asked.

"He's in shock. Anna just tried to knife him," Liam blurted out. "Oh shit. I wasn't going to tell you like this. Just get here Kate and don't hang about,"

"Is Anna all right?" she asked. Liam hesitated. "He didn't..." she trailed off.

"No he didn't. But I have to sort some things out," he said. "I have to go to Chinatown. Look I'll leave my spare key on the top of the door frame if I'm not back when you get here,"

"Good luck Liam. I'll see you later," Kate said.

Thunder was still sleeping. Liam went out and made his way

to Chinatown. He found Sonya in the restaurant where she worked. She took one look at him, took off her apron, said something in Chinese over her shoulder and took him to Kit's flat.

"This is Liam, a friend of Thunder's," Sonya said when Kit opened the door.

They went upstairs. Ling was watching TV. Kit turned it off. Kit gestured to the chair. Liam waved him away. Sonya sat next to Ling. Kit sat in the chair. Liam stood very still, braced himself and then started to speak.

"I found Anna," he started.

"When is she coming home?" Kit asked.

"Is she coming home?" Ling asked quietly. Kit looked at her angrily.

"No. She won't be coming home," Liam started again.

"I thought as much. She's gone to America. Well good luck to her," Sonya said and then rounded on Kit. "Perhaps now you'll give us all a break!"

"No, that isn't the case," Liam started again.

"Well what is it then? Don't tell me she's found herself another punter?" Sonya's voice was harsh. Kit shouted at her in Chinese. She shouted back.

"For fuck's sake - SHUT UP!!! Yer Gods..." Liam yelled at them and then stopped. He counted to ten and started again. "I found Anna,"

"You've said that. And we've ascertained that she won't be coming home," Kit said. Liam threw him a withering look.

"Kit, why don't you shut up and let the poor man speak. If you keep interrupting him we'll be here all bloody night!" Ling said angrily. Kit was about to reply, thought better of it and shut up. He sat in the chair, arms folded. "Start again Liam," Ling said to Liam. "Ignore him. We're listening,"

Encouraged Liam started again. "I found Anna, she was being held prisoner, for her own protection she believed. She came into my pub one night, that's how I found her. Krysten and I..."

"Krysten?" Kit couldn't resist.

"Thunder and I went to get her this afternoon. Thunder went up alone and when he didn't come down I went up to see what was taking so long," Kit looked as if he was going to interrupt but didn't. "Anna was shouting at him, accusing him of all sorts of things, half of which I didn't understand. Or want to. Anna has been successfully brainwashed against all of you. Her comments, that I heard, were not... complimentary. Anyway she went for Thunder. I could see the knife in her hand. He couldn't. My knife found her before she got to Thunder. I'm sorry, he may not believe she would do it but I couldn't take that chance. From where I was, it looked like she would. I'm afraid Anna is dead," Liam finished into a heavy silence.

"I'll make some tea," Ling said and went into the kitchen.

"Liam, sit down before you fall down," Sonya said, pulling him onto the sofa.

Kit buried his face in his hands and started to sob. Suddenly he jumped up and left the room. Sonya brushed away tears angrily. She shook off Liam's hand. He put his arm round her and she cried silently against his shoulder. He removed his arm before Ling returned with the tea.

Liam declined a cup. "I should go," he said getting up.

"Where is Anna now?" Ling asked quietly.

"Still there. I will make the arrangements. You can go to the police if you like," he said. She shook her head. "I know people, they will make the necessary official arrangements for you, if you'd like," he told her.

She nodded. She showed him out and watched him stride off into the darkness. She slowly closed the door and leaned against it. She didn't know what would happen now. She returned upstairs to try and bring sense to the situation and to give comfort to Kit and Sonya. Yet the cynical part of her thought that Anna being dead solved a lot of problems. It also threw up some. Namely Kit. Thunder. The future.

When Sammy came round it was evening. He pulled at the rope tying him to the stairs. After a lot of tugging and pulling at the ends with his teeth he managed to get it loose enough to free his hands. He raced up the stairs, the door stood open, no lights were on. He carefully went inside. The silence gave him the creeps. He expected noise: from the television, from Anna banging about in the kitchen or her constant moaning. He went into the kitchen and turned on the light. Anna was still lying wrapped in the blanket on the floor. Sammy undid part of the blanket. Anna's hate filled face looked up at him.

"Ho-ly shit!" he exclaimed and covered her back up. He looked round nervously but found nothing and, more importantly to him, no one. He ran out the door and down the stairs as fast as he could go. He ran up the road to Oxford Street, it was almost deserted. He ran across the street and into Bond Street tube station. At the telephones he stopped running. He dialled a mobile number.

"This is Sammy," he said when it was answered.

"I thought I told you not to ring me," a voice said.

Sammy shivered. He and Joe had met this man once and he had stayed in the shadows the whole time. Joe hadn't been that bothered at the time but he had scared Sammy. Possibly more than Thunder had. After Joe's death this man had approached him. Sammy had agreed to the job out of fear. Only now he had nightmares of shadows killing him and the few times they had spoken a vision of menacing shadows stalked Sammy bringing him out in a cold sweat. He felt like this now, the sweat ran down his back, he flexed his shoulders but the sweat still ran.

"She's dead," he said.

"Really? Who did this?" the voice intoned.

"He did. Th... Th... that man," Sammy said.

"You mean Thunder," the voice said lowing his tone. Sammy started to shake. "And what have you done about it?"

"Nothing, I ran as fast as I could," Sammy said.

"You surprise me," his tone was sarcastic, it was wasted on Sammy. He paused. "When did this happen?"

"Some time this afternoon. He clobbered me first and took the keys. Now she's dead. I've just seen her," Sammy jabbered away.

"You haven't called the police? No of course not. At least it saves you a job," the voice said.

"Me?" Sammy squeaked. "I couldn't have killed her,"

"No," the voice fell silent. Sammy waited.

"What do you want me to do?" he asked.

"Go home. I have other bait to flush him out. I will call you when I need you again," the voice said and the line went dead.

"I'll go home then," Sammy told himself. He bought a ticket and went home.

Late that night Liam returned to the building in a van with two men. He lead the way up the stairs. The two men didn't say a word as he ushered them into the flat and to the kitchen where Anna's body still lay. They unwrapped her partially, nodded a lot, then rewrapped her. One picked her up over his shoulder. They left. Liam turned off the light and shut the front door. He was half way down the stairs when it hit him. The light was on. Someone had been there.

At the bottom of the stairs the two men were putting Anna in the back of the van. Liam went under the stairs. Sammy had gone leaving the rope. Liam swore and returned to the van.

"Let's go," he ordered. They got in. They drove away up Marylebone Lane to north London and stopped at a funeral home in Kilburn. The two men carried Anna inside. One came back out to him and handed him a piece of paper. On it was the cemetery address and a time two days hence. Liam nodded and left.

He returned to his flat. It was still in darkness. He checked the flat. Thunder was still asleep in the spare room. Liam sat down to wait for Kate to arrive.

Max Cardol laid his phone down on the table thoughtfully. Sammy had confirmed what he suspected. Thunder had found Anna and eliminated her. Max smiled. It wasn't Thunder's style, he must have been seriously provoked. Anna's slavish devotion to him had worn thin after only a few weeks. She wasn't actually much use to him other than a way to Thunder. In truth Anna hadn't known much about Thunder at all. She had a vague idea what he did, she knew her brother was his contact but as to the rest, she had no idea. She didn't even know where his London flat was. All she had known was that she loved him and that he had rejected her. Once Max came into her life she had transferred her allegiance.

It was on her last visit to Kit's flat that she had managed to find a phone number but no address. Kit didn't have it. However

Max's contact had been able to trace the address and find him a cottage not far from it. He had been watching the cottage for a couple of days. Thunder was not there, but Kate was.

When he saw the taxi arrive that afternoon he immediately knew something had happened. He was in his car soon after Kate left with a small bag. They weren't difficult to follow. He parked in the car park while Kate went into the station. A path led to the platform. He went up this and stood on the platform waiting. Minutes later Kate appeared on the platform. At that time in the afternoon it was fairly deserted. It had been easy to walk up to her, knock her out and carry her to his car. He'd even returned for her bag.

He drove back to his cottage, left Kate in the boot while he packed and then drove to the place he had found. He had only just finished setting himself up there when he received the phone call from Sammy. Now he had Kate it was time to put his plan into action. He carried an unconscious Kate in and tied her to a chair. Then he sat down to wait.

At half six Liam was woken by some one shaking him. He had fallen asleep in the chair, the glass was on the floor. He opened one eye and looked up at Thunder.

"Liam! Wake up!" Thunder had been saying whilst shaking him.

Liam shook off his hand. "I like my bones where they are, thanks all the same," he said gruffly.

"I thought you were ringing Kate. Where is she?" Thunder said.

"I was waiting for her to arrive," Liam stretched.

"Well she hasn't. I even checked your room," Thunder said crossly.

"Ring her," Liam said stumbling up and across the room towards the kitchen.

Thunder rang the cottage. The phone rang and rang. Then he rang Chinatown. Ling answered. He said hello in Chinese.

"How are you?" Ling asked.

"Fine. How's Kit?" Thunder said.

"In shock. Suffering. Like you," Ling replied.

"Have you heard from Kate?" Thunder asked.

"No. I thought she was coming to you," Ling said.

"She hasn't and there isn't an answer at the cottage," Thunder said.

"She's probably on her way. Give her time to get there," Ling said.

They rang off. Liam put a cup of coffee on the table. They sat and drank.

"Perhaps she's on her way here. She might have needed time to think," Liam said reasonably.

Thunder looked at him sharply. "Why? Did you tell her?"

"It sort of came out," Liam said. Thunder gave him a withering look. "Drink your coffee, I'll make some breakfast," Liam said lamely. He disappeared into the kitchen. He put bread in the toaster and leaned on the sink unit. All he could see was roof tops. He started to swear quietly.

At about nine the phone rang. Liam was sat in the chair looking into space. Thunder was pacing. Liam snatched the phone up.

It was Kit. "We've just had word. Get Thunder over here. He'd better hear this," he put the phone down. Thunder was stood next to him.

Liam looked up. "We have to go to Chinatown,"

"I don't think that's a very good idea," Thunder said.

"They've had word. We have to go," Liam said and got up.

He got his coat, put some shoes on and was heading for the door when he realised Thunder hadn't moved. He went back and got him out the flat. They went downstairs, up the street and got into a taxi. Thunder said nothing. He was very still. He didn't look at anything, his eyes weren't focused. He didn't look like he was even breathing. They stopped in Shaftesbury Avenue and got out the taxi. Thunder stood on the pavement and waited while Liam paid the driver. Liam lead him across the road and into Gerrard Street. They went to the flat. Ling opened the door. She looked at them blankly. They went upstairs.

CHAPTER TWENTY ONE

Upstairs Kit, looking the inscrutable Chinaman with an expressionless face, was sat at the table with the answer machine in front of him. Sonya sat on the sofa, she was red eyed from crying. Ling went and sat next to Sonya. They were both red eyed. Liam leaned against the wall. Thunder sat at the table opposite Kit. They didn't say a word. Kit pressed play.

"This is a message for Thunder. I suggest you pass it on Chinaman or pay the consequences. I have his girl. Not my type, but quite nice. If Thunder wants to see her again he'd better be a good boy and do as he's told. I have her safe, for now. Lets see if he's as good as he's made out to be and can find her. A messenger will bring clues. It's not a good idea to harm the boy or you might never see her again," the voice was unmistakable. Max Cardol.

Thunder got to his feet, the chair fell backwards with a crash. He picked up the machine and threw it at the only clear wall, between the door to the stairs and the kitchen door. Liam moved quickly and caught it. Thunder threw him an angry look. Liam looked back, he showed no fear. The thought came, unbidden, to Thunder that Liam was in the same business.

"You! You murdering bastard!" Thunder's voice came out low and angry. His pent up anger gushed out.

"I wondered when it would sink in," Liam said quietly.

"You killed Anna! And probably Shelley! Now you'll kill Kate!" Thunder clenched his fist tight, the knuckles white, his arm muscles tensed.

Liam faced him unflinching. He looked at his friend with sorrowful eyes. Thunder recognised the look and immediately stepped back as if he'd been punched.

"I've been accused of many deaths over the years. Some like Anna, with good reason, but I did not kill Shelley. Your old friend did that. I would never kill Kate, but he may," Liam said softly, his Irish accent strong.

"And did you tell them how you killed her?" Thunder blazed at him.

"Yes. They know. You don't believe she would have used that knife but I did. I have no loyalty to Kit or his family. My loyalty was to a friend, and rightly or wrongly I protect my friends," Liam replied calmly. He turned to Kit. "I am more sorry than I can say that I killed your sister. I wish it had been different, but it wasn't and I didn't have the faith in her that Thunder had," he said simply.

"And I suppose that makes it right does it?" Thunder snarled at him. Liam looked back at him with a look that stabbed him to the heart. It reminded him of other faces; other times; other deaths; other friends. For some reason Rosie's face came strongly into his mind. He shook his head.

"No, it doesn't make it right. I can't change things but I would do exactly the same again," Liam's voice ended harshly.

"This isn't finding Kate," Kit said breaking the deadlock. "Ling, make some tea, we need to think,"

Ling and Sonya went into the kitchen. When they returned Thunder was sat at the table. Kit in his customary chair. Liam on the sofa. The answer machine was on the floor near Kit's feet. Ling forced a cup into Thunder's hands. He looked up at her, intense pain on his face. She stroked his cheek and then kissed him on the forehead. By then his expression had changed back to his usual mask: professional, ruthless, deadly. Ling sat on the arm of Kit's chair.

Liam took a mouthful. "Kit play that tape again. There might be some clues,"

Kit looked at Thunder briefly as he pressed the play button. Thunder was looking across the room away from them. They listened to the voice again.

"Smug bastard," Sonya said. Her hand flew to her mouth. She looked horrified at the others. She had meant to say it under her breath but it had come out louder than expected.

Liam grinned at her. "I agree,"

"There is virtually no background sounds. He could have made it anywhere," Ling said.

"We'll have to wait for the messenger," Liam said.

The phone ringing made everyone jump. Ling answered it. She spoke rapidly in Chinese. Sonya and Kit exchanged looks. Liam saw this.

"What is she saying?" he asked Sonya quietly.

Sonya looked at him. Last night she had hated him, now she couldn't. She was glad he was here, a voice of reason in the middle of chaos. "Lo Chung says there's someone in the restaurant for Kit," she told him. "I'll go and see who it is," she told Ling and quickly left.

Thunder and Kit were following her before Liam realised. "Don't hurt the messenger he said!" he yelled at them. They both stopped and looked at each other, then over their shoulders at Liam who was standing. "Harm the boy, you might not see her again. That's what he said. Do you want to risk it?"

"I have to see who it is," Thunder said.

"He's expecting a Chinese man. I'll go with him," Kit said. They left.

Ling put down the phone. "There's a young man asking for the Chinaman,"

"Sammy! Shit!" Liam exploded. "I'd forgotten him!"

"Kit will take care of him," Ling said. Liam looked at her, wondered at her meaning and then sighed.

Kit and Thunder walked into the restaurant. Sonya was sat at the back with a skinny young man. She looked up as they approached. She got to her feet.

"Well if you won't talk to me, talk to the Chinaman," she said curtly and walked away.

He looked over his shoulder with a smug look. It dropped when he saw Thunder just behind Kit. He jumped up and flattened himself against a wall. "I don't know where he is,"

"Of course you don't," Kit said in a soothing voice. "But you will tell me what you do know,"

In spite of himself Thunder had to smile. He knew that voice. Kit usually used it just before he got out his herbs, the chopping board and of course that wicked looking knife he used. Kit gestured to Sammy to sit down. Sammy sat where Sonya had been. Kit sat opposite him. Thunder stood a few feet away, arms folded, a grim look on his face. Sammy glanced at him and then he took out a piece of paper. He had written his instructions down so he'd remember. The childish handwriting danced in front of him so he kept smoothing it out staring hard at it.

"He says that he has the girl safe," he began.

"He?" Kit asked.

"He stands in shadows. I don't know his name. He didn't give one. I didn't ask," Sammy said.

"That was sensible of you," Thunder said. Sammy looked fearful at him.

"You don't need to be afraid of him," Kit said. "I'm far worse," his voice suddenly dropped. Sammy transferred his gaze.

"What are the clues?" Thunder asked

"Clues? I don't know no clues. He told me to give you this message today and tomorrow he'll give me another to give you," Sammy said.

"Oh shit. We'll be here until Christmas at this rate," Thunder said.

"What was the message?" Kit asked Sammy.

"What? Oh yes," he looked at his piece of paper, now totally smoothed out and curling at the corners. "He's not in London. He's not in Scotland. So he could be anywhere... I can't read that. Oh yes, anywhere in be teen. Don't make sense to me," Sammy read slowly.

"Well that narrows it down somewhat," Thunder said sarcastically.

"Was there anything else?" Kit asked Sammy.

"Nope," Sammy said. "His voice echoed. I only just made out that much,"

"Echoed? Like how?" Kit asked.

Sammy looked over at Thunder who was rearranging the glasses on the bar. Sonya on the other side was annoyed by it.

"For goodness sake! Leave alone!" she slapped his hand. He looked at her blankly and then turned around and leaned against the bar.

"Like what?" Kit asked.

"Like he was in a tunnel or empty room or sumink. His voice went round and returned to you," Sammy said.

"Was he on a mobile phone?" Kit asked.

"Dunno. Don't think so. I could hear his voice twice, like he had an echo," Sammy said.

Kit thought for a few minutes. "When are you coming tomorrow?"

"Dunno. When he rings me suppose," Sammy said.

"We'll see you tomorrow then," Kit said and got up, the meeting was over. Sammy legged it, edging past Thunder and out the door. He ran up the street and disappeared.

"Did that make any sense to you?" Kit asked Thunder.

"None," Thunder said heavily.

Sonya said something in Chinese. Kit smiled. He and Thunder returned to the flat. Ling and Liam was still sitting on the sofa. Thunder sat at the table. Kit sat in his chair.

"The message, such as it was, told us precisely nothing," Kit started.

"Did you expect more?" Liam asked.

"No. Cardol isn't in London and he isn't in Scotland, he's somewhere in between," Kit said.

"So he could be anywhere? Helpful," Liam replied.

"The boy did say his voice echoed, like he was in a tunnel or empty room," Kit added.

"Was it Sammy?" Liam looked over at Thunder. He nodded. "Well this was a waste of time. He's playing with us,"

"No, he's playing with me. You and Kit aren't in the equation," Thunder said tonelessly.

"Sammy will come back tomorrow when he has another message. So we wait," Kit said.

"While you've been having your little chat with Sammy, Ling and I have been doing some thinking. Now, lets assume that Kate left soon after I phoned her. Ling phoned up the railways and found out what time the trains run. There are a couple of trains soon after that so she probably went for one of them. I rang the taxi firm in the village and found out what time he picked Kate up. He also told me that the station was abuzz because a woman had collapsed and a man took her to hospital in his car. The guy at the station remembered him because he was admiring his long black leather coat. Ring any bells?" Liam said.

"What?" Thunder's attention suddenly switched on.

"I thought that would get your attention. It means that Kate didn't even get on the train," Ling said.

"Sammy said he didn't know where he was. Is there anyone else who might know?" Kit asked.

"Who knows," Liam said irritated.

"How about the man who hired Thunder?" Ling suggested.

"You could ask Palmerston-Smith if he knows if Lightman has a large office or something," Kit said to Thunder.

Thunder rang Ray Palmerston-Smith. After a few pleasantries Thunder got to the point. "Is it possible for me to talk to Lightman?"

"Carl Lightman had a heart attack a few days ago. He's in intensive care. I doubt he can talk," Palmerston-Smith replied.

"Oh!" Thunder couldn't think of anything else to say.

"Kit? Are you still there?" Palmerston-Smith's voice could be heard across the room. Ling took the phone from him.

"Hello. My name is Ling. Sarah stayed with us. Can I ask what you told Thunder?" she said.

"Oh hello. Sarah's spoken of you. I told him Lightman has had a heart attack," Palmerston-Smith replied.

"Oh, I am sorry to hear that. Do you know if he had a large office or warehouse or something?" Ling said.

"Why? What's happened? Has something happened?" Palmerston-Smith sounded worried.

"Kate has been taken by the man after Thunder," Ling explained. Kit said something angrily in Chinese. She waved at him.

"What? So the bas... Sorry. Is there anything I can do?" Palmerston-Smith said. He recovered his momentary lose of control very quickly.

"He left us a message and his messenger said his voice echoed when he phoned him. We're guessing he's in a large room or something," Ling said.

"I'll ask around," Palmerston-Smith said.

"Thank you," Ling replaced the phone.

They sat around discussing what to do, who they could contact. Mid afternoon Liam went off. Ling served dinner at seven. Thunder started drinking then. At nine Kit joined him. When Liam returned at half ten they were on the second bottle. He had no news to tell them so he joined the drinking. At eleven Ling went to bed leaving them to it.

She got up at half seven, unsurprisingly alone. Downstairs the three men were sleeping where they were: Kit in the chair, Thunder and Liam at either ends of the sofa. She went into the kitchen.

At half eight Kit appeared. She put black coffee in front of him. He sat down, put his head in his hands and groaned. Ling said nothing. A hour later Thunder staggered in. He looked terrible. Dark shadows under where his eyes should be! His skin looked grey. His hair stood out. She had never seen him look so dejected, so lifeless. Even at his worse she had never seen him this bad.

"Why don't you sit down," she said. "Before you fall down,"

Thunder slumped in the chair. Ling brewed fresh coffee. Not even that lifted his spirits. Suddenly the door banged.

"Is that real coffee I smell?" the Irish lilt positively drooled.

Ling looked over her shoulder and her jaw dropped. She had never seen anything like it! Liam looked like a heathen. His hair stood out all over the place giving him a wild and woolly look. His clothes were crumpled, like a tramp. The only difference between him and the other two was that his face didn't have that grey hung over look to it. He just smiled at her and like so many women before her: she melted. Thunder looked up at her and then over his shoulder at Liam. He laughed and then groaned.

"Liam, do something with the mane, it hurts to laugh," he put his face in his hands and laid them on the table.

Liam tried, unsuccessfully, to tame his hair. He ran his fingers through it, patted it down, tugged at it and then gave up. It was better but still wild looking. Ling put a mug of coffee in front of him. He spooned in three sugars and stirred. It sounded like a clarion bell sounding their doom.

"Stop that," Thunder said and slapped his wrist. The spoon flicked coffee across the table and onto Kit's outstretched wrist. He yelped in pain. Then Kit and Thunder groaned in unison.

Liam looked round, a beaming smile on his face. "To be sure, it's a fine morning and all," he said in his broadest Irish accent. Thunder lifted his head and looked at him daggers. Liam stared back unconcerned. "These people who can't take their liquor shouldn't drink," he added looking at Ling.

She stifled a giggle. "Anyone want breakfast?" she asked.

"Now that depends on what you're offering," Liam said. It was Kit's turn to look daggers at him but he looked innocently back.

"I thought a nice cooked breakfast," Ling said. "Sausage, bacon, eggs, fried bread, tomatoes? Or cereal and toast?"

"The first if you've got it. The second if not. Can I trouble you for some more of that wonderful coffee?" Liam said. Thunder groaned and staggered out the door. Quickly followed by Kit. Liam watched them go. "To be sure they can't take the drink. Must be the breeding,"

"I expect you started at a young age," Ling replied.

"Oh about three or thereabouts. Me da was a drinker. So I learnt the art at his elbow, so to speak," Liam was being very Irish this morning.

Ling smiled and started to cook. The smell of sausage and bacon wafted into the sitting room. Thunder put a hand to his stomach and rushed out the door onto the street. He leaned against a wall. Kit joined him shortly.

"I suggest we go for a walk," Kit suggested. "It will clear our heads,"

"Good idea," they walked off down Gerrard Street to Piccadilly.

After Liam had eaten everything that Ling had put in front of him and drank several cups of coffee he sat back and sighed deeply. "I could get used to this," he said. "Still not to be,"

"Are you in the same line of work as Thunder?" Ling asked

him.

"Now what line of work is that?" Liam asked with a smile.

"You know what I mean. Your flattery doesn't work on me," Ling said.

"You and Kate are the only two women in the world it doesn't. Well that and me ma. I'm mortified," Liam said with a hand to his chest in mock indignation.

"Huh! I doubt that. Well? Are you?" Ling retorted.

"Am I what?" Liam asked.

"I'll take that as a yes then," Ling said.

Liam leaned forward on the table and dropped his voice, losing the broad Irish accent. "You're a very astute lady, Ling. I see nothing gets past you,"

"Not a lot," she admitted. "Married to Kit and knowing Thunder, you soon catch on,"

"Thunder's been doing this a long time then?" Liam asked.

"Too long," Ling said. "This is the first time since I've known him to get so involved. He doesn't usually,"

"That what caught him out. He's involved. Bad idea, in our line of work," Liam said seriously.

"Aha!" Ling said triumphantly.

"Oh shit. I've just been caught out," Liam smiled at her. "How long have you known Thunder?" he asked changed the subject.

"About five years. Since I married Kit. We met in London. They met in China when Thunder rescued Kit and his sisters. They've been friends ever since. Other than you and Kate I think Kit is probably his closest friend,"

"Oh I think Kate got a lot closer than me and Kit," Liam said with a grin. "I've known him about five years. We met when I first moved into my flat. We became good friends after that," Liam said. "Though I always felt there was a darkness to his soul,"

"That must have been when he rescued Kit and his sisters. That wasn't a good time. I think he lost a good friend out there and possibly a woman. It made him very wary of getting involved with anyone. He tends to keep everyone away," Ling said.

"I know he has no family. Cardol senior killed them all and Thunder killed all his family and Cardol has sworn vengeance.

This is what this is all about. Revenge," Liam said.

"When this is all over, you, me and Kate will sit down and seriously discuss Thunder. We all appear to have pieces of a puzzle," Ling said sternly.

"You think we're all coming out of this then?" Liam asked.

"Of course. I know Thunder. He's like a crab, he doesn't let go," Ling said.

"You'd better include Kit. I think he has a few other pieces. Only Thunder knows it all and he won't say," Liam said. Ling looked thoughtful - in a stern way - so Liam decided this was the best time to leave. He found Kit and Thunder sat on a door step. He joined them and sat on the ground, stretching out his long legs before him. People walked round his feet.

"Your wife cooks a wonderful breakfast and has a wicked way at getting information out of you," Liam told Kit. Kit smiled and nodded. They sat and chatted about nothing in particular. Liam was in the middle of telling some story when he suddenly stopped. Thunder followed his gaze.

Strolling along, hands in jeans pockets, whistling tunelessly, eyes on the floor was Sammy, looking as if he didn't have a care in the world. So he didn't see Liam's chest until he walked into it. Literally.

He looked up quickly. "Sorry mate..." any other words died. He looked up into Liam's face.

"Now why don't you and I have a little chat, cosy like. I'm sure there's some stuff you want to get off your chest," Liam looked at him. "If you had one," he added quietly.

"I don't know anything, about anything," Sammy managed to stammer.

"The father back home used to say confession was good for the soul. I never believed him, but I'm sure it's right for some people," Liam said.

"Stop tormenting the boy. He knows zilch. If he did the Chinaman would have the words out of his mouth before he knew what they were," Thunder suddenly appeared at Liam's elbow. Liam looked at him.

"You're sure?" Liam asked.

"He is, he is," Sammy said vigorously.

"I am," Thunder said quietly. "What is the message today Sammy?"

"I wrote it down, so I won't forget," he started to look through his pockets.

"Very sensible of you," Thunder said soothingly.

Liam eyed Sammy as he searched. "Did you think to remember where you put it?" he asked in a sarcastic tone.

"Now is that any way to treat the messenger?" Thunder said to Liam.

Sammy triumphantly held up the piece of paper, scruffy, torn and smudged. "See, told you I had it somewhere," he showed it to Liam. "It's all written here,"

"Can we go in the restaurant?" Thunder called over to Kit who got out the keys and opened the door. He beckoned them in. Liam took Sammy by the scruff of the neck and frog-marched him in, his feet moved but hardly touched the ground. Thunder followed, a smile on his face. Kit and Sammy sat at a table near the back. Liam leaned his elbow on the bar and inspected his nails. Thunder sat opposite Sammy.

"Now, the message," Thunder said in a soothing voice.

Sammy smoothed out the paper and silently read the words, his lips moving.

"Out loud would be helpful," Liam remarked.

Sammy looked up at the large man. He took a deep breath and started. "Drive on the first road north until you hit a road that is a quarter score. The area west from here to a line from the bell noise to the praying bird. Fat ones and thin ones where smoke once went. That is where I am. Come alone and hurry. Your empress on the beacon will be laid at sundown on the first to get the bird. I don't understand it. What's birds got to do with it? That's it. He spoke slowly so I could write it down,"

"That makes as much sense as me flying," Liam said.

"Haven't you been in a plane?" Sammy asked him innocently.

Liam frowned at him. Sammy shrank back. Thunder looked at Kit who shrugged. Kit said something unintelligible in Chinese. Thunder cocked an eyebrow at him.

"Probably," he said. "Get a pen and paper, we'd better write this down,"

Kit went off behind the bar. Liam sat next to Thunder.

"First road north?" Liam asked.

"M1?" Thunder queried.

Kit returned with pen and paper and they wrote it down word for word as Sammy read it out again. Liam and Kit both read it again.

"Anything else?" Thunder asked.

"He didn't echo this time. I think he was in a pub. I could hear noise in the background. He rang me about half ten last night," Sammy said.

"And you waited until now?" Liam blazed at him.

"He told me to," Sammy said defensive.

Thunder laid a hand on Liam's arm. "Anything else?"

"I heard a train," Sammy tried to be helpful.

"A pub near a railway, that narrows it down," Thunder said. "If you think of anything else or he gets in touch again, ring this number," he wrote the contact number on the back of the paper. Sammy stuffed it into his pocket. Liam doubted he would be able to find it in a hour's time.

"Can I go now?" Sammy asked.

"Are there to be any other messages?" Kit asked.

"He didn't say so. He said he's given you a time limit and where to find him. It's up to you now," Sammy started to get confident.

"Don't get cocky boy, I might just forget about not hurting the messenger," Thunder's tone was unmistakable. Sammy looked scared.

"I'd get out while the going's good," Liam quietly suggested. Sammy needed no second telling. He left at great speed and didn't stop running until he reached Piccadilly tube entrance.

They returned to the flat. Ling was sat at the table reading the newspaper. They showed her the message. She read it and looked up at them.

"So? What does it mean? What's this about getting the bird?" she threw the paper on the table. "It's gibberish,"

"There's something that bothers me. Sammy said he'd given us a time limit. Do you see a time limit in that message?" Thunder said.

Liam and Kit re-read the message. Both said "No,"

Thunder took the message from them. "Listen again. Your empress on the beacon will be laid at sundown on the first day to get the bird. What bird is he talking about? And why does it have some special date?"

"The only birds I know are the ones I cook," Kit said.

"They're the only birds worth knowing," Liam replied.

"Trust you two to think of your stomachs," Ling said.

Thunder quickly interrupted them. "What birds do you eat?"

"Chicken, turkey, duck," Ling started to reel them off.

"No I mean more like game birds," Thunder said.

"Pheasant, grouse, partridge, guinea fowl," Liam said.

"That's it. Grouse. Doesn't that have a significant date?" Thunder said.

"Twelfth of August," Ling said. "First day of Grouse shooting season,"

"That's... what's today's date?" Liam asked looking at his watch. "Three days away,"

"So we have our time limit. Three days to find him," Thunder said.

"Doesn't leave long," Ling said. "He could be anywhere,"

"No, he talks about the first road. We reckon that's the M1 so he can't be that far away. Have you got a map?" Liam said.

Ling shook her head. Kit went out to buy one. The phone rang. Ling answered it. Liam and Thunder looked again at the message.

"Thunder, Ray Palmerston-Smith wants to speak to you," Ling called.

"I'm sorry about Kate," Palmerston-Smith said when Thunder came on the phone. "I've spoken to Bob Lowman and Carl Lightman's right hand man. Neither have empty buildings north of London. After that charity dance he's not likely to lie. Ring me if you need anything else,"

Ling went back to Liam who was looking pensive. "Are further?" she asked him.

"If you drive down the M1 for two hours where does that bring you? Northampton? Further? Depends on how fast you drive. According to this message you come off the motorway which cuts down the time spent on the motorway. Driving through towns and on small roads would cut down on time. I wouldn't be at all surprised if he isn't quite near the M25 you know. Mind you, anything north of London could be Scotland for all I know. I had enough trouble finding Kate's place," Liam said.

Thunder rejoined them. Kit then came in with a map which they laid out on the table and all four looked at it. After a hour they still haven't come to any conclusions. Thunder was feeling irritable. Every suggestion put forward he punched holes in.

"Lets get out of here," Liam said. "I'll borrow my mate's car and we'll drive down the M1 to see if that gives us any clues,"

Liam and Thunder spent the rest of the afternoon driving up and down the motorway. They returned later that evening. Thunder was in a foul mood and Liam not much better. Thunder's temper was bad after one hour, after that it just went down hill. Finally Liam had returned to London because he couldn't stand it any more. Ling got Thunder a black coffee and left him sitting in the kitchen looking moodily at a wall. Back in the sitting room Liam was telling Kit about the afternoon.

"Believe me, a mad man in a foul temper driving at 100 miles a hour is no picnic. I'm surprised we didn't get stopped," Liam said.

"Why didn't you drive?" Ling asked.

"I did to start with. Then Thunder decided to give it a go. At the first opportunity I drove. We've been to Birmingham and back twice. The way he drove I'm surprised I didn't see Hadrian's Wall! He drove like something possessed," Liam sounded annoyed.

"So you found nothing?" Ling asked harshly.

Liam hung his head. "Zip," he muttered.

"So now what?" she asked.

"Tomorrow, we go by train. To find that pub near the line. Would you believe. His idea," Liam didn't sound too happy about it. He started to drag his finger through his hair, got them stuck and pulled them out with a struggle. His hair stood out, wild and woolly. He sighed.

"Look, don't take this wrong but I'm going home. I can't stand anymore of this. I'll be back in the morning. Don't expect much out of him, he hasn't spoken for hours," Liam said and left.

Ling looked at Kit who shrugged. Ling cooked dinner. Thunder ate it automatically without realising what he was eating. Kit went down to the restaurant. The evening passed extremely slowly. Ling looked at the clock virtually every ten, fifteen minutes and was thankful when ten o'clock came round and she could escape to her bed. She left Thunder sat alone brooding.

CHAPTER TWENTY TWO

The next morning Kit, Liam and Thunder went off to catch trains, anything north of London. At eleven the door bell went. Ling put down the book she was trying unsuccessfully to read and answered it.

To her utter surprise it was Sarah with a tall man who she introduced as Marcus. They came in and sat in the kitchen while Ling made Jasmine tea. Sarah did most of the talking. After a few minutes Marcus interrupted her and asked about Kate. Sarah lapsed into silence. She looked at her lap and refused to lift her head. She was obviously distressed. Every so often Marcus would stroke her arm.

"Ray said last night you'd received a message. Did it say where Kate was?" Marcus asked.

Ling showed Marcus the message. Sarah looked over his arm at it. He kissed her on the head.

"Do you have a map?" he asked.

"We've looked at it a hundred times, it makes no sense at all," Ling said with a sigh but fetched it anyway.

Marcus laid it out on the table. While Sarah may have calmed down a lot over the last few months, Marcus had matured. He was no longer content to let Sarah lead and sometimes even told her what to do, which to everyone's amazement she obeyed.

"Marcus, you can't expect to succeed where other's have obviously failed," Sarah said with her old lack of tact. Her hand flew to her mouth. She looked at Ling with big eyes. Ling laughed.

"I wondered where the old Sarah was hiding," she said. "Go ahead Marcus, fresh eyes may see what we've missed,"

"Well, the first motorway north is obviously the M1," he started.

"Thunder has already worked that one out," Sarah said acidly.

"I was stating the obvious, Sarah," he was unaffected by her tone.

Ling watched them together. She decided Marcus was just right for Sarah. He didn't take offence at her tactless remarks or acid tone. He softened her sharpness, calmed her impatience and they certainly complimented each other in looks.

"Now a quarter score," he started again.

"Cricket, football, sport of some kind?" Sarah asked.

"A score is also twenty," he said.

"So a quarter score would be... five?" Sarah said.

"Right. A road maybe? Which road?" he mused.

Sarah looked over his shoulder and traced the M1 with her finger. "A5," she said simply.

"What?" Marcus and Ling said together.

"A5," Sarah repeated. "A quarter score road would be A 5,"

Ling looked at her astonished. Marcus started to curse under his breath. He looked at her finger still on the A5 junction. He handed the message back to Ling. "Can you read that bit about the area west," he asked.

"The area west from here to a line from the bell noise to the praying bird..." Ling began.

"Stop," Marcus said. "A bell noise?"

"Ring, ring," Sarah imitated a bell.

Marcus gave her a withering look. He moved his finger left. Sarah continued to imitate the bell. Suddenly he stopped. "You have that slightly wrong my darling,"

"I do not!" she retorted. "That's the sound a bell makes,"

"Quite right too but in this instance I think it should be tring, tring," he said and pointed at the map. Sarah and Ling squirted at it. Ling said something in Chinese, it was obviously a swear word. Sarah looked at her startled. "This message is very good," Marcus said softly.

"So good, four of us couldn't see it and you get it within... what?" Ling looked at the clock. It was just gone half eleven. "Thirty bloody minutes!" she fumed and muttered for several minutes and then stopped. "That's it! Simple! Too simple!" she said loudly. "We expected it to be cryptic and therefore hard to work out but it's simple, so simple a child would have worked it out," Marcus looked at her with a slightly hurt expression. "Oh not that you two are children. Well, you are compared to us lot. Well no you're not really. Oh for goodness sake, get on with it!"

"What's the next bit Ling?" Marcus asked.

"What? Oh? A line from the bell noise to a praying bird," Ling read out.

"A line from Tring to..." Marcus looked at the map. Sarah leaned on his shoulder. Keeping one finger on Tring he moved a finger on the other hand about.

"Surely it would be a line north to south," Sarah said.

"But that wouldn't be parallel to the A5," Marcus said.

"What's a praying bird?" Sarah asked.

"No idea. Isn't there a secretary bird? Perhaps it's similar," Ling said.

"A buzzard," Marcus suddenly said. "As in Leighton Buzzard,"

"A buzzard? That's not a praying bird," Sarah said.

"No, but it is a bird of prey. The spelling is wrong," Marcus said.

"Oh for fuck's sake!" Sarah suddenly said and her hand flew to her mouth. She looked at Marcus and Ling who were both looking at her in some astonishment.

"You spent too much time with Thunder," Ling said quietly.

"A line from Tring to Leighton Buzzard, the area from there to the A5. Why there?" Sarah said looking down at the map.

"What's the next bit?" Marcus asked Ling.

"Come alone and hurry. Your empress on the beacon will be laid at sundown on the first day to get the bird," Ling read out.

"That's obviously Grouse day," Marcus said. Ling gave him a withering look. "Sorry," he muttered.

"The sun goes down about half nine, ten. We've wasted one day already and those three have gone looking for a pub near the railway," Ling said.

"Pub?" Marcus looked puzzled.

"You missed a bit. That bit about fat and thin and smoke. That could be chimneys," Sarah said.

"Chimneys? Pub by a railway?" Marcus became distracted.

"Cardol rang the messenger from a pub by a railway the last time so they've gone looking for it," Ling said.

Only Marcus wasn't listening, he was gazing into the distance, unhearing. Sarah nudged him. He frowned at her.

"The bit about the empress on the beacon?" she prompted.

"What? Oh yes. The empress on the beacon," he dragged his attention back.

"He gets like this sometimes," Sarah said to Ling. "Comes of thinking on several levels,"

"It means Kate. As in Catherine the Great, she was empress of Russia," he said.

"And beacon?" Ling asked.

They looked at the map but could see nothing. Marcus finally looked at his watch. "I think it's time we went. We've done what we could,"

Ling saw them out. By now Marcus was totally distracted. He shook her hand, said goodbye and was off down the road. Sarah hugged her, asked her to phone if she heard anything and ran off after Marcus.

Upstairs Ling wrote down the answers Marcus had come up with. She hoped the three men were having as much luck. At six she found out when they arrived back. Thunder was in a fouler mood than ever. Kit looked disgruntled and Liam was surprisingly happy.

"I was stupid enough to catch a train with Thunder," Kit said.

"Bloody stupid trains," Thunder muttered.

"We caught a train from Euston. First stop Milton Keynes, it thundered through every stop. We caught another back and it stopped at some places. We got off at three. Not one of them had a pub near the line that we could see," Kit said.

"I caught the train from Marylebone to Aylesbury. Lots of nice stations, lots of nice pubs, not what we were looking for," Liam said which explained why he was so happy. He'd spent the entire time going in and out of pubs!

"Well, I did well today. I had visitors and they solved the

clues," Ling said and felt very smug. She put the map on the table and proceeded to go through the message while they looked at the map.

"If you follow the M1 from London to junction 9 you come to the A5," she emphasised A5. "As Sarah said. A quarter score road. The area west of that to a line from a bell noise to a praying bird. A line from Tring to Leighton Buzzard. Wrong spelling of praying. It should be bird of prey not the sort you do in a church! The empress is obviously Kate. As in Catherine the Great. Grouse day you know about. We couldn't find a beacon but Marcus suddenly went very distance and left in a very strange mood so anything could turn up,"

"Shit! I don't bloody believe it! Sarah? Marcus? I can believe Marcus but Sarah? Bugger me!" Thunder exploded.

"I'd rather not," Liam muttered.

"Read and weep, boys," Ling threw the paper on the table. Liam and Kit went over it again.

"She's bloody right!" Liam said to Kit.

"That can't be, it's…" Kit trailed off.

"Simple! Two kids got it! Kids!" Ling rammed home the point.

"I'm going to the pub," Liam said.

"I'm coming too. I couldn't stand Ling's smugness all night," Thunder said.

"So I get it? I've had to put up with your foul mood all day, why do I have to put up with her? Why can't you?" Kit yelled at him as they disappeared out the door.

"You can go to the restaurant," Ling said and flopped onto the sofa.

"Bloody hell!" Kit said and left.

Liam and Thunder made their way along Shaftesbury Avenue towards Piccadilly. Thunder still looked angry. Liam was too happy from a day visiting pubs to care.

"Do you want to go to the Red Lion?" Liam asked him.

Thunder groaned. "No way. I couldn't face a drinking match with Ted tonight. I'd rather go somewhere I'm not known,"

"We could go to the Coachmakers Arms?" Liam suggested. To Liam's surprise, Thunder shrugged and agreed. Liam flagged down a cab.

Thunder didn't say a word as the cab went up Regent Street, into Oxford Street, up Marylebone Lane to Wigmore Street. Thunder looked forwards the whole time. Liam looked up as they went passed Anna's prison. Neither said a word as the cab swept past the turning.

The pub was full, noisy, anonymous. The sort of place Thunder needed right now. He sat in a corner while Liam got the beers. Liam looked round the bar over his glass. "Full tonight," he said by way of conversation.

Thunder looked miles away; lights were on but no one was home. His expression was blank and his eyes unseeing. Liam nudged him. He looked round wildly. "What?"

"Crowded," Liam repeated. "The pub is crowded,"

Thunder looked round. "Oh yes," he sipped his beer. "I've lost her," he said quietly as he put the glass down, half drunk.

"Not yet," Liam said ever the optimist. "We know the area now, we just drive round and find that building,"

"It could be anywhere," Thunder said harshly. "He could be describing somewhere that doesn't exist. It could be a place in his mind. It wouldn't be the first time,"

"Yesss," Liam drew out the word. "But it could exist. Lets face it, it's you he wants not Kate. Killing Kate will achieve nothing. You'll be more pissed off than he wants you to be. Right now he wants you to find him because he's prepared. He kills Kate and you'll disappear only to pop up when he isn't expecting you. Right now is his time. This place exists," He knew he was talking sense but from the silence he realised that his friend had already gone; to a silent world in his head.

Thunder went over the last few days. There had to be a clue there. If Kate was here she'd spot it. Stupid bastard! he thought. If she was here you wouldn't be looking for her! He muttered savagely to himself. Liam leaned over but didn't hear the words. Thunder leaned back and ran his fingers through his hair in exasperation and then finished his pint.

Liam waved his glass at Neeve behind the bar. Minutes later she appeared with two more pints. Thunder drank silently. Liam talked intermittently with various people but kept his eye on his friend and made sure the beer flowed. They were still there hours later when a young man pushed his way through the throng to the bar.

"Is there a Liam here?" he asked Neeve, his English accent very out of place. He felt he stuck out in the crowd. Even though he was wearing jeans his jacket looked expensive. He drew several speculative looks.

Neeve stood with hands on hips and looked at him. "Who wants to know?"

"Half the female population, so I've heard," he said and smiled.

Neeve smiled at him and nodded in the direction of the corner. "If you're going over there you'll need to take these with you," she started to pour three beers. He waited, paid for them and took them over on a tray without a word. He put the tray on the table. First Liam and then Thunder registered the pints and looked up.

"Who the bloody hell..." Liam started.

"My God, it Marcus," Thunder said. "You'd better sit down before someone pushes you over," Marcus sat on a stool and looked round apprehensive. He was glad he'd left Sarah at home. "Liam, this is Marcus. He's Sarah's boyfriend," Thunder waved a hand vaguely in the air. His brain felt slightly befuddled.

"Hello," Marcus held out a hand. Liam shook it with one of his vice grip handshakes. Marcus managed not to wince too much.

"How's Sarah?" Thunder's voice started to slur. "Ling said you'd visited,"

"And solved the clues," Liam added.

"Bloody good that," Thunder said and leaned back running a hand through his hair once more.

Marcus looked at them both critically. Thunder was definitely starting to look the worse for drink but Liam looked like he'd been drinking orange juice. The Irish accent had been a surprise and Liam had noticed that. Marcus hoped he hadn't been wrong coming here.

"Didn't you expect a Paddy?" Liam said quietly leaning across the table. "This is a Paddy pub,"

Marcus was suddenly thrown. "No. Yes. Well, no. Well, yes. Well, I suppose so," he stuttered and then stopped. He took a deep breath. "I think I've found the place," he said quietly.

"What?" Thunder may be more drunk than sober but there was nothing wrong with his hearing. He pushed himself away from the seat and leaned forward, his elbow on the table. He steadied himself and pointed a finger at Marcus. It wavered until his eyes focused. "You have done what? Exactly?" his voice surprisingly precise.

"I think I've found the place," Marcus repeated.

"You'd better explain yourself, lad," Liam said. He gestured at Thunder. "His brain isn't working as well as it usually is," Thunder threw him a filthy look. Liam looked back steadily. Thunder shrugged and his elbow fell off the table.

"My father's company were looking for old factories to buy and convert, or something like that. We went up to Hertfordshire to look at various sites. One was an old cement factory. When Ling read out about fat and thin and smoke it sounded familiar so I spoke to my father. He faxed me the details," Marcus said and started going through his pockets.

Liam sighed. "Another one who can't find things in his pockets. Why bother at all? Why not carry a bag?" he spoke to Thunder more than Marcus who just looked at him puzzled.

Marcus went through his jeans and then his jacket. Thunder looked at Marcus and wondered how he got into the pub. He certainly stood out. Clean jeans, crisp white shirt, pale expensive jacket. He didn't look like an impoverished student tonight. Thunder was still looking unseeing at Marcus when he unfolded a piece of paper. Liam leaned forward.

"Well I'll be…" Liam suddenly said. Thunder's attention diverted, he looked over Liam's shoulder at the piece of paper he was looking at.

It was an estate agent's details. The picture was unmistakeable. It had lots of chimneys, fat ones and thin ones. It was the closest to the description in the message that they were likely to get. It had to be the place. Perhaps Cardol wasn't so clever after all.

"Well? What do you think? Could it be the place?" Marcus asked. "It's in the right area. There's a pub next to a station not far from it,"

"I think he's got it," Liam said quietly to Thunder. Thunder looked sideways at his friend. Their faces were only a few inches apart. It is said that the eyes are the windows to your soul. At that moment Liam saw tiredness and pain; Thunder saw a clever bluff that hid a quick and astute mind which told him that he and Liam were definitely in the same business. There was something else in his eyes. Something familiar. Something Thunder had seen before but now couldn't place.

"He has that," Thunder replied just as quietly. He looked at Marcus.

He was watching them intently over the glass rim while drinking his beer. He knew Thunder was a dangerous man but this Liam looked just as dangerous. When he saw Liam and Thunder both nodding he relaxed, he had done the right thing. Thunder gave Liam some money, he went to pay the bar bill. He came back to hear Marcus volunteering to drive Thunder there. He sat down.

"That's not a very good idea," Liam said. "He's not a good passenger,"

"Besides I have to do this alone," Thunder said.

"Maybe but Kit and I may have something to say about that," Liam said. Thunder frowned at him. "Besides I don't fancy this lad's chances if that man gets past you,"

"I don't need a babysitter," Thunder growled. "Marcus can take me there and go home,"

"Oh no, not this time. Sarah would never forgive me if I didn't help and Kate got hurt," Marcus said with a firmness that surprised Liam. He reversed his original thought.

"I half agree with Marcus," Liam said. "This time you're not going alone. You went alone to see Anna and nearly got knifed. This time we go for a fight. He might want you alone but what if he's not alone? I know Sammy isn't up to much but put a gun in his hand and tell him to point and shoot and he's as likely to be lethal as not,"

Thunder looked ready to argue. Liam set his jaw, his head came up, a steely look on his face. Marcus watched the power struggle go on. Thunder looked furious at Liam, a look that would have quelled most men. Liam looked unperturbed. He'd been threatened by harder and bigger men than Thunder.

"We all go. Make sure he's alone. Then you go in, finish this. We will be waiting. It's that - or nothing," Liam said quietly. He was aware he was playing with fire. Kate's life depended on this.

"Agreed," Marcus said. Thunder looked at him.

"You don't know what you're letting yourself in for," Thunder told him. "Any of you," he looked back at Liam.

"I know that you'll do whatever you have to do," Marcus said quietly.

"You go, we all go," Liam said poking him in the chest with a finger. "And that includes Kit,"

Thunder rubbed his chest without thinking. He thought about it. If he failed, Kit had his family's honour to uphold. Come to that if Thunder was right about Liam, he was more than capable of cleaning up the mess. He could just slip away but he realised that was useless, they knew where it was and could just turn up. Thunder knew Cardol wanted to see fear in his eyes when he twisted the knife and woe betide anyone who got in his way. He had a fleeting thought that Kate could already be dead and this was a trap. Far better to go prepared than steam in blind.

"Okay. We all go. But I go in alone. This is between me and him," Thunder said firmly to both of them.

"Agreed," Liam and Marcus said together.

"We'd better tell Kit," Liam said.

"If we go back to Chinatown Ling will find out and then when she can't come all hell will break loose," Thunder said.

"We won't want that," Liam said quietly.

"Why don't you pick up the stuff you need and then pick up Kit, we could be continuing the search," Marcus suggested.

Thunder looked at him in surprise. He was using his head unlike Thunder who wanted to rush in like an idiot. Thunder nodded slowly. It might work. Liam waited. If he agreed all the better. If he took off on his own Liam and Kit would be following close behind.

"Okay, lets go," Thunder finished his beer and stood up. Apparent drunkenness had been replaced by renewed energy.

They left the pub. Marcus had parked his car in Bulstrode Street. Marcus drove first to Liam's flat. He waited outside while they went upstairs.

From a cupboard in his bedroom Liam pulled out a battered canvas holdall. Thunder watched with interest while Liam collected various items. He upended an armchair and bought out ammunition. From behind the dresser in the kitchen a high powered rifle. A hidden panel in the wall unit in the sitting room he pulled out a bag. He looked through the contents, nodded and put it in the holdall. From the top of the kitchen units he got down a gun, silencer and several clips of bullets. Underneath the sink behind the soap powder was the knife he'd killed Anna with. He paused. Thunder stood at the door.

"You did what you thought best. It was a kindness, she could never return to her family," Thunder told him. He went to the spare room and changed into black jumper, jeans and mountain boots. He pulled on his leather jacket and checked his gun.

Liam handed him the knife. Thunder looked at it carefully. He looked up. "You think Cardol's going to let me close enough to use it? Give it to Marcus," he handed it back. They went down to Marcus. He didn't ask about the bag. Liam threw it in the boot. They drove to Chinatown and stopped at one end of Gerrard Street.

"You two stay here. I'll fetch Kit," Thunder got out the car and strode away into the restaurant. Minutes later he emerged with Kit. At the door to the flat Thunder grabbed Kit by the arm. Kit looked at him in surprise.

"We have to keep this between ourselves. I don't want Ling to know what we're doing. Go in, get what you want and get out. I'll wait here," Thunder said.

Kit raised one eyebrow. Thunder let go of his arm. "You think my wife would talk?"

"I know better than that. This time it's different," Thunder
said.

Kit looked at him thoughtfully. "Okay, I'll go in, get what I
need and come back,"

"Amen to that," Thunder said softly.

"You're not going religious on me are you?" Kit quipped.

"Get out of here," Thunder pushed him away.

Kit went up to the flat. Ling was watching television. Kit
spoke briefly in Chinese. Ling didn't look up. He went into the
kitchen. From various drawers he got the knife he'd given to Kate
that day, some rope, a medical kit and his herbs. On his way out
he quietly unhooked his great waxed coat. Ling suddenly looked
up and instantly she knew. Her hand went to her throat, trying to
smooth the lump there. She blinked several times and fought the
panic that was fast rising.

Keeping her voice as calm as she could she called out. "You
going out?" Kit froze at the door. He looked over his shoulder.
She was watching him.

"We thought we'd give it another go," he said lamely.

She turned back to the television. "Be careful out there," she
said. Kit gave affirmative in Chinese. "And bring her back safely,"
she added.

"We will," he said automatically and then screwed up his face
in horror. He looked over his shoulder once more but Ling was
looking at the television. He quickly headed out the door.

On the sofa Ling sat very still and let the tears fall silently, not
moving even when they fell off her chin and splashed her hand.
When she heard the front door shut she reached for the phone and
started to dial the number for the restaurant where Sonya would
be working. Half way through she put the receiver down with a
crash. This ordeal would have to be borne along. However half a
hour later Sonya arrived. She had seen Thunder come in, seen Kit
leave with him and when neither reappeared, she came to the flat.

Kit met Thunder outside. He was leaning against the wall
watching the few people about. He looked round as Kit stopped
beside him.

"Any problems?" he asked softly.

"She said to bring her back safely. I'd say she knew," Kit replied.

"Shit!" Thunder muttered. They walked to the car. Kit looked at Marcus in surprise.

"Who is he?" Kit asked Thunder in Chinese.

"Marcus," Thunder replied.

"Why is he coming?" Kit asked quietly in Chinese.

"Because he knows where we're going. I couldn't refuse," Thunder replied also in Chinese. "Beside Sarah would have his guts for garters," he added in English.

Marcus grinned at them over his shoulder. Kit groaned. Thunder shrugged. "Are we ready?" Marcus asked.

"Lets get out of here before anyone else decides to join us," Liam said.

Marcus drove off. Finchley High Street, Brent Cross, M1. He drove quickly and carefully. The roads weren't busy. At the A5 he turned off. He drove towards Dunstable. At a pub Liam told him to pull off. Marcus pulled into the pub car park. Liam looked over the seat at Kit. Next to him Thunder appeared to be asleep.

"Now what?" Kit asked.

"You drive to the factory, drop me off, drive away," Thunder said without opening his eyes.

Marcus handed Liam a map. "We need to avoid Dunstable. We'll go past Whipsnade," he said and pointed this out to Liam.

"We could feed the animals," Liam suggested.

"Or feed someone to the animals," Kit offered.

"I think the animals might object," Marcus said.

Thunder looked from one to the next. He set his jaw and tried to fight the frustration and impatience that threatened his composure - what was left of it.

"For Christ sake just get there!" his patience bubbled over.

"All in good time, my friend," Kit said soothingly. Thunder looked irritated at his friends calm voice.

"For fuck's sake," he muttered and then lapsed into the foreign language which even Kit didn't understand.

"I think perhaps we'd better put some speed on," Liam suggested to Marcus. "Before our friend explodes,"

Marcus looked in the mirror at Thunder, his face set, dark and threatening, and agreed. He started up the car and drove off, going past Whipsnade Zoo and down the hill. It wasn't long before Liam had guided Marcus onto the right road. They drove past the plant slowly. The gates were chained shut and it looked silent and dark. Marcus hoped it wasn't a bad omen.

"You can drop me here," Thunder said.

"Not so fast," Kit said quickly followed by Liam. "Not on your life,"

"You've done your bit, now leave this to me," Thunder argued.

"I think we should find somewhere to stop, have a sleep and get something to eat before you go in there, all guns blazing," Marcus said.

"What?" Thunder almost yelled. Marcus looked at him and for the first time did not shake.

"I don't think it's wise you going in there tonight, that's all. The morning won't make any difference. When the sun sets if memory serves me correct. That's tomorrow night. A few hours will not make any difference," he said quietly. Thunder frowned at him.

"He's right," Liam said. "We can't go in there guns blazing. He'd pick us off one by one. Remember he's had time to plan this," It was his turn to get the stare. Liam stared right back. After a few minutes of intense silence Thunder's gaze shifted.

"Fine," he said flatly. "A few hours won't make that much difference,"

"Good," Liam said. He leaned over to Marcus. "You can breath now," he whispered. Marcus looked startled and then let out the held breath. He hadn't realised he'd been holding it.

Marcus drove into the village and stopped at the pub. They all went in. After a pint Liam went off to talk to the landlord. He managed to get them four beds for the night and a home cooked breakfast in the morning. They remained in the bar until closing time and then went to bed. Kit and Thunder shared a room. Kit lay in the darkness listening intently. After a couple of hours he finally heard Thunder's breathing deepen into one of sleep. Only then did he fall asleep, but it was light and full of bad memories causing him to toss and turn, waking every so often when he would lay and listen for that reassuring sound of Thunder's breathing. Just before dawn he fell into a deeper sleep that lasted only a hour before he was roused for breakfast and the day ahead.

Over breakfast Liam had a good look at the property details. At the front of the factory was a large three storey office building. At each end were two big chimneys. Running virtually the length of the big building was another building. It came up half way up the office. Off this building on each side were two smaller chimneys – four in total. A metal walkway linked the one big chimney with the two smaller chimneys behind. On the side of the right big chimney was a small single story building which was like a gatehouse.

They went out to the car and Marcus drove them past the factory slowly. In daylight they got a better look. Net fencing ran along the front. In the centre of this fence was large double gates, chained and padlocked. To one end was a single gate. The office looked derelict, several of the windows were broken. They all looked at it.

Liam motioned Marcus to drive on. A bit further on he pointed to a lane. "Pull in there," he said gruffly.

Marcus pulled in. Liam got out. Kit followed. Marcus looked at Thunder who was staring moodily out the window. He got out and joined the other two. They were arguing, quietly. He heard the tail end.

"This is Thunder's area of expertise," Kit said firmly.

"He's not the only one who has some expertise here," Liam snarled back.

"Now what?" Marcus asked them.

"Thunder isn't going into a trap without some sort of back up. I don't care what he says or how expert he is," Liam said stubbornly pointing at Kit who looked as unmoving as Liam.

"If Cardol manages, by some remote chance, of killing him, who will rescue Kate?" Marcus asked.

Liam turned on him. "Do you honestly think she would want to be rescued after that?"

"Kate would want Cardol dead," Kit said quietly.

"Granted," Marcus said.

"So it will be up to us to do it," Liam said. "Besides, there is your sister's honour,"

"But he didn't kill Anna, you did," Kit replied. Marcus looked shocked.

"I protected Thunder," Liam said. "Unfortunately that meant killing Anna,"

"Unfortunately?" Marcus protested.

"You weren't there. I didn't have time to weigh things up, I just acted," Liam said defensively. With his solid build he seemed to tower over Marcus, even though there was only a couple of inches if that in height between them. Marcus sensibly kept silent, but his expression was still accusing.

"We have to have some sort of plan," Liam repeated.

"Marcus will drive me there, you two can do what you like. Cardol wants me. Alone. And that is what he's getting. Now can we get on with this? Today is Grouse Day, in case you'd forgotten," Thunder stood behind them.

They all looked round. Thunder's face was set; hard, cold like marble, ruthless, deadly. It left no one in any doubt. His presence marked him apart; a killer, professional, mercenary. He knew what he had to do and how to do it, standing around talking about it didn't help. Thunder went to the boot and started pulling things out. Liam went to help. Kit quietly stood nearby and watched. Marcus stayed where he was. Suddenly he was afraid, here were three very dangerous men, they showed no fear, they were going to work. Thunder frightened him anew. He was obviously the most dangerous. Marcus felt like an outsider, a stranger. This life was alien to him.

Thunder tucked a knife in the back of his jeans. Kit put a couple of clips in his jeans pocket. Liam and Thunder spoke in single words or nods. Kit didn't say a word. Thunder pulled on his holster and then his leather jacket. Kit tucked something in a pocket. Thunder didn't appear to notice. He checked his gun and put it in the holster and pulled his jacket together.

Liam pulled his head out of the boot. In his hand was a rifle.

He casually filled it with cartridges. It disappeared into his large coat. Marcus blinked - he didn't remember seeing Liam with that on earlier. Liam strapped a knife to his calf. He slammed the boot shut and pulled his coat together. Liam and Thunder exchanged a look, then they both nodded.

Marcus looked from them to Kit. He had a waxed jacket on. He dropped a couple of things into a pocket. Marcus realised with a sickening feeling that they were sticks of dynamite. A serrated knife was taken out, checked against his thumb and then this disappeared into an inside pocket. Marcus swallowed twice and then turned away, unable to look at them any more.

Thunder looked over at Marcus, saw him turn away and understood. "We're going now Marcus, you can start the car,"

Marcus got in. He tried to turn the key but his hand shook too much. He gripped the steering wheel tightly. His hands stopped shaking. He quickly turned the key and waited while they got in. He backed out onto the lane and returned to the factory. Outside the gates he stopped. He looked in his mirror at Thunder.

CHAPTER TWENTY THREE

Thunder looked out at the factory. He put his hand on the door handle but didn't open it. "I can smell him from here," he said in a cold grim voice that chilled Marcus to the bone.

"What will be the sign?" Liam asked looking over the seat.

"For what?" Thunder looked at him.

"For the cavalry," Liam quipped.

"What time's sunset?" Thunder asked Marcus.

"About nine," Marcus replied.

"If I'm not out by seven, come in and clean house," Thunder said grimly.

"We'll be on the village green, there's a pub there," Liam said.

"You surprise me," Thunder said coldly.

"Well, you know me, never one to miss an opportunity," Liam said lightly.

Thunder got out the car and walked away without a backward glance. The main gates were heavily chained. He walked along to the small gate which was unchained. He pushed it opened and went through. In the car they watched him.

"I don't like this," Liam muttered.

"It's his choice," Marcus said.

"It isn't his choice, he's just dancing to someone else's tune," Liam said.

"You know what I mean," Marcus replied.

"This is something only Thunder can do. Something he has to do. Something he should have done a long time ago. We can only wait," Kit said. He didn't like it any more than Liam but he knew his friend.

"And then what? Pick up the pieces?" Liam said.

"If necessary. Drive on Marcus," Kit said.

Liam looked out the window once more. Thunder had

disappeared. Marcus drove to the village and they parked up in the pub car park. Kit and Liam left their coats in the car. They bought papers, played the machines and darts in the pub and generally wasted time.

Thunder walked through the small gate and approached the main building. The main door was locked. He looked along the building carefully. The next door was also locked. He walked around the big chimney to the right. Cardol's car was parked at the back. It revealed nothing; only Kate's watch. It didn't make him feel any better.

The small building to the right of the chimney looked like a security building. However the door was locked. He gave it a hefty kick. The lock gave way and the door opened, banging against the wall. Thunder stood in the doorway and looked in. The room was bare, dust and a few bits of litter the only occupants. A solitary light bulb hung from the ceiling. He tried the switch. Nothing. There was no electricity. He wiped his fingers on his jeans and started across the room.

In the corner of the room he spotted a camera. He gave it a cursory glance and walked through the door when he suddenly stopped. Standing in the doorway he looked up. A red light flashed on and off. He frowned. If there was no electricity how come the camera worked? His eyes followed the wire from the camera. It ran through the door and along the ceiling of the corridor, loosely attached at intervals. At the other end of the corridor another camera was positioned above the door. He leaned against the wall beneath the camera and looked up. He swore under his breath and yanked out the wire. The red light went off.

He leaned back and thought. Cardol had planned this well. Putting up all those cameras must have taken time. However he didn't have time to go round disconnecting every camera, it would advertise where he was going - and shooting them would have the same effect. And waste bullets. He swore some more.

A thought occurred to him. He pushed himself away from the wall and looked outside, scanning the walls of the building. Just under the roof above the door was a camera. He ducked back in and leaned against the wall.

"Oh shit! Talk about planned! I'm a sitting duck. Bastard!" he muttered.

He sank to a squat, his elbows on his legs and thought about this, reasoning it out in his head. What game was Cardol playing? He obviously knows I'm here. He could just pick me off. So why hasn't he? Because that's not part of the game. If I follow the wire presumably I'll find him and if I don't, he'll still know where I am because of the cameras. I can't climb up the outside wall because he has a camera there too. So now what?

He dragged his fingers through his hair, linking them behind his head, head down, elbows on his knees. His thoughts chased each other around in his head. Nothing made sense. He was walking into a well planned trap; something he hated; the unknown. No escape routes, no back up, no going back for his friends would help. He unlinked his fingers, dangling his hands off his legs. He pulled out the knife and absent mindedly started to toss it, handle over blade, and catch it; handle, blade, handle, blade. Again and again. He looked into space, his eyes glazed out of focus. He only had his wits and instinct to depend on. Something he knew and trusted. He leaned his head back against the wall. So be it, he decided. He felt the frustration drain away to be replaced by a calm coldness. Cardol wanted to play games did he? Well that was fine by him!

He stood up, tucked the knife back in his jeans and with purpose walked across the room and down the corridor to the door. He put up a middle finger at the camera just before he went through the door and found himself in a large circular building, obviously one of the two large chimneys. Opposite him, across the area, was another door with a camera. He stood in the centre with his hands on his hips and looked up and round, moving in a circle.

The round walls climbed upwards. At intervals corresponding with the floors in the building next door were a series of doors, one above each other. A metal walkway went round the wall. Next to the door was a ladder going up the building through a hole in the walkway. There was a camera above the doors on the ground and first floors, beyond that he couldn't see. He sighed, dropped his hands and moved towards the ladder.

He climbed to the first floor and went through the door into the building. The door came out into a lobby. Stairs were in the corner. A door was opposite. He pushed open this door slowly. He walked along the corridor going through the middle of the building. To each side of the corridor were a series of empty offices, barren, derelict. At the far end of the corridor was another door leading into another lobby with stairs in the corner and a door which lead into the other large chimney, which looked exactly like the first. He looked over the banister and saw more cameras.

"Shit! I could be doing this all day," he muttered and banged the banister with his fist. He returned to the lobby and looked out the window at the back. To his left were stairs up and down. He could see a metal walkway leading from the top of the big chimney to each of the smaller chimneys which were behind the office. To the back of the main building was another building coming halfway up the building.

Thunder went down the stairs. His footsteps sounded loud in the silence, heightening his sense of desolation. However he mused, on the plus side there were no cameras in this stairwell.

At the bottom were several doors. One obviously lead into the large chimney. Another had an exit sign on it leading out to the front of the building; this was locked. Two doors lead into the ground floor of the office building and both were locked. The door at the back wasn't locked. This lead into a small corridor. On one side were doors to the smaller chimneys. Thunder opened one. It was very dark inside. He quickly shut it again.

There was a door in the middle of the wall opposite the doors to the chimneys. This lead into the other building. Thunder walked out under the overhang that were offices above, overlooking the main space. This lead to a huge open space, up to the ceiling, it had obviously been a sort of warehouse. In the middle of the far wall was a large roll door operated by a chain. To his left against the wall was stacks of wooden pallets, growing in height down the wall. In front of him were oil drums, stacked or in an untidy pile. He moved towards them looking around carefully. Old bags of cement lay around, some broken open, the dust had settled on everything near it. Somewhere there was an open window - or probably broken - as a slight breeze lifted some of the dust. The only sounds were of dripping water: a dull thud onto a solid bag, another onto concrete, another metallic onto one of the drums.

There was nothing else and, as he couldn't see over the drums and didn't want to waste time going round them, he decided to search the rest of the building. He was about to move away when something hard pressed him in the back.

"I don't think you'll be needing this," a voice said removing the knife.

"I wondered how long it would take you to find me," Thunder said quietly and turned to come face to face with Max Cardol.

"Well this is a nice surprise," Cardol said sarcastically.

"Long time, no see," Thunder replied in the same tone.

"Over there," Cardol gestured past the drums.

"After you old boy," Thunder said

Cardol hesitated for a second and then smiled. "Very good," he said waving the gun at Thunder.

"I see you haven't lost your sense of humour Cardol," Thunder said and walked away around the drums. Cardol followed and threw the knife away, it landed with a thump on a bag of cement.

As he walked passed the drums he saw that the other wall had tall thin windows. All were dirty and a few were broken. In the far corner was a door. To his left the pallets were stacked against the wall. In front of them in piles of varying sizes the oil drums. Against the other wall was a table. Next to it a small stove with various pots and a kettle. In front were two bed rolls. In front of this was Kate tied to a chair. She had a gag lying round her neck but otherwise looked fine. A bruise was coming up on the side of her head. Thunder frowned.

"You okay?" he asked her. She nodded.

"She's fine. We got on like a house on fire," Cardol said shoving him.

"As well as you and Anna?" Thunder asked without turning. "Or Shelley?"

"Not my type really," Cardol said. "But I suppose I could have stretched the point," he spoke lazily as if he had considered it. "If I'd been desperate enough," he added.

Thunder put his hand in his jacket. He stopped. As Cardol got near he half turned only for Cardol to bring his gun down across his shoulders knocking Thunder to his knees. Cardol put his gun to Thunder's temple.

"Hands where I can see them," Cardol said in a low voice. Thunder cursed quietly and put his hands out in front of him. Cardol pulled open the jacket and jerked the gun from its holster. He tutted and threw it away. "Over there," he said and pushed Thunder over towards Kate. "I don't want our guest to miss the action," Thunder got to his feet. He had no choice but to back step towards Kate.

He hadn't taken more than a couple of paces when Cardol suddenly hit him across the face with the back of his hand holding the gun. Thunder's head whipped to the side and he could taste blood. He looked at Cardol with a frown and wiped his hand across his mouth.

"You'll have to do better than that," Thunder said in his deadly quiet voice.

"Oh I will," Cardol promised. He turned away and walked over to the table. Thunder sprinted off behind the drums.

"Running away Thunder? Not very sporting of you," Cardol taunted. "Perhaps I'll have some fun with your friend. It wouldn't be the first time,"

He picked up a rifle and fired to the left of Kate. She screamed as the floor next to her fragmented and bits flew up. He fired to her right and she screamed again.

"You miserable bastard," she hissed at him. He fired a couple of feet in front of her feet. Kate bit her lip and closed her eyes. She didn't flinch as bits flew up.

Behind the drums Thunder heard the first shots and Kate's screams. He slumped to the floor, fists clenched, eyes screwed shut, jaw set. It was happening again; someone he loved being used as bait. He heard the third shot and silence. He was about to get up when he heard her voice.

"If you think I'm going to sit here and scream for your stupid game, you fucking arsehole, you are very much mistaken!" Kate spat at Cardol.

Thunder gave a silent sigh of relief and crawled to the end of the drums near the pallets. He looked over the last single drum and could see Cardol standing over Kate, the rifle in both hands. He couldn't see Kate's face but it was obvious she was being defiant.

"Just my little game," Cardol told her.

"Thunder's an intelligent man. I'm sure he'll work it out," Kate replied.

"Intelligent? He's sub human piece of crap!" Cardol yelled at her.

"Then you're well suited aren't you!" Kate yelled back.

Cardol backhanded Kate across the face. She looked at him coldly.

"And I suppose that made you feel a big man!" she retorted.

"It made me feel good," he told her.

"A bigger man would have made some reply instead of hitting a woman tied to a chair," Kate retorted.

"But Cardol isn't a bigger man, Kate," Thunder called out.

Cardol's head whipped round. "And you are? How many women and children did you kill in that botched job?" Thunder was silent. "You remember the one don't you? Where you were supposed to kill the bad man?"

"That was a stupid mistake. I don't do them anymore," Thunder said calmly.

"You're here aren't you? That was pretty stupid!" Cardol yelled at him.

"Killing you won't be a mistake!" Thunder retorted.

"We'll see," Cardol replied. He turned back to Kate. "I'll deal with you later, bitch," Cardol said and moved away.

"I'll be waiting, moron!" Kate replied acidly.

Cardol whipped round and hit her with the rifle, knocking her sideways to the floor. Kate didn't cry out. Thunder charged at

Cardol with a roar. Thunder's head hit Cardol in the side knocking him over, Thunder landed on top. Cardol twisted and rolled away, free. He scrambled to his feet, picked up the rifle he had dropped and kicked out at Thunder, but he had rolled away and the foot found air. Thunder rolled once more to his feet.

"Let's do this the old way. No weapons. No guns. No knives. Just fists," Thunder suggested. "If you think you're man enough,"

Cardol stared at him calmly. "But you're more at home with them. Or dynamite,"

"You hide behind that gun pretty good Cardol. Let's see how you do without it," Thunder replied.

"My father wiped your scum off this earth," Cardol said.

"Very brave against defenceless women and children wasn't he?" Thunder replied.

"We exterminate scum where I come from," Cardol said.

"He didn't do a very good job, did he? He forgot one," Thunder said.

"I will finish off what he started," Cardol said.

"Leave the man's job for the boy," Thunder sneered.

"When you're gone the world will be a cleaner place," Cardol said.

Thunder gave a snort of derisive laughter. "Cleaner place? And what will you do then? Plays with toys?"

"I'll find something else," Cardol snapped.

"Bit difficult where you're going," Thunder said.

From her position on the floor Kate couldn't believe it. They were stood a couple of yards apart, like a pair of petulant kids, trading insults. "For Christ sake you two! You sound like stupid kids! Your revenge, his revenge, actions resulting from actions that someone else did,"

"If his mother had married my father, this would never had happened. And my mother would still be alive," Cardol yelled at her, losing all control.

"But she wouldn't be your mother, you idiot! She'd be someone else's!" Thunder shouted at him.

Kate manoeuvred herself up on one elbow and looked at them with disbelief. "Is this what this is about?" she asked Cardol.

There was silence. "You're annoyed because your father had the hots for his mother and she rejected him? Is that it?" Kate blazed at Cardol. He looked at her silently. She twisted a bit more. The fall had loosened the ropes. Her hands were still tied behind her back but the ropes tying her to the chair now lay loosely round her waist. She looked from one to the other. The two men surprisingly stood waiting, watching her.

"Do you mean that because Thunder's mother rejected your father he massacred her family? Are you serious?" Kate's voice, very firm, very angry, very controlled. "You're an idiot!" she emphasised each word, her voice dripped scathing sarcasm.

"He killed my family," Cardol blazed pointing at Thunder.

"Because your father killed mine!" Thunder retorted.

"That could have been avoided!" Cardol blazed back at him.

"Oh for Christ's sake!" Kate yelled at them. They fell silent. She looked at Cardol. "Have you ever stopped to consider that you wouldn't BE you? You'd be someone else? None of this would've happened and we wouldn't be here?"

"But my mother would be alive!" Cardol blazed at her.

"BUT she wouldn't BE your mother!" Kate yelled at Cardol.

"Your mother was mad," Thunder said quietly to Cardol.

"Because my father wanted your bloody mother!" Cardol yelled, turning on him.

Kate looked at Cardol in sheer amazement. "And that's the sum total of your argument? The reason for your revenge?"

Cardol's menacing face dropped; he suddenly looked like a lost boy. Kate could see the sensitive tortured soul beneath the hardened surface.

"I never said Cardol was unintelligent," Thunder said. "He's just ..."

"Mad," she said quietly, interrupting.

"Like his mother," Thunder retorted.

"I'm going to kill you both!" Cardol blazed at them, looking from one to the other. The sensitive soul disappeared abruptly.

"Yeah right. If I'd had money every time someone said that I could buy America," Thunder said sarcastically.

"Thunder, be nice to the poor man," Kate said.

"Nice? Nice? He's psychologically impaired!" Thunder blazed at her.

"He's damaged goods," Kate said simply.

Thunder looked at her angrily. "Be quiet Kate," he started to mutter in one of his many languages.

Cardol's mask whipped back into place. "Yes Kate, be quiet. And if you're good I will kill you quicker than his last loved one,"

"Oh? And which one would that be!" Kate blazed at him. "There's been so many over the years!"

"Shut up Kate!" Thunder kept his eyes on Cardol.

"Shall I tell her about your many women?" Cardol asked Thunder silkily.

"You talk too much Cardol," Thunder said.

"But we haven't talked for so long. This is my moment," he replied.

"A moment is all you'll have," Thunder muttered. He moved towards Cardol, fists clenched, his anger visible but controlled.

Cardol waved the rifle from side to side at Thunder, as if scolding a naughty child. "I don't think so,"

Thunder backed away slightly. "Okay, lets talk,"

"I thought you would have worked it out before now," Cardol said.

"Oh I worked it out all right," Thunder said. "I knew it had to be you,"

"Sue was supposed to bring you out into the open. She could deliver the girl as well. Lightman would have got what he wanted. Maybe even gone back to the States," Cardol told him.

"To his death maybe. He can't return to the States," Thunder said.

"I could have paved the way for him," Cardol boasted.

"You'd do that for some scrumbag you hardly know? Yeah right!" Thunder said in disbelief.

"He was a friend of my father's," Cardol replied.

"I thought you didn't have anything to do with your father's friends," Thunder said.

"Some things change," Cardol sounded almost wistful.

"Not for us, they don't, Cardol. We never change," Thunder

said coldly.

"You did. You never used to get involved," Cardol pointed out, sounding almost wistful.

"Kate was a mistake," Thunder replied.

"One that you'll both live to regret. Or rather not," Cardol smiled at the irony.

"Dream on, pal," Thunder replied. "You think you can do what your minions failed to do?"

"Oh killing the great Thunder was never a task for them. They were all far too stupid," Cardol drawled.

"And expendable," Thunder said. "Sammy pushed Sue under a tube. I killed Joe and I expect some suitable revenge will be extracted for Sammy and Bruce,"

"Why should that bother me?" Cardol asked.

"What about Anna?" Thunder asked.

"She was trash. She got what she deserved," Cardol replied.

"She was having your child," Thunder said quietly.

There was a long pause. "Was she? Unfortunate then, that you killed her,"

"I didn't. That was someone else," Thunder said menacingly. He stepped towards him. Cardol pointed the rifle more firmly in his direction but Thunder carried on coming. Cardol was suddenly backing away.

"Kill me. You have the rifle. Kill me. Finish it. Wipe this scum off this earth," Thunder said angrily.

"And spoil my fun? Forget it!" Cardol snarled at him.

"You are one sick man Cardol," Thunder said.

"And you're missing the point," Cardol replied.

"Which is?" Thunder already knew the answer.

"I want you to suffer," Cardol's voice went cold.

"Do what you like but Kate goes free," Thunder said.

"No way," Cardol dropped his voice.

Thunder stepped towards him again. Cardol stepped away. His foot found Kate's. He jumped over her and aimed the rifle at her head. Cardol looked at Thunder and saw his anguish. Thunder looked at Kate. For a second their eyes locked, she smiled then closed her eyes. Thunder looked up, shrugged and turned away.

"Go ahead. I can always get another woman," he said and moved away. Kate kept her eyes firmly shut and trusted in Thunder's instinct. Thunder stopped walking when he heard the rifle go off. He looked at a spot high on the opposite wall. "Forgive me Kate," he whispered.

"You worthless piece of shit!" Cardol yelled at him, moving towards him. A couple of feet away he swung the rifle hitting Thunder across his shoulders. Thunder's knees buckled and he went down. Cardol hit him again. Thunder fell forward and rolled. Cardol stood over him, the rifle above his head, ready to bring it down. Involuntarily Thunder looked away and saw Kate still lying on the floor. Behind her there was a hole in the wall. Thunder looked up at Cardol just in time to see the rifle bearing down on his head. He twisted and wiggled away, rolled to his knees and then to his feet. He kicked the rifle out of Cardol's hands. It spun through the air and clattered on the ground.

"Now we'll fight like real men," Thunder said quietly taking off his jacket and holster. "If you can," He threw them away.

Thunder threw the first punch. It hit Cardol on the side of the jaw. Cardol stepped back a couple of paces and to his left. Thunder turned with him, facing him all the time. Cardol moved in and hit Thunder twice and moved away. Thunder hit Cardol on the ear. Cardol shook his head to clear the ringing.

They stepped in a circle facing each other, then traded a few punches. To the body, occasionally to the head. Both men were fairly evenly matched. Even so it wasn't long before Thunder was bleeding from a cut eyebrow and Cardol had a bloody nose. A few more steps, a few more punches. They circled each other warily like prize fighters. Cardol suddenly backed away, to the table where he had several things laid out, one of which was a big knife with jagged teeth. He picked it up and turned. He started towards Thunder. Thunder quickly backed away and fell over a bag of concrete. His out flung hands found a knife lying on the floor. It was the one that Cardol had pulled out of his jeans. Thunder got to his feet.

"Remember the last time we fought with knives?" Thunder

asked.

Cardol put a hand to his face. "I was lucky to keep my eye,"

"I could have killed you then," Thunder said. His voice softened a little, "But you were nothing to do with my vengeance,"

"I don't want your pity!" Cardol spat at him. He advanced on Thunder, never doubting that this time he would win; he now had the ability, he had the advantage, his hatred of Thunder burned. He swung the knife from side to side as he got nearer. Thunder jumped back as the knife whistled past his ribs.

"Close," Cardol mocked him.

"Not close enough," Thunder said in his deadly voice.

Cardol lunged for Thunder, knife outstretched. Thunder grabbed his wrist, pushing Cardol's knife higher and brought his own knife up towards Cardol's chest. Cardol grabbed his wrist and they struggled. Cardol managed to slowly bring his knife down near Thunder's face. He saw it out the corner of his eye but never took his eyes off Cardol. He put more pressure on his knife, bringing it closer to Cardol's body. Cardol lunged once more and managed to cut Thunder's check. Thunder swore loudly and spun away. He put a hand to his face, blood ran down the cheek and dripped off his jaw.

"That makes us even," Cardol said pointing his knife at him.

"I did a better job," Thunder retorted. His cheek stung, he looked at the blood on his hand and turned away slightly.

Cardol moved towards Thunder's unprotected back, his knife high. Thunder heard Kate scream his name as he stepped away and round to face Cardol, bringing his knife up and across Cardol's arm. Cardol screamed in pain, holding his arm. Thunder stepped away. Cardol moved round. Thunder stepped back one more step.

"Now we are half way to being even," Thunder said pointing the knife at him.

"How is the chest?" Cardol taunted.

"Fine," Thunder shrugged.

"Shame that idiot in China didn't do a better job," Cardol retorted.

"Isn't it just?" Thunder's voice was surprisingly calm. "But you wouldn't miss this for the world," his gesture encompassed their surroundings.

Cardol was visibly rattled. He frowned at Thunder's calmness. Thunder smiled at the perplexity on Cardol's face. He gave a theatrical bow, arms outstretched, keeping his eyes on Cardol.

"I aim to please," Thunder said. He straightened up and then stood casually, hand on hip, waving the knife as if to make a point. "Do you know I believe my mother was sensible to reject your father. He was a bully. And stupid. Just like his son!" He smiled impishly at Cardol.

Cardol lunged at him with a roar, his face grimly determined. He waved the knife like a sword. As he got closer the waving became blows. Thunder blocked the first few blows; the knives meet, locked and then separated. The sound of metal on metal echoed around the building. Cardol continued to advance, crazily now. Thunder started to back up. Cardol was like a madman and the more Thunder frustrated his blows, the crazier Cardol became. With Thunder rapidly running out of room Cardol pressed home the advantage until he had Thunder up against a stack of pallets. They rocked but did not fall. Both Thunder and Cardol looked up at the teetering stack. Thunder took the opportunity to quickly side step away. Cardol turned and followed, the flaying less wild.

Thunder realised the windows were on his left which meant that Kate was somewhere behind him. He tried to veer away but Cardol suddenly caught his hand, cutting him and sending the knife spinning away. Thunder sucked his hand and stepped firmly to his right, away from Kate. Cardol followed. Thunder stepped on a metal bar, it crunched the grit on the floor under his foot. He bent to pick it up, going down on one knee. Cardol's step quickened, bringing the knife down aiming for Thunder's neck and shoulders. Thunder held the bar with both hands and blocked the knife. He straightened up, bouncing the bar on his hand. Cardol backed away warily.

"What's wrong Cardol? You're stopped talking," Thunder said.

"It doesn't matter, you're still dead," Cardol replied.

"Funny, I feel very much alive," Thunder replied.

"Savour it!" Cardol advised him coldly.

"Likewise!" Thunder retorted. Their taunting has become childish again. Lying on the floor Kate rolled her eyes and sighed loudly, muttering obscenities. They couldn't hear the words but neither men missed the insinuation.

Thunder swung the bar around his head. Cardol ducked and edged towards the table. Thunder can see the various weapons there. That was not somewhere he wanted Cardol to go. He swung the bar once more, turning with the momentum and hitting Cardol across the arm. He dropped the knife and backed away holding his arm. Thunder kicked the knife away. Both men stood quietly eyeing each other.

Cardol's nose has stopped bleeding. The blood on his face was nearly dry. There were the beginnings of a bruise on his jaw. The scar across his eye was angry and red and the eye was beginning to close. His clothes were dusty and one sleeve was cut and bloody. Thunder knew he didn't look much better. He had dried blood on his cheek, the eye below the cut smart and he knew that tomorrow - if he lived to see it - he would be covered in bruises. His shoulders ached from the rifle earlier. Lying on the floor Kate quietly watched their encounter. Thunder didn't dare look at her.

"Let's fight like men. At least it's more honourable than the way your father killed my family and I killed yours," Thunder said and threw the bar away. Cardol stood and stared at him. He shrugged - painfully. They started to circle each other again. Both were tired, both wanted this to end, but both were prepared to fight to the death.

CHAPTER TWENTY FOUR

They traded a few punches. A punch to the head, one to the body, a kick, a knee to the gut, a push here, a thump there. Suddenly Thunder's fist hit Cardol on the jaw. Cardol stepped back and shook his head. He gingerly fingered his jaw and moved it slowly from side to side. He grunted, looked sideways at Thunder and suddenly launched a punch at his head. Bone crunched upon bone. It was Thunder's turn to step back. Cardol didn't give him the same indulgence and followed up with a couple of punches to the ribs. Thunder moved first one way and then the other as the punches hit, hard. His muscles hurt.

"You're not as tough as you used to be Thunder. You're getting soft in your old age," Cardol taunted.

"You're not so young," Thunder retorted. "Or so fit either,"

"She's feeding you too well, making you flabby," Cardol said.

"What I lack in brawn I make up in brains," Thunder retorted. They were back to their childish taunting. They heard Kate mutter but not the words.

Suddenly Cardol launched a punch at Thunder hitting him in the side of the jaw, his head jerked away to the side and blood flew out of his mouth. As his legs went from under him Thunder flung a wild punch at Cardol which caught him in the eye. Cardol quickly circled him and kicked him in the back. Thunder contorted and grunted in pain. He pulled himself up onto his hands and knees. Cardol aimed a kick at Thunder's gut. Thunder grabbed the foot, twisted and up-ended Cardol. Cardol lay sprawled on the ground breathing hard. Thunder put a hand to his back and fell, twisting to his side, also breathing hard.

They both lay there for a few minutes then both got to their feet. Thunder stood with hands on knees and heaved, the breath hurt his chest. He spat out blood and looked over at Cardol. He was standing upright but bent over, one hand gingerly feeling his eye. The skin wasn't broken but it was swelling fast and soon would close. Cardol looked at Thunder angrily.

Without a word they started to circle each other. Thunder threw a few punches, a couple made contact, most Cardol ducked. Then it was Cardol's turn. A few punches: hit, miss, miss, hit, miss. Thunder threw himself at Cardol. They both fell to the floor, rolling together. Cardol managed to roll away, his back to Thunder but Thunder held on to his shirt. Cardol's elbow caught Thunder in the mouth. Thunder swore loudly and let go. Cardol rolled away and up leaving Thunder on the floor spitting blood.

Cardol picked up a length of chain and wound one end round his hand. He brought the chain down towards Thunder's head like beating out flames. Thunder ducked one way and then another, just managing to stay out of harm's way. The sound of the chain beating the floor near his head roared loudly in his ears. Thunder rolled and rolled, finally coming to a halt against a drum. The chain caught the drum and it toppled. Thunder scrambled away at the last second.

"Shit!" Cardol swore. "Why can't you stay still long enough for me to kill you?" he said through clenched teeth.

"Sorry to be such a nuisance!" Thunder retorted as he scrambled away on hands and knees. Cardol turned on his heel and advanced rapidly. Thunder finally pushed himself up onto his feet and moved away far quicker.

Cardol swung the chain and caught Thunder on the arm. Thunder swore and cradled the arm to his body. Cardol swung the chain once more. This time Thunder caught it and yanked. Cardol toppled forward. Thunder dropped the chain and caught Cardol mid fall. He brought his knee up into the man's gut, his elbow down onto his shoulders and then his fist caught Cardol under the chin. Cardol literally flew through the air, hitting the ground with a thud.

"I said like men and you persist with these things like a coward," Thunder threw the chain away in utter disgust.

Kate lay still. The ropes were very loose now but those around her wrists were still tight. Her hands were losing all feeling. She ached. The arm under her was numb. Her face hurt like hell and she could feel her lip was swollen. She couldn't call out; she couldn't get free; all she could do was lie there and witness their fight. And listen to the taunts.

Thunder fell to the floor next to Cardol. Cardol raised a fist. Thunder slapped it down and thumped Cardol. Cardol spat blood and kicked out catching Thunder in the back. Thunder arched his back and swore, swayed and put his hand out to stop himself falling. They both breathed heavily.

"I'm too bloody old for this stupid fucking game," Thunder snarled through clenched teeth.

"Then die!" Cardol snarled back and rolled away to his feet. He aimed a kick at Thunder's head.

"I'm not that fucking old!" Thunder swotted the foot away.

Cardol fell. Then rolled to his knees and moved towards Thunder who was still on his knees. Thunder moved towards Cardol and hit him in the kidneys. Cardol grunted and fell, face down. Thunder got to his feet wearily and stumbled towards to Kate. Cardol looked round, saw where he was going and from somewhere found strength. He scrambled up and ran at Thunder with a roar, bringing him crashing down with a flying tackle that would have done a Springbok proud. Thunder kicked him away. Both lay there for a few minutes, breathing heavily. Finally Cardol dragged himself to his knees. He crawled away to the table and pulled himself to his feet.

"This ends now," he said as he picked up a gun. He pulled the chamber back as he walked over towards Kate. She saw him and tried to wiggle away but this sent shooting pains up her arm pinned beneath her.

Thunder's mind suddenly cleared when he heard Kate's scream. He pushed himself off the ground and flew at Cardol. Holding the arm with the gun they struggled. The gun suddenly went off, hitting the ground between them. They both swore. Thunder brought his knee up into Cardol's groin. Cardol grunted and his knees buckled. He managed to head butt Thunder as he fell to the floor. Thunder went down with him. They fell in a heap, Thunder holding Cardol's wrist, the gun pointed at Kate. Cardol saw the opportunity and moved his hand a few inches to get a better aim. Thunder thumped the floor with Cardol's hand a couple of times until he dropped the gun. Thunder hit him once. His fist came back a second time.

"Thunder!" it came out barely a whisper. She licked her lips. "Thunder!" she yelled. He hit Cardol. "No! No!" he hit Cardol again. "Krysten! Stop! For Christ's sake, stop!" she screamed at him. Fist in mid punch he looked at her. "Krysten. Please. Stop. He's not worth it,"

Thunder dropped his fist and crawled over to Kate. He couldn't untie the ropes on her wrists or even right the chair so he could take the other ropes off her. He crawled away towards the discarded knife.

"No!" Kate yelled. Then there was a rifle shot.

Thunder heard the two sounds. His head whipped round. He saw Cardol kneeling, a gun in his hands, he looked surprised. Then he fell forward, face down. Thunder crawled over to him. There was a hole in his back. He turned him over. His eyes looked up at Thunder, still surprised. Thunder slumped back on his heels and then closed Cardol's eyes. The sense of relief flooded through Thunder's body, giving him pain.

He looked up in the direction the shot had to have come from. At first he couldn't make it out. Finally his gaze went to the row of offices that were on the overhang. At one of the windows stood Liam, still aiming the rifle at them. His expression was thoughtful. It would be easy to kill Thunder too. Then, slowly, he lowered the rifle. Thunder didn't know whether to be surprised or grateful.

"Kate," he muttered and turned back to her. He tried to crawl over to the knife again but his strength failed him. He sat near her, his head hung down. He heard the running feet but didn't look up. Then he heard Kit's voice.

"Lie still Kate, I'll cut the ropes," Kit said gently to Kate.

Thunder looked up. Kit was cutting the ropes and helping Kate up. Kit righted the chair and sat Kate on it. She rubbed her wrists and then her arm. Kit went to Thunder and helped him to his feet.

"My gun," Thunder managed to say.

"I have it," Kit said. "Let's get out of here,"

Thunder looked up. Liam was gone. They staggered out the door. It was now evening.

Parked at the front of the building was Marcus' car. He sat on the wing staring at the building. Waiting. Arms folded. He could do no more. He felt so out of his depth he was afraid he would drown. Suddenly Liam appeared from the front of the building. He held the rifle over one shoulder.

Marcus slid off the car. He looked apprehensively at Liam. His heart hammered. "Are they ...?" his voice trailed off.

Liam looked at him as he approached the car. From round the corner of the building Kit appeared. He had one arm round Thunder who was leaning on his shoulder, his arm round Kate.

Liam walked to the back of the car and threw his rifle into the boot, as if in disgust. The others approached the car. Thunder pushed himself away from Kate and Kit and hobbled over to Liam. Liam leaned on the wing of the car. As Thunder's hand tightened on his arm, Liam looked round at his friend.

"Why?" Thunder asked softly.

"Rosie," Liam said simply.

Thunder just stared at him, his chest felt tight.

Leaving Kate with Marcus Kit went to the boot and removed a small bag. He held it out to Thunder who looked at the bag thoughtfully. He looked over his shoulder at the building and then at Kate and Marcus watching them.

"There's something I have to do," he said to her.

"Are you sure?" she asked. "He's dead, isn't he?"

"Yes," Liam said firmly. "Why bother? He doesn't deserve it,"

"It's something I promised a very great man a long time ago. This ends it," Thunder said. Kit nodded, he understood. Thunder took the bag from him and disappeared round the building.

Kit closed the boot. Liam put his hands in his pockets and hunched his shoulders, he looked unhappy. They stood and waited. Thunder came back carrying the bag; only now it was empty. He didn't say a word and looked at no one.

"Lets go home. It's finished," Kate said and got into the car. Kit and Thunder followed.

Marcus stood uncertain and looked at Liam. "Where are we going?" he asked in a strangled voice.

"Get in. I'll drive," Liam said and got into the drivers seat. Marcus got into the passenger side.

Liam drove away. He got about 100 metres up the road when there was a huge explosion. Liam stopped the car and they all looked back. The factory was no more. The chimneys collapsed in a cloud of dust, the building folded in on itself, all was consumed by a raging fire. The smoke spiralled upwards. The flames lit up the sky. Liam drove away fast. A few minutes later sirens could be heard.

Thunder sat in the back hugging his ribs, his eyes closed. On the other side of the car Kate leaned her head against the window. They all sat in silence, each in their own thoughts, until they reached the cottage.

Once there Liam herded them inside, told Marcus to get the kettle on and make tea and coffee. Thunder ran a bath and ordered Kate into it. He went into the shower. He sat with a towel wrapped round him while Kit made up one of his herbal mixtures and rubbed it into his ribs.

"You won't look too pretty tomorrow," Kit said eyeing him.

"Was I ever?" Thunder asked with a laugh.

Back downstairs with cups of tea or coffee they started to feel better.

"We'd better let Ling and Sarah know Kate is all right," Marcus said. He rang Sarah. Sarah wanted to speak to Kate. "Another day perhaps," Marcus said firmly. Sarah conceded the point.

Kit rang Ling and in Chinese told her the news.

"Are they okay?" she asked.

"We are all fine," Kit replied. Ling put down the phone.

"You never asked me where I came from," Liam said to Thunder.

"It never seemed important," Thunder said.

"I came from this tiny little place in the south of Ireland," Liam said. "You've never been there?"

"No," Thunder lied quietly. He steeled his face into stillness and waited for the expected explosion. But it never came.

"I never forget a face. Even one who hid his while we buried my sister. You thought you were invisible behind that hedge but I could see you as clearly as I see you now. Ma never found out who organised it or paid for it but it was the best funeral money could buy. Far more than we could afford," Liam said.

"What good does this do now? I could no more bring Rosie back than I could protect her," Thunder said with bitterness.

"Now there is Kate," Liam said.

"And now there is Kate," Thunder echoed heavily.

"So, it is repaid. Like it has been ever since you brought her back. You could have left her to rot in some foreign grave, unknown, forgotten, lost to her family. But you didn't. I realised long ago that you have more integrity than others," Liam said.

"I made a promise and I keep my promises. No one has been hurt since because of their involvement with me," Thunder said firmly.

"Until Kate," Liam reminded him.

"Until Kate," his voice was heavy. "That was unforeseen,"

"Unforeseen. Unplanned. Unexpected," Liam said.

"I didn't think that Rosie's family would come looking for me. What did you intend to do? Once you'd found me?" Thunder asked.

"Oh, once I had lots of ideas what I would do. Most stupid, most unlikely to happen. I found you and you weren't what I expected. Over time I realised her death had affected you more profoundly than her family. Who didn't know her at all. I loved my sister but she was too full of life for an Irish backwater, no matter how hard da tried to keep her down," Liam said.

"Maybe, one day, perhaps, we should sit down and talk about her," Thunder said tentatively.

"Maybe. One day. But not today. Right now I need a drink," Liam said.

Thunder laughed. "Now, that sounds like the Liam I know,"

Marcus and Kate came in. She carried a tray with five glasses on it. Marcus carried a large bottle of champagne. She looked at them as she put the tray down.

"Now you two have had your little chat, it's time for a drink," she said.

Marcus opened the champagne and started to pour. Kate handed the glasses out. Marcus sat down with Kit. Kate stayed standing. She looked roundat them.

"Here's to two men who should know better," she looked at Thunder and Liam. "Two men who do know better," she looked at Kit and Marcus. She took a deep breath. "And to one broken man who knew it at the end," she paused, fighting her emotion.

"And to a girl who changed our lives," Krysten said looking at Liam. He raised his glass silently.

"Here's to Kate who has also changed our lives," Kit said holding a glass up to her. They all agreed.

They drank their toast and then the rest of the bottle. The next day Marcus and Kit returned to London leaving Liam to look after Thunder and Kate.

A week later they too returned to London. Only then, in the safety of Chinatown, did Sarah, Ling and Sonya find out what had happened.

Now - finally - it was finished.

ISBN 142515466-2